WICKED HEIR

GWEN ALYSON

Garden Tub Publishing LLC

This is a work of fiction. All of the characters, organizations, and events portrayed in this novel are either products of the author's imagination or are used fictitiously.

Wicked Heir
Copyright © 2023 by Alyssa Burns

All rights reserved.

No part of this book may be reproduced or transmitted in any form or by any means, electronic or mechanical, including photocopying, recording, or by any information storage and retrieval system without express written permission from the author, except for the use of brief quotations in a book review.

First edition: 2023

Cover: BeautifulBookCovers

Published by: Garden Tub Publishing LLC
255 Simi Village Dr #940254
Simi Valley, CA 93094

Paperback ISBN: 979-8-9880027-1-0

For my 12-year-old self.
We did it.

Content Notes

Wicked Heir contains many adult themes including those that may be triggering. These themes include discussions of sexual assault and abusive family as well as attempted sexual assault on the page.

Full list of trigger/content warnings can be found at gwenalyson.com/books.

Glossary/Pronunciation Guide

Names:
Saoirse: Seer-sha
Cyprian: Sih-pree-uhn
Isolde: Ih-zohl-dah
Vasili: Vuh-see- lee
Calliope: Kah-lee-oh-pee
Cressida: Cress-i-da
Aurelius: Uh-rel-ee-us
Casimir: Caz-i-mere

Annwn (Ah-noon): Otherworld in Welsh mythology
Boireann (boy-yun): a female fae
Boireannaich (boy-yun-ak): female fae (pl)
Brigid (Brigg-id): Celtic fertility goddess
Cailleach (Cah-lech): Celtic goddess of winter and wind
Cernunnos (Ker-noo-nos): Celtic god of beasts and wild places
Dagda (Dag-duh): Celtic god of high power
Danu (Da-noo): Celtic mother goddess
Fireann: (fair-yun): a male fae
Fireannaich: (fair-yun-ak): male fae (pl)
Fomóire (fo-moir-uh): Irish mythological race of demons
Lughnasadh (Loo-nah-sah): Celtic celebration of harvest season; takes place August 1
Mo chroi (muh chree): my heart

Mo Stoirín (muh stor-een): my sweetheart

Morrigan (Moor-ih-gan): Celtic warrior queen goddess

Cat sìth (cat shoe): Celtic mythological creature, fairy creature resembling a black cat

uaislean (oo-uh-shlay-en): "gentlemen"

July 1902
Dublin, Ireland

"*Stay still.*"

Those words only made Saoirse's impulse to squirm even worse as Cressida dabbed a thin layer of berry-shaded rouge onto her lips.

"There," Cressida turned her towards the mirror, "that should make you presentable."

"A face of makeup and my chemise? That definitely will keep everyone's attention." Saoirse noticed Cressida resisting the urge to laugh, but a chortle still slipped out as she shook her head.

Cressida stepped towards the foot of Saoirse's bed and straightened the laid-out layers of Saoirse's ensemble. "You will be fully dressed for tonight's dinner."

"I would think displaying my assets would overshadow any shortcomings I have," Saoirse joked, but her fidgeting fingers gave away a different disposition. She stood as Elodie, her maid, bustled in. Saoirse cooperated as Elodie dressed her into her corset and petticoats.

Cressida watched and tilted her head from one side to another, studying Saoirse's appearance. Saoirse took slow, deep breaths to keep her hands from shaking as she mustered the courage to ask the one question she knew would shape the rest of the evening.

"Have you talked to Eamon?" she asked as she was buttoned into her steel blue skirt.

"I have," Cressida answered with a small sigh.

"And?" Saoirse flinched as her hands were batted away from her silk skirt. When she glanced at the displeased expression on Elodie's face, her gaze dropped to the front of her dress. With her mindless fidgeting, she had created wrinkles in the fabric of her skirt.

"And he hasn't changed his mind," Cressida answered.

Saoirse's heart sank, but she schooled her features to hide her disappointment like she had done for most of her adult life.

"He's adamant this is best for both of you and him," Cressida continued. "I think he's hoping you'll follow the first choice he's given you. If it's worth anything, so am I."

"And if I don't follow it?" Saoirse knew the answer, but she had to ask to confirm anyway.

"He's fairly serious about his alternative, but I might be able to convince him to re-evaluate it if he's faced with following through with it."

Saoirse could only nod in response. All she could do now was hope whatever suitor her brother had picked out would be decent enough to risk attaching herself to for eternity. There was a third option she could follow through with, but she didn't want to think about that. She clung to the bit of fading hope that this fireann was, at minimum, not as terrible as Eamon.

Cressida picked at the cascading curls of Saoirse's strawberry blonde hair, fixing them into a uniform spiral. Saoirse's sister-in-law had pinned her hair into a uniquely complicated hairstyle that Saoirse hadn't seen on any boireannaich in her twenty-three years of life. Cressida, like most fae, never adhered to a single era of style and instead mixed them to her liking. Her style and wardrobe blurred from the regency era to the present era and made it look seamlessly cohesive.

"I promise you, he doesn't *want* to implement his alternative," Cressida said gently. "But he feels he has no other choice."

"He could just not marry me off to the highest bidder," Saoirse murmured.

"You know that isn't his intention," Cressida chided. "Marrying a fireann who is well-off politically and financially is mutually beneficial for you and Eamon. He won't have to worry that you're being well taken care of, and he'll strengthen ties to England that your father sought to sever in the process."

It took strength for Saoirse to not roll her eyes. What Eamon considered "taken care of" was a bare minimum of being fed and clothed. With Eamon being the one determining what passed as care, that sliver of hope Saoirse held onto continued to dwindle.

Cressida turned to Saoirse's vanity and plucked an amber pendant from Saoirse's box of jewelry before carefully adorning it around Saoirse's neck.

"You look beautiful." Cressida grinned as the maid did the last of her fixes to Saoirse's gown. "The amber brings out the range of colors in your eyes."

In spite of the knots tightening in her stomach, the corners of Saoirse's mouth twitched into a small smile. "My mother's eyes," she said. "At least I've been told."

Cressida nodded. "Yes, and she'd be so proud of how you've grown up."

A rap on the door cut their sweet moment short, and the housekeeper's head poked into the room. "His Highness's carriage has arrived," she announced.

"Thank you." Cressida nodded to her and turned back to Saoirse. "Time to greet our guests." She handed Saoirse her evening gloves and led her out into the hall towards the stairs. As Saoirse pulled on the gloves, she tried to breathe through the nausea that rolled through her. Her standards of accepting a marriage proposal may have been quite low, but it was disturbing how easily someone could fail to meet them.

"Don't forget to smile," Cressida whispered as they reached the lower landing and walked down the hall to the entry way. There was nothing Saoirse wanted to do less than to be told to act polite and presentable.

Compared to human high society, fae nobility were notorious for having much more relaxed manners. However, her brother was the exception. He had always been hungry for control, and that extended to how Saoirse acted in the presence of guests. She wasn't purposefully being rude. She was far from it, but Eamon's expectations of her were so high, she was usually chastised once they no longer had any guests.

Saoirse and Cressida reached the entry hall and were welcomed with a tight, pleased grin from Eamon. Cressida, the ever-loving wife, tried to fuss with Eamon's jacket, but he shrugged her off with a grunt. While it was fleeting, Saoirse caught the look of hurt and frustration that crossed Cressida's face before her mask of gentle hostess replaced it.

Their attention was quickly directed to their arriving guests. Saoirse had only been given a few facts about tonight's guests, and they included her suitor's title and that he would be accompanied by another fireann for his safety.

The first to make their entrance was a fireann in an all-black, formal suit with just a hint of dark purple in the collar and cravat details. He looked young, but Saoirse knew looks were deceiving with fae. He was probably at least through his First Settling, the time before a fae turned thirty years old where their physical age was solidified, but for all she knew was approaching his Second. He wasn't extraordinarily tall, but underneath his fitted suit, he had telltale signs of a lean build. Like a true high fae, the fireann's ears came to a sharp point, but with his blonde hair and fair skin, they blurred into his hair color. Saoirse prayed to the gods that he was more than just easy to look at.

As the fireann greeted Eamon, his traveling companion came into view, and Saoirse's silent prayers ceased. The inky, dark hair and general's uniform were unmistakable, and the final sliver of hope she had been holding onto slipped a bit more from her grasp. Memories of harsh words falling from those sweet lips with ease and an empty feeling that made her stomach dip came to the forefront of her mind. Saoirse had an instinct to bolt, but she swallowed it.

She attempted to reason with her first impressions. Maybe he was part of a nearby territory and was doing this as a favor. A prince would require a companion for safety, and what better security than a general? If that was the case, this could be the last time she would have to see him. While that was one more time than she was comfortable with, she could endure a few hours of his presence for a lifetime of his absence. But if she were wrong...

"Princess," the blonde fireann said, attracting her attention away from her thoughts. He must have attempted to address her if he was resorting to forgoing her title. When she met his piercing green eyes, a spark was sent darting down her spine, and she smothered a gasp of surprise with a polite smile. She offered him a hand, and he gave her a slight bow as he brushed his lips over her gloved fingers. "It's a pleasure to meet you."

"It's a pleasure to meet you as well," she replied. Eamon cleared his throat, and Saoirse noticed a disapproving stare. "Your Highness," she added quickly. Her suitor chuckled and shook his head.

"I appreciate the formal address, but there's no need for it." The fireann slid his hand from hers, and Saoirse longed for the warmth it gave her for that brief moment.

"You allowed my brother to address you by your title," she pointed out.

"Saoirse." The warning in Eamon's voice made her stiffen, but her suitor's smile relaxed her. She knew better than to trust the way someone acted in front of guests, but something told her to trust this as genuine.

"Your brother insists on the use of titles." He slid his gaze sideways to Eamon before returning it to her. "But I'm not arrogant enough to demand the same address as human nobility does from those who aren't inclined to it. Considering you responded best to 'Princess', I assume you fall in that category of nobility."

She let out a shuddering laugh as she realized the backhanded comment he had just given her brother. Everyone around her seemed to melt away as they shared this small moment. "And what do you respond to best?" she asked.

"You can call me by my given name: Emrys." They shared another smile before Eamon spoke, essentially ending the moment they shared.

"I see you've traveled with your general. It's a pleasure to see you again, Kieran." Eamon nodded to the general with a slight grin. For anyone who didn't know the king, they would think he was indifferent to Kieran's appearance. But Saoirse knew better, and her brother was nearly giddy that the general had tagged along.

Kieran greeted Eamon with a bow. "The pleasure is all mine." He pinned Saoirse with his dark gaze and gave her a feline smile. Saoirse's stomach plummeted. Kieran wasn't a neighboring general doing the prince a favor. He was the dedicated general to Emrys's territory.

Last spring, for nearly four months, Kieran had been working closely with Eamon on something neither of them cared to disclose to her. The general stayed at the estate for weeks at a time, flirting and seducing Saoirse in his spare time. He had never shared what territory he came from other than that it was in England. The two shared an intimate relationship right under Eamon's nose and, to this day, her brother still wasn't aware of it. Saoirse hadn't even confided in Cressida about the relationship, although, she rarely shared those kinds of details with her anyway. Saoirse didn't trust her enough with those secrets and was reluctant to confess them willingly. Her sister-in-law would rather be willfully ignorant than face the truth of Saoirse's private life.

However, the relationship with Kieran hadn't lasted long. A heated argument ended their affair, and after he left the estate for good, Saoirse hadn't seen or heard from him again. His broken promises and stinging words about her age from that fight still haunted her, and now they triggered an onslaught of dooming thoughts to cycle through her mind. How often would she have to see him if she agreed to marry Emrys? Would he bring up their relationship tonight, essentially ruining her chance at freedom?

Did she even want to entertain what being part of the same court as Kieran would be like? That thread of hope was quickly unraveling, and she dug in her memory as to where she had stored her empty suitcase.

Kieran's attention turned back to her brother, and Saoirse forced herself to tear her gaze from the general and onto Emrys. The prince snuck glances towards her while he presented like he was actively listening to Eamon and Kieran. Saoirse returned them with small half-smiles as an unusual blanket of calm wrapped around her. Her worried thoughts about the general and her potential future life melted away, and she wondered if this was how the gods answered prayers. They never had answered them before, so she didn't quite have any experience to compare to.

As he concluded his brief conversation with the general, Eamon suggested they move into the dining room. Emrys offered his arm to escort Saoirse, and she took it without a second thought. The small bit of warmth his hand had given her earlier was nothing compared to the warmth his body radiated. The muscles of his arm under her fingers confirmed the strong, lean build underneath his suit, and she caught a strong whiff of a sweet yet musky scent coming off him. She had been attracted to many fireannaich in her lifetime—Kieran had no issue seducing her with his looks and charm—but none of them gave her the same feeling that Emrys did. She couldn't quite put her finger on it, but she knew she wanted more of it.

Once in the dining room, Saoirse's two other brothers appeared with their wives, most likely having been alerted upstairs that guests had arrived and dinner was about to commence, and everyone found their seats. Eamon took his place at the head of the table with Cressida at his right. Saoirse's brother, Aurelius, sat at his left with his wife, Georgiana, at his side. Emrys pulled the seat next to Cressida out for Saoirse and seated himself next to her, leaving Kieran in her line of sight at the end of the table. She let out a small sigh of relief as Emrys sat next to her and grazed his hand against hers.

"Kieran, I have to say I'm delighted to see you again," Eamon said as several servants filed into the dining room and poured wine into everyone's glasses. "I hope nothing has gone awry since we last saw each other."

"There's been some chatter, but nothing to quite be concerned about...yet." Kieran sipped on his wine and monopolized Eamon's attention as dinner was served. Saoirse caught Emrys's gaze, and he gave a dramatic eye roll as the general launched into a detailed summary of the new army leadership he had built in the last few weeks. She smirked, thankful she wasn't the only one who found Kieran's presence grating.

"Why did you bring him?" she murmured quietly so no one else at the table heard her. Her gaze flicked to his, and that spark from earlier raced up her spine. She suppressed the shiver it caused her as Emrys shared a smirk.

"I didn't have a choice," he answered. He paused to take a bite of dinner before continuing their exclusive conversation. "Trust me, if I had a say in it, spending eight hours in a train, boat, and carriage with him would not have been my decision."

Saoirse bit her bottom lip to keep from openly giggling, but her shoulders still shook. "I assume the journey wasn't boring then?" she asked.

"It was far from boring." He paused to take a drink of wine. "Going anywhere with Kieran always promises to be dramatic." Emrys glanced at the general next to him, who was still deep in conversation about his army and their role in the revolution in France decades ago. "Hence why he's made himself more interesting to Eamon than I have."

"I think that has more to do with insulting Eamon upon your first meeting," Saoirse teased. A smirk tugged on the corner of Emrys's lips, and she added, "I quite liked it."

Emrys turned his full attention to her, and they shared knowing grins before they dissolved into a fit of low laughter.

"What are you two giggling about?" Kieran asked, interrupting them. Their laughter died, and Saoirse snuck a glance at her brother.

Eamon had a disapproving scowl on his face, but she didn't have a single care about it. Wasn't this what he wanted? For her to make a good enough impression to become someone else's responsibility? Perhaps he was upset that her reaction wasn't as resistant as he expected. There was nothing to chastise her for if she went along with his plans.

She and Emrys straightened, cheeks burning from being caught in a private conversation at the table. "Nothing to concern yourself with, Kieran," Emrys answered, going back to his meal. Kieran eyed them both before returning to his conversation with Eamon. "As I said, drama follows him wherever he goes," Emrys whispered to Saoirse. "But I suppose every family has someone who is a bit overdramatic."

Family? That word made Saoirse's stomach drop and her appetite disappear. If Kieran was family, there was a higher likelihood that she would see him far more than the minimum of a general's duties in Emrys's court. But maybe he was distant family, family that only accompanied the crown prince out of career obligation rather than familial obligation.

She opened her mouth to ask Emrys how closely related Kieran was to him, but Cressida interrupted with a conversation topic of her own. "Emrys, I hadn't known you were seeking an arrangement. Your name hasn't floated around the marriage market until now."

"I've been swamped with other responsibilities over the past few decades," he answered, a hint of pink tinting his cheeks. "I didn't want to marry only to be unavailable to a new spouse."

"That's a very romantic reason." Cressida shot a pointed look at Saoirse who plastered a polite smile on her face in response. She despised the words "marriage market". It only reinforced feeling like an animal being auctioned off. It also reminded her of what awaited her if she rejected Emrys.

"Yes, very romantic," she murmured.

Dinner passed by with conversation shifting and flowing amongst the table. Saoirse had lost her courage to ask Emrys about Kieran, even with Eamon's attention mostly focused on the general giving her ample opportunities to have another private conversation at the table. If Kieran was family, she would have to find out on her own what kind of family he was. And that was as appealing as listening to her brother discuss politics with the general in question.

As plates were being cleared, the party moved into the drawing room, where Eamon continued to theorize and discuss whatever strategies he had brewing with the general. Saoirse sat on the opposite side of the room in a plush floral armchair, nursing a cup of tea. She trained her hearing on their conversation, hoping Kieran wouldn't slip the existence of their past relationship into the conversation. He was obviously getting along with her brother much more than Emrys was, and with the way the prince talked about him, Saoirse didn't doubt the general would try to sabotage the arrangement. Even if he had no idea what the alternative to marrying Emrys was, Kieran was spiteful enough to do whatever he could to harm her emotionally or physically.

As a knot of discomfort sank in her stomach, a low voice in her ear spooked her. "If it wasn't for his signature on the marriage contract, I'd think your brother was trying to persuade my cousin to marry you." Emrys's voice may have temporarily startled her, but feeling his presence so close to her gave her that unexpected calm she had felt before. She looked up at him, and the flakes of gold that rimmed the edge of his emerald green eyes glinted at her.

"Cousin?" she asked, her heart thundering. Was this the answer she had been looking for but was too afraid to ask? She prayed it wasn't, but as Emrys opened his mouth to answer, she knew her prayer wouldn't be answered.

"Kieran," he said, nodding to the general plotting with her brother.

"Oh," she said softly. She looked to her brother grinning as he conversed with the general. Kieran was Emrys's cousin. That was close enough family that Saoirse felt hope slip away. The thought of signing the arrangement and marrying Emrys now made her heart and stomach plummet. But she also knew her fate would be much worse if she refused the arrangement. She couldn't do this.

She couldn't face either choice. Her third unspoken choice would have to do. "Please excuse me," she mumbled as she set her teacup down with a clink that caught Cressida's attention.

Saoirse got to her feet and scrambled to the nearest door, trying to draw as little attention to herself as possible. She didn't dare look at Eamon, fearing that if she made eye contact with him, he would intervene. Saoirse took the stairs two at a time, her cumbersome dress nearly tripping her at the top of the stairs. She didn't pause until she was safely inside her bedroom. Panic flooded her, and she leaned against the door, gulping as much air into her lungs as she could.

She stripped her gloves from her arms as a hot crackle in her veins threatened to make her night even worse. The heat spread through her body, wrapping around her lungs and keeping her from taking a full breath. Her immediate panic did anything but soothe her body's response as her skin tingled with fire.

Her eyes darted around her room, looking for something that could physically extinguish the fire manifesting under her skin. Charred bedposts, scorched carpet, and a singed loveseat reminded her that wasn't an option. Saoirse squeezed her eyes shut and forced herself to focus on the shallow rhythm of her breathing, pleading for her magic to subside.

The grip her magic had on her lungs loosened, and she felt a sliver of control again as she took deeper breaths. Her skin felt cooler, and she was nearly calm when a sharp knock on her door made her jump. "Saoirse," Cressida's muffled voice said through the door. "Are you alright?"

Saoirse swallowed before answering, hoping the panic in her voice couldn't be detected. "Yes," she said. "I felt ill suddenly. That's all."

"Oh, I'm sorry to hear that. I'll tell Eamon you don't feel well."

Saoirse evened her breathing again, trying to plot her next plan of action. Cressida always advocated for Saoirse's wellbeing with ranging levels of success. It wasn't enough for her to spring hope again that she would come out unscathed in the morning.

"Thank you." Saoirse heard hw small her voice had become. Gods, she wished this night was merely a dream she could wake up from in the morning.

"Do you need anything?"

"No," Saoirse answered. "I just need some rest. Could you send Elodie to help me undress?"

"Alright." Cressida's footsteps receded down the hall, and Saoirse mulled over the faint details she had of her plan. After Elodie came, she'd act on it.

She anxiously waited for the maid to arrive, and once she did, Saoirse became very conscious of her body language. She went rigid as the maid unbuttoned her bodice and untied her skirts. Once her corset was unlaced, Elodie helped her dress into a nightgown for bed.

But once Elodie left the room, Saoirse pulled the nightgown off and grabbed her chemise. Her hands shook as she closed the busk of her corset and fumbled with the laces behind her back. It wasn't laced as snugly as she usually liked it, but it would have to do. Saoirse rifled through her drawers, tossing shirtwaists and petticoats she pulled towards her bed. She dressed in a brown split skirt and linen blouse and nearly forgot her stockings before yanking her boots on.

Next, Saoirse lunged towards her bed and pulled the suitcase out from underneath it. She laid it open on her mattress and haphazardly threw the garments from her dresser into it. As she packed her belongings, Saoirse fleshed out her plans. They hadn't been completely solid before now, that sliver of hope having a stronger hold on her than she wanted to admit. She also hadn't wanted to think through the implications of running away and what would happen if she wasn't successful.

Saoirse stared down at her suitcase, torn between abandoning her plan and damning whatever repercussions she may face if she followed through with it. Emrys crossed her mind and thinking of the few delightful interactions they had made her chest hurt. She imagined him with a confused and crestfallen expression the next morning as he learned she had disappeared in the middle of the night. Saoirse grabbed one of the marred wooden posts of her bed and rested her forehead against it, groaning in frustration.

Those sweet thoughts of Emrys were unfortunately overshadowed by Kieran. Saoirse felt the familiar tingle of magic creep through her arms and into her palms again. The smell of burning wood filled her nostrils and panic struck her. She squeezed her eyes shut and tried to breathe and empty her mind. Slowly, the heat in her veins receded, and she was left with the aftermath of her panic. She opened her eyes and pulled her hands away from the post, the wood of her bed frame displaying glowing orange handprints. That sealed her decision for her. She'd rather have nothing than shift her source of stress to a different person.

Saoirse continued to pack her essentials as she finalized her plan. She'd wait until the house went to sleep and sneak out the staff entrance. From there, she would assess her options to get to a train station and find a way to get onto a train to whatever destination Eamon didn't have power over. Maybe she would flee to the northern part of the island. There had been discussions of revolting for years, and if they no longer were a territory under Eamon, she had a chance of escaping his influence.

She was nearly set to close her suitcase and wait when a knock made her thoughts skitter to a halt. She looked around the room, trying to assess where the knock came from and how much time she had to stash her packed suitcase. Was Cressida checking on her again? If so, Saoirse could kiss her plan farewell. There was no possible way Cressida would be sympathetic to her dilemma.

A worse possibility hit her, and it made her blood run cold for once. What if it was Eamon coming to scold her? He usually waited for guests to leave before reprimanding her, but the weight of this evening was much more than any other dinner or event Saoirse had ruined in his eyes.

She felt frozen in place, unable to move to hide her suitcase or answer the door. Her plan to flee was about to be ruined before it even started. Her blood pounded in her ears until she heard a second knock. Time seemed to stand still as she realized the knock wasn't coming from the door that led to the hall but the one on the other side of her bed that connected to the bedroom next to hers.

*S*aoirse *furrowed her* brows at the connecting door. No one stayed in that room because of the access it gave guests to her room. Had the housekeeper placed Emrys or Kieran in that room? Surely Eamon wouldn't let a stranger stay in the room that adjoined hers. Then again, he was wholly unaware of the late night assignations she had engaged in. No one monitored the halls at night, so her safety wasn't exactly Eamon's top priority.

Saoirse felt her legs move towards the door without her instruction. There were only two possible options of who could be on the other side. She found herself praying it was the one that had her giggling at dinner and not the one that had her crying on her floor a few months ago.

A slight tremor ran through her hand as her fingers reached and wrapped around the doorknob. She cracked the door open just enough to poke her head through, and her heart kicked up when she saw it was Emrys on the other side. Relief washed through her until she realized her suitcase was most likely in his line of sight. She situated her body to block the view of it and tried to give a genuine smile.

"I'm sorry to disturb you," he said. "But I wanted to check if you were alright." He was no longer wearing his jacket and waistcoat, and the cuffs of his shirt had been folded up his forearms.

"Oh, yes." Saoirse nodded vigorously. His forlorn expression in the wake of her absence floated across her mind again, and she felt the need to satiate his concern as quickly as possible. "Thank you for checking on me." She tried to close the door, but Emrys placed his palm against it. He didn't force it open, but he pushed against it hard enough to keep Saoirse from closing it further.

"I didn't mean to startle you by telling you about Kieran." Emrys's guilty expression made Saoirse's stomach knot. Morrigan strike her. Why did he have to be thoughtful? Executing her plan would be much easier if he had a personality akin to her brother. "I honestly thought you knew."

"How would I know you and Kieran were cousins?" Her brows furrowed.

"I would think using his familial ties to the crown would be his primary means of seduction." Emrys removed his hand from the door and crossed his arms over his chest, his exposed forearms confirming what Saoirse suspected about the shape the rest of his body was in. Regardless of the plan she had committed to, she had an itch to reach out and run her hands over them.

"You know about me and Kieran?" Saoirse asked, forcing herself to keep her eyes level with his to avoid distraction.

"Would it surprise you if I told you he bragged about tupping the Irish Fae princess?"

Her cheeks burned. "And that doesn't bother you?" she asked. "I thought fireannaich leaned more territorial and didn't enjoy learning who exactly had enjoyed their intended partners' bodies." What was she saying? She wasn't intending on accepting his proposal. So why did she care?

"It would depend." He shrugged. "Do you have plans to start that relationship again?"

Saoirse wrinkled her nose at the thought. Not even if he were the last fireann on earth would she seek out a relationship with Kieran again. She'd use her own two hands to quench her physical desires in that case.

"No, never," she answered.

Emrys relaxed an inch, and she wondered if that was a true fear of his, someone using him to get close to Kieran. It was heartening to find an insecurity in an otherwise seemingly perfect fireann.

His gaze then fell and drifted down her body. His brows knitted as he brought his eyes back to hers. "Did you plan on going for a midnight stroll in the garden, or do you sleep in your day clothes?"

Saoirse looked down at herself and felt her face flush with heat again. "I..." She swallowed, scrambling to find an excuse that would explain her appearance.

Emrys looked over her shoulder, and his brows knit even further in concern. "Considering you couldn't escape the drawing room fast enough, I assume your open suitcase isn't being packed in preparation to return to England with me."

She opened her mouth, but the back of her eyes pinched. She sucked in her bottom lip and took a deep breath. "I'm sorry," she whispered.

Emrys's expression morphed, and he stood up taller, letting his arms fall to his sides. "Saoirse," he said gently. "What's going on?"

"I can't do this." Her throat felt tight as she said the words. "I can't marry into a family that includes Kieran, and I can't let Eamon send me to the Matron House."

"The Matron House?" Emrys repeated, confused.

Saoirse nodded. "Eamon told me I had no suitable place in this house, so I was either to marry the next suitor he arranged me with, or I would be sent off to work as Matron. Since I haven't Settled, he said my fertility would probably be a gift to the House."

Concern turned to disgust as Emrys shook his head at this new revelation. "That's not going to happen," he said, his tone icy.

A shiver ran through Saoirse. What did he plan to do? Barge into Eamon's office or quarters and berate him for dealing such a threat? Eamon barely listened to his own wife, let alone a near stranger.

Emrys closed his eyes and, with effort, let out a slow breath. When he opened his eyes again, he asked, "Can we talk?"

"What is there to talk about?" she asked. Defeat rippled through her. There was nothing else for her to do but flee. "I have no other options."

"I promise you there is."

Saoirse shook her head. A tear slipped onto her cheek, and she wiped at it with the back of her hand. "I can't marry you."

Emrys pursed his lips and let out another slow breath. "Can we *please* discuss it?" His voice was nearly a plea, and Saoirse felt panic rise higher in her chest. Heat flickered in her muscles, which only stoked her panic further.

No. Not again. She wouldn't let this happen again. Her fingers wove together, and she took deep, steadying breaths before she felt the heat recede. "Emrys—"

"I have a way for you to dodge both the Matron House and Kieran." Emrys said the words so quickly they almost sounded like one single word.

She stared at him for a long moment, debating. "Alright," she said quietly. "It probably won't change my mind, but I'm willing to listen."

She stepped aside, gesturing to the settee on the other side of her room. As he made his way across the room, she saw her room in a different perspective for the first time. It wasn't exactly what one would expect a high-ranking royal to live in with the wooden posters of her bed littered with scorch marks and the edges of her rugs under her settee and bed singed in black. Saoirse had become accustomed to the way her bedroom looked, overlooking the damage she had inflicted on it. A wave of embarrassment washed over her at the realization.

"Don't mind that," she murmured as Emrys paused and frowned at the frayed edges of the settee's cushion and arms. He glanced at her and studied her for a moment. His frown lifted, and he took a seat on the settee, waiting patiently for her to join. She gingerly sat next to him and smoothed the fabric of the split skirt in her lap.

"I agree that the Matron House is no place for you," he said. "You don't deserve a lifetime of lowly viscounts impregnating you to continue their bloodline."

"Well, I'm glad you have that much of a conscience." Saoirse winced as she heard the words fall from her lips. "I'm sorry."

"It's alright." He gave her a half-smile. "I know it isn't me you're upset with."

"It isn't." She shook her head and leaned back on the settee. "My brother is hard to argue with. He gets on with Kieran, and I'm sure that says more to you than it does to me." Her gaze slid to him, and she saw a muscle twitch in his jaw. "So how do you plan to keep me from the Matron House *and* Kieran?"

He loosened a breath. "If you agree to marry me," he said. "I will arrange for your departure to live wherever you'd like, by yourself."

Saoirse sat stunned for a moment. She had to give him credit. It was a plausible plan to keep her from having to move to the Matron House and avoid being part of a family that included Kieran.

No one had offered her something so good. She had been offered future favors, warm regards, and nights of pleasure, but never offered something that seemed almost unattainable. It had to be too good to be true. "How can I trust you'll follow through with that?" she asked.

"I have no urgent need to take a wife right now," he offered as an explanation. "My father is in good health. I don't need an heir to spite any siblings for the throne. And I have all the resources to make you very comfortable for as long as you desire. I give you my promise that I'll follow through with giving you your freedom."

Freedom.

It was so tempting. Having Emrys set her up for a life on her own sounded much better than what she had planned. It was weak at best, and it consisted of little more than running away with nothing but the shirt on her back. But...

"What about Kieran?" Saoirse asked. "I suppose it will take time to plan a wedding. How much would I have to see him between now and the wedding?"

"He doesn't live at the estate and only comes for council meetings," Emrys answered quickly. "He'd be around twice at the most before the wedding."

Saoirse nodded. "And we would have to travel with him back to England," Saoirse added.

"Yes, we would." His gaze dropped to the singed edge of the settee's cushion. "If it helps, he gets ill on boats, and you most likely won't see him at all."

The corner of Saoirse's lips tilted upwards. It did help a bit. "Knowing that makes him seem a bit less intimidating."

Emrys chuckled, and the sound gave Saoirse a warmth that felt different from her erratic, emotionally-driven magic. It felt like a blanket being wrapped around her shoulders with a sweet embrace.

"The choice is yours, Princess." Emrys stood from the settee, but Saoirse shook her head, reaching for his hand.

Otherworldly heat emanated from her palm, and she tried to pull her hand back, but he had already wrapped his fingers around hers. Chilly magic brushed up against her fire, and the unexplainable calm he gave her coaxed her magic to recede. It was the soothing response she desperately yearned for an hour ago.

That spark rippled through her again when their gazes met. She felt like squirming under his unwavering stare, but not from intimidation. The words lingered on the tip of her tongue, yet she still hesitated. If she agreed, she would be taking the biggest leap of faith she had ever faced.

Emrys stroked small circles on her hand with her thumb, and his soothing presence tempted her into accepting. "I'm serious with my offer," he said quietly. "You're not obligated to me at all." There was a tinge of sadness in his eyes, but his words sounded genuine. He would actually sign a proposal agreement and a marriage certificate just so that she didn't have to live under her brother or become a Matron.

It was too generous an offer to ignore.

"I accept your offer," Saoirse heard herself say.

"You will?" His expression transformed into one of hesitant joy.

"Yes," she breathed. "Yes, I will marry you." A grin spread across Emrys's face, and Saoirse quickly added, "As long as you hold up your end of the offer."

His smile didn't drop, but it paused where it was. "Of course."

They stared at each other for a long moment, neither knowing what to do next. If this was under more romantic circumstances, Saoirse would have pulled him in for a kiss. But that wasn't the appropriate response after the decision she had just given. Would a brief embrace give the same impression, or was that a safer option?

Before she could find out, Emrys slipped his hand from hers and stood. "Good night, Princess," he said, a whisper of a contented smile still on his face.

"Good night." Saoirse watched him cross the room and close the adjoining door behind him, disappearing completely from view.

She eyed her suitcase still open on her bed, then the day clothes she was dressed in. Now it seemed like a horrifying thought that she had planned to slip out in the middle of the night and run as far as she could before Eamon caught her.

She shivered at the thought of what punishment Eamon would think up in response to her fleeing. It would probably be an immediate banishment to the Matron House, and Cressida would have no hope of talking him down from it. Saoirse released a slow breath and tried to let the thought leave her mind. She wouldn't have to find out what awful punishment her brother could think up. She had a short obligation to Emrys, and then she would be free. That was enough to help her sleep for the night.

Saoirse sat across from Eamon, his dark mahogany desk littered with paperwork between them. Cressida sat in the corner to the left, waiting to bear witness to the signature on the documents. They only had to wait for Emrys to join. The minutes ticked by on the grandfather clock near the door to the office on Saoirse's right. She tried her best to keep her eyes off the door and not look too anxious. If Eamon received even a whisper of her plan with Emrys, she was sure he would shred the engagement papers in a heartbeat.

"He's only a few minutes late," Cressida said, breaking the silence. "While not very polite, it doesn't mean he's changed his mind."

Saoirse wasn't entirely sure who Cressida was trying to placate, Eamon or her, but it wasn't working for either.

"You know what his absence means for you." Eamon's gaze pierced through Saoirse, and she resisted a shudder.

"It's tardiness," Cressida corrected. "Not an absence. There isn't a time of day this arrangement expires."

Saoirse had trusted Emrys. He gave her few reasons not to. But he was related to Kieran, and that fireann had done nothing but break Saoirse's trust whenever given the opportunity. There was every chance Emrys would do the same.

Eamon sighed. "I've told you that you aren't suited to be amongst my court, let alone anyone else's. Luckily, when the

Matron House gets their hands on you, they'll teach you that you can't run people off with your grating personality. I'm sure some fireannaich would very much like to—"

Before Eamon could finish his sentence, Emrys made his appearance. The king's demeanor completely morphed before her eyes when he laid eyes on her suitor. "Your Highness," he said. All the venom dissolved from Eamon's tone, and his posture relaxed.

"I apologize for my tardiness, Your Majesty," Emrys said with a slight bow before making his way to the empty seat beside Saoirse. "I don't sleep well in unfamiliar places, and I overslept this morning."

"I'll overlook your tardiness." Eamon placed the final marriage contract in front of Emrys and held out a fountain pen. "There have been no amendments to the contract. All the contents are the same as the draft that was sent along with the arrangement request. My wife is here to bear witness to your signature."

"And Saoirse," Emrys added. When Eamon knitted his brows, he added, "Since she isn't the one signing on her own behalf, she also has the ability to bear witness."

"Yes." A tint of crimson crept up Eamon's face at Emrys's correction. "Saoirse as well."

Emrys glanced at Saoirse with the whisper of a smile on his face, and she had to work hard to not smirk. Her faith had been restored from its precarious place. She also wasn't sure which she found more amusing, Emrys suggesting her brother was no better than a human king or correcting him on his own manners.

The prince took the fountain pen and skimmed the document before putting the tip of the pen to the paper and scrawling his name at the bottom. Cressida breathed a quiet sigh of relief while Eamon's face remained staunchly unemotional. "I stand corrected, little sister," he said. "You won't be fulfilling Matron duties after all. I'm glad someone else is responsible for your disappointments now."

Saoirse caught a muscle in Emrys's jaw tic at Eamon's words, but the prince remained still. "Eamon," he said coolly. "If I may, that is my future wife you're talking to, and I implore you to think about how you speak to her."

"I still outrank you, Your Highness," Eamon sneered back. "So I would implore *you* to think about how you speak to *me*."

Emrys tilted his chin upwards, his jaw visibly tight. "My apologies, Your Majesty."

Even though it resulted in being reprimanded, Emrys had stood up for Saoirse in front of her brother again. The only person who came close to defending her was Cressida, but she folded in an instant in front of Eamon. She had the best intentions—she just never had the courage to see them through.

"Now," Emrys's thumb stroked over the back of Saoirse's hand, and she met his warm gaze, "I believe you have some packing to do."

Saoirse nodded numbly, and he turned his attention to Cressida.

"Will Her Majesty be helping you?" Emrys asked.

"Yes," Cressida squeaked. She jumped up from her seat and scurried towards the door. Stopping in the doorway, she turned, waiting for Saoirse to follow her.

Saoirse felt dizzy as she looked from Cressida to her brother to Emrys. When her eyes landed on Emrys, that spark rippled through her, and the warm sense of calm his presence brought engulfed her. He gave her a half-smile that promised her she would be defended even in her absence. She had no other evidence other than the fact he defended her without being asked, like he had a natural instinct to protect her, but she still believed it to be true.

Saoirse finally stood and followed Cressida out of the office. They made a right towards the stairs and climbed them to the upstairs hall. Once inside her room, Saoirse found Elodie pulling shirtwaists and skirts from Saoirse's armoire. Cressida started plucking clothes from the pile and folding them to put in her suitcase.

Saoirse felt as if she was watching everything from outside of her body as her belongings were folded and packed. This was truly happening. She was leaving, getting out. She no longer was going to be under Eamon's control.

Cressida stepped back as Elodie packed the sorted piles of

clothing. "I'm glad you made this work," she said quietly. "You deserve to get out of here with some semblance of independence."

Saoirse snapped her head to her sister-in-law in shock. Tears glittered along the edge of her lower eyelids, and Saoirse felt a pang of guilt. "Cressida—"

"I know you haven't been happy here," Cressida continued. "And I don't blame you. Eamon makes the otherworld seem like a quaint holiday." She gave a shaky, dry laugh. "I only wish it could have happened sooner."

"Cressida, you can still get out, too," Saoirse said, stepping next to her and folding the chemises Cressida pulled out from her dresser.

"No." Cressida shook her head. "I can't. There might have been a time where I thought I could have, but I can't fathom abandoning my mate."

Her mate. Of course. The lie her brother told to keep Cressida in line. It was a fable that described two people who were fated by the gods to be together. At least Saoirse believed it to be a fable. How did people know they had met their mate? What was the advantage of having one? No one had been able to answer those questions for her, so Saoirse had little, if any, faith in their existence.

If it wasn't for that sweet lie Eamon told, maybe convincing Cressida to leave would be achievable. She deserved better than the leash Eamon tugged her around on. Saoirse held out a bit of hope that Cressida would be inspired by her departure, but she doubted that was a realistic hope to have.

Elodie and Cressida filled a steamer trunk of Saoirse's belongings including her undergarments, dresses, and shoes. Wiping her eyes as discreetly as she could, Cressida escorted Saoirse downstairs to the entry hall where Emrys was waiting for her. Her sister-in-law vanished towards Eamon's office, leaving Saoirse alone with her new fiancé.

"What else did you and Eamon discuss?" she asked.

"Just details of your dowry," Emrys answered. "But we were interrupted by Kieran, who wanted a meeting with Eamon before we left."

That explained why her brother wasn't in the entry to see her off. When Cressida returned alone, she knew she wouldn't see her brother before she left. "Eamon is still in discussion with the general," Cressida informed her. "He has said to load into the carriage and the general will join you shortly."

"Of course," Saoirse mumbled.

Cressida acted as if she didn't hear Saoirse's comment and squeezed her into a hug. Saoirse returned the embrace and felt the tremor of Cressida's sob slip. When she pulled back, Cressida hastily wiped at her face and plastered a smile on her lips.

"I'll miss you," she said, her voice wavering.

"I'll miss you, too," Saoirse said honestly. She took Cressida's hand and squeezed it. "And I'll miss your mismatched style."

Cressida gave a watery laugh and squeezed her hand back. "Wait until you have a few more decades behind you, and you'll find yourself mixing your favorite styles, too."

Saoirse smiled and felt a light touch rest on the small of her back.

"I've been honored to be welcomed into your home, Your Majesty," Emrys said.

"You can address me as Cressida."

"Cressida," he corrected himself with a small, amused grin. "It's been a pleasure to meet you and your family."

"It's a pleasure to call you family now."

Emrys flashed a wider smile, and they made their final farewells before he led Saoirse to the carriage outside. He handed her up into it, and the two waited for Kieran to finish with Eamon and join them.

Thankfully, they didn't have to wait long and were soon on their way to the port. An awkward silence hung in the air between the three of them, and Saoirse fidgeted as she tried to find a topic to break the tension. Being in such proximity to Kieran made her uneasy, but she'd only have to endure it for the day.

"What port are we leaving from?" she finally asked, hoping it would ease their tension.

"North Wall," Emrys answered. "We have a steamer arranged to take us to Holyhead. A few other nobles will be on board as well."

"Gods forbid we travel with the unwashed masses," Kieran commented sardonically.

"If you'd like to take a ferry with humans and fae, be my guest," Emrys replied without missing a beat.

Kieran mumbled something under his breath and turned his attention to the small carriage window.

"And then what will we take when we arrive in England?" Saoirse asked.

"Wales, actually," Emrys corrected. "But we'll take a train from Holyhead to Manchester and then switch trains to get to Fearynhurst."

"So, will we arrive in Fearynhurst in the morning?" Saoirse had never crossed the Irish Sea and had no frame of reference for how big or small the British Isle was.

"We should actually arrive later this evening." He grinned at her, and that wash of calm flooded over her again.

Saoirse settled further into her seat in the carriage. She had rarely gone anywhere outside her home. Most of the nobility she had met was during dinners and long stays at her family's estate. Traveling amongst them gave her a bit of a thrill.

It took less than an hour for the carriage to reach the port. The steamer was already waiting at the port, but Saoirse and Kieran stood on the dock as they waited for Emrys to confirm their names. Well-dressed fae in a variety of colored ensembles passed by them, boarding the boat, and Saoirse felt a bit underdressed in comparison. She gravitated towards neutral colors in her daily wardrobe, but seeing her peers dressed so lively had her curious to step outside what she was comfortable with.

Emrys was still confirming their spots, and Saoirse felt her heart thudding in her chest. Being in proximity to Kieran was exactly what she wanted to avoid, but she had no other choice. She trusted that if anyone, even Kieran, harmed her, Emrys would step in and handle it personally.

"You never told me your cousin was the prince of the Northern Fae Kingdom," Saoirse said, feeling bold.

"Don't act like I neglected you," Kieran said. "I'll have you know I actually encouraged this arrangement."

"What?" Saoirse looked at him for the first time, but the general had his gaze fixed on the sea.

"I advocated for this on your behalf."

She pulled her wool shawl tighter around her shoulders. "Are you sure you were advocating for me, or was it for your close friend Eamon?"

"Eamon has nothing to do with this."

"He has everything to do with this! You know I've never had a say in any of the plans Eamon has for me. He did all the work to arrange this, not me."

"Then you should thank me for endorsing you," Kieran sneered.

Saoirse's nostrils flared, but she bit back her fiery retort. It wouldn't do her any good inciting an argument in public. He was doing the thing her brother did. He was twisting his own words to make Saoirse out to look like she was overreacting when he knew damn well she was justified in her reaction.

"I'll say this one time, and one time only," she said through gritted teeth. "Do not try to seek me out while I am with Emrys. It will not end well for you." A low chuckle came from him, and she knit her brows. "What?"

"It's adorable you think I seek anyone out," he answered. "Boireannaich have a tendency to flock to me, and I could have any one of them if I wanted."

"Good." Saoirse gave him a sickly-sweet smile. "Then go find one and don't bother me."

Kieran growled, but before he could respond, Emrys returned with their confirmed tickets. He escorted Saoirse onto the steamer, and they made their way along the outside deck to the bar where several sofas and chairs were set up. Dark wood paneled the walls and ceiling, and the lush, velvet chairs invited her to sit and enjoy the excursion. Kieran followed them into the bar, but only to sit closer to the center of the boat. He took up a dark gray armchair and crossed his arms over his chest, the pigment in his face blanching.

Saoirse bit back a grin as she watched the seasickness settle into the general. It served him right for the way he spoke to her earlier. There were a dozen fae in the room, some drinking at the bar at the back, and some playing card games at the tables near the windows on either side of the room. A whistle sounded before the steamer started to pull out of the port.

Emrys led her to two leather armchairs with a dark wood table positioned between them. They sat along the wall, the window beside them providing an undisturbed view of the Irish Sea. Another awkward silence fell between them, and Saoirse wondered how to break it. What topics did she broach with her temporary fiancé? Did she prod about his family and friends? Or was that becoming too familiar for their bargain?

Smoothly, Emrys reached into the pocket of his trousers and pulled out a deck of cards. "Familiar with the game rummy?" he asked.

She sat up straighter and nodded, thankful for the distraction. Talking seemed dicey at best, but strategizing in a card game was much safer. Emrys dealt ten cards to himself then Saoirse. They took a moment to examine their hands before beginning the game. Saoirse arranged her cards in a way that she could easily put together melds and see which cards she could safely discard and which ones she needed to be vigilant about.

She discarded her first card and picked the top card from the stockpile. It didn't match any of her half-finished melds, and she waited for Emrys to take his turn before she could discard it. They got into a rhythm of discarding and picking cards, and it eased the tension that had settled in Saoirse's shoulders.

"I'm sure this is prying too far," Emrys said. "But we don't have a conventional arrangement, and we only have so long with each other."

"If you're going to ask about my rummy strategy, you're out

of luck." Saoirse gave a cheeky grin. "I don't even share that with Cressida, and she needs all the help she can get."

The corners of his lips turned up in amusement. "I'm not interested in your card playing strategies, Princess." He swallowed the grin and lowered his eyes to his cards. "I'm more interested in you."

The air felt like it was being pulled from Saoirse's lungs. She had agreed to play cards so she didn't have to entertain a discussion. But when his emerald gaze lifted to meet hers, it had her wanting to spill all the details of her life. How in Cernunnos's Wilderness did he do that?

"What did you want to know about me?" she asked.

"How long were you Eamon's ward?"

She took a deep breath, pulling a card from her hand and placing it on the discard pile. "My mother died when I was born," she began. "I had my father for a few years until he contracted an illness while traveling. I've been under Eamon's care officially since I was four. If you could call how he treated me 'care.'"

"I would call it something else entirely, but I'm sure you don't need me ranting about that." The smirk he flashed her over the top of his hand of cards made that spark shoot through her again.

"Well, now I'm curious about *your* family." Saoirse straightened and rearranged her cards, placing her five of diamonds between her four and six of diamonds and laying the meld face-up on the table. "I know you have a cousin." She glanced at Kieran, who was slumped in his chair with a hand over his eyes. "And I'm assuming a father if your title is still 'prince.'"

"Yes, and he's...a curious fireann," Emrys said as he exchanged the card on the top of the discard pile for one in his hand. Saoirse lifted her brow at his description, but he took his time fixing his cards before elaborating. "We have an interesting relationship. He didn't have much interest in raising me after my mother died when I was young. He was more preoccupied with other things, like Kieran."

"So you were left on your own as well?" she asked.

"Not entirely," he answered. "The Head Healer of the court and her partner, the House Manager, stepped in as my caretakers."

"I'm guessing then you don't have siblings." Saoirse took the top card on the stockpile and grinned to herself as luck granted her a queen of clubs. She laid her second completed meld next to her first and waited for Emrys to take his turn.

"I do not have any siblings." He didn't display any tells as he also took a card from the stockpile and arranged his hand before picking a card to discard. "The closest I have to siblings are Kieran, who I don't think of fondly, and two of the three dukes who currently serve on our court. We're all fairly close in age, and we attended boarding school together."

"I can't imagine what it would be like growing up with Kieran."

"Yes, well, I learned early on what a rival was, and that Kieran was not one to let go of a grudge."

"What happened?"

Emrys shrugged one shoulder. "I'm not sure. He always bullied me when we were children. It might be lingering resentment over the hand life dealt him."

Saoirse knitted her brows, and after flicking his gaze up at her, he elaborated.

"His father, Callum, was king before my father. He died when Kieran was very young, and fae don't use regents. So, my father, his brother, became king, and I later came along, ultimately knocking Kieran back a place in the line of succession."

She gaped at how casually he explained court politics as if he were sharing the typical summer weather back home. He had lived it for quite some time, but Saoirse didn't think she could ever explain her family's dynamics in such an offhand manner.

"But he's had my father's attention his whole life and is treated more like the heir than I am." Emrys sighed. "He doesn't have much to complain about except something I had no control over."

"It seems like I got away unscathed in comparison." Saoirse huffed a laugh in disbelief, but her stomach clenched at the thought of continuing the subject. She didn't want to talk about Kieran, yet here she was bringing him up. "Why don't we find something else to talk about?"

They continued to play and chat about topics that couldn't possibly be linked to Kieran until Saoirse was down to three cards. She kept discarding and picking up a new third card, hoping for an ace or four of clubs. Emrys had curiously not laid down any melds and still had a full hand of ten cards. Once again, Saoirse discarded her third, and her lips tightened into a thin line as she picked another card in the wrong suit. She watched as Emrys smirked and reached for her discarded card, tucking it into his hand. He discarded his spare card before laying out his entire hand of ten consecutive cards in the spade suit.

"Rummy," he declared.

"No!" Saoirse slapped at the table. "I was so close to a fourth meld!"

"Sometimes you have to take a big risk for a big reward." Emrys shrugged, his triumphant grin unflinching.

"We're playing again." She scooped up the lot of cards and began to shuffle them.

"Don't enjoy losing, do you?"

"No," She split the cards into decks in her hands and shuffled them together. "I'm just persistent is all."

"Good, because so am I."

Saoirse kept her gaze unwavering on Emrys as she dealt their cards and straightened the stockpile. The prince didn't take his eyes off her either, but not because he was determined to beat her again. No, his gaze was hungry. It wasn't a look she was unfamiliar with. Kieran and other past lovers had given her a similar look. But there was something about it that stirred inappropriate thoughts in her mind and made her toes curl in her boots.

She finally tore her eyes off him to look at her hand. Entertaining her lustful thoughts was not an option, not with their bargain. It didn't feel right leading him into even just one night of passion only for her to leave. Emrys deserved better than that. But it didn't keep her from wondering what that night might feel like with him. What his body would feel like pressed against hers, his hands touching every inch of her...

Heat flooded Saoirse's cheeks, and she was thankful her eyes were averted to her cards. Her eyes scanned her hand, but it took her several passes to register the numbers or suits on the cards. Her mind was still stuck on that look Emrys gave her and the thoughts it evoked. She discreetly tugged at her collar as the images in her mind made her face grow hotter.

"Saoirse." Emrys's voice broke through her haze of thoughts, and she dared to look up at him.

"Hmm?" she hummed.

"It's your turn."

She glanced down at the discard pile and noticed a second card had been tossed down. "Oh," she breathed as she quickly reached for a card in the stockpile.

Her cards were still disorganized, and she tried to center herself. Dagda save her. It was going to be a long eight hours if just a look got her bothered enough to consider seeking out the nearest secluded corner on this boat. Beyond those eight hours...gods have mercy on her.

After having lunch and several more rounds of rummy, the steamer docked in Holyhead. Saoirse noticed how pale Kieran still looked as they disembarked and fought back a smirk. The three headed towards the train station nearby and hustled through the throng of people. Saoirse slid her hand into Emrys's instinctively as they wove through the mass of fae and humans. She told herself she did it because she didn't want to lose Emrys, not because she yearned to touch him.

"It wasn't nearly this crowded yesterday," Emrys said as they wove through the crowd. "Humans don't travel the train on Sundays."

"Why don't humans travel on Sundays?" Saoirse asked.

"It's apparently a holy day," he answered, tugging her as he made a left turn towards the closest train car.

"Every week?" she asked. "That seems excessive." She caught the corner of his grin as they reached the entrance of the train car.

Emrys stepped up the few stairs and turned to help Saoirse. "I should warn you, your magic will feel a little funny."

As he said so, Saoirse felt the slight hum that always vibrated deep in her veins cease almost entirely. "Why?"

"The iron," he answered. "The rail lines and train cars are entirely made of the stuff. It doesn't hurt you, but it does hinder magic. Humans only board the train with fae because of it."

Saoirse thought about her magic that manifested whenever it wanted to and found herself agreeing with the logic. Kieran grumbled something behind them, but when she glanced over her shoulder, he was still a sickly color and his eyes were glassy. He didn't have much energy to debate the topic of humans, and Saoirse was thankful for that small mercy. It was bad enough hearing her brother go on about it at the dining table. She didn't need it following her in the form of Kieran.

"This car is all ours," Emrys said as they stepped further into the train car.

The inside of it was quite luxurious. It had a small parlor with sapphire blue upholstered armchairs and a dining area with two-seat tables covered in a white, linen tablecloth against either wall of the car. The tables held dinner place settings, including all the necessary glasses placed upside down so they didn't topple over when the train began to move. Further down was a narrow hallway on the right that, Saoirse assumed, led to private compartments in the car.

Kieran shouldered past her and Emrys and trudged directly for one of the private compartments.

"He'll probably be in there for the duration of this ride and the next one as well," Emrys said as he reached for a chair at one of the tables. He nodded for Saoirse to take it, and she sat without hesitation.

"The next one?" she asked.

Emrys settled into a chair across from her and nodded. "We switch trains in Manchester. Two hours there and two hours to

Fearynhurst."

"Is there only one private compartment?"

"No, there are actually three. We can use any of them we wish."

"Do you always travel in your own private luxury car?" Saoirse asked, turning over one of her glasses as a crew member came by and filled it with water.

"The car isn't technically owned by me or my father," Emrys explained. "Any nobility can use it as long as they give enough notice for it to be added onto the train. I believe there will be more fae nobility joining us on the next train."

He sipped his water before launching into an enthusiastic history of early train travel and how much longer traveling took before the rail system was put in place, with a few personal anecdotes sprinkled amongst his facts. Saoirse quickly realized how much life he had experienced in comparison to her. Yes, he had at least a century of years on her measly twenty-three, but he had traveled for leisure and business, built friendships, and watched the world evolve. She—on the other hand—had been kept away from most everything that had to do with the outside world.

When the train pulled into Manchester an hour later, Saoirse felt the change in her magic as she disembarked one train transferred to their second one. Even with her lack of control over her magic, she could tell the difference between being on and off the train. While inside the train car, there was an emptiness she felt as if her magic had been drained from her blood. She felt strangely vulnerable, but she could see how disarmed fae would put the human passengers at ease.

Kieran once again holed himself up in a private compartment, his pale pallor easing but his demeanor still unpleasant. Saoirse and Emrys settled at one of the two dining tables in the luxury car and were joined by another fae couple. Emrys recognized them as they passed by and greeted them. He introduced Saoirse, and she learned they were parents of a duchess of the court. But she had been thrown so much new information, she barely registered their names before they settled in the parlor area as the train pulled out of the station.

The sun outside dipped below the horizon, coating the landscape with an orange glow, and Saoirse drank in the summer evening scenery. However, the serene atmosphere didn't last long as the train came to a screeching halt just a mere twenty minutes after leaving Manchester.

"Why have we stopped?" Saoirse asked.

"I'm not sure." Emrys shrugged. He stood and moved towards the door that led to the next train car. A few minutes later, he returned with an explanation. A large tree had fallen and was laying across both sets of tracks. "It's beyond the hours that anyone is available to handle it, and daylight is rapidly fading," Emrys explained. "Unfortunately, I don't think it will be handled until morning."

"So we're stuck on this train overnight?" Saoirse asked.

"Unless there's a rare high fae with an obscene level of strength on this train, the answer is yes." He frowned as he stared out the window to the quickly darkening scenery. "We will have to share a compartment."

"You sound disappointed."

He slid his gaze to her, and that spark buzzed between her shoulders. "You want to share a compartment with me?"

Saoirse opened her mouth to answer, but she wasn't sure what answer was going to come out. Want was a bit of an understatement. She had fought against her physical impulses throughout the day, and the idea of sharing a private space made her thankful for the rigidness of her corset to conceal her stiffening nipples. But she had a whisper encouraging her to keep flaming those desires, no matter how terrible of an idea she knew it was.

"I don't mind sharing," she finally said. "And I believe compartments have two beds, don't they?"

"Yes, I believe they do." He nodded slowly, the thoughts rushing through his mind apparent in his gaze. "You don't snore, do you?"

Saoirse let out a laugh and shook her head. "No, do you?"

"I've never been told so." Emrys grinned, and she noticed his body relax. "If you no longer want to share a compartment, I can find the most comfortable chair in the parlor and let you have the compartment to yourself."

"I've spent the night with worse people," she said. "You're hardly a match for them."

Emrys's grin faded slowly, and the angles of his face turned hard. Morrigan strike her. She hadn't realized how her words came across until she heard them.

"That sounded worse than I intended," she tried to amend. "I just mean I don't have any hesitance about sharing a room with you."

He nodded, and his posture relaxed again, but there was still a touch of awkward stiffness to it. Before she could continue to assure him, a dining crew member came by with two plates of dinner and an offer of a bottle of wine. Emrys nodded to them and accepted the offered wine. There was a stretch of silence between him and Saoirse as the crew member filled their glasses with wine and offered their assistance with anything else during their meal.

The two were quiet while they ate, the tinge of awkwardness seeping deeper between them. After their plates were cleared, the sun had completely disappeared and the dim light of the electric chandeliers filled the car with a soft glow. Saoirse yawned and tried to cover it, but it was too strong to be concealed.

"Sorry," she murmured.

"You have nothing to be sorry for." Emrys shook his head and stood from his seat. "It's been a long day of traveling, and it still isn't finished. Shall we retire for the evening?"

She nodded and stood, following him to the middle compartment. It was a tight space with a small vanity and an upholstered seat on the right, a single bed on the left, and a large window on the opposite wall. Saoirse frowned at the one bed and searched the ceiling for the handle to pull down the second bed.

"Emrys," she said. He turned from his open suitcase towards her and raised a brow in interest. "Where is the second bed?"

Emrys followed her gaze to the ceiling and reached up, his hand skimming the outline of what had to be an additional bed.

He found a notch that his finger could slide into and gave a forceful tug. The bed didn't budge and after two more attempts, the prince sighed in defeat.

"It seems to be stuck," he said, turning back to face her. "I could ask Kieran to switch his room with ours."

"That's assuming he isn't already asleep." Saoirse knew the general slept like the dead, and if he was disturbed, may the gods show favor on anyone who dared to wake him.

"You have a point." Emrys sighed and rubbed his hand over the back of his neck. "I could try to find that armchair if you'd like the bed to yourself."

She shook her head. "You don't have to do that."

"You're comfortable sharing a bed?" he asked.

"Emrys," she said, one corner of her lips lifting. "My sensibilities are not that delicate. You don't need to act so honorable. We both plan to merely sleep tonight, correct?"

"Yes." He nodded before sighing. "Alright." He turned back to his suitcase and popped open the lid. "But just so you know, none of this is an act."

Saoirse opened her mouth to return a cheeky comment, but she stood with her mouth hanging open as she gawked at his backside. He had slid off his jacket, and she could see the muscles under his shirt working as he unbuttoned his waistcoat.

"Well, then I wish you would be a little less honorable." The words tumbled from her lips before she could stop them. Heat filled her cheeks, and she could only stand, stunned.

Emrys paused before turning to look at her over his shoulder. She quickly spun around to the vanity and occupied her hands with unbuttoning her blouse and skirt. Her thoughts warred in her mind as she considered leaning into what she insinuated and what she felt was actually appropriate. As she reached the bare layers of her combination and corset, she pulled together the courage to ask what she felt was necessary.

"Emrys," she said, fidgeting with her fingers.

"Yes, Princess?"

Saoirse forced herself to turn around and face him as she asked her question. She found Emrys's suspenders hanging from his hips and his shirt gone, exposing his torso. Her assumptions about his physique had been correct all along. She flattened her palms on the vanity behind her and gripped the edge of it as she pressed her thighs together.

"What are our boundaries on this offer?" As she spoke, Emrys slowly stalked towards her, closing the space between them. "I know we should have discussed this last night,"—he placed his hands on the vanity on either side of her and caged her between his arms—"but I suppose now is better than never."

A slow smile spread on his face as the space between them narrowed. Saoirse's heart pounded as his gaze roamed down her body. She should put an end to this. Tell him that they should keep their distance until they were officially married, and she was on her way to her own home in the country.

When his emerald eyes returned to meet her hazel ones, Emrys licked his lips. "I hope it's obvious I'm attracted to you."

Saoirse nodded, suddenly unable to form words.

"Then I'm not going to lie. If you give me even half a reason, it will be quite difficult to watch you leave without putting up a fight."

Her ability to speak returned, and Saoirse furrowed her brows. "If I'm that much of a weakness to you, why offer me this bargain?"

Emrys sighed and dropped his gaze to the floor. "I'll admit I was a bit impulsive last night." He raised his gaze back to her, and something twinkled in the gold flecks around his irises. "I saw you in distress and couldn't live with myself if I didn't at least offer to help."

"So you offered me this out of pity?"

"No, Saoirse," he stammered. The prince closed his eyes and sighed again. "I would love nothing more than for you to stay and be my wife. But I know that isn't my decision to make. All I can do is make the idea of being my wife as appealing as possible."

"You made this offer knowing you'd possibly get nothing in return?"

"It wouldn't be the first act of martyrdom I've ever done." He gave her a dry grin. It dropped quickly, and Saoirse glimpsed an emotional mask raise on his face. "So, tell me, what are our boundaries, Princess?"

Saoirse thought over his words. She *was* curious to know what exactly Emrys could offer her if she did decide to stay. The only obstacle hindering that decision was sleeping in the compartment next door. Could Emrys alone be enough of a reason to overcome Kieran's consistent presence in her life? Or was her past with the general too much to appreciate what Emrys had to offer?

"Show me why I should stay," she said quietly. "Show me what I'd miss if I left and walked away. And I don't mean ravish me," she added when she noticed Emrys's eyes darken. "Anyone could do that. Show me why being with you would be worth it, worth putting up with Kieran."

Emrys studied her for a long moment before a soft smile pulled at his lips, and he nodded. "Alright," he said as he lifted a hand to stroke Saoirse's arm every so gently with the back of his index finger. "But I hope you know this means I won't be able to stay quiet if you ultimately decide to leave."

"I can accept that." Saoirse looked down at the hand stroking her arm, and gooseflesh rose on her skin. They stood in silence for another beat before Emrys dropped his hand and stepped away from her.

"This time would probably be a good time to mention I have a suite with a second bedroom at the estate," he said. "It's all yours for as long as you like it."

"Thank you," she said with a small smile.

"You're welcome." He turned back to organize his discarded belongings, and she caught a glimpse of the bare skin of his back for the first time. She swallowed a gasp at the crisscrossing scars blanketing Emrys's back. Fae skin didn't scar normally. With how quickly their bodies healed and the remedies healers possessed, scars were nearly impossible. Saoirse couldn't even begin to imagine what Emrys must have gone through to earn the scars let alone that many.

She was lost in her horrified thoughts, her gaze was affixed to him, until she registered the waistband of his trousers slipping off his hips. She whirled back to the vanity and tried to busy herself by fumbling with the clips on her garters. Her eyes kept peeking at the mirror, her morbid curiosity getting the better of her.

"They don't hurt," Emrys said.

"What?" she asked, flustered. The garter in her hand snapped back, and she hissed from the bite it gave her. When she peeked in the mirror at him, he was looking at her over his shoulder. He must have caught her staring.

"That's what everyone asks about my scars," he elaborated. "They're nearly a century old. The only pain they give me is remembering why I have them."

"Oh," Saoirse breathed. She didn't know what else to say. Did she tell him she was sorry he had lived with them for so long? Her curiosity craved to know how he got them, but she deemed that to be prying too deep.

The floor of their compartment creaked as he stepped closer to her and murmured in her ear, "They look much better with scratch marks, though."

Saoirse shivered as his breath brushed against her ear, and she bit her bottom lip.

"You asked me to be less honorable." He hovered behind her, and she could feel the warmth of his body radiating against her. "But to stop short of ravishing you. Is this the fine line you'd like to walk along?"

Saoirse's body begged her to say no. She yearned to lean into the sexual tension they had been building. But she knew it wasn't a good decision, and she had made that clear. Damn her and her moment of responsibility.

"Yes," she whispered. Her gaze met his in the mirror, and his grin was downright feral.

"Good to know." Emrys leaned even closer to her ear. "I would hate for Lord and Lady of Saint Clewark to learn just how much stamina the Crown Prince has." He chuckled and reached towards the pinned bun at the crown of her head. "May I?"

Saoirse nodded and watched as he pulled the pins from her hair. Piece by piece, her hair cascaded down. Emrys's fingers brushed along her neck as he gathered it over one of her shoulders. "You should know I love to touch, and it will be hard to keep my hands to myself with how beautiful you are. But, please, stop me if I cross that line you've drawn."

"I promise I'll tell you." Saoirse shivered thinking about the results of the last time she asked a fireann to stop, and how catastrophic that had ended. She pushed the thoughts away as Emrys stepped back, giving her space. Could he sense her thoughts? She looked at herself in the mirror and tried to see if her discomfort was written on her face.

She shook herself and returned to dressing for bed. Having packed all her belongings in her trunk, she would have to settle for sleeping in her combination. Her fingers nimbly loosened the laces of her corset until she could comfortably open the busk. The chill of the night brushed against her skin as she slid her stockings off and plopped them next to her other garments.

Saoirse let out a yawn as she peeked in the mirror to see Emrys in a pair of pyjamas. He was pulling back the layers of bedding on their narrow, single bed. Gooseflesh rose over her skin as she thought about being close to him again. She nimbly braided her hair before turning out the electric light and tiptoeing to the bed in the dark. Even with the amount of care she put into keeping the right amount of space between her and Emrys, the sheets were thin and didn't trap enough heat to make her comfortable. She writhed towards the only source of warmth she felt until Emrys's hand wrapped around her waist and pinned her against him.

"Stop," he rasped in her ear. "Unless you plan to rescind everything you said earlier, I recommend you stop squirming against me."

Her face heated, and she forced herself to relax against him, the heat of his body seeping through the fabric of her combination.

"Sorry," she murmured. "I promise I don't mean to."

"I know." His hand on her stomach relaxed, and he tried to pull it away.

"No," Saoirse whispered impulsively. She caught his hand and placed it back over her waist. "It was fine where it was."

A low chuckle filled her ear, and he gently pulled her closer. "Whatever you say, Princess."

Saoirse melted against him as she surrendered to his embrace, and her eyes drifted closed, sleep finally pulling her under.

Emrys *felt the* sting of ripped flesh before he heard the crack of leather. The smell of dirt and grass mocked him. The smell that he had embraced in the spring and summer. The smell that meant renewal and fresh life. A heinous, oily laugh filled the air, but he didn't dare turn to look at who had uttered it. He didn't need to.

His head swam, and his vision blurred, the blades of grass melding into a single color of green. He slumped to his knees, his chest bent over his lap. His breathing became shallower with each breath, and Emrys pleaded silently with the gods to end it. He had endured enough, he had concluded, and was ready to meet the fate of the gods.

His vision went black, and a cry came from his body until all the pain was released. He became aware again and carefully checked himself. But it wasn't his body anymore. It was a vessel that carried his soul. When Emrys lifted his head to examine his new, blank surroundings, his vessel turned numb.

Figures stood before him, each less familiar than the next. They looked neither fae nor human. They were made up mostly of light with an abstract form that resembled a body and a few defining features arranged to look like a face. Emrys stared at them in awe. Were these the gods of the Heavenly Realm?

They stared down at him with unreadable expressions, and he

had the sudden urge to beg them. But he had little control over the workings of his vessel. His tongue didn't feel like his own, and his feet refused to obey him. One of the gods stepped towards him and examined him as if he could scan through to the soul the vessel held. Burning gold eyes met Emrys's, and fear engulfed him to the point he felt as if he were physically shrinking.

This was his judgement, his final verdict to determine where in the otherworld he would settle for the rest of eternity. He'd have to confront all he had done in his life and the ultimate consequence of his actions over the last several decades. He wasn't ready to. He wasn't prepared to face the awful truth of his actions.

Emrys woke with a start, a gasp escaping him before he could stop it. He took a moment to study his surroundings. It wasn't the Heavenly Realm, but his private compartment on the train. The sweet scent of vanilla and sandalwood pulled him back to his reality, and he realized Saoirse was snuggled against his chest. She must have turned over in her sleep and now had her face buried in his pyjama top.

He relaxed into the narrow mattress and studied her features in the dim light. Her lips were slightly parted, and her face held no emotion, just blissful sleep. He had the urge to trace her features with his thumb but thought better of it, remembering that he had no idea how light or heavy of a sleeper she was.

Once again, Emrys found himself sending a silent, overly grateful prayer up to the gods. Last night, Saoirse had been a few packed petticoats away from fleeing into the night, and there was no telling if he would have found her if he waited longer than he did.

He had already planned to bargain for their marriage arrangement before he arrived. Kieran was an obstacle Emrys knew he'd have a hard time overcoming. When he witnessed Saoirse running out of the drawing room, he knew he had to offer up anything he could to appease her. A marriage in name only wasn't ideal, but he could work with it.

The gods were proving their grace today. He had hoped for an appropriate opening at some point before the wedding to bargain again with her to stay. But Saoirse had bargained for it first. She wanted him to prove staying was worth the headache of marrying into a family that included Kieran. It didn't seem like it would be hard. Emrys would woo her with his charm, and the gods would do the rest.

Saoirse sighed in her sleep, drawing Emrys's attention. He had learned bits about her throughout the day, but there was still just as much—if not more—that he didn't know. What were her favorite meals? What was the color she looked best in? What did those luscious lips taste like? His thoughts spiraled into territory that he shouldn't entertain with her in the same bed, but it was hard to resist them with her so physically close. The heat of her body was as soothing as warm tea on a chilly fall morning, and he fought the regret of giving her the second bedroom in his suite.

Emrys's arm was still around her waist, and he risked disturbing her as he gently stroked her spine. She made a small noise and stirred but didn't wake. Her hand came up and pressed against his chest. Earlier when she had touched him, he just about dissolved under her palm. Now, he could have sworn the heat from her hand was going to burn a hole in his pyjama top, and it had nothing to do with her magic. Her body became heavier in his arms, and his eyes drooped as that magical sense of calm blanketed him. The last glimpse he saw was her peaceful, sleeping face before he joined her in sleep once more.

Gray morning light spilled in from the large square window next to the bed, and Saoirse slowly came aware of her surroundings. Shadows danced around the room and a metallic sound outside told her their train was once again moving. She wasn't sure how far they had gone, but she hoped a porter would come through and announce what the next station would be.

Her attention was then caught by the feel of Emrys's chest rising and falling with his breath under the palm of her hand. Her first instinct was to pull away, but her limbs refused to move. As much as she had relished having her own bed to spread out as wide as she could for many years, there was something about being held that felt even better.

Emrys stirred, and he inhaled deeply before his eyes cracked open. "Good morning, Princess." His gravelly voice and sleepy grin made that spark zip down her spine again.

"Good morning," she said quietly. "I must have tossed around in my sleep."

He chuckled, and his thumb mindlessly traced circles on her back. "It's alright. You didn't elbow me in the throat or eye, so there's no harm done." The amused grin on his face seemed to be frozen there.

Saoirse gasped in feigned horror. "I would never." She couldn't help the giggle that escaped her throat. Her smile matched Emrys's, and a warmth settled low in her abdomen. She had an urge to kiss him, to press her body closer to his and tangle their limbs together. It would be so easy, but she hesitated. It wasn't right to give into her desires just to leave shortly after. However, with him so close, she struggled to remember why.

"Stoneblack station in five minutes," a porter outside called, interrupting Saoirse's wrestling thoughts.

Emrys sighed, and she swore she saw disappointment in his eyes. "Stoneblack is less than thirty minutes from Fearynhurst," he said as he stretched his limbs.

Saoirse nodded, reluctantly pulling away from him, and yawned as she rolled out of the bed. She recoiled as she glimpsed the state of her hair in the mirror and fumbled in her suitcase for her hairbrush. If she hadn't witnessed the way Emrys looked at her when he woke up, she would doubt he had any attraction left towards her. Once her hair was smooth and tamed, she tried to pin it into an acceptable bun. The floor underneath her creaked as Emrys got out of bed and began to dress. Saoirse kept her gaze averted from the mirror as she dressed back into the rest of her under layers. Tempting herself wasn't doing her any favors.

She wrangled the busk of her corset closed and attempted to tighten the laces behind her back. After a few minutes of struggling, Emrys asked, "Can I help you with that?"

Her gaze met his in the mirror, and her cheeks warmed from getting caught struggling. "Do you think you can do it properly?" she asked.

"I've done my fair share of undressing boireannaich," he answered with the whisper of a smirk on his face. "I think I can deduce how to tighten the laces on a corset."

"Alright." Saoirse held out the tails of her corset laces and kept her hands on her bust as Emrys pulled the lines of laces taut. She was impressed with how methodical he was at tightening her corset, and her mind wandered to fantasies of him loosening the laces and undressing her further. Her face burned even hotter as she pushed those fantasies away while his hands worked each cross of laces.

"Does that feel alright?" he asked, holding the loose tail of laces at her waist.

"Yes." She nodded. "I'm quite impressed."

He chuckled and tied her corset closed. "You should see how quickly I can unlace one."

Saoirse shivered as thoughts of him doing just that surfaced again. Between the way she woke up tangled in his arms and her wandering thoughts that had her clenching her thighs together, she wondered how long having her own room would last. If this was what every morning could be, she might just be able to keep guilt from tainting her pleasure.

Emrys led Saoirse, his hand intertwined with hers, through the small Fearynhurst station to a Brougham carriage waiting outside. He handed her up into the carriage as the footman loaded their luggage.

Once they were settled, the carriage lurched forward and began down the road. Saoirse's hand remained connected with Emrys's, and she enjoyed how comfortable it was. It was just enough touch to keep both of their desires curbed for the time being. How long it would last, she wasn't sure.

Kieran kept quiet for the short carriage ride through the countryside to the estate. Dark circles sat beneath his eyes, telling Saoirse that although the train didn't sway like the ferry, he didn't get much rest. Saoirse shifted her gaze to the passing landscape outside the carriage. The main road was sparse with homes and shops sprinkled along the roadside. Soon, the main road transitioned to a dirt drive lined with trimmed bay trees. The roofline of an estate peeked out over the top of the trees, and as the carriage rounded the end of the drive, Saoirse saw the rest of the house come into view.

Roman style columns lined a majority of the front entrance, and the sharp, clean shape of the house put Saoirse's Tudor family estate in Dublin to shame. When the carriage came to a stop, Emrys opened the door and handed Saoirse down from it. Kieran stayed in the carriage, the vehicle taking him to his final destination that wasn't the estate. Relief washed over Saoirse as she breathed easily for what felt like the first time in two days.

A pair of servants raced out of the house and towards the carriage, pulling Emrys and Saoirse's luggage from it. A stout boireann with dark hair, dressed in a plain dark plum-colored dress, stepped down onto the drive from the front door to greet them.

"Finally!" she exclaimed as she kissed Emrys's cheek and smiled up at him, wrinkles creasing around her eyes. "Did you miss every train out of Manchester?"

"No, Mamanna," Emrys answered. "We were stuck overnight. A coal train was derailed, and no one could get it back on the rails until this morning."

"Well," the boireann huffed out a sigh, "I'm glad you're home." She turned to Saoirse and gave her an equally warm smile. "And I'm glad to meet your beautiful bride." She gave a small curtsy before introducing herself as the house manager, Ada. Saoirse nodded and introduced herself in response. "Alright, well, you two must be perfectly famished. There is still food in the serving trays in the breakfast room."

Ada turned back towards the house and led them through the doors. Saoirse's shoes clicked on the dark, polished floors as she followed the house manager to the west wing of the house. They passed through the dining room, where a glossy oak table sat with nearly a dozen chairs surrounding it. Saoirse noticed the walls were adorned with plum-colored wallpaper, cream accents, and portraits of who she assumed were past family members from the last several centuries. Emrys murmured a few figures of note as they passed, and she tried to absorb their images and names as best she could.

The breakfast room was past the dining room and floor to ceiling windows bathed the room in warm light. A small round table with white linens and a vase of fresh summer flowers sat in the middle of the room. To the left of the doorway sat a white, ornately carved fireplace decorated with tall candles and various trinkets. Saoirse's wandering gaze soon fell on the sideboard to her right as the aroma of a hot breakfast vied for her attention.

Emrys pulled out a chair at the table and offered it to her. Within moments of her taking her seat, servants came into the room, filled two plates with toast, ham, eggs, and potatoes, and served them accordingly. Saoirse's stomach growled as she reached for her fork, and she and Emrys were silent for a long moment as they ate.

"Is this what I can expect every morning?" she asked, grinning playfully as she chewed.

"Ada outdoes herself every day," Emrys answered. "But if you'd like to have any of your meals upstairs, all you have to do is ask."

"That's quite luxurious."

"I'd want you to have nothing less, Princess."

Saoirse blushed. She had asked him to prove his reasons to stay with him and doting on her definitely fell into that category. Kieran finally being absent didn't hurt either.

"Danu bless you both. You've made it home." A tall and lean, but admittedly aged, fireann came through the doorway. His hair on the top of his head was absent, but his full, silver beard revealed he must have gone through several Settlings. "I was beginning to wonder if you both had decided to run off to Scotland and make your lives there."

"No, Father, if we did that, I believe any dowry that was promised would be voided," Emrys said, his words humorous but posture stiff.

Father. The king.

Saoirse quickly rose to her feet, her fork clattering on her plate, and lowered into a curtsy. Emrys had said the etiquette at his estate was relaxed, but the Northern Fae king had the power to dissolve their marriage contract if he found her unsuitable.

"Your Majesty," she said quickly.

"Oh, dear, no," the king said with a chuckle. "There's no need for that. Please, sit back down." Saoirse straightened and settled back into her seat, her cheeks burning with embarrassment. So much for a stunning first impression. "I know your brother has probably hammered those human manners into you, but they aren't necessary here. I like to keep the classic etiquette from when the fae first made it to England. Humans only created their arbitrary rules because they're all too hot-headed to remain civil at a dinner table." He punctuated his words with another chuckle.

"It's an honor to meet you, Your Majesty," she said before sipping on her glass of water and hoping her embarrassed flush would cool.

"It's an honor to meet *you*. And, please, use my given name, Alastair." He turned to Emrys and beamed at him. "You've chosen a very lovely boireann as your wife."

"I'm lucky she entertained marrying me," Emrys said.

Alastair grinned and returned his attention to Saoirse. "You look so much like your father. Obviously, much nicer to look at thanks to your mother's contributions."

Something stirred in her chest at the way he looked at her. "You knew my parents?" she asked. None of her siblings discussed her parents. Eamon shut down any conversation that talked about them, especially when the subject was their father, his predecessor.

"Oh, of course." Alastair nodded. "We worked closely with your father during the Great Famine. We were able to save many lives during that time."

A smile tugged at the corners of Saoirse's lips. While political talk wasn't her favorite topic, hearing about her father's reign made him seem less like a ghost of her past. She wanted to hear more, but Alastair didn't take up a seat at the table, giving off the idea he was only stopping by.

"Did you only come to greet us, Father? Or did you have business I needed to be aware of?" Emrys asked.

"Oh, no, I only heard you were home, and you hadn't returned empty handed." Alastair flashed another smile at Saoirse before backing away. "I'll leave you two to get settled."

"Thank you," Saoirse murmured. As Alastair turned back towards the doorway, she called out his name. "If you ever have time, I'd like to hear more about my father."

"Of course, dear." The corners of his eyes crinkled. "I can always make time."

The king vanished into the dining room, and Saoirse noticed Emrys sat silent. His movements were stiff and his jaw set, but he didn't say anything to explain himself. A few moments later, their plates were cleared, and the tightness in his posture melted just a bit.

"Shall we go upstairs so you can see your quarters?" he asked.

Saoirse nodded and stood. Emrys guided her back towards the entry to the house where the stairs separated the entry vestibule from the east wing. Upstairs, a hall on the left was lined with doors leading to various bedrooms and guest quarters. At the end of the hall was a set of double doors that Emrys guided her towards.

He opened and held one of the doors open for Saoirse to enter. She took a few steps inside before taking in the suite in front of her. Amongst other décor, a cream-colored sofa and matching armchairs sat in front of a cast iron fireplace on the left side of the room. A small piano and a bookcase that was built to the ceiling sat on the other side of the room. Potted palm plants were sprinkled around the space, and a small desk was set up near the piano. Two doors stood on either side of the room, and Emrys informed her which one led where.

"The door next to the fireplace leads to your room," he said. "The door beside the piano leads to mine. Your suitcase should be in your room already if not unpacked and your things put away."

She nodded, barely registering his words as her eyes continued scanning the room. Thick curtains were drawn back on the sides of each of the three floor to ceiling windows, allowing light to pour in and cast shadows amongst the furniture. She stepped towards the sofa and ran her fingers over the ornate top of its back.

The sound of footsteps broke through her haze of awe, and she had the urge to ask Emrys about his demeanor downstairs. She had hesitated downstairs in case Alastair was still nearby and was in range of accidentally eavesdropping on them. But when she turned around in the sitting room, Emrys had disappeared. She felt the weight of his absence as she circled to the front of the sofa and sat down. Her brow rose as she noticed a round black form on the seat next to her.

It had white splotches and streaks, and she carefully reached out to touch it. When it popped its black and white head up and yawned, showing off its small fanged teeth, she realized it was a cat. The pattern of his fur made her think of the formalwear that fireannaich wore to special occasions.

"Hello," she said as she reached over to pet it. The cat sniffed at her fingers before bumping the top of its head towards her hand, begging for attention. She petted it and heard the low rumble of a purr.

"I see you've met Owen." Emrys's voice startled her, but she recovered before he could notice.

"Owen, is it?" She gave the cat's chin a scratch, and he squinted his eyes shut in appreciation. "He's very affectionate."

"Oh, he'll let anyone who gives him the time of day pet him." Emrys moved to the front of the sofa, and Owen rose, arching his spine before stretching out his back paws. He bumped his head against Emrys's legs, and Saoirse heard the purring intensify.

"He's very fond of you."

"He has a special affection for me."

She watched as Owen flopped back onto the sofa cushion and turned to expose the white strip of fur that ran from his nose to his belly. "I never had a pet," she confessed. "The closest I had was a wild cat sìth in our garden. But it merely chased me through the trees whenever I went looking outside to play. It was nothing like Owen."

"Well, Owen will quickly adopt you." Emrys grinned.

The feline moved towards her and flopped against her thighs, his loud purring still audible. Saoirse grinned and scratched under his chin again. Emrys remained in front of her, watching her and the cat, and she knew she wouldn't have a better time to ask about his father. She swallowed as she searched for the right way to bring it up.

"Emrys," she said softly. She lifted her gaze to him, and a small jolt of that spark sizzled between her shoulder blades. "I know you told me your relationship wasn't easy with your father when you were growing up, but he seems to have come around."

Emrys blew out a breath and dropped down onto the sofa next to her, his gaze fixed on Owen. "He has somewhat," he said in an equally quiet voice as hers. "But it's still complicated. The last few months he's treated me like the son he actually sired. However, it's only been in private. As if he doesn't want anyone else to know he's fond of me. In council meetings, he still favors Kieran." Emrys lifted his gaze to her again. "You've been the first person he's acted like that in front of."

"Oh." Saoirse couldn't think of anything else to say. Eamon had been controlling ever since she could remember, whether or not family or guests were present. She couldn't imagine if he was reasonable when no one else was around and then acted like he had no use for her in front others. Thoughts of Eamon's behavior made her think of another question. "Does your father know about my past relationship with Kieran?"

"Most likely." Emrys shrugged. "I thought he would bring it up earlier, but he might have chosen to ignore it for your sake."

"Well, that's a small blessing," she murmured.

He nodded before giving Owen's stomach one last scratch and rising from the sofa. She could feel the heat of his body radiate towards hers. "Have you looked at your room yet?"

"No." Her voice cracked, and she cleared her throat. "Not yet." The thought of going back to an empty bed after sleeping so soundly in Emrys's arms had her delaying the visit to her room. But it was for the best. She had to stop tempting herself or else she would never find the courage to walk away when she needed to.

Emrys held out his hand, and she took it without hesitation.

"I'll go inspect it now," she said, standing. He let her hand go once she was on her feet, and her heart squeezed. Danu's tits, she needed to get herself together. Keeping a healthy distance was in both their best interests. She crossed to the door Emrys had pointed out earlier, and tears immediately pinched the corners of her eyes as she opened the door.

The floors were polished and pristine. A thick silk quilt was spread on the bed to her left and was layered with Witney blankets. More quilts in an array of pastel colors sat on a cedar chest at the foot of the bed. A dresser and vanity free of scorch marks sat together in the corner across from the door and the rug on the floor under her bed was still nicely woven without a single blemish.

Saoirse sank onto the bed and wiped at her eyes. It was silly to cry over a room without damaged furniture, especially when she had been debating on turning it down moments ago. But her threshold for thoughtfulness had been set so low she was overwhelmed.

The frame of the doorway creaked, and she gave another hasty swipe at her face before looking up. Emrys leaned against the doorframe and gave her a half-smile. Her delight in the room turned sour when she remembered she was set to leave soon. This room would only be hers for a week at most. Sure, Emrys would ensure whatever home she wanted was as pristine as this room, but she was quickly becoming attached to it.

"You can be honest," Emrys said. "You can tell me you hate the curtains. It won't hurt anyone's feelings. I think Ada would even agree with you."

A laugh bubbled to the surface, and Saoirse's grin kept the rest of her tears at bay. "No." She shook her head. "It's perfect. For the time being, anyway. Thank you."

His smile faltered a bit, but he quickly recovered. "My pleasure, Princess." His gaze did a sweep of the room before landing on her again. "I'll let you enjoy your perfect room. If you need anything, I'll be downstairs."

Saoirse nodded. Once he disappeared from her doorway, she shucked off her boots and picked up her feet, hugging her knees to her chest. She was one step closer to her freedom. So why did she feel so hollow?

aoirse spent her first night in the Fearynhurst estate tossing and turning, unable to get her body comfortable or her mind quiet enough to sleep. While her room was more than she could have asked for, it wasn't familiar. At one point, she became tempted to sneak across the suite to Emrys's room, but the longer she hesitated, the less she was willing to disturb him. Instead, she took the spurts of sleep she was granted until the sun rose and streamed through the cracks of the curtains.

She was barely awake when someone knocked twice on her door and entered her room. A tall boireann briskly walked across the room, her chatelaine jingling on her hip, and pulled the curtains open. Morning light flooded in, temporarily blinding Saoirse.

"Good morning, Your Highness," the boireann greeted with a curtsy.

"Good morning," Saoirse replied.

"Would you like me to draw you a bath before breakfast?" The boireann continued to pull open the curtains, tying them back neatly.

"No, after breakfast is fine." Saoirse yawned and looked at the boireann more closely now that her eyes had adjusted. She had pale skin and caramel colored hair. She didn't look plain, but her servant's attire didn't do her any favors. "I'm sorry, I didn't get your name."

The boireann turned and smiled. "Rory," she answered. "I'm the housekeeper of the estate."

Saoirse didn't know all the intricacies of overseeing servants as that had fallen to Cressida in Ireland, but she was fairly sure the housekeeper wasn't obligated to lady's maid duties. "Do I not have a lady's maid?" she asked.

"That will be me," Rory said. "Ada is finding a lady's maid to hire, but for now, I've volunteered to fulfill those duties."

That made Saoirse curious as to whether or not Emrys shared the details of their bargain with anyone in the house. If she was to leave, it didn't make sense for Ada to hire a lady's maid right away. On the other hand, it could just be a coincidence in timing. She and Emrys did have less than a day of official courting before they became engaged. That was quite a short notice to have a lady's maid hired and trained.

Rory rummaged through Saoirse's dresser and wardrobe and placed the clothes she picked at the foot of the bed. Saoirse rose and worked alongside Rory to dress. The housekeeper had chosen a simple white shirtwaist and a matching jacket and skirt set in a burnt orange color. Rory helped Saoirse slide her feet into her boots and buttoned them closed. The housekeeper checked if Saoirse needed anything else before curtsying and making her exit.

Saoirse poked her head into the sitting room and found it quiet with the curtains drawn back. She ventured out of her room and saw Emrys's door across the room was left wide open. She peeked inside to find his bed empty. He must have already made his way downstairs.

She made her way to join him and when she came to the breakfast room, Emrys was already seated in the small dining room with a plate of food. He glanced up as Saoirse walked through the doorway and gave her a half-smile. She nearly jumped when the spark jolted through her. If she wasn't awake before, she was now.

"Good morning," he greeted.

"Good morning," she replied, taking a seat next to him.

A servant breezed into the breakfast room and served her a

plate of food similar to the one she had the day before. Emrys took a bite of food and seemed like he was preparing to ask a question after he swallowed when Ada joined them.

"Good morning, sweetheart." The boireann took one of the empty seats as she held a leather-bound notebook and a pencil. She flipped a few pages until she came to a set of blank, lined pages. "Emrys, I know that you have business to catch up with this morning, so I won't keep either of you too long. But I did want to settle a few details for the wedding with both of you."

"Of course." Emrys laid down his fork, turning his attention to Ada.

Saoirse nodded and watched Ada scribble something down in her notebook. The house manager then launched into a series of questions about florals, place settings, and meal courses. Saoirse, having no experience in any kind of party planning, was at a loss of how to answer her questions. Emrys kindly explained the differences between her options, giving her the power to make a final decision. She was unsure of her answers at first, but when neither Emrys nor Ada questioned her, she grew more confident in her choices.

"Mistress." Rory burst into the breakfast room, interrupting their planning. "Oh." She stopped short when Saoirse and Emrys turned their attention to her. "My apologies," she bobbed a quick curtsy, "I forgot you were with the prince and princess." Rory turned to leave, but Ada halted her.

"Aurora, did you need something?"

"It can wait." The housekeeper's face was beginning to redden. "It's just something with Rhys."

Ada let out a sigh. "I'll be just a moment longer. I'll find you when I'm finished."

Rory nodded and bobbed another curtsy before vanishing.

"Rhys is our butler," Emrys murmured to Saoirse before she could ask.

"Yes, and I can't get him and Aurora to get along to save my life," Ada added. She hovered the tip of her pencil down the list of notes she had made before scribbling something else. She quickly pivoted their conversation back to where it was before the interruption. "Emrys, have you decided on the guests that should be invited?"

"Yes." Emrys nodded and sat a bit more upright. He listed off only a dozen names, a small variety of dukes, duchesses, lords, and ladies. Having never attended a wedding in her lifetime, Saoirse learned from their conversation fae weddings were small and intimate, with only the closest peers in attendance as witnesses. This was apparently in contrast to human weddings where it was a large celebration that included peers that were only vaguely acquainted with the bride and groom.

"And Saoirse?" Ada asked.

"Me?" Saoirse was taken aback. No one had ever asked her for her list of guests. But she also had never had one before. She hadn't really made any lasting friendships in her life to warrant invitations to social events.

Ada nodded and waited for her share who she wanted invited.

"I guess my brothers," Saoirse answered. "Although I don't believe they planned to come. Other than them, I don't have anyone else that comes to mind."

The house manager gave her a soft, empathetic smile. "That's no problem, dear." She scribbled down a few more things. "Well, I think that will be all for today. I'll let you both enjoy the rest of your day." Ada closed her notebook and scooped it up as she stood. "If either of you need me, I'll be keeping the peace amongst the staff." The house manager hurried out of the breakfast room, leaving a heavy quiet in her wake.

"Do you have to scurry off as well?" Saoirse asked after another beat of silence passed between them.

"I do have business that needs attending, but it can be delayed as long as I want it to be." He flashed her a grin, and Saoirse let a giggle slip. "Do you have any plans for the day?"

"No, I'm not quite sure what to do with myself," she answered with a shrug. "Usually, Eamon gave me a task without much instruction and then reprimanded me for doing it poorly by the end of the day."

Emrys's grin fell, and a muscle in his jaw ticced. Saoirse was sure if he were given the chance, Emrys would hunt her brother down for sport and not have a single regret. "Well, you won't have that here," he finally said. "Whatever you desire to do, you're welcome to."

Freedom. Even though their bargain hadn't been fulfilled yet, she was still freer than she was back home. She could return to bed and try again to sleep. She could take a survey of the books in the library, collect the ones that interested her, and read them at her leisure. There were so many possibilities she couldn't decide where to begin.

"I think I'll take a stroll through the back garden," she announced. "It seems to be shaping up to be a lovely day. I'd hate to waste it inside."

"That sounds like an excellent idea." Emrys set his utensils down, his plate left with only crumbs. "I do hope you plan to wear a hat. I would hate for you to be scorched by the sun."

The word "scorched" made Saoirse's skin prickle. "I'm sure your Head Healer has a remedy if I get sunburned."

"True." He reached towards her and stroked her cheek with his thumb. "But it's quite an unpleasant remedy, and I think I'd be beside myself to watch you endure it." He paused before leaning towards her. His breath ghosted over the shell of her ear as he whispered, "There are much better ways to get that flush on your skin."

Gooseflesh rose over Saoirse's neck and chest. "I'm not sure where my hats have been placed," she said softly. "But I'll make sure to mind how long I'm in the sun. I promise."

"Good." Emrys brushed a kiss so lightly to her temple, she wasn't sure if his lips had actually touched her.

The closeness eased the tension in her body regardless. Her mind drifted back to the restlessness she experienced throughout the night. She now regretted not giving into her desire to join Emrys. He gave her a calm she had never felt before nor could explain.

"If you need anything," he continued, "Ada welcomes any request, and you can find me in the library. Enjoy your stroll."

Saoirse murmured her thanks, but her body wouldn't obey her to stand. Even after Emrys left the breakfast room, she found herself still squirming in her chair. She had to remind herself that she had asked for this from him. He was showing her what she could expect if she decided to stay.

Conflict warred in her mind. She had been trying to keep the mindset that this was merely temporary and to keep herself at a distance from everyone. But then she had moments where she let herself imagine staying. Ada and Rory were sweet, attentive staff, and Alastair had welcomed her like a new member of the family. Then there was Emrys.

She couldn't deny the physical spark between them and the way his seductive comments made her stomach flutter. She was coming to enjoy the feelings and imagining herself walking away from them made her heart hurt a little.

Saoirse took several deep breaths, and once she calmed her mind, her limbs agreed to cooperate. She stood from the table and made her way to the terrace, looking out over the lawn. The Fearynhurst estate was like most country homes: it dedicated much of the grounds to wide-open lawns for picnics, garden games, and shooting rather than massive gardens full of florals. There was a single well-manicured rose garden tucked in the corner of the lawn as a small herb garden set up on the side of the house near the backdoor of the kitchen. Trees were sprinkled through the lawn, providing small respites of shade.

Saoirse breathed in the warm morning air and walked down from the terrace, wandering towards the rose garden on the east side of the lawn. July had brought an array of bright and colorful flowers to bloom in the small garden. As she got closer, she saw there was also a variety of flowers and shrubs to complement the pink, orange, red, and white roses. Arbors of lavender-colored clematis provided bits of shade in the otherwise uncovered garden.

As she walked through the other side of the garden back onto the lawn, Saoirse heard soft thuds, like someone was making contact with leather repeatedly. As she rounded the corner, she saw Kieran, half-dressed in only a pair of trousers, sparring with a freestanding leather punching bag.

Saoirse's muscles tightened, and her breath was stolen to the point of pain. What was he doing here? Emrys had warned her Kieran might be at the house a couple of times before the wedding, but she didn't imagine she would see him so soon. Her only other thought was to place as much distance between her and Kieran as she could. Saoirse quickly turned and headed straight back for the house.

Her heart pounded as she stepped inside, her feet carrying to an undecided destination. All she knew was that she couldn't tolerate being near Kieran. In her haze of panic, Saoirse didn't register anyone else around her until her shoulder bumped into someone else.

"Oh, Your Highness," Rory said. "My apologies."

"Oh, no, I should be the one apologizing," Saoirse said. "I wasn't paying attention."

"It's alright. We all get lost in woolgathering from time to time." Rory smiled at her, but then her expression turned into concern. "Is everything alright?"

"Um." Saoirse hesitated, debating if she should rope Rory into her past problems. Her mind circled through her options until an idea came to her. "Yes, but I think it would be in my best interest to get a full tour of the estate. Is that something you would be able to help me with?"

Rory's face lit up. "Yes, Your Highness, that is definitely something I can do for you. Would you like me to take you around now?"

"Yes, please," Saoirse said.

"Then we'll start with the drawing room." Rory motioned her towards the front of the house, and Saoirse sighed in relief.

Her reasoning behind her request for the tour were two-fold. First, if Kieran crossed her path, at least she wouldn't be alone.

She had told him to stay away from her, but she didn't hold much faith that he would abide by it. Her second reason for the tour was to learn where she could escape to if she needed. Was the drawing room secure enough to keep Kieran out, or would the kitchen be a safer hiding place?

Rory showed her the drawing room before they entered the library, where they found Emrys working. He sat at an oak secretaire, several papers spread out in front of him.

"Our apologies, Your Highness," Rory said, moving towards the door.

Emrys turned his attention to them and flashed a welcoming smile to Saoirse. "No need for apologies."

Saoirse felt drawn towards him, and her feet moved before she could stop them. She came up beside him, and he slipped his hand into hers.

"How was your stroll in the garden?" he asked.

"It was..." She contemplated telling him about Kieran. It wouldn't do much good. Kieran didn't even notice her before she fled back into the house. It had only shaken her.

"Is everything alright?" Emrys asked.

"Yes." Saoirse nodded, attempting to smile. "I had found Kieran in the garden earlier."

Emrys's face fell. "I'm sorry. I didn't even know he was here. Would you like me to say something?"

"No, it's alright." An easier smile pulled at her lips. "I don't even think he noticed me. I came back inside when I found him."

"Would you like to join me?" Emrys asked. "It's a bit of mundane work to observe, but I won't balk at having company."

"That's a lovely offer," Saoirse said, her gaze drifting towards the doorway. She noticed Rory had moved and stationed herself just outside the door. "However, Rory is giving me a tour." Saoirse covered her mouth as a yawn escaped her. "And then I think I'm going to retire to my room for a bit. I didn't sleep very well last night."

Saying it out loud made her think of the night she got the

best sleep of her life. She could feel the weight of Emrys's arm over her waist and the heat of his body against hers. She chewed on her bottom lip, the request sitting on the tip of her tongue.

"I won't argue with those plans then." He gave her a cheeky grin and squeezed her hand.

Saoirse returned it and took a deep breath. "May I ask something?" Her voice was quiet, and she hoped she wouldn't be overheard.

"Of course."

"If I wanted to not sleep alone, could I..." She swallowed and peeked at where Rory was standing. The housekeeper quickly averted her gaze from them and fiddled with the watch on her chatelaine. Saoirse felt her cheeks flush with heat. "Could I join you in your room?" she murmured.

His smile widened. "Always."

"Even if it's the middle of the night?"

"Yes, you're allowed to join me any time you'd like."

Saoirse exhaled in relief. Giddiness rushed through her, and she couldn't help herself. She leaned down and pressed a kiss to his cheek. His skin was warm under her lips, and she had to refrain from slipping her free hand around the back of his neck and kissing him properly on the lips. She wouldn't be able to stop herself then.

"Thank you," she said softly.

"You're welcome." Emrys squeezed her hand three times before she slipped it away and followed Rory out of the library.

While she tried to listen to the housekeeper's information, Saoirse's mind was elsewhere. It kept wandering back to Emrys and the feel of his skin. She wondered how far she could wander into that physical territory before she would snap and surrender everything to him. Each time she thought about, it became harder and harder to remind herself why that would be such a poor idea.

The house *was* quiet long after dinner. Saoirse had taken her meal upstairs in their suite and kept to her room for most of the afternoon and evening. Emrys didn't blame her. Here he had promised minimal interaction with Kieran, and she had stumbled upon him her second day at the estate. Emrys hoped, as he wandered through the first floor hallway, that this encounter didn't seal her decision to depart after their wedding.

The thought was what had him slinking through the dim hall to the kitchen. He hoped he would find some remnants of dessert to distract him, but he found Ada scrubbing furiously at the countertop instead.

"Why are you scrubbing the counters?" Emrys asked.

With a huff, Ada tossed the cleaning brush onto the countertop, and the wooden handle made a sharp *smack*. "Rhys thought it would be a brilliant idea to tell the scullery maid that her appearance was shabby and it wasn't a surprise her work took on the same aesthetic," she answered. "She then locked herself in her chamber sobbing, and I could only console her by promising her I would take care of cleaning the kitchen tonight."

"Mamanna," Emrys said with a sigh. "Why don't you dismiss him from the staff? You have the power to do that, you know."

"Other than saying the wrong thing from time to time, he is a competent butler, and it would take me weeks to find someone to fill his position." Ada picked up the scrubbing brush again and used the flat edge of its handle to scrape something thick and sticky off the counter that Emrys didn't even want to begin to guess at. "I don't suppose you came looking for me just to watch me clean counters."

"No," he said sheepishly. "I was hoping there was still a bit of cake left."

Ada chuckled and dropped the brush into the sink. She wiped her hands on her apron, leaving streaks of wetness on the otherwise white cloth, and strode to the end of the long counter. "I'd usually scold you for hunting down sweets so late at night, but I'd rather this be eaten than forgotten in the icebox." She pulled a glass dome cover from a silver serving tray and plated the single slice of chocolate cake that was left standing. Grabbing a fork from a nearby drawer, she returned to Emrys and handed him his evening indulgence.

He put a reasonably-sized bite on his fork, restraining himself from devouring the sweet as quickly as he could.

"I'm surprised you didn't take that back up with you to share with your sweetling." Ada teased. "I know you like to spoil your maidens with romantic gestures."

"Please, don't call them maidens." Emrys said, his face growing hot. Ada had always been the one to pry into his relationships, always with the best intentions. When she got wind of his marriage arrangement with Saoirse, she wrung every detail from him.

Ada giggled with pride at getting under his skin. "Maidens, sweetlings, lovers, no matter what you call them, you have a penchant for showering them with indulgences."

"Well, she's learned enough undesirable details about me. I don't need her to know the extent of my fondness for sweets just yet."

"She'll learn soon enough. She's accepted your marriage contract, which is more than I can say for that Highland lass."

Emrys sighed. "You know that wasn't her fault."

"It wasn't yours either." Ada wagged a finger in his direction.

"Yet you moped about like she was the last boireann on earth."

He poked his cake with his fork. "Well, it's obvious I was being dramatic and misguided at the time. The gods had this planned, and I fought against it. I deserved to be a little heartbroken."

She snorted. "You deserved a good smack upside the head."

Emrys shot her an unamused look. They slipped in a comfortable silence as he scraped the last bits of cake and frosting from his plate. Ada plucked the dish from the counter and took it straight to the sink where she rinsed the remnants of the dessert off. "Have you told Saoirse yet?"

"About Magaidh?" he asked, confused as to why Ada would inquire if he had shared details of a former relationship to Saoirse.

"No," Ada said, her tone restrained. "About why you proposed this marriage."

"No," he answered shyly, dropping his gaze to a scratch in the countertop. When he lifted it again, his adoptive mother gave him a stare that told him she was waiting for an elaboration. "I'd rather like to go back to talking about Magaidh at the moment."

"We've concluded she's no longer relevant." She crossed her arms over her chest and, even being a good eight inches shorter than he was, stared down her nose at him. It was an impeccable ability. "Why haven't you told Saoirse?"

"Because..." He stalled his answer. He hadn't told anyone that he had promised Saoirse could leave if she went through with the marriage. "I might have made a promise to her that I would set her up with a home of her own if she married me."

"You want to give her a house?" Ada's brows furrowed. "What does that have to do with telling her she's your mate?"

"Mamanna." Emrys admonished, looking around to make sure no one was listening. He had only told the court and his adoptive mothers about the mating bond the gods gifted him. Letting it slip further than that circle scared him. "No, I told her she could leave if she married me."

"Emrys," she scolded. "Why would you do that?"

"Because," he said defensively. "She used to be involved with

Kieran, and it didn't end well. He's already harassing her here, and her only other option was being sent to the Matron House."

"A Matron?" Ada asked in horror. "Her option besides marrying you was becoming a Matron?"

"That or running away, which she nearly did."

Ada's face softened with empathy, and she sighed. "Have I ever told you how much of a martyr you are?"

Emrys huffed a laugh. "I'm well aware of that." He fiddled with the signet ring he wore on his pinky. "There's hope she'll stay."

"You promised her something better than a house?"

"She asked me to prove that it would be worth her effort to stay."

Ada's brow rose. "And telling her you are mates won't do that?"

Emrys sighed. The bond was only part of the reason he wanted to marry Saoirse. Yes, it had led him to her, but she had already won his heart in a matter of days. He wanted her to feel the same way. "I want her to make the decision on her own, not because of the bond."

"And if she figures it out on her own?" she asked.

"If she hasn't figured it out already, I doubt she will on her own." He shrugged. When he first met Saoirse, he caught the tiny flinch in her body when their eyes met. She had to have felt the mating spark like he had. Unlike Saoirse, Emrys had been expecting it and was able to disguise his reaction better. "Don't misinterpret my words. I'm not mocking her intelligence in any way. If I hadn't known before meeting her, I doubt I would have caught on either."

"You don't think she finds the symptoms of it odd?"

Emrys wrinkled his nose. Outside the mating spark, the other signs of the bond were subtle.

"Mamanna, it's not a disease," he said. Ada arched a brow still waiting for his answer. "They're very close to feelings of attraction, just a bit stronger. She probably assumes that's what she feels."

"And has she acted on any of it?"

"Mamanna!" Emrys ran a hand over his face to hide the color that was creeping up his cheeks. Ada had no inhibitions when it came to asking about his private life—unlike Seraphina, who instructed him on the anatomical basics but refused to hear any details of any boireann he took to bed.

Ada giggled and plucked the brush she had disposed in the sink, rinsing off soap and the grime she scrubbed at. "Then when do you plan to tell her?"

"If she decides to stay, I'll tell her," he said, thinking through his reasoning as he spoke. He hadn't exactly thought through his plan of how he was going to share the information. "That way, she's still chosen the marriage and won't feel obligated to it."

"You can turn anything into a diplomatic answer." Ada shook her head and chuckled. She shut off the water in the sink and wrung her hands on a nearby cloth. "Alright, I'll quit my prying. Besides, I think Saoirse might be a little more inclined to be loose-lipped than you." She punctuated her statement with a wink.

Emrys emitted a groan of dread and stared up at the soot-covered ceiling, sardonically praying the gods would end this misery.

"I have one last question before you go off and plot the ways in which you could fire me once you eventually inherit the throne," she said, leveling a stare with him. "What will happen if she rejects you when she learns the truth?"

"I've tried not to think about that," he murmured. "But I'll still love her. I've promised her freedom, including from me. She's allowed to take it however she sees fit."

Ada reached up and cupped his cheek. "Romantic martyr," she repeated. Emrys rolled his eyes, but he couldn't hold back his grin. "Promise me," she continued, "that if that happens, you won't do what you did last time."

Emrys winced at the dull pain in his chest that thinking of the last time gave him. It took him literal decades for him to recover from Magaidh ending their relationship. While he knew why Ada was bringing it up, he also knew Saoirse happened to be the remedy that helped him recover from that heartbreak. He had endured it for her.

"I promise," he whispered.

"Good." Ada stood on her toes to press a kiss to his forehead. "It's getting late now, and you have a quite a morning ahead of you tomorrow. Off with you. And give something to Saoirse so she can indulge me with the details."

"I will absolutely not." Emrys shook his head and turned towards the doorway. "And I'll be swearing her to secrecy from you."

He heard Ada's amused laugh as he walked out of the kitchen.

If he had a choice of a fitful night of sleep or no sleep at all, Emrys would have much rather had no sleep. He retired to bed shortly after his conversation with Ada in the kitchen, but not long after he fell asleep did he wake again. He squinted at the mechanical clock on his bedside table and noticed he had slept two hours at most, yet he felt like he had only blinked his eyes.

The soft click of his doorknob turning made his pulse kick up. A slight orange glow spilled into the room from the fire that was still smoldering in the sitting room, and it framed Saoirse's silhouette.

"Emrys," she whispered.

A grin tugged at the corners of his mouth. "Yes?"

"I'm sorry if I woke you."

"You didn't."

There was a pause, and her shadowed figure took a step into the room towards him. "I couldn't sleep, and I—may I join you?"

"Yes." He couldn't help the smile that continued to spread on his face as Saoirse closed the door behind her and tiptoed towards his bed. He pulled back the layers of bedding in front of him, and she gingerly slid beneath them. As he tucked the sheet and blankets over her, he wrapped his arm around her waist and held her where she was.

Her body relaxed into his, and her calming effect mixed with her sweet scent quickly soothed him. He knew it was thanks to the bond, but he was thankful regardless. Saoirse's warmth against him was exactly what he needed to sleep through the night.

"I promise I appreciate my separate room," Saoirse said. "But I didn't sleep well in it last night."

"It's alright." Emrys pushed his luck and dropped a kiss to the base of her neck. Her body didn't tense in response, and one of her hands even laced with the one over her waist. "I'm sure you'll find a use for it." She giggled and squeezed his hand she held.

He had to restrain himself from burying his face in her hair and sighing happily. His earlier conversation with Ada echoed in his mind, and a spike of anxiety hit him. The wedding was in less than a week, and there was a potential he would lose his opportunity to tell her about their bond completely. Her sleeping in his bed wasn't a guarantee she would choose to stay.

"Well, don't you know how to treat a boireann well," Saoirse said, her playful tone pulling him back to the present.

"I've been on this earth for a hundred and ninety-two years. I would hope I know a bit about how to treat a boireann well." He gave in and nuzzled her neck. He heard her give a short hmm. "What?"

"Nothing," she said, her shoulders vibrating against him. "I just think you're quite spry for your age."

Emrys gave her side a squeeze, and she answered with a little squeal and laugh. Saoirse twisted in his arms and faced him. Even in the dark, he could see the amused smile on her face. He wanted to kiss her and taste that smile. He wanted to do much more than kiss her, but for now he'd settle for tasting only her lips.

Saoirse's smile slowly faded, and she reached towards his face. But before she could touch him, she seemed to think better of it and pressed her palm to his chest. "I hope I get to find out all the ways you like to spoil boireannaich," she whispered.

She tucked her head under his chin, and her body grew heavier in his arms. Emrys let his eyes close as he listened to the steady rhythm of her breathing. He let it quiet his mind, letting the flood of sultry thoughts wash away. Slowly, he slipped into sleep, his last thought before sleep being the smile on Saoirse's face as he spoiled her in all the ways he wanted to.

Saoirse was finding herself waking in unfamiliar beds increasingly common. It took her a moment to clear the morning fog from her mind and recognize where exactly she had woken up this morning. It wasn't until Emrys crossed in front of her vision that she remembered where she was. She found herself eye level with the trouser-covered curve of his arse, and she had half a mind to reach out and cup her palm to it. Part of her was sure he wouldn't reject the gesture, but before she had the chance to act on her impulse, Emrys turned and spotted her awake.

"Good morning," he said in a smooth voice. It was far from the husky voice that made her shiver when she woke up in his arms on the train. His hands worked at his collar, wrapping and knotting his tie.

"Good morning," she mumbled as she propped herself on her elbow and glanced at the clock on the bedside table. "Do you always dress this early, or is that for my benefit?"

He chuckled and tightened his silky tie around his neck. "I have a council meeting with the court today, and I wanted to get to breakfast early. I hope the valet, Lachlan, and I didn't disturb you this morning."

Saoirse shook her head. "A council meeting?" she repeated. Emrys nodded. "The dukes you told me about will be coming?"

"Yes." A muscle in his jaw fluttered briefly before he added,

"And Kieran."

Saoirse's heart only dipped into her stomach briefly. The reaction was less visceral than she thought it would be. Maybe it was because she knew he would be at the house this time. Or maybe it was because of how she handled herself with him the day before.

"I expect he would be, considering his position." She pushed herself upright and fidgeted with her fingers as she swallowed the apprehension of her next question. "Can I join you?"

"In the council meeting?" Emrys asked, his brows flicking upwards in surprise.

She nodded. "My brother, while he wanted me to do his menial tasks, never allowed me into meetings with his court. What he doesn't know is that I seduced the visiting dignitaries when he wasn't paying attention." Saoirse's smirk at the memories quickly morphed into molten embarrassment as she realized who she revealed that secret to. "I probably shouldn't have mentioned that last bit."

Emrys huffed a laugh and dropped his attention to the brass buttons on his waistcoat. "Do I want to know the reasons you did that?"

"Mostly defiance," she answered sheepishly. "It was made very clear to me I wasn't supposed to interact with them. But the visiting company hadn't been informed of that." Another smirk tugged at her lips. "I never interacted with them in front of Eamon, but they occasionally sought me out at night, and I wasn't going to deny them. I only got caught once and received a lecture for it. But it's hard to care about being reprimanded when you've spent a night being worshipped." Her cheeks burned again, but Emrys merely chuckled.

"Well, if you plan to sleep with any of the dukes," he said with a cheeky grin. "I must warn you about the wrath their wives will inflict on you."

"I didn't plan on doing any such thing." She tried to keep her voice light, but she was overwhelmed with a sudden fear that he thought of her differently now. "On second thought, I shouldn't have asked. Never mind my request. I wouldn't be useful there, anyway."

As she fumbled with the bed linens, a warm hand embraced her cheek, and her attention was pulled towards Emrys. He pressed a kiss to her forehead before she could protest her own inquiry further. Gooseflesh rose over her skin at the touch, and she fisted the sheets to keep from grabbing at his collar and pulling him for a true kiss.

"I would be beyond thrilled if you joined our meeting today," he said.

"Alright." Her voice was small, and her face still burned with embarrassment, but Emrys was being genuine as he always was. He wanted to be her included. That set a different kind of warmth pulsing through her body, and she took deep, quiet breaths to keep that heat from manifesting into more than just desire.

He pulled his hand away from her and stepped back. "Shall I send up Rory and wait for you downstairs at breakfast?"

"Yes, I would appreciate that." Saoirse watched as Emrys disappeared out of the bedroom. She took one last deep inhale of his scent that lingered on the sheets before rising and crossing the suite back to her bedroom.

After breakfast, Ada intercepted Saoirse for a few moments to confirm details concerning the menu at the wedding. Saoirse told Emrys to continue on and she'd meet him in the council room. He kissed her temple before parting from her, and Saoirse was beginning to anticipate and welcome his kisses. Part of her was waiting for the day he'd slip up and kiss her lips. That would likely be the day that she chose not to leave.

Once she was finished with Ada, Saoirse made her way to the council room on the other side of the house. She had no earthly idea what she expected the room to look like, but she was surprised to find it as rich yet mundane as the rest of the house. Bookcases crafted from dark mahogany sat along the walls, and trinkets from around the world littered the shelves. A large, intricately carved table sat in the middle of the room, taking up a majority of the space. Celtic symbols were carved into the edge of the glossy table, and a thick plum-colored rug sat between the table. In fact, Saoirse could barely see the dark parquet flooring because the rug ate up so much footage of the room.

Around the table were eight chairs, four of them already occupied by fireannaich. Saoirse reached for the chair next to Emrys's, but he quickly sprung to his feet and pulled it out for her. "Uaislean, I have an introduction to make," he announced to the room. The three fireannaich, who she assumed were the dukes Emrys had spoke of, devoted their attention to Saoirse, and she felt moisture collect on the underside of her arms. "This is my betrothed, Her Highness of Irish Fae, Saoirse."

"It's a pleasure to meet you all," she said with a small smile. She took the seat Emrys had pulled out for her and smoothed the lap of her dark brown skirt. She had tried to imagine what she would have worn if any of her brothers had invited her to a court meeting. Her finest shirtwaist and skirt with just a few touches of jewelry were the best she could put together without a decent frame of reference.

"Emrys, I didn't know we were bringing our partners to council now," another duke said. Saoirse's attention turned towards him, and she observed his dark hair and angular features. He was dressed in a black brocade waistcoat that, in contrast to the other duke, was straining to smother his broad chest. "You know Isolde would jump at the chance to have a say in our meetings."

"Well, when she is next in line for queen, she can join us." Emrys chuckled and smirked at the duke. "Until then, Cyprian, I implore you to not be rude to my future wife."

The duke's high cheeks turned a bright shade of pink as he cleared his throat. "My apologies, Your Highness," he said, his face still flushed. "I should have introduced myself before making jests. I'm Cyprian, Duke of Stoneblack. It's a pleasure to meet you."

"Hello, Cyprian." Saoirse gave a polite smile, and something in her felt free. Everyone else in this room skipped the constant honorifics and passed over politeness for fondness. It was freeing to sit at a table and not have to worry how she was sitting or how she addressed the rest of the court. "And I forgive you. Your wife sounds like someone who would punish you enough in my name." She received a nervous laugh from the duke before he averted his gaze away from her.

"Trust me, we all apologize on his behalf," one of the other dukes said from across the table. His deep, tanned complexion complimented his black hair. He wore a navy blue waistcoat with silver trim around the collar and buttons and cuff links that matched. "I'm Laszlo, Duke of Cogwick. May I offer you a drink?" He held up his small glass tumbler filled with an inch of warm amber liquid.

"No, thank you," Saoirse answered.

"You do realize it's my liquor you're offering to pour, don't you?" Emrys asked, crossing his arms over his chest.

"Actually, I believe it's your father's." Laszlo corrected.

"Ah, well, in that case." Emrys rolled his eyes, but the upward tilt of the corner of his mouth gave away his lack of seriousness.

"I do wish Andromeda was here," Laszlo drawled. "She would have a field day with Cyprian putting his foot in his mouth and the witty responses Her Highness has to them." He winked at Saoirse, and the Duke of Stoneblack gave him a glare. Saoirse stifled a giggle by chewing on the inside of her cheek.

"Well, I'm not one to follow in Cyprian's footsteps either," the last duke said. In contrast to the other two dukes, he had a slender build and a dark brown and gold brocade waistcoat. It complemented his pale complexion and dark hair and eyes. "I'm Vasili, Duke of Donheath. And unlike these two, I don't think my wife would find any of these meetings interesting. She'd be much more at home with Seraphina."

"The Head Healer?" Saoirse asked.

Vasili nodded. "Calliope, my wife, is a High Healer and would much rather discuss remedies for measles than remedies for the economy. Although I don't think even those two could find a cure for whatever disease plagues Cyprian to say stupid shite."

"Alright, you've all had your fun," Cyprian ground out. "We don't need to mock me for the rest of the meeting."

"We're sorry, Cyprian, but you make it too easy." Laszlo nursed his drink, hiding his amused grin, as a few snickers echoed in the room.

"Well, again, it's a pleasure to meet all of you, poor impressions and all." Saoirse didn't glance at the duke, but she heard Cyprian sigh in relief. "I hope my presence doesn't interfere with your work."

"You won't be a hindrance, Your Highness," Vasili said in assurance. "If anything, everyone will be falling over themselves to look impressive today."

Tension she hadn't realized that was sitting in her shoulders loosened as she realized how at ease she was in a room full of fireannaich. None of them gave her a reason to be intimidated nor showed any signs of wariness from her presence. She was assumed and accepted as an equal.

An equal.

That revelation hit her the hardest. Eamon had always assigned her to tasks that he felt were too menial for him. The fact he never explained how to complete them was a completely different argument altogether. But no matter how well or hard she worked to complete his asks, he still found ways to demean her and convince her it was her fault that she failed. For a while, she believed him.

But sitting in this room, a room full of very competent, albeit comical, fireannaich, she was being respected as an equal and finding fewer reasons to choose to leave. Choosing Emrys meant she would be choosing these people as well. They barely knew her, yet they accepted her and welcomed her into their fold. It was enough to tip the scales further in the direction of staying.

"Well, we're a boisterous bunch today." A deep, rumbling voice broke through the laughter in the room, and attention turned to Alastair in the doorway. He made his way to one of the empty chairs near Saoirse and gave her a closed-lip grin. "Saoirse," he said, his eyes softening. "I'm glad to see you join us today."

"I appreciate being allowed to join," she said in return.

Alastair's face fell in horror for just a moment before he quickly recovered with a smile. "You're always welcome to join. I hope none of these four have told you otherwise." His eyes drifted over the room, and the dukes shook their heads vigorously.

"No, not at all," Saoirse said before someone opened their mouth and accidentally incriminated themselves with poorly chosen words. "My brother has been the one to tell me I'm unwelcome at court meetings. These uaislean have been nothing but kind since I've sat down."

"Good." Alastair sat back in his seat, and Saoirse could feel the atmosphere in the room had shifted.

She glanced sideways at Emrys and noticed his posture had become stiffer. Kieran hadn't even arrived and already Emrys was on edge. She reached for his hand and brushed her thumb over his knuckles. The tension eased in his hand, and he turned his palm upwards, clasping her hand.

An uncomfortable silence fell over the room until the last member of the court joined the room. Kieran swaggered in and took a seat next to Alastair. No one spoke, but everyone's line of sight confirmed they registered his presence.

The general's gaze swept over the room, and it was Saoirse's turn to stiffen as his dark eyes met hers. She squeezed Emrys's hand and received three light squeezes from him in return. She glanced at him, and he communicated his encouragement to her silently. The spark that continued to strike her in his presence shot up her spine, and it was enough to muster the strength to not dash out of the room.

Kieran's acknowledgement of her presence was fleeting as he pulled his pocket watch from his plain, black waistcoat and checked the time, stroking his thumb over the face of the watch. "Apologies for my tardiness," he said, bored. "I just received the news about Donheath."

"I'm sorry," Vasili blurted. "What news?"

"You haven't been told?" Kieran asked, a bit of astonishment in his tone.

The duke shook his head, a puzzled expression creating a crease between his brows.

"You oversee everything that happens in your territory, do you not?" Kieran's tone shifted into condescending.

"Kieran." A quiet growl came from the back of Emrys's throat, warning him.

"Let him answer, Emrys," the general said coolly. "I want to confirm that he's competent in his position."

Emrys's fingers twitched in Saoirse's hand. At least she wasn't the only one who was easily agitated by Kieran.

"Yes, Kieran, I am fully aware of what happens in Donheath," Vasili answered.

"Then why do I know about a sighting of Fomóire in your territory before you do?" Kieran inquired. "I think that's a bit concerning."

Fomóire? Why would Fomóire make their presence in England? Saoirse might not have known much of what went on in the world outside her family's home, but she was educated on Fomóire and other beings of that sort.

They were rock-like creatures that dwelled in the ocean and mostly kept to themselves. The last time they were seen on land was centuries ago during the Great Conquest where the fae and gods clashed, Dagda's treasures being the prize for the winners. The god had carelessly left his treasures on earth, allowing them to be found by anyone.

When fae began to uncover them, a war broke out between the fae races and gods. The Fomóire were on neither side but attracted to the war due to the treasures. They became such a threat to both gods and fae that the two groups banded together during the Great Conquest to battle the Fomóire and banish them back to the sea. What was done with Dagda's treasures after the war was murky. Legends were crafted to explain where they rested with one suggesting the treasures were hidden on earth again.

Was the legend true? Were the treasures still on earth and attracting the attention of Fomóire?

A scrape of chair legs and a soft thud caught Saoirse's attention, and she turned to Emrys to find Cyprian's large hand clamped onto his shoulder. Emrys's jaw was set and his arm muscles twitched against his physical and self-restraints.

"Emrys," his father warned.

"Do you have a comment, Emrys?" Kieran asked, his snake-like smile making Saoirse's skin crawl. There was a gleam of mischief in his eyes, and she had a very bad feeling about his intentions with this information.

"It is troublesome that Kieran has been alerted to this matter before you, Vasili," Alastair commented, his tone shifting from warning to concern.

"I promise you, Alastair, I am given notice of every matter that happens on my lands," Vasili said. "I have not heard a single word about this sighting."

"Regardless of whether you knew of it or not, you need to act, Vasili." Kieran's finger circled the face of his pocket watch again as he spoke. "We know what Fomóire can be capable of. Bloodshed could be imminent. We have a unit that can be deployed immediately to defend against the Fomóire, so no harm comes to our population."

"Hold on," Vasili said, putting a hand up. "I need to investigate this further. If I truly have missed this information, I need to find out why."

"There isn't time to investigate," Kieran pushed. "What if more than just a sighting happens while you're knee deep in paperwork, trying to puzzle out who failed their duties to you, and a life is lost? I think the people of Donheath will be more upset at that than a few soldiers present around the borders."

Saoirse looked to Alastair, who looked restrained. His jaw worked as if he wanted to say something, but his mouth never opened. It was curious that he wouldn't step in to reel Kieran in, even if he did favor the general the most.

"No," Vasili said, the firmness in his tone wavering. "I need to—"

"You *need* to act, Vasili!" Kieran's fist hit the table, filling the room with a resounding thump.

"Enough, Kieran," Laszlo said sternly, jumping to his peer's defense. "You may have military expertise, but you have no authority to demand anything from us. Vasili knows what is best for the people he has been entrusted with."

"Yes, but—"

"The matter is settled, Kieran," Cyprian chimed in. "You can suggest and advise, but you aren't allowed to intimidate anyone. There are rules for how these meetings are to be conducted. I shouldn't need to remind you of that as if you were a misbehaving child."

Kieran slumped back in his seat and tucked his pocket watch back into his waistcoat. The comparison Cyprian had drawn between the general and a child that had been refused their wishes was plainly evident. Saoirse saw Alastair's jaw relax and his demeanor shift. He let out a breath as if it had been held in his lungs against his will.

"I believe that matter is settled," he said. "Let us move onto other business, shall we?" A few strange glances were exchanged between the dukes, but they obliged their king. They transitioned to topics such as agricultural contracts that were about to expire and a new expansion of the city center in Stoneblack that was coming along nicely. While the discussion of the Fomóire sighting at the start of the meeting was full of drama and tension, the rest of the meeting was quite dull.

Saoirse hated to admit it, but she was now grateful she hadn't been forced to experience these types of meetings at her home estate. She imagined the ways she would have hid and excused herself from them if she had been expected to attend. Having sex with the visiting dignitaries was much more fun.

Alastair finally concluded the meeting and commented his appreciation for Saoirse's appearance before excusing himself from the room. Kieran followed without a parting word to the rest of the court, and Saoirse let out a breath she hadn't realized she had been holding.

"Saoirse, will you be joining us at our next council meeting?"

Laszlo asked.

"Oh, I..." She trailed off, searching for a polite way to excuse herself from the next meeting.

"It's alright," Cyprian chimed in. "You can be honest with us. We understand the content of court meetings are quite dry. If it weren't for them, Isolde would demand to join."

"I'll admit I did begin to lose interest once the topic shifted to contracts and construction," Saoirse confessed.

The fireannaich chuckled at her admission.

"You aren't obligated to attend these meetings," Emrys said. His composure had relaxed since Kieran and his father left, and she was happy to see the sweeter side of his personality again.

"Am *I* obligated to attend these meetings?" Vasili asked, his feelings of defeat apparent on his face.

"Unless you think Calliope can manage the status of Northern English agriculture, yes, it is," Cyprian answered.

The Duke of Donheath's shoulders sagged, and Laszlo patted him on the shoulder in sympathy. "Kieran only thinks he can get under your skin because he doesn't understand how important your role is in the court," Laszlo told him. "I think you have the right idea investigating why you missed something so vital in your territory."

"Would you do the same given my circumstances?" Vasili asked.

"Of course." Laszlo nodded. "I would have slipped a bit more profanity into my argument, but I absolutely agree with your decision. It's important to find the root of the issue so it doesn't happen again."

"Agreed," Cyprian added.

Saoirse watched as confidence thrummed through Vasili again. He sat up a bit taller, and he looked much less defeated than a few moments ago.

The legs of Saoirse's chair scraped the floor as she scooted back to rise to her feet. "Well, it has been absolutely lovely to meet all of you, and I hope to meet your better halves fairly soon."

"Emrys, what if we brought them with us the next time we

meet?" Laszlo asked.

"You really want to watch just how chaotic this room can get with Andromeda added to the mix, don't you?" Cyprian asked.

"No, no," Laszlo said, waving his hand to dismiss the notion. "I meant so they can mingle with Saoirse while we have our meetings."

"That sounds excellent," Saoirse said with a wide grin.

"I agree. I like the idea." Vasili nodded. "The ride to Fearynhurst and back can get lonely."

"Well, if that's your reasoning..." Cyprian gave a knowing look and Vasili's complexion flushed. Emrys jabbed the Duke of Stoneblack with an elbow.

"I wish I had something small enough to throw at you," Vasili said.

"A bit of your magic is always an alternative." Laszlo suggested. "A blast of air can reach that far, can't it?"

Emrys snickered.

"No, no." Vasili shook his head. "I promised Calliope I would use my magic for productive things."

"I didn't," Emrys said, placing two fingers behind Cyprian's ear.

He yelped and smacked at the prince's arm, complaining of the cold touch. The dukes erupted into more laughter, and Saoirse giggled with them. The way Emrys and the dukes acted reminded her of her brothers. Eamon was always a poor sport, but her two other brothers never missed an opportunity to tease and mock each other.

Saoirse gracefully rose from her seat and slipped her hand from Emrys's. She immediately missed the assurance it gave her.

"Emrys, be careful. You're driving your bride away with your childish antics," Vasili said with a cheeky grin.

"No," Saoirse said, giggling and shaking her head. "I would love nothing more than to stay and learn what other ways you three can come up with to torment Cyprian, but I have an appointment for a dress fitting."

"Well, then we look forward to seeing you again at the

wedding," Laszlo said. "And I must warn you not to let Andromeda talk you into any strange herbs or furniture arranging that help fertility. I swear that boireann is going to turn our house upside down before we have a child."

"I'll try not to." She couldn't help but grin as she left the council room. There was something new and warm that ran through her blood as she walked through the house. It felt as if daylight was cracking through a gray afternoon, and she was discovering what the sun felt like on her skin for the first time. Her magic tingled in her palms, but it didn't manifest any further. She felt like her magic was communicating to her that it liked this feeling, this feeling of happiness.

Friends.

She had friends—at least she would if she ultimately chose to stay. The urge to stay had never felt so strong. Weighing her two options, staying came with more rewards. She would have Emrys, the dukes, and a household that genuinely cared for her. Leaving and living on her own would give her the ultimate taste of freedom, but she would be alone, more alone than when she was in her family's estate.

A pang of anxiety hit her chest as she entertained the thought of staying with seriousness. She would be agreeing to attach herself to a family and court that included Kieran. But the rest of the people she would be attaching herself to cared enough about her to make her decision worth it. Saoirse took a deep breath, hoping her next leap of faith would pay off.

Three days passed by quickly, and Emrys woke on his wedding day with Saoirse in his arms and her sweet scent in his nose. Each night since she first slipped into his room to share his bed, she had joined him earlier and earlier in the night. Last night she had dressed for bed in the other bedroom and joined him less than ten minutes later. Emrys hoped tonight there would be no need to prepare for bed, and he and Saoirse could share more than just sleep after the wedding.

It was a far-fetched hope seeing that she hadn't given any indication she planned to stay. He had made arrangements for her in case she chose to follow through with their initial bargain, but Emrys had been praying those arrangements would go unused.

A sigh came from Saoirse, and he greeted her with a kiss to her shoulder. "Good morning," he said, hearing the gravel in his own voice.

Saoirse shifted to face him, and her sleepy smile made the mating spark jump. That was another matter altogether. If she chose to stay, he promised himself—and Ada—that he would tell her. Once she agreed to stay and sealed their marriage, he wouldn't fear she would mistake it for coercion. From there, she could choose what they did with the bond.

"Good morning." Saoirse yawned, pulling him back to the present.

He kissed her forehead and savored the warmth of her skin beneath his lips. He had been inching towards kissing her properly, hoping she would make her decision before he did so. His stomach knotted at the idea of sharing sweet, passionate kisses with her just to lose her.

"It's our wedding day." he said, running his fingers over her exposed arm.

"It is." Her eyes lingered on his chest. Emrys watched her throat work as she swallowed. "Emrys," she whispered.

This was it. She had made her decision. He wanted to keep his mouth shut and let her say whatever she was going to say. But he couldn't. "Saoirse, you don't have to decide right now," he said. "You can enjoy the day and make your decision tomorrow."

She stared at him blankly. Slowly, she shook her head. "I was going to ask if you were going to give me a proper kiss to seal our marriage today."

"Oh." Emrys wanted sink into his mattress and never emerge again. He should have kept his mouth shut after all.

"But since you mentioned it, I've already made my decision. I made it after the council meeting." She chewed on her bottom lip, and Emrys felt his heart lodge in his throat. "I want to stay."

He had to have misheard her. "You want to stay?"

She nodded, a bright smile spreading across her face. All the tightness in Emrys's chest unraveled, and he pulled her close to him. She let out a soft giggle and wrapped her arms around his neck. He wanted to cry from joy, and take a lap through the house, to tell everyone the good news. He had done it. He had convinced her that staying with him was worth whatever trouble Kieran created.

Saoirse pushed herself up to meet Emrys's gaze. Her eyes darted down to his lips as her tongue ran over hers. Until now, he had successfully restrained himself, but between just having awoken and the way Saoirse was staring at him, he couldn't keep his body's response under control. If she shifted her legs over him at all, she'd know exactly how she affected him.

She inched closer towards his face, and Emrys resisted threading his fingers through her messy hair and pulling her down to his lips. He lay still, waiting for her to make contact, but she moved painfully slow. She torturously tested his self-control with every second she wasn't touching him. Her breath ghosted over his lips, and the air hitched in his lungs.

A boisterous knock caused both of them to abruptly pause. Emrys knew who it was and what it was for. He had arranged their breakfast to be brought up so that time wasn't wasted moving up and down the stairs before preparing for the wedding. Maybe they would leave the food outside the door and this moment with Saoirse wouldn't be interrupted indefinitely.

Instead, the door clicked open, and Emrys heard two voices. Rhys and Rory had both come to deliver breakfast and run through their morning chores with Emrys and Saoirse. As Rhys entered Emrys's room, a feline shape leapt onto the bed. Owen crawled up beside Emrys as the butler went about the room, opening the curtains.

"Good morning, Your Highness," Rhys said before briefly glancing over his shoulder and correcting himself. "Your Highnesses."

"Good morning," Emrys murmured. "Rhys, do you mind fetching my dressing gown and then leaving us alone for an hour?"

"Of course, Your Highness." Rhys nodded and pulled a plum-colored satin dressing gown from Emrys's wardrobe.

"And ask Rory for one of my tea gowns?" Saoirse asked, her voice small. Although she had been in his bed the last few days when Rhys came in the mornings, Emrys felt she wasn't used to being found in his bed quite yet.

"Of course, Your Highness," Rhys said. The butler vanished from the room, and Emrys reluctantly slid Saoirse off of him. He wrapped himself in a dressing gown, hoping it would hide the evidence of how the morning had affected him.

Rory came in a moment later with a maroon tea dress, and Saoirse slid out of bed to be dressed in it. Emrys decided to move into the sitting room to make sure breakfast was done correctly.

When Saoirse emerged from his bedroom, he tried not to mourn the moment that he lost thanks to the staff. She made herself comfortable on the sofa, and Emrys sat next to her.

"You know, I've never been to a wedding before," she said, reaching for a knife and the jam. "Let alone had one." She glanced sideways at him with a half-smile.

That soothed his grief over losing their intimate moment. "Not even your brothers' weddings?" he asked.

Saoirse shook her head. "Eamon and Aurelius were already married by the time I was born, and Casimir married when I was an infant. But I don't count that one. No one remembers what happened to them when they were infants."

"Are any of your brothers and their wives mates?" Emrys tried to keep his tone casual with the question. Priming her for his future reveal wasn't wrong. It could help him gauge her reaction and plan accordingly.

Saoirse wrinkled her nose. "Cressida seems to think she and Eamon are."

"She *thinks?*" he asked.

"Eamon lured her into marrying him by telling her that." She stabbed at the food on her plate, and Emrys tried not to show his panic. "I for one don't believe anyone could be handpicked from the gods to paired with someone else."

"Oh?" Emrys's thoughts raced as he scrambled to remain calm.

"It's a bit ridiculous to me. Anyone could claim to be someone's mate to force them into a partnership or marriage or to keep them in a relationship. I think it's a load of hogwash and wish the concept wasn't so..." she twirled her fork in the air, "romanticized."

Emrys stared blankly at the low table in front of him. Any confidence he had from Saoirse sharing her desire to stay was now burned to ash. There was a good chance she wouldn't accept the bond if he told her. At least not any time soon. He had built her trust enough to stay, but not enough that she wouldn't accuse him of manipulating her. He'd have to continue to keep it to himself for a bit longer, as painful as it was.

Shaking him from his frozen trance, Saoirse gasped. "Owen!"

Emrys blinked and caught the feline sinking his teeth into his sausage link just before pulling it off his plate. Emrys clapped one hand onto the back of Owen's head and held his jaw. He pulled the piece of meat from him, but not without a chunk of it ripping off and getting eaten up by Owen. Emrys tore off another bit that had been claimed by the cat's mouth and tossed it to him.

"Damned little thief," Emrys muttered.

Saoirse was overwhelmed by a fit of giggles and doubled over from them. Her laughter eased the bit of dread that was stirring in him, and he tried to make peace with his new plan.

Emrys turned to the black and white cat and caught him licking at the sides of his mouth in satisfaction. He had to admit, Owen's pattern of fur made him look like he was dressed appropriately for today's formal occasion. All he needed was a tie and top hat to complete the look. "Are you proud of yourself?" Emrys asked him. Owen blinked and licked his lips again as if to answer "yes." Emrys sighed and stabbed at his eggs, willing himself to eat them despite the pit in his stomach.

"Reminds me of all the times Casimir and Aurelius would steal food off each other's plates like they were children." Saoirse's giggling had subsided, but her amused smile remained. "They act much like you and the dukes did after the council meeting."

"Well, I'm glad to know I'm not exaggerating when I compare them to actual brothers."

"I hope their choice in wives is where they differ." Her smile faltered a bit.

"Do they not treat you like a sister?"

"Not at all." Saoirse shook her head. "Cressida would probably be the closest to one, but with how loyal she is to Eamon, I only shared whatever I was comfortable with Eamon possibly knowing."

"And the other two?"

"Georgiana, Casimir's wife, is too prudish to have any fun. What my brother sees in her is beyond me." She rolled her eyes. "And Aurelius's wife...I've actually never met her. I know he's married, but I've never seen her or even heard him talk about her. Now that I think of it, I think they might have an arrangement like ours." She let out a small huff as she took in the realization. "I guess I had more in common with her than I thought."

Emrys gave a half-grin. "Do you wish they could have attended today?" he asked cautiously. He was the last person to question anyone's family dynamics, but for such an important day, he was surprised Saoirse's family had turned down the invitation.

Saoirse shrugged. "If I'm being honest, I'm glad they aren't attending. I've had a whole week away from Eamon and have never felt more at ease. I haven't had to fear looking over my shoulder to find him disapproving of something new." She looked at him sideways with a half-smile, and all the disappointment and anxious thoughts Emrys had collected that morning drifted away. At least for now, Saoirse was happy with him and that was enough to keep him from spiraling.

Emrys felt a soft hand slip into his palm, and he glanced down to see Saoirse's fingers intertwining with his. "Have I thanked you yet?" she asked, leaning closer to him.

"Thanked me for what?" he asked.

"For giving me freedom." She breathed a laugh and pressed her forehead against his. "No, freedom seems like too simple of an answer." The gold flecks in her hazel eyes danced as she met his gaze and searched for an answer that better described what she felt. "I feel...safe. Safe to be myself. Safe to make my own choices. No one has ever made me feel like this."

"There's no need to thank me," Emrys told her. "But I would do it all again without a second thought."

The corners of Saoirse's lips tugged upwards, and Emrys felt the tip of her nose graze his. Her warm breath licked at his lips, and he found himself once again feeling like time stalled. The anticipation was agonizing, and yet he didn't dare force it. Saoirse's bottom lip barely touched his when the door of the sitting room was thrown open, and the screaming meow from Owen echoed in the room as he greeted the intruder.

"Good morning, lovebirds," Ada singsonged. She marched through the sitting room with Rory holding a mass of cream lace both in her arms and trailing behind her. "I apologize for interrupting, but I have a bride to dress and you," she pointed to Emrys, "have somewhere else to be."

He took a deep breath. "I asked Rhys to give us an hour."

"Well, we don't have an hour to spare you." Ada shrugged. "Now, get to the spare bedroom so Lachlan can dress you."

Emrys had to remind himself of everything Ada had given him throughout his life. Otherwise, he would succumb to his urge to kick her and the cat out and lock the door behind them.

Saoirse's hand squeezed Emrys's, and he forgot they still had that connection.

"I guess we'll be sharing our first kiss with everyone else," she said in a low voice.

"Not that they haven't barged into this room all morning already," Emrys muttered.

Saoirse let out a breathy laugh and kissed his cheek before slipping her hand from his. He missed the feel of it immediately. "I'll see you at the ceremony." She followed Ada into her bedroom, and Emrys took a moment before rising to his feet and finding the spare bedroom he had been banished to. He had been patiently waiting for this day for several decades. What was a few more hours?

Saoirse watched as Rory tugged and teased at her locks of strawberry blonde hair. Since Ada had commenced preparations for the ceremony, Saoirse had been sent into a whirlwind. She was ordered into a bath and then immediately pulled to the vanity afterward. She noticed as Rory ran her fingers through her wet hair, it dried in an instant. The housekeeper had to have mid fae magic. Mid fae had more passive, practical magic skills. It was why they were commonly found amongst house staff and other labor jobs. Sometimes, Saoirse envied their magic. Mid fae didn't need to worry about it manifesting when it shouldn't and causing harmful repercussion.

"Mistress Ada tells me this is the first royal wedding since His Majesty married his late wife several centuries ago," Rory said, bringing Saoirse's attention away from thoughts of magic.

"I imagine that's why she's flitting about the place like a rogue chicken."

The boireannaich giggled, and Saoirse felt a bit of that same warmth she had when she spent time with the dukes after the council meeting. Being able to joke and tease without the worry of harsh glares and imminent lectures felt freeing. As the minutes ticked by, she was more and more content with her decision.

"She's quite excited about witnessing her final son get married." Rory pinned Saoirse's hair as she intricately braided and twisted it at the crown of Saoirse's head. "Don't misinterpret my words. Ada and Seraphina treat us all like their gods-given family, quarrels and all, but the prince surely has a special place in their hearts."

"I've been told a bit about his relationship with them." Saoirse tilted her head to the side to sneak a glimpse at her hair, but Rory corrected her back. "I'm glad he has such supportive people."

"The same couldn't be said about the rest of his family," Rory muttered more to herself than Saoirse, but her voice was still loud enough that Saoirse caught every word. She debated asking what exactly she meant by that but held her tongue. She knew Kieran would be brought up, and he was the last person she wanted her thoughts to dwell on today.

Instead, she occupied her thoughts with Emrys and how close they had come to sharing an actual kiss. With the morning's interruptions, it seemed like they'd be sharing their first kiss at their wedding after all. It wasn't the worst way to share a kiss, but Saoirse would have preferred a bit more privacy.

"There," Rory said as she slipped the last pin into Saoirse's hair. Saoirse was finally able to move her head freely and study Rory's work. She smiled at herself and the housekeeper at the intricate hairstyle that framed her face and the crown of her head. "Just need a bit of rouge on your lips and cheeks and then we can put on your dress."

Rory, who Saoirse had never seen wear a stitch of cosmetics, was quite apt at applying it. Saoirse's lips looked like they had been bitten to a rosy shade, and her cheeks gave the impression that she had spent a good hour under a warm afternoon sun. It was a romantic look, and the idea of sharing her first kiss with Emrys in front of an audience didn't seem as off-putting anymore. Kissing him as a bride seemed fitting.

Actually, the more she thought about it, the more she just wanted to kiss him. She wanted to kiss him during their ceremony, find a quiet room afterwards to kiss him more, take turns unbuttoning each other and kissing more than just lips...

"Saoirse?" Rory's voice broke through Saoirse's daydreaming.

"Hmm?" she asked. "Sorry."

"It's alright. I don't blame you for your woolgathering today." Rory gave her a knowing smile in the mirror. Saoirse's cheeks deepened beyond the artificial hue the rouge gave her. "I asked if you wanted me to fetch Ada so we can dress you?"

"Oh, yes." Saoirse nodded. "That would be wonderful."

Rory's chatelaine jingled as she made her way out of the room. Saoirse heard the sound quiet to near silence as Rory moved further towards the hall, but it soon became louder as she and Ada drew closer. The house manager opened the row of small satin buttons on the back of Saoirse's wedding dress as Rory prepared the under-layers. Saoirse stood and let the housekeeper lace her into her corset and layer on several petticoats. Rory untied the ribbon straps of Saoirse's chemise and tucked them into the top of Saoirse's corset to keep them secured.

Once her base of shaping layers was on, it was time for her final ensemble addition. Rory helped Ada lift the gown over Saoirse's head and carefully dress her into the delicate garment. Saoirse pulled her arms through the lace and ruffles of the elbow-length sleeves and tried to peek at herself in the mirror, but she was at a difficult angle while Rory buttoned her into the dress. The housekeeper closed the buttons at Saoirse's collar and turned the bride to face the floor length mirror next to the vanity. As she laid eyes on herself,

Saoirse felt the world stop.

Saoirse had only seen herself in the dress once, but it was different seeing herself in it with her hair done and cosmetics added. It was an image she had only dreamed of. But it wasn't ever a dream of finding love and happiness. It was a dream of escaping her previous life and hoping whoever she was handed off to was at least a shade better than her brother. Now, however, Emrys had changed that dream. First, it was complete freedom to be on her own, but now, it was the idea of a life that included him and a family that brought her happiness.

Saoirse gingerly ran her finger over the details on her dress. Her collar and neck were sheerly dressed in Swiss dot and heirloom lace, while creamy white satin peeked out from beneath more lace that ran from her bust to the floor. Rory added a finishing touch of a blush-colored satin sash around Saoirse's waist and tied it into a bow at her back. She adorned her neck with a single strand of pearls that Saoirse had brought with her. They had been her grandmother's for centuries and passed to Saoirse when her mother died. It was one of the few pieces she had of hers. Even if she had no memories of the boireann, at least she had a physical piece of her to carry.

"You look stunning," Ada said softly.

"Thank you." Saoirse smiled at her in the mirror, unable to take her eyes off herself.

"Emrys is going to be speechless." Ada fluffed the tulle of Saoirse's sleeves and skirt.

"Hopefully not speechless enough he can't say his vows," Rory snickered.

"I'm sure it won't be the last time I make him speechless today." Saoirse smirked, but then remembered who the company was that she was saying this to. Her cheeks brightened again, but Ada and Rory just shared cheeky smiles with her. After taking one last glance at herself in the mirror, Saoirse was led downstairs.

The dining room table had been set up for over a dozen people, and rich floral centerpieces in plum colors and soft yellows sat in the center. Rory handed her a matching bouquet before leading her onto the terrace. Several chairs were set up and filled with people, including a few faces Saoirse recognized. Her heart ached a bit when she remembered none of her family had made an effort to attend. It was most likely due to Eamon barring them from attending, but it still hurt wondering if either of her brothers had pushed against him or just rolled over and allowed him to dictate their lives.

Rory squeezed Saoirse's arm and vanished back into the house, most likely to make sure the reception was being prepared properly. The murmuring among the guests quieted as a few string musicians began to play. Saoirse drifted down the aisle and her vision suddenly tunneled to only see Emrys in his plum-colored uniform jacket. His hair had been neatly combed, and his smile made the gold in his eyes dance.

Saoirse couldn't decide if he looked more handsome well-groomed and in uniform or hair mussed and half-dressed like he was this morning. Both made her want to grab for him and end the tension that came with delaying their first kiss. But it would have to continue to be delayed as she closed the distance between her and her groom and the druid priestess commenced the ceremony.

The priestess began with a blessing that was first spoken in the Old Language and then in the common tongue. Saoirse listened along as she spoke of commitment and partnership. A week ago, she was looking forward to moving to a home that was all her own, free to do whatever she pleased. Emrys, however, had proved himself worthy of taking the leap to stay with him instead.

There was an exchanging of rings after the two vowed to uphold the commitment the priestess outlined in her blessing. The ring Emrys slid onto her finger had a band made of silver in the pattern of a Celtic weave. A large, bright amethyst sat in the middle and glinted in the summer sun. Diamonds were scattered through the woven pattern of the band, accenting the points where the weave crossed over itself.

A slight panic settle into Saoirse as she realized she was never given a ring to place on Emrys's finger. He squeezed her adorned hand and procured a wedding band with a matching Celtic weave from a pocket on his jacket. She smiled with relief and placed the ring on his corresponding finger.

The priestess gave a final blessing and made the announcement of their union. Emrys took her face in one of his hands and brushed his thumb along her cheek as he lowered his head towards hers. There was no one to interrupt them this time. It was tradition and expected that they would kiss. Her heart pounded in her chest as his scent enveloped her and his lips brushed over hers. The spark bounced erratically in her body and before she could stop herself, she reached for the front of his jacket and pressed her lips to his, deepening their kiss.

The small crowd witnessing their vows let out cheers and Saoirse was reminded where they were. The lawn and guests around them had dissolved for a moment, but she now was made very aware of her surroundings. She pulled away from Emrys, and his matching silly grin told her all she needed to know about their first kiss.

Emrys slipped his hand into Saoirse's and guided her back down the aisle. The faces around them blurred as he led her towards the house, and Saoirse was thankful he had some type of hold on her. She felt both dizzy and like her mind had every thought she could imagine racing through it at the same time. Her thoughts didn't steady until Emrys pulled her into the council room and quietly shut the door behind them. He wrapped his arms around her waist and pulled her close.

They stood catching their breath for a long moment before he asked, "Are you alright?"

"Yes." She nodded, her smile from the ceremony still tugging at her lips. "Are you?"

"Yes," he answered, with a breathy laugh. "We're married now."

"We are."

Emrys traced the curve of her jaw with his finger and tipped her chin up to press a kiss to her lips. "You've gained your freedom. No one can take it from you now."

"Thank you," she breathed.

He chuckled and kissed her again. "I told you. You have no need to thank me."

"I believe I do." Before he could argue the point further, she dropped her bouquet to the floor and drew him in for a long kiss. The heat of his body pressed against hers radiated through her dress, and she wished they didn't have a reception to attend.

Saoirse ran her tongue over the seam of his lips, and Emrys didn't hesitate to welcome it into his mouth. His hand still on her waist wandered over her hip and wrapped around to her arse, clutching it. The sensation made a small moan escape her, and she ground her hips against him without thinking. Devilishly, she grinned against his lips when she found how quickly his body was reacting to their kissing. She reluctantly pulled away, taking his bottom lip between her teeth as she did, and stared at him through hazy vision.

"I believe we have a party to get to," she said, her voice raspy with desire.

"They can wait," Emrys responded, capturing her lower lip between his.

Saoirse gave an amused giggle and gently pushed him back. "I think they'll begin to suspect we're doing something scandalous."

"Well, we are married now. It's a bit expected." He gave her a cheeky grin and tried to kiss her again, but Saoirse turned her head so he made contact with her cheek. "Alright, let's go put any unsavory rumors to rest." Emrys pulled his hands away from her and reached for her bouquet that had been abandoned on the floor. "I'm sorry we had to share our first kiss in front of an audience." He scooped her flowers up off the floor and leaned close to her ear to whisper, "I promise to make up for it later."

Heat flushed through Saoirse's body as his breath tickled the shell of her ear. Gooseflesh rose over her skin, and she narrowed her eyes as she caught the smug look on Emrys's face. He had only done it to torment her in response to halting their moment alone.

"You're a cheeky cad," she murmured, taking her bouquet back.

"Ah, but I'm *your* cheeky cad now." Emrys kissed her cheek and offered his arm to her. "Shall we see how Cyprian chooses to embarrass himself today?"

"I would love nothing more." Saoirse wrapped her hand into the crook of Emrys's arm and let him lead her to the dining room where their guests awaited.

S*aoirse sighed as* she toed off her shoes and leaned back against Emrys. They had retreated to their suite as their reception was winding down. They left to a round of cheers and whistles, many of the guests quite deep in their cups. Once upstairs and inside their suite, Emrys shed his heavy jacket laden with medals and pins, and the two flopped onto the sofa, exhausted.

A fire crackled in the hearth, and Saoirse felt her magic hum in sync with it. She hadn't been this tired in quite some time, and she had forgotten how much energy she exhausted each day to keep her magic from manifesting inappropriately. Saoirse didn't necessarily allow her magic free, but she did let it thrum alongside the fireplace.

"Of all the weddings I've attended, I believe this was the best," Emrys remarked as he casually adjusted his arm so his hand rested on Saoirse's waist.

Saoirse snorted. "I would hope our wedding was the best you've attended."

"Well, considering none of the dukes had a proper wedding, the standard is fairly low."

A lazy smile pulled at Saoirse's lips, and she reached for Emrys's hand. She traced his knuckles with her finger as she collected her thoughts. There had been so many introductions, courses of food, and traditions to execute that Saoirse's mind had barely been able to take it all in. "I agree," she murmured as she reflected on the congratulations and attention that had been showered on them. "I think our wedding was the best." She yawned and let her head lull to the side, her cheek pressing against Emrys's chest. "I am disappointed I didn't get the chance to meet the duchesses."

Emrys's chest rumbled with a chuckle underneath her head. "You did," he said.

"I did?" Saoirse swiveled her head to face him.

"Yes, you did." Emrys dropped a kiss to her forehead. "But it was in the receiving line after dinner, so I don't blame you if everyone's faces and names blurred together."

"Well, I guess I'll meet them again later this week at tea, then." Saoirse turned again to gaze into the fire. The crimsons and golds danced over the charring wood, and the soft crack and pop in the otherwise quiet room gave her a sense of peace. "Emrys," she murmured. "Can I ask a personal question?"

Emrys reached for her free hand that was adorned with her wedding ring. The amethyst and diamonds winked and glistened in the firelight. "I believe this ring means you can ask about anything you'd like to know about me." He kissed her knuckles before returning her hand back to where it had been resting.

"Cressida mentioned you only recently expressed interest in marrying," Saoirse recalled. "Why now? Did you not have any interest in marrying before now, or were there not any prospects you fancied?" She chose to ignore the mentions Kieran made about persuading Emrys to marry her. He most likely fabricated it, and she didn't find it worthy of bringing it up.

Emrys's fingers at her temple stilled for a moment before answering. "There had been one boireann I nearly married," he said.

Saoirse felt a bolt of jealousy course through her. It was a strange feeling. Rationally, she knew there was no reason for it. That marriage hadn't come to fruition, and Saoirse was his wife he was legally bound to now. And yet...

"She was the daughter of the Highland Fae king, and we were close friends," Emrys continued. "But my plan to marry her fell through. Her father had arranged her with someone else before I could arrange myself as a suitor. I haven't seen or spoken to her since she told me she was arranged."

"How long ago was that?" Saoirse wanted nothing more than this jealous feeling to pass. Maybe if it wasn't recent, her emotions could ease and her night wouldn't be soured by irrational feelings.

Emrys stroked her arm, and the consistent motion helped a bit. "About fifty-four years," he answered with a bit of melancholy in his tone. Her jealousy became replaced with sympathy. It seemed like this boireann hadn't just been someone he sought out to have as a partner to produce an heir like many royals did. Emrys had been hurt and heartbroken.

Saoirse reached for his hand and threaded her fingers with his. She squeezed his hand three times before bringing it to her lips and pressing a kiss to the back of it. Emrys squeezed her hand back and swiped his thumb along the side of hers. "I nearly gave up on marrying altogether after that," he murmured.

"What made you decide to seek it out again?" She held her breath, hoping he wouldn't bring up Kieran's name.

Emrys took in a deep breath and slowly let it out. "The dukes urged me to see who was eligible. I didn't plan to send any proposals, but you stood out to me. It was like the gods kept pointing me towards you."

Saoirse relaxed. Kieran had been lying after all. "I guess I have them to thank, then."

Emrys chuckled, and the two slipped into a comfortable silence. It was odd to think of herself as married, as a wife. For a long while, she saw it as a path to freedom. "Wife" would only be a title she took to escape Eamon and produce an heir for someone.

But with Emrys, nothing felt like an obligation. She felt free and content. There was nothing more she wanted than to be here, tangled with him on the sofa. Even if she was beginning to itch from the seams of her dress.

"Can I ask a favor of you?" she mumbled.

"Always."

"I need help getting out of my dress." Saoirse sat up and a long pause hung over them. "Do you mind unbuttoning me?"

"Of course." Emrys reached for the line of buttons that held her dress closed, and Saoirse worked to keep her breathing even.

She knew what asking that question could lead to, and she wanted it. No longer did she want to dance around what was inevitable. Saoirse trusted him, and she wanted him to know that.

Emrys began to carefully unbutton the back of her dress and, as her back was slowly exposed, the warmth of the fire seeped onto her skin. She felt a pop in her veins and fought with what little energy she had left to keep it at bay. Emrys's fingertips grazed the bare skin of her neck as he opened the bodice buttons, and the simmer in her veins was overshadowed by sparks darting through her from his touch.

"There," he said as he reached the final few buttons just above her hips. "Do you need help with the corset, too?" She nodded and closed her eyes as she concentrated on grounding herself. There was only the soft sound of laces being pulled through the grommets of her corset and the beat of her thundering heart to drown out the anxiety filling her. The garment layer sagged, and she took a deep breath, filling her lungs and belly. The crackling in her veins was subsiding back to the hum it was before, but the buzz of that spark lingered.

Emrys pulled his hands back from her body. "There, now you're free." Saoirse shed the clothes off her shoulders and attempted to shimmy out of them as she turned to face him again. Her foot caught on the lining of her dress, and her body flew forward, her gaze staring straight at the arm of the sofa as she fell.

An arm wrapped around her waist, and the next thing she knew, she was being pressed against a warm body. Emrys gave an amused smile and suppressed a chuckle. "Are you trying to throw yourself at me, Princess?"

She covered her face with her hands, but her shoulders shook with silent laughter. "No, but I don't think I'm as graceful as I think I am." She felt his chest vibrate as he lifted her upright in his lap. His hands wrapped around hers and gently pried them from her embarrassed face.

"I didn't marry you for your gracefulness."

She realized how close they were now, and her eyes lowered to his lips, unable to move them back up. "What did you marry me for?"

She watched his throat bob as he swallowed. Another beat passed before he answered. "We'd be here all night if I listed them all out."

The corner of her mouth tilted up, and warmth spread through her body, pooling in her abdomen. She drifted closer to him and felt the spark run along her spine as she brushed her lips against his. Fingers slipped into her hair, and she felt pins being removed from her locks. They both parted their lips without any coaxing, and Saoirse clutched his shirt to pull herself even closer to him. She felt her chemise drift downward and hang precariously just above her nipples. She lost her ability to care about being exposed and pressed herself against him.

"Emrys," she breathed between kisses, "touch me. Please." His lips trailed along her jaw and neck before he responded.

"Touch you how?" he asked.

Her body became even more bothered at the question. She reached for the hand he had on her waist and dragged it over her hip to just between her thighs. "Here," she said. "And I would hope you know how to touch me effectively."

His lips smiled against her skin as his fingers found the clips of the garters keeping her stockings on. He slid the silk garments off her legs and slid his fingers up to the hem of her chemise. "I'll be more than effective, sweetheart." His hand warmed the bare skin of her thigh, and gooseflesh erupted in the wake of his touch. She shifted in his lap until she was straddling him. Their eyes met as they shared panting breaths. "Are you sure you want this?" Emrys whispered.

"Yes," Saoirse said with a nod. His darkened gaze locked on hers as her hem was pushed further towards her hips, and his thumb danced along the sensitive skin of her inner thigh. He teased her as he slid both hands onto her ass and squeezed. She bit her bottom lip and gave an impatient noise. "Emrys."

"Yes?" he asked as he kissed her jaw and kneaded her flesh.

"You're a terrible tease."

His chest rumbled against hers as he chuckled. He gave one last squeeze to her rear before running his thumb between her thighs. She whimpered at the intimate touch, and her body became hungry for more.

"Oh, Saoirse, you're soaking wet." He groaned as he circled her clit with his thumb. "And it's all just for me."

Points of her body became slick with sweat, and her desire was growing desperate. Never had someone aroused her to the point of groveling. She undulated her hips over his hand, and he finally gave her what she wanted. Two fingers slid inside her, and she gasped as her body tightened. He moved his fingers at an achingly slow pace, and she mewled her approval.

"Do you want me to go faster?" he asked as he nipped at her bare shoulder.

"No." She shook her head. "Not yet." Her eyes fluttered close, and she relished the slow build-up he was creating. Past encounters with lovers had been quick and dirty, both her and her partner looking to find release and move on. But Emrys was wholly concentrated on her. He teased and explored and relished her responses.

Her orgasm built to a point that teetered on release. She bucked her hips against his hand as her breathing became labored. "Emrys," she pleaded. Without another word, he moved with short, quick strokes until her body felt like it was about to tear apart. Every muscle in her body tightened and then shuddered as her release crested and broke over her.

Saoirse's nails dug into his shoulders as she rode out the rest of her orgasm, her body shaking and her lips unable to form words. Emrys captured her bottom lip between his teeth and kissed her as he slowed to a stop. Her body slumped against him, and her kissing became lazier.

She finally broke from his lips and gulped the air. Beads of sweat rolled down between her shoulders and her thighs were dewy. Emrys lifted his fingers to his mouth and wrapped his lips around them. His eyes closed, and he hummed as if he was tasting the sweetest honey in England. As he slid his fingers out, his eyes slowly opened, revealing how deeply they had darkened with lust.

"Now I get to dream of how you taste." While he stared at her as if he were hungry to devour her further, he remained restrained. His gaze drifted over her body, and he let out a labored breath. "Gods, you're beautiful."

Saoirse's cheeks flushed all over again, and she smiled shyly. She met his gaze and caught the flush creeping up his neck. He stared at her hungrily before he shut his eyes, confliction written on his face.

"We should stop," he said, the husk in his voice still present.

"Why?" she asked. His pants strained under her with an obvious erection. "We've all but tupped in a bed together."

"You deserve better than to be *tupped* tonight."

"What if that's what I want?"

"It might be what you want, but have you taken a contraceptive?"

Saoirse shook her head. It hadn't crossed her mind to do so when she hadn't been entirely sure about staying until this morning.

"Then we stop here," Emrys said, kissing her collarbone. "And you'll sleep in your own bed."

Her brows furrowed. "Why my own bed?"

"Because if I have you within arm's reach, I will ravage you and most likely give us an heir before we're prepared. Unless you want one mere hours after being married."

Saoirse shook her head, her eyelids growing heavy.

"Then your own bed it is." He pressed a kiss to her forehead.

She sighed. Her lust-addled brain wanted nothing more than for Emrys to carry her into his room and satisfy her fantasies. But she had to admit she was thankful one of them had a fraction of responsibility present.

A yawn escaped her, and she rested her forehead against Emrys's. She felt his hand gently run up and down her back before both of them slid around the back of her thighs. She wrapped her arms around his neck as he stood from the sofa and carried her to her bed.

Emrys sat her on the mattress, and she took her time pulling her hands from him. Saoirse watched with heavy-lidded eyes as opened one dresser drawer after another until he found what she assumed was a nightgown. He placed it on the bed next to her and disappeared into her bathroom. She heard running water as she opened the busk of her corset and slid her chemise off.

Her head had poked through the opening of the nightgown when Emrys returned with a wet cloth.

"I might have kissed most of your cosmetics off, but I'm sure you'll want to remove the rest." He handed her the damp cloth, and Saoirse caught a peek at herself in the floor length mirror nearby. She scrubbed at the various smudges of rouge on her face while Emrys pulled the rest of the hair pins from her hair. Her hair fell to her shoulders and, after running his fingers through it to loosen any tangles, Emrys braided it clumsily.

Saoirse handed him her soiled cloth and tried to tuck the stray pieces of hair into the braid Emrys had made. When he returned from rinsing the cloth in the bathroom, Emrys's lips grazed Saoirse's forehead and lingered there.

"Good night, Emrys," Saoirse said.

"Good night, Princess," he whispered against her skin. He stepped out of her reach and disappeared from her room. Saoirse allowed her exhaustion to take her over, and she barely got under the layers of bedding before sleep pulled her under.

Emrys woke with a start and glanced around his dark bedroom. Everything was still, but his heightened hearing picked up the sound of cries. He threw the sheets off himself and hissed as his bare feet touched the cold wooden floors. Opening his door, he surveyed the dark sitting room that also sat quiet save for the last few dying embers of the fire. More cries came, and those were less muted. Panic washed over him as he stepped towards Saoirse's room and heard another cry come from the other side of the door.

He threw open her door and looked for her in the dim room. His eyes had adjusted to the lack of light and, with a sliver of pale light from the moon, he could make out her silhouette sitting upright in her bed. She cried out, her words mangled between her gasps for breath. Her skin glowed unnaturally, and she cried out louder as he noticed the tips of her palms and fingers began to be engulfed in flame. He hurried over to her and knelt near her bed as he tried to wrap his hands around hers, but the fire bit at his skin. In his panic, his magic had stalled, and he swore as he tried to concentrate enough to get it back.

He held onto her forearms and focused his mind on his own breathing as he tried to soothe her. She continued to gasp for air as if something was choking her breath. He felt his icy magic crawl through his veins, and he carefully placed his hands around Saoirse's. The flames extinguished one by one, but her breathing still hitched as panic wracked her body. His chest tightened as he heard her gasp and choke.

"It's alright," he said softly, his thumbs tracing gentle circles on the backs of her hands. "You're safe. I'm here."

Her eyes focused on him, and while her breathing was still rapid, she was no longer crying out or gasping. Emrys watched her as the fear in her eyes began to settle. Her hands were still warm but no longer scorching from the flames, and her skin began to return to its normal, pale hue. Saoirse steadied her breathing, but her face contorted and a sob escaped her lips.

The tightness in his chest became worse at the sight of tears staining her face. He rose from the floor and wrapped an arm around Saoirse. "It's going to be alright," he murmured against her temple. "You're safe."

Saoirse's body shook as she cried and Emrys wanted to get her out of this room. He slid an arm under her knees and gently lifted her off the bed. Saoirse's hands that had clung to his now grasped at his bare shoulders. Her fingers pressed against his skin, and Emrys could feel the anguish in her grip. He carried her out of her bedroom and into his, sitting on the bed with her in his lap. He held her close and brushed his fingers over her hair as she continued to sob.

At a loss of how else to comfort her, he began to hum a melody he didn't know he still remembered. It was to a ballad about fireannaich soldiers returning from war and the families that welcomed them. He hadn't thought of the song in decades. It was one Ada sang to him when he was young and inconsolable like Saoirse was. Eventually, Emrys softly sang the lyrics out loud as he ran his hand over Saoirse's arm.

Her sobs slowed to a quiet and were replaced by hiccups. Her breathing evened, and Emrys could feel her head become heavier on his chest. Her grip on him slackened, and her hand slid to tuck into her chest.

Emrys returned to humming the melody as he watched her body fall into sleep. He noted how peaceful she now looked. His mind tried to piece together what had happened and his stomach churned at the reasons why. The screams he heard and the panic he saw in her eyes were more than just the result of a nasty nightmare. She didn't have any kind of control of her magic, something fae learned at eight or nine years old and honed until they were Settled. He had been suspicious of her control on her magic from the way her bedroom in Ireland looked alone. He tried to convince himself it was from the distant past, but after tonight, he couldn't deceive himself any longer.

The thought that Eamon neglected to get her a tutor for her magic made Emrys sick. He pressed a kiss into the crown of her hair and sighed. Saoirse hadn't been shy about sharing how awful her brother was, but Emrys hadn't imagined it was this terrible. Putting Saoirse out into the world with untrained magic wasn't just harmful to others, it was dangerous to her own wellbeing. His charm had led her to stay, but he was quickly learning he would have to put in a serious effort to make sure she stayed safe. But he didn't care how much work it took. He would go to the ends of the earth to protect her.

Saoirse woke with the dawn, feeling her swollen eyelids fight against her as she tried to open her eyes. A pounding headache battered against her skull. The night terror that awoke her and sent her into an attack of hysterics had been the worst she had in months. She should have seen it coming with how her magic fought against her will after the wedding. But her magic usually only crept through her arms and fingers, threatening to emerge, but had never resulted in physical flames. Real flames hadn't manifested since her argument with Cressida ages ago.

She moved her foot, but it came in contact with something solid. She squinted and looked around the dim room, recognizing it wasn't the one she had fallen asleep in. The warm body next to her told her where she had been moved to. Saoirse cautiously lifted her head and glanced at the foot of the bed to see Owen curled up and fast asleep. The corner of her lips tipped up, but a bolt of pain struck her temple and buried her head back into Emrys's side.

Saoirse's body was still exhausted from her midnight magical exertion, and the sweet warmth of Emrys's body against hers enticed her to join him back in slumber. She closed her eyes, but flashes of her nightmare kept her mind awake. She finally abandoned her attempt at returning to sleep and instead kept her eyes cracked open and her breathing attuned to Emrys's.

His musky scent with that hint of bergamot brought Saoirse back to their night before she went to bed. She had let him touch her, taste her. She could only imagine the things he had wanted to do with her if she'd had a modicum of forethought and took a contraceptive tonic before the wedding. Those memories felt bittersweet now that she had ruined the rest of his night. She had probably screamed and woken him up. Her cheeks flushed in embarrassment as she imagined him waking in the middle of the night and seeing her in distress.

This was supposed to be her first official day of her freedom, but she still had the shackles of her past holding her back.

Emrys began to stir and drew in a deep breath before she felt his hand come to life, stroking her arm. She lifted her gaze to his, and he gave her a sleepy grin. "Good morning, Princess," he said, in that gravelly voice still laden with sleep.

"Good morning," she murmured before groaning and burying her head again.

He brushed her hair back, and Saoirse peeked up at him. "I hope it's alright I brought you here." His expression was pained, as if he was reliving the night in his mind. "I felt somewhere that wasn't your room would help."

Saoirse nodded. "It did. Thank you."

"I guess we really can't stay in separate rooms if we tried." Emrys chuckled, but Saoirse could hear the nervousness in it.

"I'm sorry," she murmured.

"You have nothing to be sorry for." His fingers brushed over her hair rhythmically, and her mind calmed. "We don't have to discuss it either."

Saoirse held back her immediate response in order to think it through. She wanted to dismiss that idea and tell him she was fine with discussing it. But was she? She felt safe with Emrys. She had felt safe enough with him to divulge details about her life. Was this any different? "No," she said quietly. "I want to discuss it." She traced the path of his ribs with her finger, buying herself time to muster the courage to begin the discussion.

"Then can I ask you about something?" His voice was low and gentle. She nodded, and her finger slowed to a halt on his skin. "Is... is your magic untamed?"

The question caught her a bit off guard. She hadn't thought he wanted to discuss her magic. She had never disclosed how she managed her magic with anyone. Tears pinched the back of her eyes and threatened to fall down her cheeks as she nodded her answer. Emrys pressed a kiss to the crown of her head, and the tears slipped down her cheeks.

"I was never given a mentor to teach me how to control it." She sniffed and haphazardly wiped at her face. Emrys's fingers stroked over her cheeks, brushing the tears away. "As I've already told you, my parents died before my magic manifested, and my brother didn't bother with getting me a mentor. I don't know if my other brothers volunteered to teach me, but I wouldn't be surprised if Eamon refused them. He had another hold on me if I couldn't safely manage my magic. But he got tired of me bothering him, and I believe that's why he started arranging me. He wanted me to be someone else's problem. I'm sorry you're the one who now has to suffer because of it."

His fingers hooked under her chin and gently lifted her gaze to him so that he knew she was listening as he spoke. "Do you hear me complaining?" His voice was soft and gentle, but there was a firmness to it. She shook her head, but she knew his question was rhetorical. "I don't see your magic as a burden. I don't see *you* as a burden."

Another tear rolled down her cheek at his words. While no one had ever told her she was a burden, no one had ever confirmed she wasn't one either. Her mind had come to those conclusions on its own. Her interactions with her family had convinced her of it, but she hadn't realized how heavy those thoughts weighed on her until Emrys relieved her of them.

"If you want, I'd be happy to mentor you with your magic," he said as he wiped the tear from her cheek.

"You shouldn't have to." She attempted to argue, but she knew it was useless. Emrys had made it clear he took her as she was and he'd do anything to keep her safe. "You didn't ask for this responsibility."

"I don't care if I didn't ask for it." That gentle but firm tone came out again. It reminded her of Ada. "You can't live with untamed magic. I'm more than happy to mentor you. I've done it for nearly a century."

"You've mentored young fae with magic?" Saoirse shouldn't have been surprised. He had revealed to her that he was much older than she first suspected. There was much more to his life she had to learn than he did of hers.

"I have and still do." A shimmer of pride flashed in his gold-rimmed, emerald eyes. She took a moment to weigh his offer. She hated that her brother was still getting his way regarding her life, but Emrys was selflessly offering his time to benefit her wellbeing. Again.

"Alright." She nodded, accepting his offer. "Thank you."

"You're welcome." The corners of his lips perked up as he stroked Saoirse's arm in satisfaction. "But we're not going to start today. I want you to rest. I'll tell Ada to deliver your meals and have Seraphina check on you...if it's alright that I share the details of your magic with her."

"That's fine."

"Good, then she'll check to make sure you don't have any injuries and that you're strong enough to start training tomorrow." A smile stretched on his face and Saoirse smiled back. It was the first genuine smile she had that morning. Emrys kissed her forehead, and her body relaxed under the tender touch. It hadn't occurred to her how tense her shoulders and core were until she released them with an exhale. She nuzzled her face into him once again and relished the feeling of safety she felt. She hoped he didn't have to leave for the day. Maybe if she asked in such a way she didn't come across as needy, he would stay with her.

Before she could open her mouth to speak, he slipped his arm out from under her and swung his legs out of the bed. She wanted to reach out and grab for him, but she stopped herself.

"I have some work I have to complete since nothing was done yesterday, but I'll try to check in later today and make sure you're alright." He replaced the sheets and blankets he had disturbed next to her and tucked her in.

Saoirse grabbed for him before he stepped out of her reach. "When you come to check on me, will you have time to stay with me?"

He gave her a half-smile and kissed her forehead. "I'll make time." He kissed her lips and let the touch linger for a second longer than it needed to.

Saoirse watched as he readied himself for the day. He moved swiftly and was fully dressed in a matter of minutes. Even in her achy state, her eyes roamed over his body, appreciating how his clothes complemented his physique.

"I'm serious when I say I want you to rest," Emrys said, making his way to her door. "Your body needs it. Not just from the magic, but...everything else."

She blushed at what he insinuated. What they had engaged in hadn't been too wild last night, but it was enough that rest was tempting.

"Take a nap, have a bath, read a book if you'd like. Understand?" He paused in her doorway and waited for her to respond. She nodded and nestled further into the bed, hoping her mind was calm enough to sleep a few more hours.

"Good." His eyes glanced at the foot of the bed and his smile widened. "If you do anything that is not resting, Owen has permission to snitch on you." She laughed, and it made her feel lighter. "Have a good day, Princess." He vanished from her doorway, but she noted he left the door ajar for Owen.

Silence overtook the room, and Saoirse turned over and sighed. She hoped she could sleep now and her thoughts wouldn't linger on her nightmarish episode. As much as she wanted to enjoy Emrys's company when he eventually returned, she wondered if that would be the only time her mind could quiet and she could relax enough to sleep. Saoirse let her eyes drift close and tried to succumb to sleep. It took a bit of coaxing, but she was finally pulled under.

S*aoirse awoke a* few hours later to a thud at the foot of the bed. She jumped as her eyes flew open. She squinted from the sudden flood of light and saw the shape of someone rummaging through a brocade bag.

"Didn't mean to startle you, dear," the boireann said, a Scottish lilt in her voice. "I thought you were already awake. Emrys made a fuss to get me up here he failed to tell me you'd be asleep."

Saoirse's eyes adjusted, and she could make out more detailed features of the boireann. The pointed tips of her ears peeked through her silver-white hair that was braided down her back and nearly reached her waist.

"It's alright." Saoirse rubbed the sleep from her eyes and yawned.

"Oh, dear, I believe I've been rude." The boireann placed a few vials of different consistencies and colors on the nightstand nearby. "I believe this is the first time we've met. I'm Seraphina, the Head Healer. Well, the only healer in this house, but that just means I can title myself whatever I want." She gave Saoirse a wink.

"I assumed as much." Saoirse attempted a genuine smile, but she could feel how heavy her face was with exhaustion. "But it's nice to officially meet you."

"Ah, I see Emrys has given me a reputation with you already." Seraphina chuckled. She smiled at Saoirse before reaching for the layers of blankets that covered her. "Can I examine you for injuries?"

Saoirse nodded and sat up higher in her bed. She extended one arm at a time to the healer, who took special care to rotate her limbs slowly as she inspected them. No one had taken this much time to check her over so thoroughly. The experiences she had with healers were minimal at best.

Unlike Alastair, Eamon didn't keep a resident healer and only called one if there was some sort of disaster or grave illness. Saoirse could count on one hand how many times she had been seen by a healer. It was usually only when either she or Cressida begged Eamon to call one to the house. Even then, they had briefly glimpsed over her, forced an unknown potion into her hand, and left with little to no other instructions.

Seraphina was far from any of those healers. The fact Emrys's first instinct was to request her to examine Saoirse as well told Saoirse all she needed to know about her decision to stay. She could only imagine what would have happened to her if she had experienced this while she was on her own. Others could have been harmed. Or she could have lost her first home on her own. A shiver ran down her spine at those catastrophic thoughts.

"Emrys told me you woke in the middle of the night with your magic manifesting." Seraphina said as she closely examined Saoirse's arms.

Saoirse nodded but didn't elaborate.

"May I ask what you were doing before going to bed?"

"Um." Saoirse's face flushed, and she saw Seraphina pause.

"You don't need to answer that," the healer quickly amended. "I should have known better." She shook her head before asking her next question. "How long have you been training with your magic, dear?"

"I..." Saoirse searched for an answer without outright admitting the issues she had dealt with for the past several years, but there was no way to dance around it. "I haven't."

"You haven't?" Seraphina's snowy white brows knitted together in concern. "What do you mean you haven't?" Saoirse chewed on her bottom lip and Seraphina, noticing her embarrassment decided to ask a different question. "How old are you?"

"Three and twenty," Saoirse murmured.

"You're three and twenty and you've never had any training with your magic?" Seraphina tried to hide her horror, but Saoirse noticed it.

She swallowed and tried to paste a cheery smile on her face to assuage the healer. "Can't quite train my magic when I don't have the means to find a mentor."

What she intended to be humorous only made the healer more horrified. Seraphina slowly took a seat at the foot of the bed. "Who kept you from getting trained?" Her voice had lowered to a gentle tone, and it caused Saoirse's guard to slip just a bit.

"My eldest brother," she quietly admitted. Her eyes dropped to her hands in her lap as she rubbed circles in her palm with her thumb. She pressed firmly into the center of her hand, creating enough stimulating pressure to keep herself grounded. "He didn't want to invest in a mentor to help me learn about my magic. He told me that having untapped magic would make me more appealing to suitors. I wanted to leave home, and marrying a suitor was my only viable option my brother would give me. But I've come to realize he was just unbothered to find a mentor for me. Having uncontrolled magic has only caused me more problems." A sting behind Saoirse's eyes warned her that tears were close to spilling again. She pinched the side of her hand and forced herself to keep her emotions at bay. "Recently, he's been trying to push me off so that I was someone else's problem."

"My dear, you are not a problem," Seraphina said. She gently placed her hand on Saoirse's knee and gave it a squeeze. Saoirse lifted her gaze to the healer and saw warmth reflected in her eyes. "I won't lie to you. It's difficult to manage magic that isn't trained, but it doesn't take any value away from you."

Saoirse gave a watery smile and wiped the few tears that had rolled down her cheeks. She could see now where Emrys's response to her confession that morning came from. He didn't treat her like a burden because Ada and Seraphina never treated him like one.

They didn't have to raise him, but they loved him enough to strain their patience and every ounce of their time to shape him into who he was now. She should have felt envious, but she only had admiration for their influence on him.

"Thank you," Saoirse whispered.

"You're welcome." Small wrinkles creased around the healer's eyes as she smiled. She stood from the bed and finished examining Saoirse's arms and legs. She asked a few other questions that were related to how Saoirse felt physically, and when she mentioned a persistent headache, Seraphina dove into her carpetbag. She came back up with a tonic that she began to mix at the bedside.

"Magic has a funny way of making a mess of our bodies," Seraphina said as she mixed the liquid. "It's as if the gods weren't satisfied enough our bodies could be injured and break that they had to add magic to them and leave us on our own to figure it out." She gave Saoirse a cheeky grin that she had seen before. It was Emrys's.

"Luckily," Seraphina continued, "they had mercy on us, and our bodies heal in half the time it takes humans to heal from the same ailments." The healer handed a glass of amber-colored tonic to Saoirse, who looked at warily.

The strong scent of bitter black tea and rosemary hit her nose, and she cringed in response. It reminded her of the time Cressida tried to cure a skin infection with a similar concoction. That was one of the few times Eamon actually requested the help of a healer if only to rid his wife and household of the bitter smell.

"Don't think too hard about it." Seraphina gave her shoulder an encouraging squeeze. "Just hold your breath and swallow it in one go."

Saoirse took a deep breath and held it as she tipped the liquid into her mouth, attempting swallow it before her tongue could register the taste. The bitter flavor burned her throat, and she sputtered a bit as she handed the glass back to the healer.

"I have to say you took that better than Emrys does." Seraphina chuckled as she took out a small cloth from her bag and began to wipe the remaining droplets in the glass. "Sometimes I just let him live with the aches that plague him when I'm not in the mood to fight with him to take it. He may be nearly two hundred years old, but some days he could convince me otherwise."

Saoirse let out a soft laugh and another wave of loving warmth washed over her. While she hadn't witnessed either Ada or Seraphina interact with Emrys directly, she had no doubts their love for him ran deeper than the Atlantic. Now that she was married to him, their love extended to her as well. She didn't let herself linger on that fact, otherwise her emotions would overwhelm her again.

"Emrys told me you and Ada raised him," she said.

"Aye, we did." Seraphina nodded as she packed her things. "Ada and I have been partnered for, oh, close to four centuries now. We've taken care of many wayward children. But Emrys gave us a run for our money."

"He told me that, too."

"Aye, well, he was the last child we took in as our own, and for good reason. He was the sweetest little boy but...I think losing his mother began to catch up with him when he started working with his father." Seraphina's face faltered to a bleak expression. Saoirse was about to sympathize when the healer continued. "His mother was very close with Ada and I, almost like a sister. For a time, she had a sinking feeling something was going to happen to her. She couldn't quite put her finger on it, but it was a terrible inkling she had. She came to us and asked us to take care of Emrys if anything were to happen to her. We tried to calm her and put her at ease, but unfortunately, her instinct had been right."

"If it's any consolation, you both have raised a wonderful, thoughtful fireann," Saoirse offered.

"Aye, we think so, too." Seraphina gave her a wink and patted her blankets. "Well, I'd better let you get some rest." She closed her bag with a snap and turned for the door.

"Can I ask for one favor?" Saoirse asked.

"What do you need, dear?"

"A contraceptive tonic." Saoirse's cheeks burned. Even if she hadn't come to Saoirse's bedside, Seraphina was the healer

Saoirse would have gone to for the tonic. She didn't know why it embarrassed her.

Seraphina let out a little chuckle. "Of course. And I'll have Ada send up a tea for you. She knows the best ones to get rid of the aftertaste from tonics."

"That would be lovely. Thank you." Saoirse watched the healer disappear from the room and felt the sharpness in her head begin to subside.

It wasn't long before Rory brought up a small vial and a large mug of sweet-smelling tea. Saoirse swallowed the contents of the vial and took a tentative sip of the tea, sighing in contentment. The housekeeper fluffed her pillows and straightened her blankets. She mentioned something about sending dinner up, but Saoirse was too lost in thought to register what she said. Rory slipped out of the room as Saoirse reflected on what she had gained in the last week. She may have lost most of her family, but she was realizing how the Fearynhurst estate was feeling more like home than Dublin.

Emrys scanned the document in front of him for the third time, hoping he would finally absorb what the subject of it. His mind had been elsewhere all day and had made finishing his list of tasks take that much longer.

"Emrys." His father's voice caught his attention. He was seated across the council room table, drafting a letter. "Are you alright?"

The truth was that Emrys wasn't. He kept thinking about Saoirse alone in their quarters all day. Had he made the right decision and let her rest on her own while he worked? Or should he have shirked his responsibilities for another day to stay with her?

A gentle knock on the door pulled him from his thoughts, and he almost jumped out of his seat at the sight of the visitor in the doorway. Saoirse stood in a lilac tea gown, her hair in disarray with bits of her strawberry blonde hair having fallen from her braid, framing her face. Even in such an imperfect state, she was beautiful.

"Oh," she said softly when her eyes scanned the room. "I thought you would be alone. My apologies for disturbing you." She turned to leave, and Emrys bolted out of his seat without a second thought.

"Wait," he said, following her into the library that sat adjacent to the council room. He caught her hand, and she stopped in her tracks. "Are you alright?"

"Yes, I've been feeling better." She gave him a smile, and he noticed the redness around her eyes and nose from earlier had faded. The tightness in his chest eased at that observation.

"Good." He brought her hand to his lips and brushed a kiss over her knuckles. "Did you need something?"

"I was going a bit mad being in the suite all day, that's all."

The tightness returned at her words. He had been so worried about her that his work dragged to the point he hadn't found time to check on her. "I'm so sorry," he said weakly. "I'll be done in ten minutes."

"Emrys, it's alright." Saoirse rose up on her toes and pressed the gentlest kiss to his lips. "I thought I would sit with you while you worked, but I didn't realize your father would be with you."

"You can still join me," Emrys said quickly. "My father wouldn't mind."

"I'm not exactly dressed to be in others' company." Saoirse waved her hand over her hair and tea dress for emphasis. "I'll find somewhere to wait for you."

Emrys leaned down to her and gave her a long, lingering kiss. "Ten minutes," he repeated. "I promise."

"Come find me then." Saoirse slipped her hand from his and disappeared from the library.

Emrys returned to the council room with a new determination to finish the day's work. However, after he sat down, his father decided those ten minutes needed to stretch further.

"Is everything alright?" Alastair asked. "It's only the first day of your marriage. I would hope there isn't trouble already."

"No." Emrys shook his head as he concentrated on the handwriting on the parchment in front of him. He swore silently at the loopy and elongated writing, wishing some fae would take up some of the modern tools like typewriters. "Saoirse, um, had an incident."

"Oh?" Alastair's brows furrowed.

For a long moment, Emrys debated informing his father of the status of Saoirse's magic. She had been fine with him sharing that with Seraphina, but would it upset her to make her father privy to it as well?

"It's her magic," Emrys finally answered. "It isn't quite tame."

"What?" Alastair's dark eyes grew wide. "Don't tell me Eamon never..." His statement trailed off as if it was too terrible to voice out loud.

Emrys nodded in confirmation. Alastair dropped his fountain pen on the table and sat back in astonishment. While Ada and Seraphina had been the ones to arrange a mentor for Emrys's magic while he was growing up, Alastair had never interfered with it and had a basic understanding of the importance of managing magic. Eamon made him look like a model parent in that regard.

"Who knows?" Alastair asked in a hushed tone.

"Seraphina," Emrys answered. "And most likely Ada as well."

"Keep it like that," Alastair ordered. "You can't let anyone else know, especially..." He shut his mouth and looked around the room and out the dark windows. His voice lowered even further as he said, "Especially certain members of this court. They would jump at a chance to take advantage of untamed magic."

Emrys knew who the "certain members" were without having to ask. He shivered at the possibilities of what Kieran would have done with Saoirse's magic if he hadn't broken his promise to her. There was no chance Emrys would share that information with Kieran, even without his father's ominous warning.

"Emrys." His father's tone had dropped to a serious octave. "Keep her safe. Whatever you have to do, make sure she and her magic don't fall into the wrong hands."

Emrys nodded slowly. It was odd for his father to give him such a serious command, especially in regard to his partner. He had taken no interest in his previous relationships and little interest in the proposal he wanted arranged with Saoirse. Why was he so adamant about this now?

Emrys didn't let his thoughts linger on his father too long, however. He did promise Saoirse he would be wrapping up his work quickly to join her. Skimming the document, Emrys signed his name at the bottom and passed it onto the pile of completed work. With a brief parting word to his father, he set out to find where Saoirse was keeping herself occupied. He checked the library only to find it empty, and the dining room was also void of her presence.

Boireannaich voices coming from the kitchen caught his attention, and he followed them, hoping he would find Saoirse amongst them. He breathed a sigh of relief when he saw Saoirse sitting with Rory, a genuine smile on her face as the housekeeper imitated the stern voice of Rhys. A giggle rang throughout the room, and the sound melted the worry that still plagued Emrys.

"Good evening, Your Highness," Rory greeted him.

"Good evening," Emrys returned.

Saoirse turned to him and calm wrapped around his anxious heart. She thanked Rory for the conversation and wove her fingers with Emrys's.

"Did you want to return upstairs?" he asked.

She shook her head. "Do you mind if we go outside in the garden for a bit?"

"Not at all." With his hand in hers, they made their way to the terrace where the cool night air greeted them. The night was quiet with only a few noises of owls and other nocturnal creatures interrupting the peacefulness.

Saoirse stepped up and leaned on the stone balustrade of the terrace, Emrys's hand still tucked in hers. She seemed at least well enough to venture outside, and Emrys took it as a sign that she had followed his urging to rest for the day. Saoirse's fingers from her free hand skimmed over their interlocked fingers, and she gave a shaky sigh.

"I know you said I don't have to talk about it," she said softly. "But you should know last night wasn't the first time my magic has manifested like that."

Emrys remained silent, waiting for her to continue. She continued to fidget with their entwined fingers, and he caught the slightest wobble in her lower lip. He didn't know if he should change take her into his arms or keep their connection to just the hand she held.

"I'm not sure what Eamon put in his letter when he offered me as a bride, but you're not the first suitor I had been arranged with."

Emrys tried to keep his breathing even and not let a wave of jealousy wash over him. There had been no mention of any other attempts to marry Saoirse in the interest letter Eamon had sent several weeks ago. It had been a very brief letter, and Emrys had read it several times over, searching for any other inklings that Saoirse was his promised mate. Instead, it highlighted very little of Saoirse and focused on what Eamon was offering in exchange, an odd way to propose a marriage. Emrys satiated his sudden pang of jealousy by looking down at their interwoven hands. The glint on her wedding ring reminded him those other suitors weren't successful.

"I never asked to be arranged," Saoirse continued. "What I had asked from Eamon was to no longer live under him. I had hoped that would mean being sent off to a distant relative and living a quiet life with them, or something of the sort. But I shouldn't have dreamt so greatly." She let out a shaky laugh and squeezed Emrys's hand. "Instead, he arranged me with a lord."

"I assume it didn't go well?" he asked.

Saoirse shook her head. "No, he was a kind fireann, but he refused to marry me because of my age."

"I'm not sure I want to know how old you were."

"I was fifteen."

Emrys's blood ran cold, and he had the urge to storm back to Ireland to pummel Eamon until he was unrecognizable.

Fifteen.

Gods, he remembered what he was doing when he was fifteen, and it wasn't being arranged with potential brides. He was mastering his magic and playing shinty with his school friends. To imagine

Saoirse being thrown into an arrangement instead of having a childhood made him shiver.

"I'll need you to excuse me for a few days. I have a need to teach Eamon why arranging a fifteen-year-old with untrained magic is a barbaric idea," Emrys said sardonically.

Saoirse gave a low laugh and squeezed his hand three times. "Oh, it gets much worse."

Her tone was light, but her words were heavy. Emrys could think of only a few things that would be worse than being arranged as a child.

"Eamon didn't take the rejection well," she continued. "It looks poor on his part to have his ward be rejected by a low nobility."

"It was Eamon's fault," Emrys muttered. Another squeeze hit his hand.

"That was Cressida's argument," Saoirse agreed. "She tried to advocate for me and somehow convinced Eamon I should be closer to an adult age before I'm arranged. I believe she first suggested I finish my First Settling, but I don't think Eamon wanted to have to deal with me through that ordeal."

The more he learned of how Eamon acted behind closed doors, the more Emrys wanted to throttle him. It was made even worse when he remembered how well Kieran got on with her brother. Another shiver ran through Emrys.

"I endured a few more years until I turned nineteen and nearly begged Eamon to arrange me." The corner of Saoirse's lips tipped up in a brief dry smile. "It seemed like the easiest way to escape him, and my age was no longer a mark against me. He finally complied with my request and arranged to marry me to a duke in the northern part of the island."

"An improvement from a lord," Emrys tried to joke.

Saoirse didn't smile at his humor. Her hand tightened on his and her face twitched. "His name was Odysseus. He was much older than the lord I had been arranged with prior. He was putrid and old-fashioned." Disgust colored her face as she described him. "At every turn, he reminded me of how interested he was in the purity of my body. I fully regretted my plea to Eamon. I tried everything to get out of the arrangement, but nothing scared him off. At eight centuries old, I'm sure he had seen just about everything and wasn't amused with any of my antics." Saoirse closed her eyes and inhaled a shaky breath.

"I was desperate to break off the arrangement. The night before he was to sign and send off the contract to my brother, I told him my virginity was a lie. I said I had taken one of my brother's friends to bed and kept it a secret to myself." Her lip quivered as she spoke. "That was when he struck me across the face. He called me a whore and tore the contract apart. Then he grabbed me and threw me to the floor and told me that since I was already ruined, he would at least get to enjoy me before I left." Tears rolled down her cheeks, and she twisted her face in pain from reliving what sounded to be an unimaginable nightmare. "I fought against him, and after a few lucky blows, I was able to get out from under him and flee. I felt like I ran for miles, but it was probably only several feet before a groom found me. He arranged a carriage to get me home."

Emrys moved without thinking and slipped his hand from hers so that he could pull her close to him. Saoirse leaned against him, and her voice shook as she continued even further with her story.

"When I got home, Eamon was furious. Odysseus had obviously told them what I had said, and my brother was livid that I had fled from what I had begged for." She swallowed and blew out a shaky breath. "Cressida didn't help matters this time. She didn't exactly reprimand me, but she tried to convince me that what Odysseus had said and done to me wasn't what I had actually experienced. That was what triggered my magic." Saoirse's face crumpled, and she clutched at Emrys's waistcoat. "That's why my room back home is scorched. My magic unleashed itself and fed on my panic and anger."

Emrys thought back to the marred bedroom, and the ache in his chest returned as he pictured the scene. He rested his chin on the crown of her head before thinking again and pressing a kiss there instead. He stroked her back until her breathing settled and she relaxed against him.

"Cressida and I never spoke of it again." She sniffed, but her voice was steadier. "She most likely did it out of fear. But I believe she's the one who convinced Eamon to make suitors come to the house to keep anything unwanted from happening."

Emrys closed his eyes and took deep breaths to ease the tightness that had returned in his chest. He turned a bit so he could lean his back against the railing and held Saoirse a little tighter. She sunk deeper into his chest with a sigh.

"Saoirse, I'm so sorry," he said. His voice wavered, and he forced himself to hold his emotions together. "You didn't deserve any of that. No one deserves that."

"I know you probably have questions." Her fingers traced the seam of his waistcoat pocket as she spoke. "You can ask them if you'd like."

Fresh questions sprung up in his mind, but he hesitated to voice them. Even if she said she was ready to talk about them, he knew first hand that wasn't always true. Letting her reveal those traumatic moments was one thing but prying into details about them was another.

"Are you alright?" he asked gently, and a breathy laugh came from her lips in response.

"I'm getting there," she said. "It's taken me a long time to even retell it from start to finish. Every time I think of telling it, the pain of reliving it floods back, and I hesitate. I keep telling myself it was easier to just push it away and forget about."

"Is it?" he asked, knowing the answer. He had his own painful memories he didn't like reliving, but he knew the relief of sharing the burden with others who cared.

"No, it's scary to tell it, but I feel like it's less heavy on me."

Emrys grinned to himself and began to gently brush his fingers over her hair.

"I imagine this is also what triggered your magic last night?"

She nodded and sighed against him. Her body became heavy as her limbs relaxed. "I wanted you to know."

She trusted him. She had told him she felt safe with him. But sharing this vulnerable bit of herself, it meant more than any words of reassurance she could give him.

"Thank you for sharing that with me," Emrys whispered.

She lifted her head, and his gaze locked on hers. He felt the spark shoot violently through his body again, and he schooled his features to hide his shock from it.

"Thank you for listening."

Her eyes glistened with appreciation, and the tightness in his chest threatened to strangle him. He wondered how many times she had just wanted someone to listen to her and believe her. How many people had swept her experience aside? How many interjected their own opinions to discredit her?

Emrys placed a kiss to her forehead, lingering on her warm skin. Saoirse gave a small smile before resting her head on his chest again. "Would you feel up to working on your magic tomorrow?" He worried that just one day wasn't enough to recover. It was more than just her magic running wild in the middle of the night. Her emotional trigger was much worse than he had imagined. "You don't have to. We can take another day."

"No, I want to."

"Very well. I have my entire afternoon clear so we can work on it then."

"Thank you." He heard the sigh of relief in her voice.

"Anytime, Princess."

They stood in silence for a long moment, and Emrys was content to hold her as long as she wanted. He would stay out on the terrace with her for an eternity if she allowed it. In the quiet, something tugged at his mind. It whispered to him that sharing what he knew would relieve the strain they both felt of holding onto secrets. But he knew it wasn't right. Knew it was something she wouldn't believe him even if she did trust him as much as he thought she did. The irony of the thought wasn't lost on Emrys, and he pushed the idea of that confession aside. He had to gain more of her trust—enough to keep her with him even after his admission.

13

Saoirse made her way through the house towards the back terrace and reached for the door when a voice cut through the quiet of the house. "Good afternoon, Your Highness," Kieran said from his seat in the anteroom.

She froze, her hand held out towards the knob of the door. Her heart kicked up as she slowly turned to face him.

"Good afternoon," she said, trying to keep her words steady. She turned the knob but paused when he spoke again.

"How is married life treating you?"

She gave him a puzzled look over her shoulder. She noticed a thick book in his lap, and he wasn't dressed in his general's uniform like he had been the last time she saw him. He looked quite casual, as if he lived at the estate. Frustration boiled in Saoirse's veins. Emrys promised to be more vigilant about visitors, especially Kieran. How did he keep slipping into the house without anyone knowing?

"Why does it matter to you?" she asked.

"I want to know how my investment is doing."

"What does that mean?" Saoirse crinkled her brow.

"I convinced Emrys to marry you."

Rage simmered in her belly. He was still prattling on about this. She didn't believe a word of it. Emrys had told her Kieran treated him poorly ever since they were children. Saoirse doubted he would ever listen to Kieran's urging on anything.

"You're lying," Saoirse said bluntly. "You're lying to me and you're lying to yourself. Emrys and I made that decision together."

"Come now, Saoirse." Kieran stood and slowly closed the space between them. "Do you really think a Crown Prince would willingly enter a marriage arrangement with a boireann who hasn't even Settled yet?" He reached for one of her loose waves of hair and wrapped it around his finger.

"Just because you found that unappealing doesn't mean he does." She swallowed, her gaze watching his fingers fidget with her tendril of hair.

"I never said it was unappealing." Kieran stepped closer to her, the space between them barely a breath wide. "Admit it, Saoirse, Emrys deserves better than you."

"And what do I deserve?" she asked, her words quivering as he inched closer to her.

"You know exactly what you deserve." He cupped her face, and her heart sped up as he closed the distance between them. His lips merely brushed hers before she realized what he was doing.

Saoirse lifted her hands to push him away, but a strong gust of wind knocked him in the side of the head and ruffled her hair. Kieran stumbled sideways and rubbed at his face as if he had been slapped. His gaze snapped to the hall, and Saoirse followed his line of sight, finding nothing there.

When he turned back to Saoirse, she grabbed the door handle and swung the door open, rushing outside.

The warm summer breeze rustled her skirt as she stepped outside. She was grateful for whatever—or whoever—had caused that gust in the house. There was no predicting how far Kieran would have gone without something intervening. As she got her rapid heartbeat under control, she scanned the lawn for Emrys and spotted him near a tall oak tree. Her legs still wobbled as she walked down the steps to the grass.

She finally gained her composure as strolled across the lawn. As Emrys came closer into her view, she noticed he was without a waistcoat and his sleeves were rolled to his elbows. While Kieran had been subtly casual, Emrys was distractingly casual. He looked like he had on their wedding night, and it sent a shiver down her spine. It was too public of a space to reenact that night, but it didn't mean her mind could stop thinking about the way he touched her and the words he spoke to her.

"Are you alright?" he asked.

Saoirse swallowed and nodded. "I'm fine," she said. This wasn't the time or place to tell him about Kieran. Emrys would most likely rush into the house and, based on how he reacted to Kieran berating his friend during council, commit violence against the general.

Emrys studied her for a moment, looking like he wanted to say something, but decided against it. "Alright, well, I think this will be a good place to practice," he said. "No one is usually around at this end of the lawn, so we shouldn't run into any interruptions."

He dropped to the ground and took a seat, motioning for Saoirse to do the same. She knitted her brows but sat in the lawn across from him. The fresh summer blades of grass tickled her hands, but she focused on her mentor and his instructions.

"We're only going to focus on understanding your emotions today." His voice turned firm, and she raised a brow at the objective he gave. "Magic feeds off emotions. If we don't understand how our emotions manifest, our magic can't be controlled and wielded to be effective. The first thing I want you to do is to close your eyes and examine what emotions you're feeling right now."

She did as he instructed and shut her eyes, trying to navigate what emotion she was feeling. She predominantly felt anxious and felt her magic pop in her veins along her shoulders. Her anxiety grew and fed the magic infusing into her veins. It burned along her muscles, and she clenched her hands into fists, trying to keep it from growing further. This was how it felt before it manifested fully, and she couldn't stop it. Her breathing picked up, and she felt whatever control she had slip.

"Saoirse." She heard Emrys's voice. "Look at me." Her eyelids flew open, and she let loose the breath she hadn't realized she had been holding. He placed a hand on hers and felt her magic begin to dwindle and recede in response.

"Sorry, I panicked a bit," Saoirse said, catching her breath.

"It's alright. Now you know how fear manifests. It's not the most ideal emotion to draw magic with. Magic can grow from it without intending to feed the emotion and makes your magic difficult to contain. So, this time, I want you to handle both your fear and your magic. Soothe your fear while it's still small and let your magic flow."

"I don't think that's a good idea." Saoirse shook her head adamantly.

"You'll be alright."

He squeezed her hand, and she closed her eyes again, concentrating on not letting her fear overfeed her magic. As she tapped into the anxious feeling, her magic began to rush through her again. Saoirse panicked again and tried to physically shake the magic out of her hands. Instead, it did the exact opposite of what she intended. Flames danced between her fingers, and she opened her eyes as she felt a cool touch wrap around her hands.

Emrys was gently gripping her hands, his thumbs gliding over her fingers. "Listen to me," he said calmly. "Only let your fear feed as much of your magic as you feel you can handle. Find something that will soothe your fear and keep your magic steady."

Saoirse nodded and closed her eyes, focusing solely on minimizing her fear. She felt Emrys's hands pull away from hers as she searched for something, anything that would relieve her anxiety. Emrys's touch was the only thing she could focus on, and she tried to use it to soothe her emotion. She thought of all the little touches he enjoyed giving her. The mindless circles he drew on her skin. Kisses to her temple. The way he traced the curves of her body with his wandering hand.

The thoughts calmed her anxiety enough to allow just enough of it to feed her magic and let it manifest. For once, Saoirse felt a control she hadn't before. Her magic idled with only a few nips here and there as it waited for her command. She attempted to manifest her magic on her own terms and it coursed through her, warming her palms. It flickered just under her skin and, imagining the little touches Emrys gave her, held her magic to where it was.

"Now draw it back." Emrys's words almost startled her, but she managed to keep herself calm. She used the thought of the more intense moments of touch Emrys gave her, and her magic receded back up through her arms and spine, leaving her to feel the cool summer breeze as it lapped around them. She sighed as it fully receded and opened her eyes, exhausted.

"Good," Emrys said with a smile. "Now do it again."

"What?" She was still breathing hard, the exercise leaving her winded. It had taken all her strength, her focus, her concentration to do it once, and he wanted her to immediately do it again?

"You thought you would practice summoning your magic and pulling it back once and be done?" He huffed a laugh. "You felt how difficult it was, right?" She nodded and knew what he was going to instruct next; she was going to be doing the same thing dozens of times over that afternoon. "Then you need to do it until it's as easy as breathing," he said.

Saoirse gave another sigh and shut her eyes. She no longer felt anxiety but annoyance and a tinge of anger. It summoned her magic more abruptly than anxiety did, and she suddenly battled panic and anger at the same time. Her chest tightened and burned as she felt the flames lick through her layers of skin and rise into the air at her palms and fingertips. She opened her eyes and stared at Emrys helplessly.

"Soothe the panic," his steady and smooth voice said. "You just did it. Whatever you pictured or said to yourself before, do it again. It should calm the anger as well."

She shouldn't have been surprised that he had picked up on her annoyance with him, but she followed his instructions as he gently wrapped his cool fingers around her hands to extinguish her magic again. Saoirse gulped for air and honed her senses to his touch.

It wasn't enough. Her fear and anger were feeding off each other and rejecting anything she tried to soothe them with. "I can't do it," she said weakly. Emrys's icy touch intensified as she felt her magic becoming more unruly.

"Yes, you can," he affirmed. "What did you use to soothe your anxieties before?"

Saoirse swallowed. "You."

"What is it about me that helped? You don't need to answer out loud. Just focus on that answer." He gently caressed the heat in her hands with his magic and Saoirse reflected on what it made her feel.

She felt safe when he touched her like that. It reminded her that she wasn't on her own any longer, and she could trust someone to care for her. The thoughts brought her to the quiet moments on their wedding night when they were sitting together on the sofa. She had felt content and safe that night, a combination she had rarely felt.

The memory soothed her panic to a minimum, and her anger extinguished. Her magic receded like the fading heat from the smoldering embers in the fireplace that night. Finally, her breathing evened, and she felt the hot curls of magic wane in her limbs. The tightness in her chest loosened, and she panted as her body finally felt under control.

"I'm done," she said between heaving breaths.

"But you did it." Emrys excitedly cupped her face and pressed a kiss to her temple. "You controlled it. You should be proud of yourself." He tried to pull her into an embrace, but Saoirse, feeling overwhelmed and exhausted, placed her hand on his chest and kept him at an arm's length.

"I'm not proud of myself. That felt like the pits of the Otherworld, and I hated every moment of it."

"Saoirse," Emrys's voice dropped to a gentle tone.

She felt hot tears pinch her eyes and shook her head.

"Why aren't you proud of what you just accomplished?" he asked.

Saoirse's lip quivered, but she whispered. "Why should I be? I did it terribly." Eamon had never acknowledged her efforts on the tasks he gave her, especially when he omitted important instructions and she had to decipher them herself. There was never room for her to be proud of her work. Instead, she was blamed when something went wrong because she couldn't execute perfection to please her brother.

"Because yesterday you didn't know how to safely control your magic, and today you just did it," Emrys answered.

She dropped her chin to stare at the grass, but her vision swam and the blades of grass blurred into a pool of green color. She felt his fingers gently clasp her chin and lift it until she was forced to meet his emerald gaze. His eyes were full of care, and she hated that he had to witness her reacting like this.

"Yes, it was messy, and it wasn't perfect, but you did it," he said with a soft smile.

"But it took too many tries to get it right."

Emrys's smile dropped, and his brow creased in concern. "I never expected you to do it correctly the first time. I don't expect you to know how to control your magic intuitively. If you did, you wouldn't need me."

"I'm not a waste of time?" she asked, her throat getting tighter. A fat tear rolled down her cheek, and Emrys didn't hesitate to wipe it away. She closed her eyes, and more tears fell. She had finally slipped out of Eamon's grasp, yet his venomous words still echoed in her mind and held her hostage.

Emrys's hands framed her face, and he continued to swipe tears from her cheeks. "You're not a waste of time," he said firmly. "I will always have patience with you. I would rather sit here and watch you try a hundred times before getting it right than witness you nearly burn down your bedroom again." He gave her forehead a kiss. "I am giving you an ocean's worth of grace and I need you to give yourself at least a spoonful."

Saoirse let out a watery laugh and nodded. She wrapped her hands around his forearms and lifted her gaze to his. "I hate that you're burdened with having to fix what Eamon broke."

"You aren't broken." He shook his head and pressed his forehead against hers. "You aren't a burden either. You're my wife, and I will do everything in my power to help you realize you have more inherent worth than you think you do."

Saoirse genuinely smiled and lifted up on her toes to brush a kiss to his lips. A new emotion flooded her limbs. It was warm, like the hearth from their wedding night. It felt exciting yet comforting as it enveloped her. Her magic bubbled in response, but it halted as if waiting for her to give a command.

Emrys pulled back and looked down at her with an expression that mirrored how she felt inside. "Do you want to keep going?" he asked.

"Yes," she said in a small but assured voice.

She pulled out of his grasp and closed her eyes again, filling her lungs and exhaling slowly. She let the new emotion coursing through her feed her magic and it obeyed her with little effort. Her magic rushed through her arms and stopped at the tips of her fingers.

Saoirse pulled it back, imagining the glowing ashes of the hearth and savoring the emotion that coated every corner of her body. It still took an effort to make her magic ebb and flow in her body, the emotion dimming and brightening as other emotions tried to overshadow it. But for once, she felt fully in control. She had a say in where and how her magic manifested itself, and it was the freshest taste of freedom she had felt yet.

Saoirse collapsed on the sofa in their sitting room. She had practiced her magic for several hours, feeding off her emotions until her body was exhausted. Emrys vanished into his bedroom while Saoirse lay unmoving on the sofa. She had fortunately pushed her thoughts about Kieran from her mind while she worked her magic, but now they flooded back to her. She had accepted that he would come by the house whenever he liked, and she had no power to stop him. But if she had a little warning, she could at least avoid him.

"Shall I ask Ada to bring up her steel scraper to peel you off the sofa?" Emrys asked with a chuckle.

Saoirse craned her neck to look at him and winced when her muscles screamed in protest. "Have you already bathed?" she asked.

"I don't need to bathe," he answered. "Not as badly as you do."

She scowled as he chuckled. If her body wasn't so sore, she would brandish a vulgar gesture in his direction.

"I'll fetch Rory and let her know she should also bring up dinner," he said once his giggling subsided. He dropped a kiss onto her forehead before moving out of her eye line.

"Wait," she said, pushing herself upright and ignoring the cry from her muscles. "I need to ask a favor of you."

He pivoted and returned to the arm of the sofa. Resting his forearms on it, he leaned towards her. "Yes?" His emerald green eyes met hers, and that spark ran through, making her shiver.

"Can you please inform me when Kieran is at the house?"

Emrys's brows knit, and he frowned.

"We crossed paths before our training session." She chewed on her lower lip. "And he kissed me."

"What?" Emrys's face completely fell. "Why didn't you say anything?"

"It was barely anything." Saoirse waved her hand. "And I didn't want it to interfere with our training time."

"That's why you looked so spooked," he said. He swore under his breath in the Old Language, a mixture of Gaelic and fae languages. "I'm sorry. If I had known—"

"You don't have to apologize," she said, stopping him. "I would just like a bit of warning before I run into him at the house."

"Of course." Emrys nodded. "I'll make sure Rhys informs so I can make you aware."

"Thank you." She gave a half-smile.

He pressed a kiss to her forehead before slipping lower, hovering above her lips. "Why don't *I* run you a bath."

Saoirse let out a small laugh. "Do you know how to?"

He opened his mouth in exaggerated offense but laughed before retorting, "I'll have you know I not only know how to run a bath, but I'm quite skilled at many things that can happen in a bathtub."

She snorted a laugh. "You told me I smell, so I think I should take it alone."

"Are you sure?" he asked with a cheeky smirk. "I could help you reach the birthmark between your shoulder blades—the one in the shape of an eight-point star."

Saoirse gasped and reeled back. She was quickly reminded of how sore her body was. "How do you know about that?"

"Your underthings only cover so much, Princess."

She giggled as he swooped in for a kiss. She continued to laugh as she reached up to cradle his face and kiss him again. Her earlier encounter with Kieran melted away, and Saoirse felt like she and Emrys lived inside a bubble of warmth and happiness. Anything could be thrown at her, and she would be able to conquer it with him beside her.

Saoirse woke up with a deep feeling of contentment. The sheets she was wrapped in smelled like Emrys, and the room was quiet. When she cracked her eyes open, she found she was alone. It wasn't surprising. Somehow, she was able to sleep through Lachlan and Emrys starting the day every morning.

She reluctantly pulled back the bedding and swung her feet onto the floor. After trotting to her room, she gently rang the bell pull. Rory appeared moments later and helped her dress for the day. A cream-colored blouse with a cameo broach and a navy blue skirt was her choice of outfit for the day.

Saoirse felt like she was floating as she made her way downstairs to the breakfast room. Soreness lingered in her body, but it was nowhere close to how debilitating it was the day before. She couldn't imagine when she would feel better without her rapid fae healing. How humans lived with days if not weeks of pain, she didn't know.

It didn't hurt that Emrys ran her an herbal bath and massaged some of her muscles before they went to bed. He didn't push it farther than innocent touching, but Saoirse's mind kept wandering to less innocent thoughts. Memories of their wedding night had flashed in her mind, and she had to work to keep from squirming whenever she did.

Her contentment came to a halt when she glimpsed a guest at the breakfast table. Kieran sat with a plate of half-eaten food in front of him and an unbothered expression on his face. Her mind scrambled to devise an escape plan, but before she could turn around and flee to her room, he looked up and grinned at her.

"Good morning, Your Highness," he said.

"Good morning," she mumbled. "Why are you here?"

"Alastair requested my presence today."

"And he needed you first thing this morning?" Saoirse began to scream internally. Where was Emrys? Why hadn't he warned her or at least left something like a note informing her? If she knew Kieran was at the breakfast table, she would have asked Rory to bring up a tray.

"Saoirse," Emrys's voice startled her. His hand gingerly rested on her hip, and he was breathing heavily as if he had sprinted across the house to find her. "I'm sorry. I forgot to tell you about today. I didn't remember he'd be here until Rhys told me."

"Your Highness, did you ask your beloved to warn you of my presence?" Kieran asked.

She shot him a glare.

"I guess your wishes aren't high on his priorities," he continued with a shrug and sip of his tea. "Don't you think if he saw you as worthy of his affection, he would make you his primary concern?"

Saoirse felt dizzy and had to grip the doorway to feel stable. She fought off Kieran's words, but they were slowly sinking their talons into her confidence. She knew he could weave a fabricated idea as easily as she could breathe, yet it still didn't help stop her from entertaining his words. She couldn't stay in this room any longer. She had to flee. Saoirse turned abruptly and squeezed past Emrys.

"Saoirse," she heard him call after her. "Wait."

She got as far as just outside the dining room before she was willing to stop. She spun to face him, and he at least had the decency to look apologetic. "I asked you to warn me so this wouldn't happen." She folded her arms across her chest and leveled an angry stare with him.

"I'm sorry. I forgot my father had arranged this meeting yesterday and invited Kieran. When Rhys came to tell me he was here, I rushed to find you."

She dropped her head back and sighed, staring up at the ceiling. She wanted to forgive him, give him the benefit of the doubt. But the thought of being unworthy of him to the point he didn't prioritize her was eating at her. It was so easy to feed that lie like panic and anger fed her magic. She needed to get more distance between her and Kieran, and the hallway wasn't far enough.

When she picked up her head, he gave her a forlorn look. "Please, have Rhys inform me whenever Kieran comes," she told him. "Rhys at least thinks I'm worthy of following through on my requests." She couldn't help flicking him on the raw. It made her feel better, at least for a short moment.

"That's not it at all," Emrys argued, but Saoirse didn't want to hear any of it right now.

"We'll discuss this later," she said mildly. "Please, have Rory bring up my breakfast." With that, she made her way across the house.

Trudging up the stairs, she let out a frustrated exhale. Part of her felt like forgiving him was the right thing to do. He gave her a space that was her own, listened to her, and volunteered his time to mentor her magic. They were all reasons to overlook this hiccup, but something whispered she shouldn't.

Not worthy.

Saoirse shook her head and rushed to her quarters, shutting herself inside. She flopped in one of the armchairs and groaned. A few moments ticked by before a sharp knock startled her, and Rory entered with a tray of breakfast. Saoirse pushed herself upright and accepted the tray. Rory quickly disappeared back into the hall, leaving Saoirse to eat her breakfast in near silence. The only noise to keep her company was her doubtful thoughts.

Emrys watched Saoirse round the corner towards the stairs and growled in frustration. He could rip Kieran in half for what he said to her. To undermine everything Emrys had done to build her trust and confidence and in front of him was a brazen choice. If he didn't strike Kieran for his own sake, he would do it for Saoirse's.

Emrys stormed into the breakfast room and glared at his cousin, holding himself back. "Upstairs," he barked. "Now."

"Are you commanding me?" Kieran asked.

"Obviously, polite invitation isn't enough to direct you where you're supposed to be, so, yes, I am." Emrys felt his heart racing in his chest. He usually tried to be cordial with Kieran, but his protective instinct from the mating bond was infiltrating his actions.

"You're not being a very gracious host, Emrys." The general sipped his tea. He carefully placed it back on the table and sighed. "But since I've finished my breakfast, I'll overlook it." He stood to his full height, which was a few inches taller than Emrys. It was enough for Emrys to feel the looming presence Kieran had. "Don't command me again. I promise it won't end well for you."

Kieran sauntered out of the room, and Emrys took a moment to pull himself together. If he had followed Kieran immediately, he probably would have incited unnecessary violence to work off his frustration. But Emrys knew that wouldn't solve anything between him and Saoirse. He would have to do a fair bit of groveling and pray he could convince her to see Kieran's words for what they were, a bitter lie.

After a few deep breaths, Emrys made his was upstairs to his father's office. The door to the office was open, and he saw his father sitting behind his oak desk. It was angled perpendicular to the door with two brown leather chairs on the opposite side of the desk.

As Emrys made his way inside, he took inventory of several fountain pens strewn across Alastair's desk, as well as the paper and leather-bound books stacked on one side. His father was in his typical day attire of a crisp white shirt, black waistcoat, and black trousers. In his hands, he held an official-looking letter.

Alastair ran a hand over his face and sighed as Emrys took a seat on the other side of the desk. Kieran was already seated in one of the plush brown leather chairs and gave Emrys a warning glare as he sat down. Emrys avoided his gaze and crinkled his nose as the smell of diluted vinegar hit his nose. He hoped the smell wouldn't rub off onto his clothes. The last thing he wanted was to smell like pungent furniture cleaner when he begged for Saoirse's forgiveness.

Out of the corner of his eye, Emrys saw Kieran check his pocket watch, his thumb stroking the face of it. Alastair's eyes flicked up from the letter in his hands, and he set it down in front of him.

"I've received the official report from Donheath," Alastair said. He flashed an apologetic look to Emrys before settling his gaze on Kieran. "Your information was correct." He nodded to the letter and allowed Emrys to reach out and read it.

It was addressed from Vasili and not only outlined the details of the Fomóire sighting, but the slip up of why the information was delayed to him. Emrys knew the explanation wasn't necessary, but Vasili had a habit of feeling obligated to over-explain. It was a quirk of his that the court had just accepted about him.

"I'm glad you finally acknowledge that," Kieran said. "Can we proceed with action this time?"

"I don't want to make any decisions regarding Donheath without Vasili's input," Alastair answered. "He gave no indication that he desired military action in his letter, and I have to respect that."

"We should still prepare ourselves." Kieran said. "Expanding the army doesn't interfere with the territory. It merely prepares us to act in case the Fomóire threaten to strike in Donheath."

"Do we have the resources to do that?" Emrys asked. "The Royal Mere army is the largest fae army already. If we expand it further, it might put a strain elsewhere."

"That's just a price we would have to pay for safety." Kieran shrugged.

"Potentially starving the territory in the name of military intimidation doesn't sound very safe," Emrys retorted.

"Kieran, Emrys has a point," Alastair interjected. "Where do you propose we pull resources from in order to expand the military?"

Kieran furiously fidgeted with his pocket watch. "There has to be an area that has some fat we can trim in order to finance the expansion. Resolving the threat of the Fomóire is a top priority, isn't it?"

Alastair sighed. "I'll have Laszlo put together a financial report and evaluate where we have extra funds. We'll reassess this at the next council meeting."

Kieran tucked his pocket watch back in his waistcoat pocket and stood. "Thank you, Your Majesty, for wasting my time to tell me there's nothing we can do." With that, he left without another word.

Emrys watched a muscle in Alastair's jaw flex as if he was fighting against an invisible gag. His face relaxed once Kieran was out of sight, and he sighed with relief. "Will you draft a letter to Laszlo asking for a report?" Alastair asked, glossing over Kieran's inappropriate parting words.

It didn't surprise Emrys. His father had always overlooked Kieran's indecencies, including those that directly affected Emrys.

"Yes, I will," Emrys said flatly. "Is that all you need from me?"

"I do have one more matter," Alastair said. "I want to ask how Saoirse is."

A flare of jealousy kindled in Emrys's gut. His father had an interest in anyone except his own son. The only silver lining was that if Alastair had a genuine interest in Saoirse's wellbeing, he would likely step in to keep her safe if needs be.

"She's doing better," Emrys answered tightly. "We've started training, and I think she'll be just fine."

"And...no one else knows about it, correct?" Alastair gave him that serious gaze again and with the way his volume dropped to nearly a whisper, Emrys could safely assume his father was worried about Kieran learning of Saoirse's magic.

"No more than Seraphina and Ada still."

"Good." Alastair nodded and turned his attention to some papers that were on his desk. "Please give her my regards."

"I will." Emrys gave a half-hearted attempt at a smile and rose from his chair. He took a step towards the door before a thought struck him. "Father, can I ask for a favor?" Alastair turned his attention, and Emrys quickly added a detail he hoped would secure his agreement. "It's for Saoirse."

Alastair raised a brow. "What is it?"

"Will you tell Kieran not to come to the house when he isn't invited?" Emrys asked. There was no way Kieran would obey Emrys's request, but he had a better chance if it came from Alastair.

His father's expression dimmed. "I will do my best."

"Thank you." Emrys nodded to his father before making his way out of the office. With his mind calmer, he felt better prepared to talk to Saoirse. He hoped his effort to keep Kieran out of the house was enough to earn her forgiveness. But Emrys's calm was tested when he was intercepted in the hall.

"Kieran, whatever petty argument you want to pick, I don't have time for it." He tried to push past the general, but Kieran stepped with him to block his path.

"No arguments here," he said. "I only wanted to inform you that your little mate is quite chatty."

Emrys's eyes widened when Kieran uttered the word mate. He glanced over Kieran's shoulder and hoped the walls in this house were thicker than he assumed they were.

"You haven't told her?" Kieran's gaze studied Emrys's face as if formulating something in his mind. A slow smile spread across his face a moment later. "Sweet, naïve Emrys, don't you know keeping secrets from your wife is in very poor taste?" Kieran's rumbling chuckle made Emrys's blood boil. "I would hate for you two to have a falling out over such an easy conversation."

"Kieran, stop." Emrys clenched his jaw, holding himself back from grabbing Kieran's collar and connecting his fist with the general's nose.

"I promise I won't speak a word of it," Kieran continued, ignoring Emrys's command. "For a price."

Emrys closed his eyes, weighing his options. Telling Kieran to get lost in Cernunnos's Wilderness would put him in the position of having to be constantly vigilant of the general's interactions with Saoirse. Which was difficult when Kieran enjoyed coming by without notice. His other option was to tell Saoirse, but with the way he had already tarnished some of her trust, he risked losing her altogether with the truth.

"What is your price?" Emrys murmured.

"Nothing too steep." Kieran shrugged. "Silence for silence. When the time comes for me to inform Vasili of my military plans in Donheath, you don't say a word. You don't have to sell him the idea if he's unsure of it, but you don't outright object to it either. In return, Saoirse stays blissfully unaware of your little secret."

Emrys sighed. Betraying his friends was nearly as painful as betraying Saoirse. But Vasili would eventually understand. Besides, maybe he could build Saoirse's trust again—and his courage—to tell her, and Kieran's deal would be completely moot.

"Fine," Emrys huffed. "But when it's no longer a secret with Saoirse, this deal is off."

"That's only fair." Kieran turned to descend the stairs but paused. "I hope you know the longer you wait, the worse her reaction will be. So, you either take this secret to your grave or break her heart. The choice is yours."

Emrys lost his hold on his self-control and made to lunge for the general, but a gust of wind smacked him in the chest.

Kieran's element of magic.

Emrys faltered for a moment until he got his footing and seethed at the general. "Uh-uh," Kieran taunted. "You can't assault me either."

"You can't change the terms after we've agreed on them."

"Would you like me to find your wife now and nullify our entire agreement?" Kieran offered. When Emrys stayed silent, the general flashed a toothy, devilish grin. "I didn't think so." Kieran swaggered down the stairs, leaving Emrys to deal with his mix of emotions where he stood.

Saoirse inwardly groaned when she heard the door to the sitting room open. She was just about to finish her breakfast when Emrys came up beside her.

"Is now a better time to discuss this morning?" he asked quietly, squatting down beside her chair.

Against her better judgment, she turned to look at him and saw his look of remorse. She didn't know what to say to him. Her thoughts still echoed Kieran's words, and she was struggling to shake them.

"Or can I grovel for forgiveness?" He lifted one corner of his lips in a half-hearted grin.

"The latter sounds more appealing," Saoirse said.

"I'm sorry I didn't tell you Kieran would be here today," Emrys said. "There are several things I should have done, but I can't go back and change it now. I can only apologize and do better in the future. I've already asked my father to tell Kieran to only come when he's invited."

"You asked your father?" She knew that had to be difficult for him. Alastair didn't exactly favor Emrys enough to warrant considering a request like that.

"I asked for your sake," he answered. "I knew Kieran would disregard anything I asked of him, but if it came from my father, there's a higher chance he'll heed it."

A smile tugged at Saoirse's lips. He acted to amend his slip up without her even asking. Only someone who was a high priority to him would get that kind of treatment. "Is he going to follow through with it?" she asked.

"He said he'll try," Emrys answered. "Kieran has some kind of hold on him. I can't quite explain it, but..." He stared off in puzzlement for a moment before shaking his head. She knew what he was referring to. She had seen it in the council meeting, the way he acted like he had an invisible restraint on his voice. "Anyway," Emrys continued, "the point is he agreed to it. He cares about you and your wellbeing. I might have mixed feeling on the fireann, but I won't upset the applecart if your wellbeing is looked after."

Saoirse's smile grew a little wider. Kieran was a cad for insinuating she wasn't anyone's priority. Emrys was proving him false and so was Alastair. They both cared about her immensely and prioritized her happiness.

"Thank you," she said. "I know that must not have been easy."

"Nothing I do for you is difficult." The whisper of a grin he had slowly faded. "Which is why I'm sorry for how badly I blundered this morning. Will you please forgive me?"

Saoirse leaned over and kissed his forehead. "Yes, I forgive you."

His posture melted in relief, and his smile returned.

"But," she said, a Cheshire Cat grin spreading on her face. "I could do with some more groveling."

He chuckled and kissed her, rising to his full height. "You're too late. You've forgiven me. I can be a cheeky cad once again."

"*My* cheeky cad." She stood, giggling, and wrapped her arms around his waist. The heat of his body radiated against hers, and she wanted nothing more than to melt against him. He ran his hands over her arms, and the strength of his grip made her sigh with that contentment she woke up.

"I think this will benefit both of us," he said. "Not seeing Kieran unless it's a council meeting isn't the worst thing in the world."

"As someone with family who I'd be happy to never see again, I don't blame you."

The twinkle in the gold flecks of his eyes dimmed. "That's not exactly why."

Saoirse crinkled her brows. "What is it?"

The muscles in his jaw worked for a minute before he swallowed. "He's the one who gave me my scars."

Her stomach plummeted at his confession. She didn't know how to respond. She wanted to tighten her grip on his waist, or kiss every inch of him until the sadness in his eyes disappeared— anything to ease the pain she saw in his expression.

"I'm sorry," she whispered.

Emrys pressed his lips to her forehead and let them linger on her skin. He didn't open up further about his scars, but Saoirse knew how difficult it was to open old wounds, so she didn't press him for details. Knowing they were inflicted by Kieran told her enough.

Emrys slowly kissed down to her lips, his touch languid. She dug her fingers into his waistcoat and sighed. While she loved the urgency that came with hot passion, there was something to be said about taking their time. She deeply felt every graze and grope they shared, and the spark made itself present with every new sensation that touched her.

He picked her up into his arms, her legs wrapping around his hips, when an untimely knock interrupted. Their lips pulled apart, and they shared heavy breaths.

"I'm going to undermine Ada and fire every staff member in this house," Emrys murmured.

Saoirse couldn't help but giggle as he gently placed her back on the ground. A maid curtsied before scurrying in and making a beeline for Saoirse's breakfast tray. She picked it up without a word and quickly made her way back to the hall. Saoirse rested her head against Emrys's chest, her fit of giggles still bubbling inside her.

"Well, this is a terrible time to be reminded I have work that needs to be done," he grumbled.

Devilishly, she grazed her thigh over the hard bulge she felt at his groin. "How badly do you need to work?" she asked in a sultry tone.

He grunted in frustration. "Staving off an attack by rock creatures from the ocean is fairly pressing." He dropped a kiss to the crown of her head. "I'll just think of the time I witnessed Cyprian treating an infection in his toenail. That usually calms everything down."

Saoirse pictured the fireann using one of Seraphina's remedies on unnaturally yellow toenails. It, too, calmed any flicker of passion in her body. Emrys gently lifted her head so she could meet his gaze, and while passion had been extinguished, that spark continued to ripple through her.

"Shall we continue this later?" he asked.

"If I can get that image of Cyprian out of mind, yes."

"You can also join me as I work. I'd never reject company."

"Will you get any work done with me around?" She raised a brow.

He lifted a shoulder in a shrug. "If I don't, I won't be upset."

"You'll have to explain why you slacked off to the court tomorrow in your council meeting."

"The dukes would understand," he said in a low voice.

Saoirse gave a low laugh and shook her head. "You'd better work alone. Otherwise you'll have to think of something much worse than infected toenails."

Emrys sighed in exaggerated defeat. "How dare you be responsible."

She giggled again as he gave her another kiss. But he also acted responsibly and slipped out of her grip before disappearing into the hall.

15

S*aoirse straightened the* trays of sandwiches and biscuits in the drawing room as she anxiously awaited her guests. She had been spending hours training and was looking forward to spending an afternoon doing something other than flexing her magic. Over the last few days, the soreness in her body seemed to compound instead of ease, and spending a whole afternoon sitting and enjoying tea sounded heavenly.

The three duchesses were set to arrive at any minute, and while Emrys swore to Saoirse she had met them at their wedding, she still had little recollection of it. She was looking forward to meeting them properly and spending the afternoon with them. Ada and Rory had decorated the low table in the drawing room with a linen tablecloth and had arranged a variety of finger sandwiches, scones, tea, and spreads. They had also plated delicious-looking biscuits, but had lost track of them amidst the preparations.

"Good afternoon," a light voice sang.

Saoirse turned to see a boireann with dark almond eyes and long hair that spilled over her shoulders like liquid onyx had entered the room. Her porcelain skin popped against her sapphire blue skirt and matching jacket. Saoirse grinned as she noticed the fuchsia pink necktie the duchess wore at her collar.

"Good afternoon," Saoirse returned.

The duchess plopped herself in the armchair adjacent to Saoirse and leaned towards the low table to inspect the food. "Ada and Rory have outdone themselves."

"I'm sure they'd love to hear that themselves."

The duchess plucked a tea sandwich from a tray and took a dainty bite. She hummed her satisfaction and nodded. The corner of Saoirse's lips twitched up as she imagined Eamon's reaction to the duchess's manners. If this had been in his presence, he would have been horrified by the duchess's lack of decorum by tasting the spread before the rest of the guests had arrived. But in this court, the relaxed manners made Saoirse less anxious about doing the wrong thing.

"I must apologize," Saoirse said sheepishly. "But I was terribly busy on the day of the wedding, and I don't remember meeting you or the other duchesses."

The duchess giggled. "No need to apologize. You and Emrys looked quite infatuated with each other that night. I wouldn't blame you if you forgot your own name." She winked knowingly, and Saoirse's face heated. "I'm Andromeda, Duchess of Cogwick. Laszlo's wife, if you need your memory refreshed as to which of the dukes belongs to me."

"It's a pleasure to meet you…officially." Saoirse grinned.

"Something smells delicious." Another voice drifted into the room and two boireannaich appeared in the entry. "Andromeda, have you started eating without us?" The duchess who spoke had golden hair pulled into a prim pompadour at the crown of her head and wore a blush pink skirt and an ivory lace blouse adorned with a cameo. Her attire was a stark contrast to Andromeda's loud combination of colors.

"I was merely tasting," Andromeda shrugged. "Someone has to assure that the food is edible."

"It sounds more like you wanted to ensure none of the cucumber sandwiches made it onto anyone else's plate," The third duchess that joined them said, pointing her polished wooden cane at Andromeda. Most of her brown curly hair was pulled back into a bun, but a few short tendrils hung to frame her face. A burnt orange jacket and skirt set complimented the rich brown complexion of her skin.

"I do adhere to the rule of whoever finds something first is entitled to it." Andromeda took another irreverent bite of her sandwich.

"That seems to be the only rule you adhere to." The blonde duchess reached her hands towards Andromeda's hair, but they were batted away. "Are you ever going to wear your hair properly?"

"No, you know how terrible my hair looks teased," Andromeda protested. "I absolutely detest what the humans have set as a trend. I miss the hair during Victoria's years."

"At least let me pull it back and put a bow in it."

Andromeda sighed and let her fellow duchess gather her hair at her nape. A black velvet ribbon was pulled from the fair-haired duchess's skirt pocket and was used to tie Andromeda's hair back.

"Do you always have a ribbon on your person?" Saoirse asked.

"I always have it when I know I'll be around Andromeda," the duchess said with the whisper of a smirk on her face. "I know better than to assume she's put her hair in a proper pompadour."

Andromeda rolled her eyes. "Thank you, *Mother*," she said. "Before you two continue to reprimand me about my social faux pas, why don't you introduce yourselves to our host?"

"Did we miss introductions at the wedding?" the blonde duchess asked.

"No," Saoirse said. "I believe we did meet, but with the dozen or so people I met that evening, I wasn't paying attention to everyone who gave me well wishes."

"Oh, that's alright." The duchess waved her hand as she sat on the sofa on the other side of the low table. "I'm Isolde, Stoneblack."

"Cyprian's wife," Andromeda murmured to Saoirse.

"And I'm Calliope," the other duchess said. "Duchess of Donheath and wife of Vasili. It seems our husbands have made a bigger impression than we have."

"Well, I'm sure you three have spent an hour with them all in the same room." Saoirse snickered. "It's enough to leave quite an impression on anyone."

"I believe that," Andromeda said with a huff of a laugh. "Those boys are about as inseparable as oxygen in the air."

"And yet if they were locked in a room for over a day they'd murder each other." Isolde snorted.

"I've witnessed them locked in a room for over a day," Andromeda said. "And they *did* nearly murder each other." She turned to Saoirse and added, "I was schoolmates with Emrys, Cyprian, and Laszlo. I know too much about those three fireannaich, so if you ever need leverage against Emrys, just let me know."

"You attended school with them?" Saoirse asked.

Andromeda nodded. "My parents knew if they sent me to finishing school, it might not still be standing by the time I left. Luckily, fae don't follow the precedent set by humans, and I was eligible for boarding school, even though I wasn't set to inherit my family's title." She reached for the pot of tea at the end of the table and began to fill cups of tea, passing them amongst the guests.

"Andromeda's manners are in rare form today," Isolde teased. "It's usually the hostess who serves tea."

"Oh," Saoirse said, her face flushing with embarrassment. She had only attended a handful of afternoon teas hosted by Cressida and hadn't paid much attention to what she was doing. Saoirse had mostly been counting down the minutes until she could leave.

"Ignore her." Andromeda handed Saoirse a cup. "I assume you've never hosted anything before."

Saoirse shook her head shyly.

"My apologies," Isolde said. "I only meant to harm Andromeda's feelings."

Andromeda briefly stuck her tongue out at the duchess causing an eruption of giggles.

"Is this Ada's black tea?" Calliope asked.

Saoirse nodded, and the duchess sighed in satisfaction.

"This spread is quite impressive," Calliope remarked. "I do wonder why there are no seed cakes though."

"There were some," Saoirse said, surveying the trays. "They

must not have made it to the table."

"Cyprian probably stole them." Isolde shrugged and sipped at her tea.

"It's not the only thing he's stolen." Calliope giggled, and Isolde shot her a glare before quickly changing the subject.

"So Saoirse, how have you found married life?" she asked.

"It's been..." Saoirse dug for an answer. How did one explain they had a minimally intimate wedding night that turned into a magic and panic-inducing nightmare resulting in years' worth of magic training in just a few days and a relationship strain from one's former lover—now cousin-in-law—all in the first week of their marriage? Well, apparently, that's how one would explain it, but Saoirse wasn't quite comfortable divulging all of that. "It's been something." She tried to add a smile, but she was sure it came out more like a grimace.

"Marriage is hard," Calliope said, assuring her. "It doesn't get any easier when you've been arranged. Give it some time. And if it still isn't great, well, you have three females who will happily take you in."

Saoirse gave a more genuine smile at that. "How were you all arranged?" she asked, diverting attention from her rocky relationship.

"Isolde was kidnapped," Andromeda said breezily.

"Kidnapped is a bit of an exaggeration," Isolde argued.

"Did you ask him to take you to his home?"

"Not exactly."

"And did he let you go home?"

"I was allowed to, but I was safer with him. He was protecting me."

Andromeda rolled her eyes and turned to Saoirse. "Kidnapped," she whispered.

"It's not kidnapping if I willingly got in his carriage." Isolde seemed determined not to let Andromeda have the last word in this argument. "Who wouldn't get in a carriage with that fireann?"

"Whatever gets you to orgasm at night," Andromeda said

sweetly.

Calliope snorted and quickly hid her amusement when Isolde shot her another glare.

"What about you, Andromeda?" Saoirse asked around her stifled giggles. "How were you arranged with Laszlo?"

The room went eerily quiet, the amusement on Andromeda's face falling. Isolde dropped her gaze to her tea, and Calliope mindlessly studied the wall of built-in bookcases. "Did I say something wrong?" Saoirse asked.

"No," Andromeda said hastily. "Laszlo and I...we've had quite the relationship. But all that matters now is we're together and we love each other."

"I'm glad to hear that." Saoirse smiled at her and noticed how Andromeda's returning smile had a whisper of pain in it.

"Vasili and I are the most boring," Calliope said, diverting the conversation. "He had broken his arm and a few ribs in a horseback riding incident, and I was assigned to heal his injuries."

"Calliope's a High Healer," Andromeda quickly explained.

Saoirse nodded her understanding. High Healers had a rare magic that could break and heal bones.

"I don't do any formal work anymore," Calliope added sheepishly. "But I do volunteer in the Matron House and Healer Care Units quite a bit."

High Healers were in constant demand, and Calliope removing herself from the profession would have most likely been a controversial decision. Saoirse could sense she had an inkling of guilt that led her to volunteer her time and magic.

"I may be in need of your services soon, Calliope," Andromeda said. "Laszlo and I have started discussing children."

"Does he want to start trying?" Isolde asked.

"Oh, no, we only talked about some things but didn't make any plans." Andromeda shrugged, causing Isolde to snort.

"I doubt you didn't make any plans," she said. "As long as I've known you, you always have some sort of plan."

"Well, it's not like we're not trying." Andromeda had a

mischievous glimmer in her eyes as she sipped her tea. "We haven't used contraception in years, and I don't plan to use it again any time soon."

"At least you've talked about it," Isolde said with a sigh. "Cyprian avoids the topic like it's the next plague. I swear one day I'll have to hold him down and force him to discuss it. Actually, discuss several things while I'm at it. Nine decades of marriage and it's still a struggle to get him to discuss certain things."

The boireannaich giggled and reached for more sweets on the table to taste.

"Saoirse," Calliope said. "I don't believe I mentioned this to you, but you looked stunning at your wedding."

"Thank you." Saoirse smiled and felt that warmth that was becoming familiar to her.

"Your dress was beautiful. Andromeda, did you design it?"

Saoirse turned her attention to the duchess who nodded with a proud smile.

"You designed my dress?" Saoirse echoed, stunned.

"I did indeed." Andromeda's smile nearly reached her ears. "And I have to say my girls at the shop are the true heroes. They worked overtime to have it ready in under a week."

"I'm at a loss for words." Saoirse had never had anyone close to her go so beyond what was asked of them, let alone a complete stranger. "Thank you."

"It was my pleasure. I think it was some of our best work."

The other duchesses nodded their agreement.

"Do you own a shop, then?" Saoirse asked.

Andromeda giggled. "I own several."

"Several!"

Isolde and Calliope giggled.

"Andromeda owns almost half the shops in Cogwick," Isolde informed her.

"And you have time to come here and have tea?" Saoirse asked.

Andromeda let out a genuine laugh. "I have managers employed at all my shops. I don't need to be running around town making sure everyone is doing their job at all hours. I put in my time doing that long ago. It's much easier to pay others to do that."

"What kinds of shops do you operate?" Saoirse's curiosity was getting the better of her. The duchesses had much more exciting lives than she imagined. She was absolutely enthralled with their work and stories.

"A dress shop, hat shop, cigar lounge," Andromeda tapped her fingers as she named off her storefronts, "cobbler shop, bookstore, and I just opened a penny bazaar."

"My, all you need is a gaming hell." Saoirse giggled.

"Don't tempt her," Calliope joked.

"I think Laszlo would have an apoplexy if I opened a gaming hell." Andromeda reached for another tea sandwich. "The thought of me running a club for elite fireannaich would have him tearing half of them apart."

The boireannaich giggled, and Saoirse basked in the company around her. The dukes had made her feel welcomed, but the duchesses made her feel like family. They joked with her and tossed their manners aside to make crude comments without a second thought. Tea with them felt like nothing she had experienced back home. She was comfortable enough to let her guard down just enough.

The few hours they had passed too quickly. Soon, the biscuits and sandwiches were nearly gone and there was no tea left to pour. As the afternoon wound down, Saoirse found she didn't want her new friends to leave.

"What would you ladies say to doing this every time the fireannaich have a council meeting?" she asked.

"I have no objections to that," Isolde said.

"Me neither," Calliope added.

"If it means a delicious spread by Ada and Rory nearly every week, I won't object to it either." Andromeda chuckled.

Saoirse grinned. Like Emrys, she would have her own meeting with peers. Granted, their discussions would not have as high of stakes as those in the council meetings, but Saoirse didn't care. She needed an entertaining discussion every once in a while.

"Emrys is holding out on us," Cyprian's deep voice rumbled from the doorway. He strolled into the drawing room and helped himself to the sweets that were left. "You ladies have a much better arrangement."

"Cyprian," Isolde said, accusation in her voice. Her husband froze, the piece of chocolate halfway into his mouth. "Did you steal the seed cakes that were meant for our tea?"

"No," he said in a small voice before cautiously biting into his piece of chocolate.

Isolde narrowed her brows at him.

The duke swallowed and straightened. "It's time for us to go."

Isolde let out a small huff and stood, waving her farewell to the other boireannaich and taking her husband's hand. Laszlo and Vasili were next to escort their wives to the carriages waiting outside. Saoirse leaned back in her armchair and sighed contentedly. She relived the conversations from the afternoon, and a smile grew on her face that refused to waver. Her little village of support was growing even wider, and she held onto it as a defense against any doubts she had about herself or Emrys.

"Where was my invitation to the party?"

A cold finger of dread ran down her spine at that voice. She didn't need to turn to learn who was in the doorway, but she did anyway. Kieran loomed in the doorway dressed in his proper uniform like he had been for the last council meeting. The dukes and duchesses had left several minutes ago, so why hadn't Kieran?

He snapped his fingers and strode further into the drawing room. "Oh, that's right. You don't want me near you so badly that you asked Alastair to ban me."

"You aren't banned," Saoirse argued, realizing her mistake too late. "You just need an invitation." She shouldn't have taken his bait. All he wanted was to get a rise out of her, and he had gotten just that.

"And will you ever extend an invitation to me?" he asked, approaching her. He leaned down to her eye level and waited for her answer.

"I have no reason to extend an invitation to you for anything." She leaned away as far as she could from him, but he continued to push closer to her.

"Really?" he asked. "Not even if you were pushed aside by your beloved husband?"

"Emrys has never pushed me aside."

"Not yet." Kieran shrugged. "But time is ticking until your relationship is set to expire, once he finds how unworthy you are."

"You don't know what you're talking about, Kieran." Saoirse frowned and pushed herself up to her feet, stepping away from the general.

"I don't? I've only known the fireann for nearly two centuries. I know he has high standards, and you, my dear, fall short."

She shook her head. He was at it again, twisting her thoughts and convincing her of things that weren't true. She thought of what Emrys told her yesterday about his scars and used it to shield herself from Kieran's words.

"If I fall short, then why do you say you advocated for me?" she asked, hoping it would trip him up. She crossed her arms over her chest and lifted her chin.

"Because I was the only one who had ever interacted with you. My support held more weight than whatever nonsense your brother wrote on that proposal."

"And why should I believe Emrys listened to you?"

A wolfish smile tugged at his lips as he stalked towards her. "Because I can be very persuasive, enough that even *he* can't argue with me." Kieran's hand grazed her hip and slid behind her.

Saoirse tried to back away out of his reach, but her calves hit the low table, and she froze. He had backed her into a spot that gave her no means of escape. Short of fighting him, all she could do was stand petrified under his touch.

"You want to know my real motivation?" he asked in a low, husky voice. "It was to get you. I knew he'd find out how much of a mess you are and tire of you eventually. That was when I planned to come save the day and keep you for myself. He wouldn't argue either. In fact," he placed a finger under her chin and tilted her head up to meet his gaze, "I think if I held out long enough, he would beg me to take you off his hands."

Saoirse swallowed and shook her head. She told herself it wasn't true. Emrys had shown her nothing except his desire for her, but that seed of doubt had made its home in her mind. How long would he put up with her? She had already proven she was the mess that Kieran described her to be.

"Kieran." Emrys's bellow caused the general to freeze.

Kieran slowly turned, his hands slipping off Saoirse.

"I'd prefer you to keep your hands off my wife," Emrys growled.

The general held up his hands in surrender. "As you wish." He stepped away from Saoirse and with one last knowing glance at her, quit the room.

Saoirse felt her heart pound in her chest as Emrys stared down the general until he was out of the drawing room. He quickly shifted his gaze back to Saoirse and hurried towards her. "Are you alright?" he asked, his voice dropping to a gentler tone.

She could only nod. If she opened her mouth, she was sure she would vomit. Emrys's arms came around her and pulled her into an embrace. She closed her eyes and buried her face in his chest, breathing in his scent that she now equated with peace. Along with his tender touch, calm enveloped her, and she sighed. It felt like the first exhale she had made since Kieran made his presence known, and it was a relief.

The chatter of Kieran's words echoing and the thoughts trying to argue against them hushed as she stood in Emrys's embrace. It contradicted everything Kieran had just told her, and Saoirse was thankful for it. She wished she could stay like this forever and shut out the rest of the world. But she could barely shut out Kieran, and that fact haunted her.

S*aoirse spent the* next few days in her new routine. Emrys trained her magic for several hours, and then she took a day off to recover before starting the cycle over. She grew more confident in how she handled her magic and hadn't had it flare since she started training with Emrys. It was a relief to have something in her life under her control. Unfortunately, he couldn't say the same about other aspects of her life.

Kieran's words surfaced in her mind daily, and Saoirse wasn't always successful at shaking them. She couldn't help but agree with some of the things he said. Since the day she Emrys she knew he deserved better than the mess of herself that she could offer him. But every time Saoirse hinted at it, Emrys did something to quickly squash her doubt.

Even with those genuine actions, thoughts of her worth still plagued her. She found herself curious on more than one occasion of what it would be like if she left. Would she finally be relieved of her tormenting doubts? Was it best for Emrys that she disappear from his life? She knew she was irrational for believing she saw inklings of Emrys having just mere tolerance for her when they weren't there. But it was exhausting to constantly fight herself especially when she was alone.

Saoirse chewed on a fingernail while she gazed out the window in the quiet sitting room, the silence a blessing and a curse. Emrys came up behind her and ran his hands over her arms.

"Hello," he greeted with a kiss to her cheek. "How are you feeling today?" He squeezed the muscles of her upper arms, and she thankfully didn't wince in pain.

"I'm feeling alright," she answered blandly.

"Good," he murmured in her ear. "Because I have the rest of the day for us to do whatever we desire."

That spark rippled through her, and she found the strength to shove away any remnants of her doubts. It was easier to put them aside when she was around Emrys. But there was a small voice that still whispered to her, wondering how long that would last. She was becoming convinced that at some point it would fade.

Emrys wrapped his arms around her waist and nuzzled his head into her neck. Gooseflesh rippled over her skin as his lips grazed the column of her throat. She laid her hands over his arms and tried to surrender to his touch. But her mind was distracting her too much.

She gave a wince, and Emrys froze.

"Are you sure you're alright?" he asked, his voice muffled against her skin.

Saoirse wanted to nod. She wanted to push through the endless cycle of thoughts that plagued her. Dagda save her, she wanted Emrys to ravish her until she could no longer remember her name let alone the nonsense that Kieran spewed to her.

But she couldn't. Kieran's words taunted her.

Unworthy...tire of you...beg me to take you...

"Saoirse." Emrys's voice rattled her from her thoughts.

"Hmm?" she hummed, a sinking feeling heavy in her stomach.

"If you're not feeling up to it, we can spend time another way." His words hit her ears, but she barely registered them.

She turned in his arms and stared up at him. The gold flecks around the emerald green of his eyes glinted, and she swallowed. "I think I need some time to myself," she heard herself say.

"Oh." His hands slowly slid from her waist. "Alright. I'll leave you be, then."

"No," Saoirse whispered. "I mean I think I need to leave."

Emrys's face morphed from concealing his disappointment to outright shock. "What?"

A pain twisted in her chest. "I need to leave for a bit, a few days, weeks maybe."

"Why?" Emrys's voice cracked.

They stared at each other for a long moment, Saoirse feeling like she would vomit if she opened her mouth to explain.

"Does this have to do with Kieran?" Emrys finally asked.

"Maybe." Saoirse felt a sting behind her eyes. She didn't want to leave, but being in this house just made her thoughts echo louder and louder. "I keep doubting you and myself, and it's becoming too much."

"What are you doubting about me?"

"Everything," she confessed. "I wonder how long it will be before you tire of me. Or how much more of my mess you're willing to take on before you say it's enough."

"I can promise you that time will never come." Emrys tried to step towards her, but Saoirse took a step back.

"I want to believe that promise." She clutched at the collar of her shirtwaist. "But I can't do that here. I need time alone."

"Where do you plan to go?"

That was the burning question, wasn't it? She didn't have anywhere to go. She certainly wasn't going to go home to Ireland. She'd rather escape to Kieran's barracks than return to her family home. However, the thought of her family brought an idea.

"Is our bargain still good?" she asked.

"What bargain?" Emrys's brows furrowed.

"The one where you get a marriage on paper and I get to live away from my brother."

"Saoirse—"

"Just answer me. Is it still good?" she demanded.

Emrys looked at her with a pained expression. It took him a moment before he answered. "Yes, always."

"Then I'd like to follow through with it." She swallowed. "Just temporarily. I need some time away from you and Kieran."

"You promise you'll come back?" His voice cracked on the last word.

"We shouldn't promise each other anything." Saoirse's cheek twitched, and she knew if she didn't flee to her bedroom, she'd find herself sobbing in Emrys's arms. "Will you please have a carriage readied for me?" She didn't give him time to answer as a tears welled in her eyes. Quickly, she spun towards her bedroom, the tears rolling down her cheek.

She hurried the few steps into her room and shut the door, hoping Emrys wouldn't attempt to talk her out of this. This was the right decision. She needed space to decipher what was the truth and what was fabricated. Besides, it would give Emrys a reprieve from her mess for a few days.

With blurry vision and falling tears, Saoirse dug around her room for her suitcase. She dug through her dresser and put her folded petticoats and chemises in her suitcase. Her tears fell faster until she had to grip the sides of her suitcase, the pain in her chest threatening to crack her open.

A sob slipped from her, and she lost herself in emotion. She grieved how naïve she was to let herself reach this point. She shouldn't have let herself believe she was worthy of Emrys's time and affection in the first place. It was only hurting her in the presence.

She cried in frustration of her circumstances that put her here. If her brother hadn't made a mess of her life, if maybe her parents were still alive, she might have had a better outcome with Emrys. But she couldn't change those things. Her life was what it was: a tangled mess that couldn't be smoothed out. She just hoped she wasn't being too naïve again to believe time apart would resolve everything.

Emrys stood stunned in the sitting room. What had he just witnessed? Saoirse had seemed out of sorts since he found Kieran with her. She had been acting distant during their time alone but assured him she was fine. Obviously, her thoughts were getting the best of her. There was only one person who could feed her the lies she was repeating.

Kieran. Emrys didn't know exactly what the general said to her, but it made enough of an impact to give her the desire to leave. Even if it was temporary, she was still leaving. Panic rose in his throat as the thought of Saoirse never returning crossed his mind. It was a real possibility. If she found peace living by herself, that was it. He would lose his mate for good, and there was nothing he could do about it.

Emrys took a deep breath, trying to settle the impulse to beg her to stay and make promises he might not be able to keep. He moved towards her door and gently rapped his knuckle on it. He waited in anticipation for her to answer, but she never did. Instead, he heard the distinct sound of sniffling and shaking sobs on the other side of the door.

"Saoirse," he said gently. He still did not receive an answer. And maybe that was for the best. His instinct was to plead for her to reconsider, but that never worked out in his favor. He had to think of something before making any kind of sweeping gesture. He thought of what he could do in the present. Suggesting anything tonight was obviously out of the question. And tomorrow he was going to Stoneblack to—

An idea formed, and with a renewed vigor, Emrys knocked on Saoirses's door. "Can I talk to you?"

Her sobs quieted, and Emrys heard soft hiccups. There was silence for several beats, and he prayed it was in his favor. Finally, he heard soft footsteps and then the click of the doorknob turning. Saoirse cracked the door open just enough to show her face. Her undereyes were swollen and most of her face was red and blotchy. He wanted to pull her into his arms and hold her, but he refrained.

"Emrys." Her voice was low and scratchy. "Unless you have arrangements for me, there isn't anything to talk about."

"That's exactly what I have," he said. "Tomorrow I'm visiting Cyprian in Stoneblack, and if you'd like, you could come with me and decide if you'd like to stay there. Kieran has never stepped foot in their house and I rarely visit outside of high holidays."

Saoirse eyed him warily. "Don't you think they'd be a bit biased?" she asked. "Cyprian is one of your closest friends. I would imagine he'd be filling my head with all your worthy qualities."

"On the contrary." Emrys tried to resist the urge to grin, but he couldn't help it. A half-smile pulled at his lips. "He would tell you nothing but my shortcomings. It's why he was not at the top of my list of potential escorts during our arrangement."

The corner of Saoirse's lips twitched, and Emrys held his breath.

"Come with me tomorrow and see if it's where you'd like to stay," he offered. "Isolde could give you a full tour and give you an idea of what it would be like to stay there. If it doesn't seem to suit you, I'll make arrangements for you to stay by yourself, away from the household and court."

Saoirse chewed on her bottom lip. He hoped an afternoon with one of the duchesses would either ease her worries or convince her to stay somewhat close. He wasn't lying when he said Cyprian would make him out to be the lowliest cad, but Emrys knew he could somehow persuade Saoirse to shake whatever nonsense Kieran fed her.

He could feel his heart pounding against his ribs as he waited for her answer. It felt like hours passed before she finally spoke.

"Alright," she said quietly. "I'll go with you to Stoneblack. But if I decide to stay there, I'm not coming back here. I'll ask you to arrange for my things to be sent there."

Emrys nodded even though the thought of bringing her along and then leaving her behind cut him deeply. She was confused and in pain, and the best way he could relieve it was to let her make this decision. Regardless, he sighed in relief.

"I plan to leave after lunch," he told her evenly. "You can meet me in the entry way."

Saoirse nodded and gave a small flinch of her lips, a gesture he took as an attempt at a grateful smile. "I'll be spending my night alone," she told him. "But I will see you in the afternoon before we leave for Stoneblack."

"Very well." Emrys watched as she slowly closed her door.

His relief was short-lived as worry overpowered him. He thought winning Saoirse over would be easy at first. He had charmed his way out of more difficult situations with more success. But those situations also didn't have Kieran stepping in to ruin everything.

Kieran. That bastard. He had threatened Emrys with his blackmail information and then sowed this crippling doubt into Saoirse. It not only was pulling them apart, but it interfered with Emrys's confidence in sharing the truth about their bond. Without her denial of mates, this doubt would just be an obstacle. With it, her doubt was a battle, one he was currently losing.

Emrys slunk to his bedroom and flopped onto his bed. Saoirse's sweet and fresh scent still lingered on his sheets, and his heart ached. Tonight would be his first night in nearly two weeks he would be sleeping alone. He did not look forward to the fitful sleep he was about to have. All he could do was send up a prayer that the gods would intervene and help Saoirse shrug off her doubts for good.

Saoirse felt a pit in her stomach as she walked down the stairs to the entryway. She hadn't slept well at all as her thoughts circled around the things Kieran had said to her, the way Emrys looked when she told him she wanted to leave, and where she was going to stay. She wished she could battle her thoughts without leaving, but distance was the only viable option she could think of to help relieve her mind.

Emrys greeted her in the entryway as she approached him and escorted her outside. She wiped her sweating palms on her skirt and followed him to the carriage. A footman extended a hand to her, offering to hand her up into the carriage. With a nod, she took his hand and stepped up into the carriage. Emrys followed her inside and sat across from her, shifting carefully to keep his knees from touching hers. A snap was heard outside the carriage, and she caught Emrys flinch. But he didn't acknowledge it as they lurched forward.

Saoirse watched the landscape roll by from the small window of the carriage, keeping her eyes on anything but Emrys. He was dressed in his usual tie and waistcoat but had added a jacket, making his figure look a bit bulkier than it usually was. She tried not to remember what he looked like underneath all the layers of fashion he wore, or the way the heat from his body felt against her. It only reminded her of how she slept alone last night, tossing and turning as she tried to succumb to sleep. Against her better judgment, thoughts about him slipped into her mind. Had he experienced the same fitful sleep? Or did he relish a bed to himself?

"Has Isolde told you how she and Cyprian met?" Emrys asked, shaking her back to the present.

"Not exactly," she answered sheepishly. She wasn't keen on conversing with him, but the thought of rudely ignoring him didn't sit well with her either. "Andromeda mentioned something about kidnapping."

Emrys snorted, then a grin settled on his face. "Don't mention that word to either of them. But with a few key details omitted, it could come across as kidnapping."

"So, her marriage is consensual?" Saoirse asked, her curiosity too strong to end the conversation politely. "She's not being held as a duchess against her will?"

A rumbling chuckle filled the carriage. "Yes, it's consensual and no, she isn't being held against her will. Although, if you stayed the night, you'd think differently from what you hear coming from their bedroom."

She bit back a grin. "So, how did they really meet?"

"They met at a ball nearly a century ago, and Isolde was looking for any way not to marry a fireann that her parents wanted her to," he explained. "I'm not sure what happened between her and the fireann, but she found Cyprian and asked him to take her home. However, Cyprian took her to *his* home instead of hers."

"And she trusted him enough to do that?" Saoirse asked, shocked. So it wasn't an entire exaggeration to claim that Isolde was kidnapped.

"Isolde has a tendency to make impulsive decisions." Emrys shrugged. "She took a calculated risk and, luckily for her, it paid off."

Saoirse was a bit stunned. From the way Isolde had chided Andromeda for not adhering to societal rules at their tea, she would have thought the duchess would have been extremely careful with the way she chose her partners. Instead, she was an impulsive risk-taker. Saoirse liked her even more after learning that bit of information.

She hoped staying with Isolde and Cyprian would be the key to resolving all her problems. At the house, she was alone except for Emrys and rarely had anyone to discuss her relationship with. Tea with the duchesses was the first time she had the freedom and outlet to do so. Living with Isolde for a period of time was becoming more and more ideal.

Emrys recounted another story about the couple, and Saoirse tried to relax. She made a conscious effort to listen and not let her mind wander to worry and despair. Just as she was settling into the rhythm of Emrys's stories, the carriage rolled to a stop and a footman was opening the door. He offered to hand Saoirse down from the carriage, and she graciously took it. She stepped onto the gravel path in front of a beautiful brick manor and took in the entire aesthetic of the house.

Half the exterior was covered in climbing ivy, and wildflowers overflowed from the flower beds under the windows. The manor looked like it was several centuries old yet meticulously maintained. If Emrys was nearly two centuries old and grew up with Cyprian, Saoirse could only begin to guess how old the manor was.

"Welcome to Brennan Hall," Emrys murmured to her. "This house has been in Cyprian's family for four centuries." He grinned at her, and Saoirse shyly returned it.

She followed him towards the large wooden front door where they were greeted by one of the duke's footmen. Emrys gave him their names, and they were ushered into the drawing room to wait for the duke and duchess. Saoirse sat stiffly on a loveseat while Emrys took an armchair near her. Before he could strike up another conversation, a large dog with long brown and black fur trotted into the room. It was tall enough that its head could reach Saoirse's lap. It sniffed eagerly at her as if looking for something on her person.

"Hello," Saoirse said, tentatively petting its head. She noted how soft and plush the dog's fur was and how it didn't balk at her petting it.

"Hades," a deep voice said sternly. "Come."

Saoirse looked up to see Cyprian in the doorway. The dog turned in Cyprian's direction and trotted over to him. The duke commanded Hades to sit, and the dog obeyed immediately.

"My apologies," Cyprian said. "I thought he was in the garden."

"It's alright." Saoirse waved away his apology. "He's quite friendly."

"I didn't know you were also coming." The duke shot a look at Emrys whose face became red-tinted. "I'll have Delya, the housekeeper, fetch Isolde. I believe she's just freshening some of the guest rooms."

"That would be lovely. Thank you." Saoirse gave him a polite smile.

Cyprian gave Hades a command, and the two disappeared from the room for a moment. When he returned, Isolde accompanied him and hurried to greet Saoirse with an embrace.

"This is such a lovely surprise!" she squealed.

Saoirse returned the embrace and caught a whiff of Isolde's delightful scent that smelled like honey and apples.

"Why don't you show her the house?" Cyprian suggested. "Show her all the fun projects you've been working on."

Isolde let go of Saoirse and rolled her eyes before looking over her shoulder at her husband. "You can admit you like the new bedding," she said. "You don't have to have this air of mystery when it comes to liking linens."

The duke gave her an unamused stare. "Emrys," he said, turning his attention away from Isolde. "Shall we go to my office and discuss whatever it is you needed to consult me on?"

"Gladly." Emrys nodded to the boireannaich and his gaze lingered on Saoirse before following Cyprian out of the room. The spark raced through her, and she tried to school her features.

Isolde allowed a moment to pass before ushering Saoirse into the hall. She started her tour with the dining room and then the music room. When they reached the end of the hallway, she turned to Saoirse and asked, "So, what happened to you and Emrys?"

Saoirse's jaw went slack. Neither Isolde or Cyprian knew she was coming, so how did Isolde know something happened?

"What makes you ask that?" Saoirse looked over her shoulder to make sure no one was overhearing this conversation.

"Oh, don't be alarmed." Isolde waved her hand. "I have a secondary magic."

"Oh." Saoirse knew many high fae had secondary magic. Her brother, Aurelius, could shift into a hawk form, but she didn't know there were other types of secondary magic.

Isolde leaned against the doorway to a room that Saoirse assumed was a guest room. She drew that conclusion from the four poster bed and nightstand she could see over the duchess's shoulder. Would that be her potential new bedroom?

"I'm a Thread Weaver," Isolde told her, pulling Saoirse from her wandering thoughts. "Well, the name isn't actually all that accurate because I don't weave any of the threads. I can just see them. They connect to people and certain shades denote what kinds of relationships they have. Their thickness also tells me how strong the relationship is, and the romantic one between you and Emrys looked fairly strong at your wedding, but just now it seemed quite fragile."

Saoirse chewed on her bottom lip, and her gaze dropped to the floor. She would have to tell Isolde eventually if she decided to stay with her. "Something did happen," she confessed quietly.

"Well, I suppose I should say something is *happening*." The duchess crossed her arms and remained quiet, patiently waiting for Saoirse to continue. "I'm having doubts I should stay with Emrys."

"Why?" Isolde asked, her blond brows knitting.

"Because..." Saoirse debated how to explain the inferiority she felt. "I don't feel worthy of him as a partner."

"You?" Isolde reeled back, stunned. "Of anyone, Emrys should feel unworthy of you. What makes you think you don't deserve him?"

Saoirse's gaze followed the intricate pattern of the floral wallpaper next to her as she contemplated how to divulge her past.

It wasn't something she really wanted to continue dwelling on. "Kieran," she murmured.

One of Isolde's eyebrows quirked in curiosity. "And what does he have to do with you and Emrys?"

Saoirse took a deep breath, letting it out in a heavy sigh. "Before Emrys and I were arranged, I had a relationship with Kieran."

"You tupped the general?" The corner of Isolde's mouth lifted, but she visibly fought it.

Heat crept up Saoirse's cheeks. "For about three months."

The duchess's jaw morphed from fighting a grin to dropping entirely. She scrambled to compose herself and looked down the hall over Saoirse's shoulder. "I know the fireann is a despicable cad," she said in a low voice, "but he is easy to look at and I'll admit I'm quite curious."

Saoirse stifled a chortle. If this was Isolde's reaction to finding she and Kieran shared an intimate relationship, she could only imagine how the other duchesses would respond. She was half-tempted to reveal it at their next tea just to find out.

"You're correct about him being a cad," Saoirse said. "He was a decent lover, but..." she bit her bottom lip, her mind wandering to her wedding night with Emrys. While she had been the only one pleasured, it was much more than Kieran had ever done for her.

A slow, knowing smile crept across the duchess's face. "I'm glad to hear you found better in bed."

Saoirse's blush intensified.

"But I suppose Kieran is a bit jealous?" Isolde asked. "From what I know, the fireann doesn't enjoy sharing, let alone watching someone else flaunt what he can't have."

"I'm not sure if that's it." Saoirse sighed. "He's the one who broke off our relationship in the first place. He had suggested marrying me and then changed his mind, blaming me and my age for his decision. I can't explain why he would want to ruin my relationship with Emrys to have me again. "

"It doesn't sound like it's solely you that he wants," Isolde commented carefully. "Coming from someone whose former partner tried to ruin her marriage, it's not that they want you so much as they want what you symbolize. You as a person they could take or leave." She muttered something in the Old Language under her breath that sounded like a curse.

"And what do I symbolize?" Saoirse asked, her curiosity piqued.

Isolde's shoulder lifted in a shrug. "Power, possibly? I'm not as familiar with Kieran's position in the court as Cyprian, but knowing where Emrys stands, it wouldn't surprise me if he envies the power Emrys holds. Power that you now hold, too."

"Kieran only sees me as an object of power," Saoirse said to herself. Suddenly, her doubts washed away, replaced by anger at the general. Of course his words were never about persuading her to give him a second chance at a relationship. It was to bully Emrys from a new angle. In Kieran's eyes, she was never a person who needed to be cared for and nurtured. She was merely an object to manipulate.

"I don't usually share this," Isolde said. "But I had doubts with Cyprian, too. He was obstinately against marriage, believing he wasn't fit for it, and I had spent endless time and energy convincing him he was worthy. But my former partner tried to poison my thoughts when he learned about Cyprian's insecurity. He nearly convinced me I had wasted all my efforts."

Saoirse felt stunned. She wasn't the only one haunted by her past. It was strangely comforting to have someone else in the same club that no one wished to be part of.

"But none of it was true," the duchess continued. "He merely did it to impede the arrangement Cyprian and I were finalizing so he could gain the dowry my parents were offering."

"What convinced you they weren't true?" Saoirse asked.

Isolde grinned broadly. "Cyprian marrying me without thinking twice. And he didn't do it just to spite my former partner either. He did it because he loved me."

That warmth she hadn't felt in almost a week seeped back into her chest. She wasn't alone in what she was experiencing. She had friends that understood her position and were available to lean on. That was enough reason to contemplate staying.

"I also learned the fireann was a complete fraud," Isolde added. "That helped me see through his nonsense he tried to feed me about Cyprian."

The boireannaich laughed, and Saoirse felt light. She didn't need to stay with Isolde. She just needed to silence Kieran before he could start talking again.

"If Kieran still gives you issues..." Isolde scanned the hallway over Saoirse's shoulder again. "I'm not supposed to suggest this. Cyprian doesn't like when I speak of things that are outside of the law, but if you needed it, Cook is well-versed in lethal herbs."

"Isolde!" Saoirse tried to sound scolding, but the laugh in her throat undermined her. There was that calculated impulsivity again.

The duchess gave an innocent shrug. "If he's scheming to pull you away from me and the other duchesses, he deserves repercussions."

"I agree, but maybe less lethal repercussions." Saoirse giggled.

"Then maybe I can convince Cyprian to show Kieran his shifted form."

"Cyprian can shift?" Saoirse's eyes lit up as Isolde nodded. "What's his shifted form?"

"A bear," Isolde answered with a giggle. "He doesn't shift often, but I think for your sake he would make an exception."

Saoirse shared in the duchess's amusement as the weight of her anxiety was quickly replaced with contentment. This was what had convinced her to stay with Emrys in the first place. She didn't just marry Emrys. She married into a family that cared for her and friends that wanted her to stay around.

She tried to muster the desire to leave that she felt last night, but it had evaporated. She wanted her life with Emrys, any lingering whispers of doubt and all. If Kieran wanted to ruin that, he'd be asking for a fight from more than just Saoirse.

18

Emrys *followed Cyprian* down the hall and into his study. Hades, who had been laying in the hall, followed on his heels all the way inside. Emrys noticed some of the small decorations he passed in the home had changed since the last time he had paid a visit. Hydrangeas and dahlias had replaced the peonies and primroses in the various vases in the hall to match the season. Emrys knew that had to be Isolde's work. When Cyprian was living a bachelor life, it was a miracle if the wallpaper in the hallway matched.

The duke closed the door behind them and turned to Emrys. "What did you do?" Cyprian asked.

Emrys tucked his hands into the pockets of his trousers. "It's nice to see you, too, Cyprian. How are you? How is your wife?"

"Emrys." The duke gave him a stern look. "You rarely pay me personal visits, let alone accompanied by your wife. Tell me, what did you do?"

"In my defense, I didn't have a wife until two weeks ago."

"Emrys." Cyprian growled his name. His patience with Emrys's cheekiness was obviously dwindling.

"I need you to do me a favor," Emrys finally confessed.

The duke sighed and ran a hand down his face. "I'm going to bill you for whatever I have to fix."

"Hopefully it won't require that."

Cyprian crossed the room to his desk. "The last time you said that, I was working day and night to keep your arse from being sent to a Welsh prison."

"It's nothing close to that," Emrys promised as he shook his head.

The duke sat behind his desk and gestured for Emrys to sit. Hades lay down next to his master and rested his head on the floor between his paws. Emrys took the seat Cyprian offered and tried to decide how to word his request.

"How do you prove someone is blackmailing you to a court of law?" Emrys asked.

Cyprian's stern glare turned to disbelief. "What in Annwn did you do?"

"I—I did nothing." Emrys swallowed hard. "Kieran learned I haven't told Saoirse about our mating bond yet and has threatened to tell her if I argue against his plans in Donheath."

The disbelief turned to puzzlement on Cyprian's face. "Then why did you bring Saoirse with you here? I'm not complaining. Isolde was giddy all morning knowing Saoirse was coming, and I reaped the benefit of that." The duke gave a cheeky grin. "But if you're just here to discuss the legality of blackmail, why bring Saoirse?"

Emrys dropped his gaze to his fingers that were fidgeting with the seam of his chair arm. "Saoirse wants to leave."

"I shall reiterate my previous question. What did you do?"

"Why do you think I did something?" Emrys glanced up at the duke with a scowl, but Cyprian only crossed his arms and sat back in his chair, waiting for him to answer. "It has to do with Kieran. He's been slowly whispering in Saoirse's ear to convince her I have such high standards that she's unworthy of my affection."

Cyprian let out a bellowing laugh. "You? She thinks she's unworthy of *you*?" He let out another laugh and took a moment to collect himself. "My apologies, but that was quite a lark."

"I'm glad the low points of my relationship are so amusing to you," Emrys said flatly. "Meanwhile, my wife is about to leave for good."

The duke cleared his throat, settling himself. "So Kieran is both blackmailing you and sowing doubt in Saoirse's mind about you. To what end?"

"I don't know." Emrys shrugged. "I thought maybe he's jealous of my marriage with Saoirse, but he's placed the doubt on her rather than undermining me altogether."

"And luring her to leave you as well," Cyprian added.

"Um...no," Emrys said slowly. He hadn't told anyone other than Ada the bargain he had made with Saoirse. Everyone assumed it was a run-of-the-mill arrangement with the added element of a mating bond.

"What do you mean 'no'?" Cyprian leveled a heavy stare with him.

"Saoirse and I—" Emrys swallowed. "We made a bargain over the marriage contract."

A dark brow rose on Cyprian's face.

"The night I met Saoirse," Emrys elaborated, "I found her packing to escape in the middle of the night. I learned her brother had given her an option to marry me or she would be sent to the Matron House."

Cyprian's skepticism flashed to disgust.

"She had a previous relationship with Kieran, which I was aware of, and to no one's surprise, it had not been a very healthy one. She couldn't bring herself to marry me knowing Kieran was my cousin. So I made her a bargain."

"What kind of bargain?" Cyprian asked, his words slow and hesitant.

"I..." Emrys rubbed at the back of his neck and stared at the polished floor. "I told her she could leave if she married me." He cautiously dragged his gaze up to his friend, aware of the possible disapproving reaction from the duke.

Cyprian stared at him in disbelief, breaking his unfazed barrister exterior. "Your tendency towards martyrdom disturbs me."

"I know. And you're not the only one to tell me that."

The duke let out a long breath and ran a hand down his face. "So how long has she threatened to leave?"

"It hasn't exactly been a threat." Emrys felt sweat gather at his hairline. "She announced last night she wanted to leave. She says it's temporary, to get her head right."

"And you brought her here why exactly?"

"I offered her to stay with you and Isolde instead of by herself."

Cyprian leaned back in his chair and pinched the bridge of his nose in frustration. "Cailleach's quim, I need a drink."

Emrys wilted, embarrassed by his ploy. But he didn't know what else to do. Cyprian and Isolde's home was the best he could come up with as an alternative to making arrangements for Saoirse to live on her own.

"Does anyone else know Kieran is blackmailing you?" Cyprian asked.

"Just you," Emrys answered. "I can't exactly explain why Kieran is blackmailing me to Saoirse."

"You know you could just tell your wife you're mates, and then Kieran has no upper hand."

"Yes, I will just tell the boireann who has expressed her desire to leave me that we've been fated by the gods, a concept she's expressed to me that she doesn't believe in," Emrys said sardonically. "Incredible idea, Cyprian. I'll go find her and do that now."

"You're going to have to tell her at some point," the duke argued. "If not now, when?"

"I'd like to have her committed to staying first."

Cyprian sighed. "I'll do what I can about Kieran. If anything, I'll help buy you time until you tell Saoirse, but I need you, for the love of all things sacred, tell her about the mating bond as soon as you can."

"And you'll let Saoirse stay here if she chooses?" Emrys asked anxiously.

"Of course."

"Thank you." Emrys let out a breath, a slight weight easing from his shoulders. "And I promise I'll tell her when I can. Kieran will only make good on his threat if I raise an argument against him in regard to Donheath. I would need you to argue on my behalf."

"That will be easy enough." Cyprian shrugged. "I hate almost every proposal from that fireann. I don't need much incentive to argue against him."

"Thank you, Cyprian. I truly appreciate it."

"You're welcome." Cyprian gave him a half-smile. "Now, I recommend once you get your wife into a better place, give her a good enough time that I get the secondhand details from Isolde."

"Have you always been such a gossip?" Emrys chuckled.

The duke shrugged again. "Isolde makes it interesting enough that I live for whatever good gossip she brings home."

"You're incorrigible." Emrys shook his head and rose from his seat. "But I promise I'll take your advice."

Cyprian also got to his feet and made his way towards the door of the study. The dog quickly stood and eagerly followed the fireannaich.

"You'd better," Cyprian said, opening the door and motioning for Emrys to exit.

Emrys rolled his shoulders back, his hope renewed. Cyprian would keep Kieran from exposing his secret for now and buy Emrys enough time to dissolve Saoirse's doubts. He just hoped she would give him the chance to do so.

Emrys and Cyprian exited the study to find Isolde and Saoirse giggling as they descended the stairs. Emrys's heart kicked up seeing her smile. He tried to prepare himself for Saoirse's decision, but he knew his heart would sink either way. She was set on leaving. It was just a matter of where she was escaping to.

"You seem like you two are having a fine afternoon," Emrys said.

"We are." Saoirse smiled up at him.

"I take no responsibility for any changes in decor that are made at the Fearynhurst estate," Isolde said with a cheeky smile.

Emrys tried to return the pleasantry, but all he could think about was that there was no mention about Saoirse staying in Stoneblack. It could only mean she had chosen to stay by herself elsewhere. His heart slowly sank at the thought.

"Have you and Cyprian finished?" Saoirse asked.

"Yes." Emrys nodded. He held out hope for one more moment. "Shall we return home?" He had never wished for her to say "no" more than he did now.

But his wish didn't come true as she nodded.

"Yes, I'm ready." She began to reach her hand out towards him, and he stood frozen in confusion.

Awkwardly, he offered his arm, and she wrapped her hand into the crook of it. She and Isolde shared a brief embrace before Emrys escorted her towards the entryway. Confused but grateful, he led her to the carriage waiting in the drive and handed her up into it.

When she broke the connection, Emrys had to take a deep breath to settle himself. His panic had been strangely relieved, and he could only blame the bond because he wasn't naïve enough to believe she had changed her mind from one afternoon.

After he was seated in the carriage to return home, he folded his hands in his lap in order to not fidget. He heard the whip before the carriage crawled to a start and winced involuntarily. It had been several decades since that sound meant anything other than travel, but he still equated it with his nightmares.

Saoirse's gaze was fixed on him, and he tried to straighten to combat his habit of shrinking at the sound of a whip. Her hazel eyes remained on him as the carriage rolled onto the main road. He had two options. He could either explain the reaction she had witnessed or broach the other subject that sat heavily between them.

But he didn't need to choose. As he opened his mouth to attempt resolving one of them, Saoirse took him by surprise.

"Emrys, I want to stay," she blurted in a whisper.

His entire body froze in shock. "Excuse me?" he asked in disbelief.

"I want to stay," she repeated.

His mouth made several attempts to form words, but he was

too stunned. He took a deep breath and composed himself. "What changed your mind?" he asked curiously.

"What Kieran has said to me isn't about desiring me," she said. "I'm merely a pawn for him to play with."

"So, just like that, your doubts are gone?" What was he saying? He shouldn't be questioning her intentions. Instead, he should be celebrating his relief.

"Not entirely." Saoirse sighed. "Since our night on the train, I've thought how you deserve better than what I can offer. And that was long before Kieran started to amplify those thoughts."

Emrys's renewed hope deflated a bit. Her doubts weren't anything new. They had just reached a peak. "I want you to know that's not true."

She nodded in acknowledgement. "I'm still fighting my doubts, but they're with me, not you."

"So this might happen again?"

Saoirse leaned back against the seat of the carriage, withdrawing a bit. Emrys kicked himself for asking the question. He had to amend it. He had to take action and prove she was nothing short of a blessing to him.

"What if we went back to our second bargain?" he suggested tentatively.

Saoirse's brows knit.

"Give me a second chance to prove why you should stay." His heart pounded in his chest, once again waiting for her to accept his offer.

She stared at him before shifting her gaze to the window. Emrys could almost see her thoughts running rapidly in her mind. His breath caught in his lungs when she finally looked back at him.

"Emrys, I—"

"I know Kieran has taken a knock to your confidence," he interrupted. "Let me help you rebuild it and prove you are worthy of everything good."

The corner of her lips tipped upwards. "Even if that means we start over?"

"Maybe not completely over." He felt his heartbeat in his throat. "We can start back at where we were on the train, little more than strangers with a strong attraction to each other."

A blush rose on Saoirse's cheeks. "You felt that, too?"

"How could I ignore it?" Emrys huffed a laugh. "If you hadn't implemented the caveat that I couldn't solely ravish you to persuade you to stay, I would have stripped you bare and tupped you in that sad excuse of a bed."

The blush on her face darkened, and she bit her bottom lip. He reprimanded himself for giving such a cheeky answer, but her reaction gave him the inability to remember why. Nothing he agreed to with Cyprian said he couldn't still use his charm. He just needed to put in more actions than words.

"So, will you give me a second chance?" he asked.

Finally, a true smile spread on her face. "Yes," she said with a nod. "I'll allow you a second chance."

Emrys's shoulders sagged in relief. The worst was over. Saoirse wasn't leaving. He had an opportunity to prove staying was a good choice. A new spring of hope flowed over him, and while he still had work to put in, all was right in his world.

The next day, Saoirse and Emrys quickly settled into their new bargain. Saoirse chose to sleep in her own room again, her sleep only slightly better than it was the night before. Although, she was beginning to regret the decision. The absence from Emrys's bed must have given him the impression that she no longer desired his touch. He had reduced his physical contact with her to only small, innocent touches. Not that she was wishing to be fully ravished, but she desired a bit more than a pat to her shoulder.

Her doubts still hadn't vanished, but her vigor to fend them off had been renewed. Instead of undermining Emrys, Kieran was chipping away at her confidence. It was a sinister tactic, but Saoirse was and always had been aware that he wasn't empty-headed. If he was going to use her as a pawn in his games, she would just have to make the pieces harder to move.

"Hello." Emrys leaned his forearms on the back of the chaise in the library. Saoirse had been trying to read in order to occupy her thoughts with something other than him, but had been failing miserably.

"Hello," she greeted.

"I was thinking, if you were up to it, we could pick up with training sessions tomorrow."

She gave him a genuine smile. "Yes, actually, I would really like that."

"Great." He grinned back and leaned closer to her. His lips paused inches away from her temple. Saoirse silently urged him to make contact.

Instead, he pulled back and tried to recover with a wonky smile. "I'll meet you on the lawn tomorrow afternoon." His words weren't nearly as confident as they had been previously.

Trying to mask her disappointment, Saoirse nodded her agreement. "I'll see you then," she said, hoping her smile reassured him.

Awkwardly, he squeezed her shoulder before leaving. She sighed once he was out of earshot and found herself restless. She should have been thankful that he was being careful and respectful. But a part of her yearned to be touched by him. Hadn't he warned her during their night on the train that he enjoyed making physical contact? From there he had eased into holding her hand and kissing her cheek until they reached their wedding where they allowed the tension to explode between them.

Saoirse hadn't realized she had become accustomed to a certain level of intimacy until it was cut off almost completely. If anything, she just missed kissing him. His scent, the feel of his hands on her, the way he could communicate more in a single kiss than any amount of words—she missed it.

She shook herself and forced her attention back to the book in her lap. She shouldn't be thinking of kissing Emrys. It only made her miss it more. But in her defense, it at least kept her thoughts distracted from her doubts. A smile tugged at the corner of her lips. Fighting off Kieran's lies with Emrys's kisses felt poetic. All she needed was to find how to silence her doubts about herself for good. She had a feeling it would take a bit more than kisses to do that.

Emrys was placing wooden stakes into the ground when Saoirse stepped onto the lawn that afternoon. He placed them in a triangular formation—with the stakes closer to her clumped together and the ones further away spread several feet apart.

"If your intention is to burn the entire lawn, I don't think Ada will appreciate it," she said as she approached him.

He looked up from his work and grinned. "Let me worry about that," he said.

She quirked an eyebrow at him, skeptical the lawn would remain lush and green by the time they finished. Their last few sessions had been working on her manifesting her magic and releasing it from her grip. More than once, a rogue flame had made its way to the grass, singeing it until Emrys extinguished it with his magic.

She crossed her arms over her chest, watching him finish his work. "What are the stakes for?"

"Since you've been working on forming and releasing your magic, I thought aiming it would be a natural next step." He took a few steps to a nearby stake and placed his hand on top of it. "I want you to summon your magic and aim for this stake. Don't think about how I've just placed kindling all over the lawn. I want you to get comfortable aiming your magic."

He removed his hand from the stake and stepped aside. Saoirse took a moment to shake out her hands and focus. She stared at the piece of pine standing in the grass and felt the anxiety wash through her. Singeing small patches of grass was one thing, but aiming her magic purposefully so close to the lawn terrified her.

"Imagine the stake is Kieran." Emrys's words cut through her haze of thoughts, and her eyes shot to him. "We can turn this into a cathartic exercise."

"I thought using anger was frowned up," Saoirse countered.

He shrugged. "It's not a viable resource for magic, but sometimes it needs a bit of a release."

"Anger isn't exactly what I'm feeling at the moment." She shook her head and fidgeted with her wedding ring.

His gaze dropped to her fumbling fingers, and he stared for a moment before he turned to the stake. He put his palm out and gray-blue magic drifted from his fingers. He aimed it around the base of the stake and up the length of wood until the ground and stake were covered in ice. "Does that help?" he asked.

Saoirse gaped for a moment at what she witnessed before

nodding. Her worry was slowly replaced with that emotion she couldn't quite name, the one that her magic responded to best. With the feeling fresh in her mind, she summoned her magic and siphoned it through her muscles.

The action was becoming easier, like second nature, and within seconds, flames were licking her palm. She filled her lungs with a deep breath before pulling her hand back and surging it forward. A sad, crackling ember sputtered a few inches from her palm and turned to ash at her feet. She looked to Emrys, who was biting back a laugh as he strode over to her.

"I didn't think I'd need to cover the grass at your feet in ice as well," he teased.

Saoirse shot him an unamused look.

"You had the right idea," he said as he moved to behind her. "It's not much different from when you were aiming it upwards. It just needs to move forward now." Emrys gingerly reached for her hand.

Saoirse let him carefully position her arms and body. One hand rested on her hip while the other wrapped around her forearm of her dominant hand. Emrys brought it up to chest height and pulled it back, her elbow nestling into the area between his bicep and ribs. This was the closeness she didn't realize she would miss so much. The bit of worry over the lawn going up in flames quieted, and her magic danced in her veins, ready for another attempt.

"Think of pulling your magic back like a bow." His voice was low, and his breath ruffled the loose hairs on her neck. That spark raced up Saoirse's spine, and she had to work to breathe evenly. "Don't keep your magic in your fingers. Keep it just inside your hand at your palm, and when you push forward," he moved her arm forward in a swift motion, "push it as quickly and as far forward as you can. Let's try it together."

Saoirse nodded and focused on her magic rather than the points of her body where she could feel Emrys touching her. His grip relaxed, but his hands remained on her. She conjured her magic into her veins and held it in the area of her palm. She pulled her elbow back towards Emrys again before thrusting her arm forward and letting go of the leash on her magic.

Amber flames sprung forward, and a thread of panic weaved through her. She quickly drew back her magic, creating a watermelon-sized fireball that went spiraling towards the stakes. Without thinking, she leaned back into Emrys and watched in horror as the fire dissipated and melted the ice off the stake, leaving a light burn mark on it.

"That's alright," he said calmly, his thumb tracing soothing circles on her forearm. "That's what the ice is there for."

"I made it too large," she said, panicked.

"And that's alright," he assured her. "You're in control of how much magic you use. If you want to make it smaller, cut it off sooner."

She nodded and shifted her weight back onto her feet, her panic finally waning. He slipped his hands from her and for a moment, she considered grabbing one of his hands to remain on her. She reluctantly thought better of it and shook off the dismay of her last attempt. Her thoughts focused on the feeling Emrys gave her from being close to her, and she let it feed her magic. She pulled back her arm again, took in a deep breath, and threw it forward, letting her magic manifest until she had finished exhaling.

A fireball, the size of a grapefruit this time, hurled towards the front stake. It hit it squarely in the middle, leaving another dent in the layer of ice Emrys had covered it in. Melted ice dripped down to the frozen grass and Saoirse stood staring at it.

Excitement thrummed through her, and she let out a stunned laugh. "I did it," she whispered. She turned to Emrys and repeated with a smile spreading on her face, "I did it!"

"Yes, you did." His grin was equally as wide as hers.

Without a second thought, she threw her arms around his neck and embraced him. He tensed for a moment, but before Saoirse could let go of him and face the awkward fallout, he relaxed and wrapped his arms around her waist. She tightened her hold on him and buried her face in the crook of his neck, inhaling his musky citrus scent.

For the first time since working on her magic, Saoirse felt accomplished instead of frustrated. She could finally feel her progress, and it was a relief. There were still parts of her life that had earmarks of her brother's handiwork, but this part of her was shedding that evidence, one afternoon at a time. And it was with Emrys.

He was undoing part of the hurt and pain that Eamon had inflicted on her. Emrys was building her confidence piece by piece and doing everything but contributing to what she already struggled with. And he did it without hesitation. Using her brother as a standard of care was a low threshold to hurdle, but Emrys was exceeding it at every turn. A doubt whispered to her that she wasn't worthy enough for it, but she combatted it with the way Emrys's fingers were currently stroking along her back. He didn't care what she brought with her into their relationship. He wanted her as much as she needed him.

Saoirse and Emrys stood embracing each other for a moment longer, both of them basking in accomplishment. When Saoirse finally loosened her grip, she saw a conflict of emotions in Emrys's eyes. He still had a proud smile on his face, but it no longer reached his eyes. His hands pulled away from her, and he stiffly stepped around her and towards the stakes on the lawn.

"Shall we do it again?" he asked, his voice cracking awkwardly. He refused to turn back in her direction, and she bit back a grin. At least she knew she wasn't the only one who was affected physically by their proximity.

"I have a feeling you won't let me leave until I've struck every stake," she said.

He looked over his shoulder with a smirk. "You know me too well."

She giggled as she stepped up beside him and bumped him with her hip. He swayed a bit but didn't stumble from the contact. He angled the lower half of his body away from her, and Saoirse resisted the urge to torture him further.

"Just for that, I'm going to make the next one that much more difficult for you." He gave a cheeky half-grin. "You're going to use your other hand."

Saoirse gave a horrified gasp but couldn't hide the grin that was still stretched across her face. "You're abhorrent."

"I've been called worse." Emrys shrugged, but amusement still twinkled in his eye.

Maybe it wouldn't take as long for them to reach where their relationship was previously as Saoirse thought. Maybe she would be wrapped in his arms under his sheets sooner than expected.

E*mrys walked through* the doorway of the council room, dreading the day's meeting. He never anticipated council meetings with giddiness, but he hadn't ever wanted to feign illness as strongly as he did today. Not that it would convince anyone. He would have to be profanely ill to be excused from council.

"You look like you haven't had a good night's sleep in a week," Laszlo remarked as Emrys took his seat at the table. "Marriage must be treating you quite well."

Emrys glared at the duke, and Laszlo recoiled.

"Have things not improved?" Cyprian asked.

"What does he know that I don't?" Laszlo demanded. "Are you and Saoirse already bickering?"

"I didn't take Saoirse as being the type to bicker," Vasili chimed in.

Emrys ran an annoyed hand down his face. "We're not bickering," he corrected. "We're working through a hiccup, and she's been sleeping somewhere else."

"And you told Cyprian first?" If Emrys didn't know better, he would have thought Laszlo was pouting.

"I didn't intend to tell him." Emrys glared at the duke in question. "I had other business to discuss with him, and he pulled it out of me."

"You brought Saoirse with you," Cyprian argued. "How was I

supposed to ignore that fact?"

"What did you do?" Vasili asked.

Emrys sighed. He guessed being interrogated about his marriage was better than being asked what he went to Cyprian for. "I didn't do anything. It was about Kieran," Emrys confessed. "He and Saoirse were involved before we were arranged, and he's been trying to convince her to leave me because she isn't worthy enough."

A silence fell over the fireannaich as they digested that information. Emrys didn't know if he preferred silence or laughter as a response. Cyprian's amused reaction was annoying, but the silence made him itch.

"Kieran?" Laszlo asked, sobering. "Does she know about..." He trailed off but Emrys knew what the duke was inferring.

"Not entirely," he answered. "She knows he's responsible for my scars. That's about it."

"Have things improved?" Cyprian asked.

Emrys opened his mouth to answer but was interrupted by the presence of Kieran.

"Speaking of," Vasili murmured.

"You were speaking of me?" Kieran gave a slimy grin. "I hope it was all good things." The general took his seat and flashed a knowing grin at Emrys.

"That would be a very short conversation," Cyprian commented offhandedly.

Kieran's grin fell, and he glared at the duke. Before any kind of discourse could break out from Cyprian's comment, Alastair joined and commenced the meeting.

Last week, they had sorted out a budget to expand the army. While Kieran got his way once again, at least it hadn't come at a detriment to any of his friends. Today, he most likely wouldn't be so lucky. His stomach plummeted as the meeting started. He no longer had time to run if he wanted to. If Kieran had a plan to implement the army in Donheath, Emrys would have to sit and keep his mouth shut. Cyprian had agreed to argue against anything that was beyond Kieran's given authority on Emrys's behalf, but not being able to step in was going to be torture.

"Kieran, how is recruitment coming along?" Alastair asked. "Are we meeting the numbers you foresee us needing?"

"Yes, they're excellent," Kieran answered, fiddling that damn pocket watch between his fingers.

"How much longer until they're ready to for possible deployment?" Alastair asked.

"I've been able to bulk the recruits in record time," Kieran said. "They can be deployed by the end of the week."

"How?" Emrys asked before he could stop himself.

Kieran narrowed his gaze at him in warning. "I've incorporated an enhancement. It's a secret little formula that's between me and the lovely boireann who gave it to me."

"You're giving the army a potion?" Cyprian asked.

"Nothing gets past you, does it?" Kieran gave a smug half-smile.

Emrys clenched his jaw. Never had he wanted to commit violence on the general as much as he did right now.

"And why is that necessary?" Danu bless Cyprian for being able to converse with Kieran so eloquently. There was a reason he was the barrister for the court.

"Because we're setting up camps at the end of the month," Kieran answered.

"That was never decided," Vasili said in surprise.

"It certainly was." Kieran turned his gaze to the duke, and Emrys found the calm expression on the general's face unsettling. "In times of war, the crown overrules the overseer of the territory."

"We aren't in a time of war," Vasili argued.

"Not yet." Kieran shrugged.

"Kieran," Cyprian said, his tone a warning. "We haven't declared war. Therefore, that clause cannot be enacted."

"We might not have," he turned his attention to the barrister, "but the Fomóire have, and if we don't act, we may experience devastating losses to our kind."

"The Fomóire are beasts," Laszlo chimed in. "They can't declare war."

"Their threat of devastation is enough reason to declare war on our part." Kieran's voice was becoming agitated, and Emrys saw him clutch his pocket watch tightly. "I'd rather us secure our lands before we're wiped off the British Isle."

"Kieran, we can't declare war on beasts," Cyprian said. "We can only create contingencies to implement if they strike."

"Cyprian, I appreciate your legal perspective, but this is a military matter." Kieran turned his attention to Vasili. "And neither of you have military experience."

"Emrys has military experience," Vasili argued. The duke's pleading gaze turned to Emrys. "You think we should hold off on implementing camps until we have more evidence, don't you?"

Sweat collected at Emrys's brow as he looked between Kieran's intimidating gaze and Vasili's desperate one. His mouth opened and closed like a fish as he weighed his options mentally. He couldn't let his friend be trampled over by Kieran, but he also couldn't let his relationship with Saoirse be ruined even further by the general. They were still in a precarious position. He could always find a way to earn back Vasili's respect at a later time, but he might lose Saoirse altogether if he decided to speak up now.

"Emrys," Vasili said. "What are your thoughts?"

Emrys looked to his father, whose cheeks were twitching. He wasn't stepping in either and looked to be held in silence against his will.

Emrys swallowed before responding. "I don't have any. I trust you to make the decision on your own merit."

Vasili's brows knitted. "Emrys, what does that mean?"

"His Highness has spoken," Kieran interrupted. "Either you grant me the power to your territory or risk the cost of delaying it."

Vasili gave one last confused glance at Emrys before facing Kieran. "Are you absolutely sure this is the best course of action?"

"The longer we wait, the more lives we risk." The general shrugged. "Our subjects are in your hands, Vasili."

The duke sighed in defeat. "Alright, I concede."

"Excellent decision." Kieran smirked and turned to Alastair.

"We'll have the first camp set up on the north side of Donheath by the end of next week. We'll increase our recruitment again and have the border of the territory secured before Mabon."

"That's excellent to hear," Alastair said, his mouth finally forming words. After giving his jaw a roll, he quickly moved on to the next order of business. For the rest of the meeting, Emrys avoided Vasili's gaze.

His heart didn't stop racing, and the sweat collecting at his brow didn't evaporate. He would have to explain himself at the end of the meeting, and it scared him nearly as much as facing Saoirse if she were told about their bond. But his marriage had to take precedent over friendships, right? The dukes would understand, wouldn't they?

The meeting concluded after the more mundane matters were wrapped up, and Alastair and Kieran vacated the room almost immediately. The dukes, however, didn't budge.

"What in Cernunno's Wilderness is wrong with you?" Vasili directed his question to Emrys, and the outburst took him off guard. Vasili was usually slow to anger and not at all hostile. But Emrys had really muffed his friend's trust.

"I'm sorry, Vasili," he said. "I couldn't say anything about Kieran's military plan."

"And why is that?" Laszlo asked, narrowing his eyes.

"He..." Emrys chewed on the inside of his cheek. "He's blackmailing me."

"Blackmailing you?" Laszlo repeated. "With what? You don't keep secrets."

"Well, I have *one*, and Kieran found what it was and is exploiting it."

Laszlo's puzzled expression deepened until realization struck his features. "You haven't told Saoirse you're mates?"

"How did you deduce that?" Cyprian asked, stunned.

The Duke of Cogwick shrugged. "Emrys doesn't hide much, and he told us earlier he hasn't told Saoirse about what Kieran did to him. Why would that be what Kieran leveraged against him?

That led me to think of the only other thing he might keep from Saoirse, and that's their bond."

The barrister stared at him. "What are you doing in business? You'd almost make a better lawyer than me."

Laszlo slowly grinned with pride. "Thank you."

"You put my territory at risk because you didn't tell your wife about your silly little bond?" Vasili's voice rose, and the room fell silent.

Emrys's sweat intensified, but his mouth went dry. "I'm sorry, Vasili, but if Saoirse found out from Kieran, I would lose her completely."

"And you couldn't have just told her yourself?" The disgust on the duke's face made Emrys's stomach knot.

"I can't tell her yet."

"Why not?" Vasili demanded. "It's a simple conversation. And if it came from you, she'd be less likely to rebuke it."

"It's not that simple, Vasili."

"Yes, it is!" The duke rose to his feet. "You're a being a selfish cad because you don't want to be uncomfortable. Instead, you make my life unbearable. Friends don't do that, Emrys."

"Vasili, I really am sorry. I—"

"No, I don't want excuses. You had a chance to do the right thing, and you didn't. I can't believe I considered you a friend who supported me." Vasili stormed out of the room, leaving an awkward silence in his wake.

"You made Vasili...angry," Laszlo said. "I didn't think he could be angry."

Emrys groaned. "I ruined a lot, didn't I?"

"You let Kieran ruin not only a friendship but a precarious political situation as well," Cyprian remarked. "I would consider that a lot."

Emrys thudded his head against the table.

"It could have been worse," Laszlo said.

"How?" Emrys growled.

"Vasili could have tried to swing at you."

Emrys picked his head up and glared at the duke. "Vasili acting in violence is your idea of worse?"

"As I said, I didn't think the fireann could feel anger, so yes, violence would be worse." Laszlo shrugged.

"Leave," Emrys said flatly.

"But—"

"Both of you, take your wives, and leave."

The sound of chair legs scraping echoed in the room, and the dukes shuffled out with little more than a mumble of farewell, leaving Emrys to sulk on his own.

Saoirse settled into her armchair in the drawing room and patiently awaited her friends. Her afternoon with Isolde earlier in the week had her eager for their scheduled afternoon tea with all the duchesses. Talking to Isolde had helped Saoirse feel a little less isolated in her relationship. It was something she never could have done with Cressida when she was with Kieran. If she had revealed her involvement with the general to her sister-in-law, there wasn't a single possibility where Cressida wouldn't have shared that with Eamon. And if Eamon knew about them...

"Good afternoon." Isolde's melodic voice broke the spiral Saoirse was about to slip into. The duchess wore a soft green blouse with lacy details around the collar and a matching dark green jacket and skirt. A pale gold pearl comb was nestled in her blonde bun and glinted every time the light caught it.

"You're a bit early," Saoirse said.

"It's Cyprian's fault," Isolde grumbled. "He kept getting on to me all morning about being ready to leave and we wind up arriving early." The duchess rolled her eyes, annoyed. "It's like he doesn't trust me to be on time to anything. But enough about my pain in the arse of a husband. How have you and Emrys been?"

"Are you starting without us?" Andromeda interrupted, walking through the door. She wore a beautiful, delicate white lace ensemble with her hair pulled up into a period appropriate pompadour.

Calliope trailed behind her, her cane absent today. Her attire looked the most subdued in a cream-colored blouse and blush pink walking skirt. But with her rich brown skin, it popped just as much as the dark green Isolde wore against her pale complexion. The two duchesses settled on the settee and Saoirse, having learned her lesson from their last tea, began to pour tea and pass the cups around.

"So, what have we missed?" Andromeda asked.

"Well, I was complaining about how my husband was badgering me all morning that we ended up arriving early, but it looks like I wasn't the only one." Isolde daintily stirred her tea.

"Vasili has been a bit more anxious than usual," Calliope supplied. "It was either arrive early or spend hours later tonight trying to ease him."

"Hours?" Andromeda asked, arching a brow. "I didn't think the fireann could go more than thirty minutes."

Calliope shook her head. "Sex is the last thing he's interested in when he's like this. He usually ends up needing near complete silence and a hot bath that is nearly scalding. I don't mind it, but not being able to do anything else to alleviate his anxious state makes me feel helpless."

"That's understandable," Isolde said. "Cyprian has had to deal with my moments like that, and coming from the person who has been in Vasili's shoes, we hate that we can't have you do more either."

"This is becoming a bit depressing," Andromeda commented. "I was looking forward to riveting conversation about someone's sex life. Could we move onto that? Saoirse, you're still a newlywed. You must have something titillating we haven't heard yet."

"I'm sorry to disappoint you," Saoirse said. "But Emrys and I have been going through a rough period."

"Already?" Andromeda asked. "Over what?"

Saoirse chewed on her bottom lip and glanced at Isolde. The duchess sipped her tea and shrugged.

"They've been through worse if it makes you feel any better," she said. "Andromeda alone—"

"Has gone through a lot," Andromeda finished for her. "And I don't plan on discussing it today." The duchess shot a look at Isolde who, quickly tightened her lips.

"Well, there's no use in delaying it then." Saoirse let out a long exhale. "It has to do with Kieran." She glanced at Andromeda and Calliope whose expressions were a mix between piqued curiosity and surprise. "I used to have a relationship with him. It ended several months before Emrys and I were arranged. But he's been trying to convince me I deserve someone like him more than I do Emrys. Unfortunately, I let his words resonate too much with me and pushed Emrys away as a result."

"How did Emrys respond?" Andromeda asked.

"He put up a good fight to keep me from pushing him too far." Saoirse gave a small smile. "He's also been working tirelessly to keep me from believing anything that comes out Kieran's mouth."

Calliope swooned. "That's the protective trait of mates for you."

"No," Isolde said quickly. "Anyone can feel protective. I would be protective of Cyprian if that past lover of his tried to convince him he was a terrible husband."

The duchesses shared several looks with each other, and Saoirse knit her brows. "You believe mates exist?" she asked.

"They have to," Andromeda answered. "The gods must get bored watching society pair themselves off. Sprinkling in mating bonds gives life a bit more spice for them."

"Do you three believe your spouse is also your mate?" Saoirse followed up. She didn't believe for a moment mates were true, but she was in the mood to entertain her friends.

Andromeda let out a snort. "Laszlo and I have known each other since we were teens. If we were mates, I would think we would know by now."

Saoirse saw Isolde stiffen from the corner of her eye. She was about to ask if she was alright when Calliope weighed in on the subject.

"Mates are fairly rare," she said. "A mating bond is considered a gift from the gods, and they're very picky on who they bless with a bond."

"Well, it seems like all you have to do is be a self-absorbed arse to be someone's mate." Saoirse let out a sardonic noise. "The only mates I'm aware of are my brother and his wife, and I know it's a blatant lie he told her so she didn't leave him."

"That's only one couple," Calliope argued. "The mated pairs I've encountered are very loving and would never lie to each other."

"Mates can never lie, actually," Isolde chimed in. "It's one of their traits."

That tidbit didn't sit right with Saoirse. There had been a few moments when she had been inclined to be honest while talking to Emrys. But that was because she trusted him with the truth. Wasn't it?

"So while mates can't lie," Saoirse continued, entertaining the idea just a bit further, "someone could lie about being a mate? How does that help anyone decipher what's true and what's not?"

Isolde shrugged. "There must be other signs. I would think they would share something physically that would indicate a bond."

"Didn't you tell me you could see threads of relationships between people?" Saoirse asked. "Wouldn't you be able to tell if a couple were mates or not?"

Isolde froze again and shook her head vigorously. "I've never come across any mates." She slurped her tea and avoided everyone's gaze. "I wouldn't know what shade those threads would be."

"Isolde learned a while ago not to meddle with relationship threads," Andromeda explained. "She nearly ruined a century's long marriage between the Dukes of Frigrave."

"I simply mistook their romantic thread for their platonic one," Isolde said, trying to defend herself. "I truly had the best intentions in mind."

"Yet you learned to stop meddling because of it." Andromeda sipped her tea as she stared down the other duchess.

Isolde glared at her but didn't argue otherwise. Saoirse pondered the workings of Isolde's secondary magic. How did she know she had it? Was it something she had from an early age, or did it develop along with her primary magic? Her curiosity about Isolde's ability distracted her enough to put the argument of mates aside as the conversation shifted back to the current status of her relationship with Emrys.

"So, you said you and Emrys are mending your marriage," Andromeda said.

"We've been working through it," Saoirse replied. "We're slowly rebuilding what we lost."

"I'm glad to hear that." Isolde smiled at her, and Saoirse couldn't help but return it.

"Yes, and I've heard fucking is an excellent way to rebuild a relationship," Andromeda added.

"We're nowhere close to that." Saoirse stifled a giggle. "He barely touches me beyond a pat on the shoulder."

"Emrys?" Calliope asked. "The fireann who can't keep his hands to himself even with our husbands? That Emrys?"

Saoirse giggled. "The exact one. I had to tug him into an embrace yesterday."

"Emrys enjoys physical touch, but he takes consent very seriously." Andromeda bit into one of the macarons. "If you told him what you're comfortable with, he'll follow through with it."

Saoirse sat back and contemplated the suggestion. Maybe she could also put in an effort to assure him his work wasn't a waste. Her thoughts wandered further to what kissing Emrys again would feel like. Yesterday reminded her of how far they had come before it crumbled. She wanted to reach that point. She wanted it so badly it physically hurt her.

"I know that look," Andromeda said, pulling Saoirse from her introspection. "That look usually leads to fucking on the sofa."

Saoirse couldn't hold back her laugh this time. The duchess had sniffed out her craving for more than just a kiss. Even though Saoirse had been quenching her thirst for desire on her own, it didn't compare to what she had shared with Emrys and what more they could indulge in.

"Oh, it's definitely going to lead to fucking," Isolde giggled.

"Promise us you'll share some details at Calliope's anniversary dinner that Andromeda is hosting."

"Anniversary dinner?" Saoirse repeated. This was the first time she was hearing about such a dinner.

"Yes, it's on Lughnasadh," Calliope said. "I'm guessing in the midst of your rough patch Emrys forgot to mention it."

"Yes, he did." Saoirse nodded. "But I'm looking forward to it now."

"Good." The duchess grinned.

Chatter about the event erupted and excitement bubbled up in Saoirse's chest. It was one thing to spend time weekly with these boireannaich, chatting and gossiping to their hearts' desires, but the feeling was elevated being included in their personal celebrations. Sure, it was partly out of obligation because of Emrys's connection to their husbands, but they made it clear they genuinely wanted her included.

Tea wound down and was brought to an end when Vasili came to collect Calliope. She stood from her seat but quickly grabbed for her husband's arm. Her balance wobbled, and she breathed deeply until she was steady again. "The one time I decide not to bring my cane," she muttered.

"I told you to take it even if you don't think you need it," Vasili chided. "I know you don't want to acknowledge it, but you're reaching a point where I don't think you can go without it even for outings like this."

"I know you're right." Calliope looped her arm with Vasili's. "I just don't want to give up the idea of independence."

"For a High Healer, you're quite stubborn about your health." The duke pressed a kiss to her temple. "Let's get home before you make yourself worse."

Calliope bid farewell to everyone before disappearing into the main hall with her husband. Lazlo and Cyprian followed behind shortly, and they were in much lower spirits than the last time Saoirse saw them.

"Did council not go well?" she asked.

"Your husband upset Vasili," Cyprian answered.

Saoirse was surprised to hear that. "But Vasili was just here and didn't seem upset at all. If anything, he was worried about Calliope's health."

"Vasili has a tendency to mask his emotions, especially in front of others," Laszlo explained as his wife rose to her feet and smoothed her skirt. "He'll be alright, and Emrys will find a way to make up for it. But your husband might need a little extra attention tonight."

Andromeda smacked his shoulder. "They're not fucking at the moment."

"All the more reason." The duke shrugged before his wife smacked him again. "Alright, alright, let's get home before I no longer have an arm."

Andromeda waved as Laszlo escorted her out. Isolde gave Saoirse a quick embrace before having Cyprian do the same with her. Then Saoirse was left alone with a new assortment of thoughts. What could have Emrys done to upset Vasili? Was it a misunderstanding? Surely he couldn't have done it intentionally.

Her thoughts spiraled as she sat by herself in the drawing room. It led to her being startled when Emrys called her name. She jumped in her seat before turning and finding him in the doorway.

"Are you alright?" he asked.

"Cyprian and Laszlo told me about Vasili," she answered.

Emrys went still. "What did they tell you?"

"That you upset him during council."

"Ah," he said, the tension in his posture relaxing. "It was a political quarrel that I take the blame for. I plan to rectify it soon."

That eased Saoirse's worry a bit. He owned up to his blunder like he had with her. It helped silence the lingering doubts she still fought. He was flawed just like everyone else. He may not be a mess like she was, but he wasn't perfect either. It made the argument of her deserving of less even more ridiculous.

"I'm glad to hear that." Saoirse gave him a small smile, and he attempted to return it. "Would you like to have dinner together tonight?"

That question perked him up. "I'd enjoy nothing more."

Saoirse rose from her seat and crossed the room to him, wrapping her arms around his waist and enveloping him in an embrace. He hesitantly returned it, the warmth of his hands seeping through her blouse.

"What is this for?" he asked.

"I was told you might need it," she said, her voice muffled by his waistcoat. Emrys embraced her more tightly, and she sighed against him. "And it was suggested I tell you something." She lifted her gaze and rested her chin squarely in the middle of his chest. The spark rippled through her, and she couldn't help but give a sedated smile. "I like it when you embrace me."

He quirked an eyebrow.

"And I'd like you to do it more often."

A smile tugged at his lips. "I can manage that."

Emrys *took a* day to think through his apology to Vasili. He weighed risking Kieran spilling the truth about his bond with Saoirse. Whether he lied about telling Saoirse or spoke up against Kieran in council, he took a gamble on her finding out from someone that wasn't him. But he couldn't let this conflict with Vasili linger either. He had really miffed the whole situation.

He paced the length of the sitting room, scratching at the nape of his neck, until Saoirse's door opening caught his attention. He whirled in her direction and felt the mating spark rush through him. She stepped out of her room and greeted him with a gentle smile.

"Hello," she said.

"Hello," he echoed.

"What are you doing?"

Emrys let his arm drop and sighed. "I'm working on how to apologize to Vasili."

"Are you going to Donheath?" she asked, her expression hopeful.

"Eventually." He gave her a half-smile. "But I think Calliope is volunteering the rest of this week, so she won't be there if you're thinking about visiting with her."

"Oh." Saoirse tried to hide her disappointment, but Emrys saw the excitement in her eyes dimmed.

"But speaking of Calliope, I believe Andromeda would love to make you a dress for Vasili and Calliope's anniversary dinner."

Joy lit her face again. "Will you accompany me to Cogwick?"

He shook his head. "I want to be surprised."

She smiled shyly at him. "As you wish." She took a few steps forward, and he assumed she was headed for the hall. But she surprised him and stepped in his direction, closing the distance between them. She rose on the balls of her feet, and her lips grazed his stubbly cheek. He had declined a shave that morning since he hadn't been spending close time with Saoirse lately. But now he regretted it.

She reached up his cheek and rubbed her fingertips over his stubble, a questioning look on her face.

"I didn't expect you to kiss me, so I'm not shaven," he explained.

Saoirse giggled and buried her face in his chest. Emrys brought his arms around her and pressed a kiss to her hair. Maybe he wouldn't have to risk Kieran telling her. They were making decent progress. At least that's what Emrys thought. And he had been plucking up the courage more and more to tell her himself.

He stroked her cheek, coaxing her to look at him. She slowly pulled away so their gazes could meet. "I'm going to go to Donheath today," he told her. "And tomorrow we can go to Cogwick together."

"What about being surprised?"

"I'll sit in Andromeda's shop with a blindfold the whole time."

She giggled again. "I can go myself. It's alright."

"Are you sure?"

"Yes." She nodded and leaned closer to him. Her gaze dropped to his lips, and he could feel her chest rising and falling against his with each breath. "I want to see your reaction the first time I wear it," she whispered. Her eyes flicked up to him, and she stepped back. "I hope you have a safe trip to Donheath, and I'll see you later today."

Emrys nodded, his body as taut as a violin string. He watched Saoirse disappear into the hall, and it took him several minutes to collect himself before he followed to request a carriage to Donheath.

Even while inside Vasili's home, Emrys could still sense the distinct smell of livestock. It wasn't pungent, but it definitely lingered. The duke hadn't given up his lifestyle when he came into his dukedom over fifty years ago. He had scaled back how many animals he raised and kept over the years, handing off the ones he could no longer care for to other farmers in his territory. The animals he did raise were no longer used to generate his income but to sustain his household in dairy goods. Instead, he did it because he liked it. But Emrys admired that about the fireann. Vasili participated as a duke because he was obligated to, but he kept and raised his animals because he loved them.

Emrys sat in the small drawing room, waiting for the duke to greet him. *If* he would greet him. Emrys would not be surprised if Vasili refused him outright. He had every reason to. Emrys had chosen to preserve himself rather than defend his friend. His secret was getting out of hand, and now his friends were paying the price for it.

"Emrys," Vasili said, standing in the doorway. His clothes were beyond what Emrys imagined as casual. He wore a tan striped collarless shirt, brown trousers, and no waistcoat to conceal his suspenders. His sleeves were rolled, and his hair looked like it had been flattened under a hat all morning.

"Vasili." Emrys stood. "Thank you for seeing me."

The duke shrugged. "It would look a bit cantankerous of me to refuse you." Vasili's expression was unamused, and Emrys knew he had to jump straight for his apology.

"I'm sorry, Vasili," he said. "I should have stood up for you, but I didn't."

"You chose to be selfish," Vasili countered, crossing his arms over his chest. He had always been honest, but never so harshly. "You don't want to face the consequences of telling Saoirse the truth, so you let Kieran bully me and the court into getting his way."

"I know." Emrys sighed, his gaze pleading. "But I'm changing that. I'm going to tell her."

The duke raised a brow. "Are you actually going to tell her, or are you just saying that to placate me?"

"I'm being honest," Emrys promised. "I'm going to tell her before the next council meeting."

Vasili studied him for a moment before sighing in defeat. "It's not completely necessary," he murmured. "After the meeting, I spoke to some of the local people, and they were enthusiastic about having the military watching our borders. They said they felt safer knowing there was a defense in place."

"Everyone is that shaken by the Fomóire sighting?" Emrys asked, intrigued. Vasili hadn't shared any reactions from his territory in council meetings, but that might have been something Emrys would have coaxed out of him to counteract Kieran's strong-arming.

Vasili nodded. "We've never had such a lethal threat. Everyone is willing to do anything to keep that threat away. I've done some thinking as well, and it wouldn't hurt to have a bit of protection in case they come close again. I'd rather do everything I can than look back and wonder what else I could have done."

Emrys stood stunned. "So you agree with Kieran's decision?"

"As much as any of us hate to admit it, yes, I agree with him."

As shocking as it was, Emrys understood Vasili's position. He had more than his pride to take care of. He had a territory to keep safe, and he was able to put aside his feelings about Kieran to decide what was best for everyone in his care. It was more than what Emrys could say about himself.

"You're a better fireann than me," he said, attempting to be light-hearted. "I'm still sorry. I chose myself over what was actually best for everyone. And whether or not this worked in your favor, Kieran bullied you into the decision, and I could have at least stopped him."

"Thank you," Vasili said with a half-smile. "I appreciate you recognizing that."

"So, will you forgive me?" Emrys asked. His heart pounded in his chest as he waited for Vasili to answer. Even though this ordeal had been beneficial for the duke in the end, Emrys still wasn't innocent.

Vasili took a deep breath, letting it out slowly. "Under one condition."

"Name your price," Emrys said. "I'll happily pay it."

"Tell your wife the truth," the duke said. "I've been told Calliope nearly ruined it for you at tea, and as much as Saoirse enjoys my wife's company, I think she'd take it much better coming from you."

"I promise I will." Emrys breathed a sigh of relief. "I was serious when I said I was going to tell her before the next council meeting."

"I'll believe it when it comes from Saoirse's mouth." Vasili smirked.

"You have no faith in me?" Emrys asked, feigning offense.

"Next to none." Vasili chuckled. "But I hope you prove me wrong. I have five hundred pounds on you telling her before Lughnasadh."

"Are you three taking bets on me?"

It wasn't the first time his friends had bet on one of them. The last was on Laszlo for when he would tell Andromeda how he felt about her. Isolde had won that jackpot.

"Four of us, actually," the duke corrected. "Andromeda overheard about it from Calliope and placed a bet of her own."

Emrys shook his head. His friends were brutal, but they kept him tethered to what mattered most. "Well, I hope to make you happy and wealthy soon." He chuckled. "Now, if you have time, why don't we craft a plan to make Kieran's army camps work in your favor?"

A wide smile spread on Vasili's face. "That sounds like a fine way to spend an afternoon."

S*aoirse tugged on* the hem of her jacket, smoothing it over
her bust. She was giddy at the thought of taking a carriage to
Cogwick to craft a dress with Andromeda. During the planning
of her wedding, she had made decisions about her dress, but they
were from fabric samples and ideas that Ada jotted down in her
notebook. She hadn't physically gone to the duchess's shop during
that process.

The heels of Saoirse's boots clicked against the wood floors of
the vestibule that led to the entry. She was preoccupied with tugging
on her gloves and hadn't noticed the figure that had crossed her
path.

"Your Highness." Kieran's voice made her gaze snap up at him.
"Traveling alone, are we?"

"By my own choice," Saoirse answered, her heart pounding in
her chest. She was determined to keep Kieran from twisting and
poisoning her thoughts any further. She was going to make it to
her carriage, and she would stomp on his foot to get there if need
be.

"It's for the best." The general shrugged. "Emrys is terrible
company."

"He's fine company," she said sharply. "But he has other
business, and so do I, so if you don't mind." She tried to shove past
him, but he caught her arm, yanking her around to face him.

"A lovely boireann like you shouldn't be traveling alone," he said. "Let me accompany you."

Saoirse clenched her jaw. "I'll be fine, thank you," she said through gritted teeth. "Let me go."

"Your Highness, I have no ill intentions." The saccharine sweet tone of his voice grated on her nerves. "I would hate for something to happen to you."

"I'll be fine," she repeated as she tried to wrench her hand away. His fingers tightened around her arm, and her heart beat erratically in her chest. The way he was restraining her, and the tightness of his grip, was sending her mind back to when Odysseus tried to do the same thing. Her lungs felt tight, and she couldn't move. The feeling in her hand was being cut off, and she couldn't summon her magic to defend herself if she tried.

"Kieran!" A shrill Scottish voice caused the general's grip on Saoirse to lax just enough for the feeling in her hand to return. Seraphina stormed towards them, murder glinting in her eyes. "Let go of her."

"This is none of your business," Kieran sneered.

"It is my business when you're giving Her Highness bruises," Seraphina spat at him. "Let go of her before I pull you into my office and experiment on you with some elixirs."

Kieran flared his nostrils at the healer but dropped Saoirse's arm unceremoniously.

"Good, now get your arse out of this house." The healer pointed a finger towards the front entry. "And don't return unless you've been asked."

Kieran didn't budge. "I'll have you know I was here on business. I had an urgent report for Alastair, and I will deliver whatever in Annwn I want."

"No, you won't." Seraphina looked like she was close to having steam flood from her ears. "I don't care if you have to send your most trusted errand boy, you will not step foot in this house unannounced again. Unless you want your arse scorched."

"You and I both know you don't have elemental magic." Kieran smirked devilishly at the healer, challenging her, but Seraphina's gaze was sharp and unflinching.

"No, but nothing is stopping me from branding your arse on the stove."

The general's stare turned to shock in response to the threat. Quickly, he stole a glance at Saoirse before growling and storming towards the front door without another word.

Saoirse felt the breath return to her lungs, and her hands shook as she rubbed at her forearm. She tried to calm herself, but the tremor continued to run through her. Seraphina cautiously approached her, the healer's expression softening once the general was gone.

"Are you alright, dear?" she asked.

Saoirse nodded, but her body still vibrated with the sudden rush of distress that had hit her.

"Why don't we get a cup of tea, hmm?" Seraphina shepherded her towards the kitchen and pulled a chair out for her at the small wooden table in the corner of the kitchen. It was crudely made with uneven edges, but the top was smooth and varnished.

Saoirse sat in the little wooden chair and tore off her gloves. Her breathing became more rapid as she unbuttoned her jacket with her shaking fingers and shrugged out of it. When she finally felt like her clothes weren't suffocating her anymore, she focused her attention on the rhythm of her breathing.

She heard whispering before Ada placed a cup of tea in front of her, and she noticed Seraphina was gone. With a deep breath, Saoirse reached for the teacup and found her hands were still shaking. She supported it with her other hand so as to not splash any tea on herself. She successfully brought the cup to her lips and sipped it slowly. The honey flavor was a small comfort, and she continued to sip at it.

Her mind raced with thoughts, ranging from digesting what happened to berating herself for what she failed to do in response. Self-pity set in, and she tried to ward off the tears, but they swam at the bottom of her vision. She felt a tightness in her chest, and the ability to take a full breath escaped her. The feeling didn't subside until the chair next to her was occupied and a familiar scent immediately soothed her.

Emrys watched a carriage he recognized pull away from the house as he approached the front door. Kieran. Agitation hit him instantly. It was only made worse by his involuntary flinch as the sound of a whip struck the air. He let out a low growl, hoping it would help work off his frustration. He turned towards the front door and only got a few steps inside before Seraphina's Scottish brogue bombarded him.

"Emrys," she said sternly.

The hair on the back of his neck stood up at the tone she used. It was a tone that never led to anything good.

"Come with me, my boy." Seraphina waved to follow her.

"What happened?" he asked, following the healer through the house towards the kitchen.

"Kieran grabbed Saoirse, and she's not hurt, but she is spooked."

Emrys's blood ran cold. Damn that bastard getting away with touching Saoirse again. "Why did you let him go?"

"Because I wanted him as far from Saoirse as possible," Seraphina answered. "And I threatened to brand his arse if he came back."

Amusement from her threat was lost on him as all he could focus on was Saoirse. Kieran had put his hands on her again. Maybe it was for the best that Seraphina had run him off. Emrys would have probably hunted him down and broken his fingers one by one. He had come between his relationship with Saoirse too many times now.

Seraphina led Emrys into the kitchen, where he found Saoirse sitting and clutching a cup of tea in her hands. Ada was standing behind her and plucking pins from her hair. Once her hair was free, Ada ran her fingers through the loose waves, combing them. She began to braid Saoirse's hair, sliding her fingers through the strawberry blonde locks and pulling in bits as she braided the strands.

Emrys sat next to Saoirse and noticed she was trembling. "Are you alright?" He wanted to reach out and touch her, but he knew better than to do that after Kieran had grabbed her without her permission.

Saoirse nodded, but it was unsteady. Her arms shook as she placed her cup of tea on the table. She flattened her hands on the wood surface and took several shaky breaths.

"Being strong doesn't mean you can't show emotion," Emrys said softly. "If it did, it would make you Cyprian."

She breathed out a laugh, but she quickly sucked in her bottom lip. Her eyes closed and tears fell, leaving wide, wet tracks on her cheeks in their wake. When she opened her eyes, she turned to him, and Emrys's heart squeezed. That same pain he saw when her magic manifested from her nightmare was in her eyes now. He felt helpless watching her have to handle the aftermath of being touched without her permission.

In one swift motion, Saoirse reached out and wrapped her arms around Emrys's neck and buried her face in his collar. She softly cried, and her body vibrated with the emotion. Emrys wrapped his arm around her back while he wedged his other under her legs. He shifted her onto his lap, and her grip on him tightened.

"I froze," she said, her voice thick. "I didn't know what to do, so I stood there, letting him keep hold of me."

"That's a completely normal response," Emrys told her. He ran his hand up and down the length of her spine, hoping it provided at least some comfort to her. He had the urge to use the bond to relieve her pain, but this wasn't the time or place to explain that. "He caught you off guard. It's why he did it. He didn't want you to react."

"I don't want it to happen again. I *can't* let it happen again. I can't."

Emrys knew she wasn't talking about Kieran merely touching her arm. The thought of that fireann trying to force himself onto her...his thoughts were nothing short of murderous.

"I won't let that happen," he told her. "I'm going to do

everything in my power to keep that from happening."

Saoirse's breathing was labored, but it was even. Her face was still buried in the crook of Emrys's neck. The feel of her body in his arms was bittersweet. She was so warm and smelled of vanilla and sandalwood, but the circumstances that put her there made his chest feel tight. He tried to see the silver lining, that she wanted him to comfort her, that she didn't push him away because she felt unworthy of his comfort. She trusted him, but the realization was vastly overshadowed by what she had experienced.

His mind churned with thoughts, some of them consisting of the unspeakable things he wanted to do Kieran. But most of them were ideas on how to protect Saoirse. He couldn't stand guard at the door, barring Kieran from entering. He couldn't hover over her all hours of the day either. For one thing, she would most likely get tired of the act of shielding her constantly and tell him to piss off. For another, he had a job to do and couldn't sacrifice it to keep tabs on her or act as gatekeeper.

He needed to supply her with the tools to respond with action. Kieran was refusing to listen to anyone and stay away like he should. Emrys would have to equip Saoirse with a way to ward Kieran off. She had a decent control on her magic. Teaching her how to wield it to protect herself wouldn't be a bad start. He had just started plotting the lesson in his mind when Saoirse pulled back.

Her cheeks were stained with tears, and he held off the urge to wipe them away. She felt so small and vulnerable in his arms. If he could, he would hold her until they rotted away with the earth.

"Emrys," she said, her voice soft and hoarse. "I—" Her eyes flicked behind him, and he knew it was in awareness of Ada and Seraphina who were still hovering nearby. She leaned closer to him, their faces nearly touching. "I don't want to be alone tonight."

"You don't have to be." He finally slipped the leash on his self-restraint and wiped at the tear stains on one side of her face. "You don't ever have to be alone."

She pressed her forehead against his. "Thank you," she whispered.

Something felt so normal about the way they were touching. It was intimate and raw. Saoirse was trusting him enough to let him touch her, hold her, comfort her. She wanted to sleep by him again. That was something Emrys didn't think he'd do again until—gods, he didn't know when he would earn that simple joy again. He didn't feel deserving of it, yet he wasn't going to deny her when she needed it.

He still felt they had a long way before their relationship reached the state it was prior to it crumbling from Kieran's meddling. But he was dedicated to putting in his effort and staying patient. The pay off was slow, but incredibly worth it.

Emrys *bounced on* his toes as he waited for Saoirse to join him outside. He hadn't been this anxious to train her since their first lesson. While learning to aim her magic was a useful exercise in controlling said magic, it wasn't a useful skill. At least, not in their current circumstances. Most of what was taught to fae were skills whose uses had long since gone extinct. They had been living in a time of peace for over two centuries. Combat magic skills weren't necessary and were only taught so students had practice manifesting and controlling their magic.

Today's lesson, however, was necessary, and Emrys wished he had planned it earlier. The thought of Saoirse feeling helpless triggered a heightened protective reaction thanks to the mating bond. But Saoirse would most likely tell him to find the Hounds of Annwn if he followed her around at all hours of the day in the name of safety. Teaching her how to use her magic to defend herself was his next best idea.

In the distance, a figure emerged from the house, and as it drew closer, Emrys's heart skipped. Saoirse looked much more put together this afternoon. Last night, she had slept in his bed with him, and it was the best night of sleep he had in over a week. But he heard her sniffles and the shaky breaths she took during the night as she fell asleep. It had gutted him to lie there, helpless to ease her further. He had pulled her in as close as she would let him and sagged in relief when he felt her body finally grow heavy and still. Now, Saoirse strode across the lawn, and Emrys gave her an easy smile.

"No stakes today?" she asked, one corner of her lips lifting.

"No, not today." He shook his head. "Aiming your magic is all well and good, but I want to give you some practical ways to use it."

"Like what? Starting a fire in our hearth?"

"Like defending yourself."

Any hint of a smile on Saoirse's face fell. "Is this about yesterday?" She crossed her arms over her chest, and her gaze dropped to the toe of her boot digging into the grass.

"This is about the times you've told me you didn't know what to do." He took a step towards her, and she looked up at him sheepishly. "It's normal to freeze, but I want to give you at least one tool to help you."

"Only one?" she asked, arching a brow.

"Well, I plan to teach you several." Emrys reached out and placed a hand on her shoulder. "But if you remember and execute at least one, you have a good chance at snapping out of being frozen."

Saoirse's whisper of a smile returned, and she nodded, dropping her hands to her side. "What do you have for me first?"

"First, a few actions that can be done without magic." He reached for Saoirse's arm and lifted it as he wrapped his hand around her wrist. "If fear petrifies you, you may not be able to call your magic. So knowing how to get out of a grip without it is important." He tightened his grip and felt Saoirse go still. "If you're taken by the arm, you're going to want use your free hand and grab onto my pinky finger."

Saoirse wedged her fingers under his and gripped his pinky.

"Now, twist my finger."

She carefully twisted it, and he responded by releasing his grip.

"Move your arm away and twist my whole hand towards my body until my palm is facing up and my arm is behind my back."

She followed his instructions and disarmed him by pinning his arm behind him.

"Good, now, let's do it a little faster and with a little more conviction." He wrapped his hand around her arm again, and she murmured his steps aloud as she repeated what he had taught her. With each attempt, she did it more fluidly and with a vigor that had Emrys's finger nearly sore.

"Alright, let's give my pinky a break." He shook out his hand and flexed it a few times. "Why don't we work on escaping a few other holds?"

Emrys taught her a few more strategies for if she was grabbed by her waist or her hair. With each repetition, he noticed her growing more confident, yanking his arms into their disarmed state with more unmitigated force. He wasn't sure who was going to be more sore by the end of this session, Saoirse or his limbs. If only it would be for a more pleasurable reason...

He stopped that train of thought before it could go further. He and Saoirse were nowhere near revisiting physical intimacy. And he wasn't going to be the one to bring the subject up even if they were. He'd have to keep those thoughts for when he was alone and uninterrupted.

"How are you feeling about disarming someone without magic?" Emrys asked.

"I feel good about it." Saoirse smiled, and it made his heart leap in his chest. "But I think I'd feel better if I knew how to add magic."

He slowly grinned. "We can add magic." He unbuttoned the cuffs of his shirt and rolled them up to his elbows, exposing his forearms. "Anything I just taught you can be enhanced with magic and disarm someone completely by its mere use. If you can summon it, your magic is your best tool to escaping someone trying to restrain you."

He gripped her arm again and pulled his magic to his fingers. He didn't let ice manifest on his palms but held it just under the surface of his skin like he had taught Saoirse in previous lessons. "I want you to summon your magic and hold the fire in your palm."

Saoirse nodded, and he watched as her breathing slowed. Heat brushed against his ice, and he smiled. An orange flame flickered on her palm and the tips of her fingers. The heat of her magic seeped further through the thin sleeves of her blouse and into Emrys's hand. When he felt it creeping towards a temperature that he knew would bring consequences, he released his grip.

"Good!" he praised.

"I didn't hurt you?" Saoirse asked quickly.

"You won't hurt me," he promised. He held up his bare arm to her. "Pull back your magic and feel my skin."

The flame in Saoirse's hand dissipated, and she gingerly ran her fingers over his skin.

"Not only is my magic protecting me, but I know when to pull away before it gets too hot."

"What if someone used their magic to protect them like you are?" she asked. "Mine wouldn't be useful then."

"Unless someone with an ice element knows you have a fire element, your magic will work just fine."

Saoirse's fingers lingered on his skin, and she nodded absently. His brief intimate thoughts from earlier crept back, and this time it was harder to rein them in. She touched him so delicately, and while his magic was keeping him from feeling most of her touch, it was enough to feed his imagination.

He shook himself and slowly pulled his arm away. "Are you ready practice some new grips with your magic?"

Saoirse nodded, and he stepped around to stand behind her. He slid his arm over the front of her chest and held her against him.

Saoirse stiffened, and Emrys wasn't sure if it was from the way he was restraining her or if she could feel his ill-timed arousal against her. He swallowed that embarrassment and tried to speak his instructions evenly.

"Take one or both hands and grip my arm," he said.

She did as he instructed and firmly grabbed his arm with both her hands. A little proud smile twitched on his lips. She was committing to his instructions without hesitation. Her confidence in her abilities was growing, and he couldn't help but be proud of her progress.

"Since your palms are on me this time, manifest your magic to where it's sitting just below your skin." He felt warmth begin to brush against his arm. "My arm might be protected by magical frozen temperatures, but my skin is still susceptible to an open flame."

Saoirse's shoulders vibrated in silent amusement, but she let it dissipate as she summoned her magic. Heat rapidly licked against Emrys's arm, and his grin of pride stretched further.

"Excellent," he murmured into her ear. His nose brushed against her hair and he caught a whiff of her sweet scent. He was so tempted to drop a kiss into her hair. It would be so brief and light. She might not even notice it.

Suddenly, he felt a sting on his arm that rapidly turned to a scalding burn. He hissed as he pulled his arm out of her grip and clenched his jaw in pain. He didn't dare swear out loud, lest he let Saoirse think she harmed him.

But it was too late. She spun and gasped at him. He forced himself to look at her and found her staring at him in shock and remorse.

"Emrys, I'm so sorry," she said. She began to reach for him, but then pulled her hands back, an expression of fear and guilt on her face.

His heart sank. It was his own fault he got burned. He wanted to blame the bond for distracting him, but it was his own bodily desire that took his thoughts somewhere they shouldn't have been. "I'm fine," he said, shaking his head. He flooded more of his own magic into his arm and cringed at the pain it brought. "You didn't hurt me. The heat startled me was all."

"Emrys, your arm is blistering."

He looked down at his arm and sure enough, bright pink blisters in the outline of Saoirse's hands were bubbling on his skin. "Right." He sighed, holding back a grunt. "I should, um, have Seraphina make sure it's not serious." He turned back towards the house and heard footsteps trail alongside him.

"I'm coming with you," she insisted.

"You don't have to," he countered. "It'll be five minutes of me complaining about the way her ointment smells, and then she'll probably bandage my arm for good measure. It's anything but exciting."

"But it's my fault," Saoirse said, her voice dropping lower. "I want to make sure you're alright."

Emrys wished he could assure her that it wasn't her fault in the slightest. He wanted to pull her close and kiss her deeply to get his point across. But that would cause more issues than there already were.

"You're more than welcome to come along," he conceded. "But please don't think it's your fault."

She stayed quiet as she trailed behind him into the house and through the hall to Seraphina's office. When they walked through the doorway, Emrys's nose was hit with the pungent scents of the herbs and oils the healer kept. He already dreaded the remedy she was going to use. It wasn't going to be pleasant, but he guessed that was what he deserved for letting his mind slip to where it shouldn't.

He stood on one side of the large work table in the middle of the room, Seraphina on the other side at her desk facing the wall. "Afternoon, Mamanna," he murmured.

The healer turned in her chair, her expression going from pleasant surprise to scrutiny. "To what do I owe this visit?"

Emrys extended his left arm towards her and revealed the blistered skin. "I think this might need attention."

Seraphina stood and leaned over the table to inspect his injury. "Well, you're right about that." The healer bustled over to a cabinet and glasses clinked as she dug through its contents.

"I tried to fix it with my magic," Emrys confessed.

Seraphina sighed. "Then it's too late to tell you to not soothe it with ice." She pulled out a jar with a light pink cream inside it and brought it back to where Emrys had his arm extended. "Ice will make it harder to heal." Seraphina popped open the jar lid and scooped out a dollop with three fingers. She spread it over the blistered skin and Emrys let out the grunt he had been holding back. It stung his tender skin, and he silently swore at himself for letting it happen.

"It was my fault to begin with," Saoirse said quietly.

"No, it wasn't," Emrys argued. "It was mine. I wasn't paying attention and didn't pull away when I should have."

"I believe that much more than Saoirse maliciously burning you," Seraphina said as she carefully covered his injury with her remedy. "Probably was letting his groin think more than his brain."

"Mamanna," he growled. His face heated, and he didn't dare look over at Saoirse.

But to his surprise, her soft hand slipped into his free one, and she wove her fingers with his. He squeezed it three times, and she gave a single squeeze in return. His shoulders relaxed from her touch, and he drew circles with his thumb on the back of her hand.

Seraphina finished lathering his injury with ointment and wrapped it in gauze to keep it clean. "See me tomorrow for a fresh bandage," she said as she tucked the tail of the gauze into itself. "It should take two or three days to heal. Maybe a bit more. Using your magic on it will slow down the healing by a day or so."

"I'll remember that for next time." Emrys flexed his arm and bent it to evaluate how tight the bandage was and if it hindered him at all. He had most of his range of motion, and the sting in his arm was dissipating. "Now that I'm bandaged," he turned to Saoirse, "We can return to our lesson."

"No." She shook her head. "I think you taught me enough for today."

"Saoirse, I'm fine," he tried to argue. But she stubbornly shook her head again.

"I'm not continuing today. I don't want you to make your injury worse or give you another one. We can pick up lessons again when you're healed."

Emrys looked to Seraphina who gave him a look that told him she wasn't about to intervene. He was on his own with this one. "Alright," he said. "We'll pick up lessons again in a day or two."

"Thank you," she murmured. She lifted the hand she held to

her lips and pressed a kiss to the back of it.

Her gaze lifted to his, and the mating spark roared to life inside him. Her next movements were swift, and Emrys barely had time to register them. She slid her free hand to the back of his neck and pulled him towards her, their lips meeting. The kiss felt soft and precious. And incredibly fleeting. Saoirse pulled away from him slowly, her hand sliding to his chest.

Her eyes were focused on his throat, and she chewed on her bottom lip. Cailleach's quim, how he wished he could be the one to do that to her lip.

"Saoirse," he whispered.

"If yo two are going to make sheep's eyes at each other, you'll need to do it elsewhere." Seraphina's sharp brogue interrupted them.

Emrys slid his gaze to her and saw the withering stare she gave him. Stifling a chuckle, he slipped his hand from Saoirse's and wrapped it around her waist, pulling her close and pressing his lips to her forehead. They then shuffled out of the office and into the hall.

A lilting giggle slipped from Saoirse as she pulled him into a corner of the hall. Her teeth sunk into her bottom lip as she gazed up at him. Another giggle trickled out from her, and Emrys couldn't help but grin at her.

"What?" he asked softly.

"I haven't felt this giddy since our wedding," she said.

His grin grew wider. "I'm happy to re-enact that night with you."

She shook her head, amusement glittering in the gold flecks of her eyes until she looked down at his bandaged arm. Her smile fell a bit. "Once you're healed," she whispered. "Then we'll re-visit that topic."

He kissed her forehead again. "As you wish, Princess." Emrys's heart felt light and his head a bit fuzzy as he let his lips linger on her. This was the first time since they started mending their relationship that Saoirse had entertained out loud anything physical. His earlier thoughts crept back, and for a moment, he let them. The taste of her, the flush of her skin, the sounds he knew she could make, they flooded his mind like a dam had broken.

He might have made a poor choice to allow the thoughts to overwhelm him. If he didn't pull himself together, he would embarrass himself in front of more than just Saoirse. Emrys took a deep breath and pushed his carnal thoughts aside. He would get to live them out eventually. Saoirse had all but guaranteed it.

Saoirse tried to sleep alone, but she ended up flopping onto her back and kicking her bedding off her legs. She stared up at the ceiling and let out a sigh. The reason she chose to sleep in her own bed was similar to why Emrys had insisted she do the same on their wedding night. She would certainly do something beyond what she was emotionally prepared for if she shared the same bed as Emrys.

But laying in her own bed only allowed her thoughts to run wild. She thought through the afternoon and guilt sunk in her stomach. She had lost her concentration when Emrys stood behind her and wrapped his arm around her shoulders. His body had been so close to hers, and his lips had barely brushed her ear. It was enough to distract her and forget how far she was supposed to let her magic manifest. It had resulted in burning Emrys's arm to the point it blistered.

He had tried to assure her it hadn't been her fault, but it was hard for her to convince herself that was true. Seraphina had hinted that Emrys was distracted for the same reasons, but he wasn't the one manifesting magic that could harm someone.

But even though she had been weighed down by guilt, her arousal was still strong, and she had acted on impulse. The moment her lips touched his, the guilt had washed away. He confirmed in that kiss what Seraphina had alluded to. He had been just as bothered as she was.

Saoirse kicked the rest of her bedding off and swung her legs over the side of the bed. The cold floor bit at her bare feet, and she quickly scurried to her door and across the sitting room. She took a deep breath as she wrapped her fingers around the doorknob of Emrys's room and slowly turned it. She peeked into the dark bedroom and saw Emrys shift in her direction.

"Can you not sleep either?" he asked, his voice thick with exhaustion.

Her heart kicked up. "No," she responded feebly. "Is it because of your injury?"

"My injury is just fine," he said. "You can come see for yourself."

Saoirse stood in his doorway, contemplating his offer.

"Saoirse." His voice became firmer. "Come here."

She heard bedding rustle as she took a step into the room. It only took a few more steps before she reached the edge of his bed. She craned her neck, but the room was too dark for her eyes to adjust to see anything on his body.

"Lay down," he urged.

"But—"

"I know you're not here to check my wound. Last night was..."

"Was the first night since I told you I wanted to leave," Saoirse finished. Sleeping on her own after her incident with Kieran wasn't going to be comforting. When she was sitting in the kitchen, fending off her urge to sob, the only person she wanted near her was Emrys. She couldn't explain it, but his presence alone was a comfort.

Then there was the physical way he comforted her. He didn't press her to calm her emotions or offer a minimal pat of sympathy. No, he had held her and wiped her tears, things he had done since shortly after they had met. He didn't treat her like a burden in those moments. He showed her something that no one else had, and she was beginning to cast her doubts away and believe she deserved his care after all.

"Yes," Emrys said. "And I hope I'm not the only one who noticed my sleep was better than it has been for the past few weeks."

Saoirse couldn't argue against that. While her thoughts still bit at her, causing her to spill more tears, once she had fallen asleep, she stayed asleep.

"You don't have to stay," Emrys added. "But if you—"

Just like with their kiss earlier, Saoirse slid into the bed before she could second-guess herself. She lay on her back and immediately felt the warmth of his body next to her. She could see Emrys a bit better being this close, and he was on his side with his head propped with one hand. His bandage stood out against the dark figure of his body, and she reached for it. She intertwined her fingers with his and pulled his arm in front of her. While she inspected his arm, she paid attention to any winces or whimpers of pain. When nothing manifested, she brought his arm to her lips and brushed them against the gauze.

"I can't begin to describe how I've missed those kisses," he purred in her ear.

"Don't you know kisses are full of secret healing magic?" She grinned and leaned her head towards him.

"Seraphina has never shared that bit of healing expertise with me." Emrys chuckled. His fingers that were woven with hers fidgeted and traced shapes on the back of her hand.

"Emrys," she whispered. "I really am sorry about injuring you."

His fingers stilled in her hand. "I appreciate that, but you have nothing to be sorry for. I lost my attention for a moment and paid the price for it."

"I...I did, too," Saoirse confessed.

Another chuckle erupted from him. "I think that kiss you gave me earlier told me that."

Her face heated, and she buried it in the crook of his neck. Emrys kissed her forehead, and she sighed. Her eyes grew heavy, and the arousal she thought would overtake her lay dormant. All she wanted was to be held by Emrys and sleep.

"Saoirse," he asked groggily. "Can we make this a regular occurrence again?"

"I'd like nothing more," she whispered back.

He slid his hand from hers and wrapped it around the dip of her waist. He kissed her shoulder and ran his fingers over the side of her ribs in a rhythmically movement, lulling Saoirse further towards sleep. She sighed before fully relaxing against him and surrendering to slumber.

Emrys *signed his* name for the fifteenth time on a piece of parchment that would be sent along with a stack of letters addressed to various nobles. Every year he was invited by over a dozen different types of nobilities and each year he had to decline their invitations. Lughnasadh was Calliope and Vasili's anniversary, and each year they chose to celebrate with the rest of the court. Snubbing his friends was not something he was in the business of doing, especially with how fragile his friendship with Vasili currently was.

Emrys had chosen to do this task in the council room as the afternoon light was warming that side of the house. As he placed his weighted stamp on top of hot, plum-colored wax on the closure of an envelope, he heard a commotion that sounded like a hoard of birds being disturbed outside. He stood and crossed to the room to the ceiling height window that overlooked the lawn behind the house.

Sure enough, there was a flurry of black birds flying out from the line of trees on the edge of the lawn. Emrys knitted his brows, wondering what had disturbed such a massive flock. Out of the corner of his eye, he saw more movement, but this time it was on the lawn. He slid his gaze in that direction and a grin grew over his face. Saoirse had found fresh stakes and planted them in the lawn in various patterns. Next to her feet was a bucket, and he assumed it was full of water since she was practicing alone and he wasn't around to extinguish any rogue flames.

Saoirse was shaking out her hands. She must have let loose a bit too much magic, hence the frantic flock of birds. Emrys watched her roll her shoulders before she pulled her arm back and let a grapefruit-sized ball of fire shoot from her palm. It hit what he assumed was its intended target, and he caught her little motion of victory.

Emrys chuckled to himself as he continued to watch her practice. She hadn't let him train her for the last two days since his injury still hadn't fully healed. Her paranoia about hurting him again had waned, but she had made it clear she wanted him completely healed before he got near her with her magic again. He respected her request, but he had been apprehensive. He worried this incident would cause her to refuse their training sessions altogether, but that worry was relieved watching her practice on her own.

"How many Lughnasadh invitations did you receive this year?" His father's voice made Emrys nearly jump. He turned to find Alastair studying the stack of sealed envelopes.

"Over two dozen," Emrys answered.

"Everyone wants to have the royal newlyweds at their celebrations," Alastair remarked. He ambled to an empty chair and sat, plopping his portfolio he had brought with him onto the polished surface of the table. "Vasili and Calliope are fortunate you accept their dinner invitation every year."

"I wouldn't ever choose anyone else over my friends," Emrys replied. "Besides, Saoirse has grown fond of the duchesses of the court."

"Has she?"

Emrys nodded, and with one last long look at Saoirse outside, he took his seat at the table again. "I don't think she had anyone like them back home."

"You think?" Alastair's brows raised in surprise.

"From what I've learned about her brother, I pray the fae of Ireland are shown mercy by the gods."

"Eamon is a bit of an arse." Alastair pulled a stack of paper from his portfolio and flipped through the pages. "I hope Saoirse doesn't miss him too terribly."

"I don't think she misses him at all." Emrys punctuated his statement with a chuckle. "He's left quite a mark on her, though."

"How so?" Alastair asked. "Did he lay a hand on her?"

"No." Emrys shook his head. "At least, I don't believe he did. He's done more damage to her mind and confidence. It seems he emphasized perfection at all costs with her and if she fell short..."

"She took all the blame for the fallout," Alastair provided.

Emrys nodded. "I think she's started to unlearn at least a bit of it, but the marks of that pressure are still there."

Another round of squawking outside caught Alastair's attention, and he startled. "What in Cernunnos's Wilderness is going on outside?"

"Saoirse is practicing her magic," Emrys answered. "Every once in a while, she manifests a bit too much of it and startles the wildlife."

"Why is she practicing alone?"

Emrys swallowed. "It's a long story."

Alastair craned his head towards the window. "I think you should go out there."

"She's alright." Emrys waved off his suggestion.

"Emrys." his father's voice dropped to a serious tone. "Go out there."

"Father—"

"Take this advice not as your father but as a fireann who has loved and lost. Go outside and join your wife. Cherish any and every moment the gods give you with her."

Alastair's steel blue eyes pierced through Emrys. He wasn't going to let Emrys argue any further. When it came to Saoirse, his father was nearly as protective as he was but in a much stranger way.

Emrys finally conceded and stood from his seat. He entered the hallway and made his way to the nearest door that led outside. He stepped out onto the terrace and came up to the railing.

Saoirse was concentrating and had one stake left untouched. Wisps of hair fell around her face, a few pieces sticking to her sweaty forehead. Her chest heaved as she stood catching her breath. With a deep, cleansing breath, she reeled her arm back and shot out a strong blast of fire. It struck dead center on the stake and she exclaimed in excitement. A smaller flock of birds emerged from the trees in response and flew over the house.

"It looks like the birds are celebrating with you," Emrys said.

Saoirse startled at his voice, but her surprise was quickly replaced with glee. "How long have you been standing there?"

"Just a few minutes," he answered. "But I saw you earlier from the council room window."

She looked over her shoulder in the direction of the council room. "You were watching me?"

"A bit." He shrugged. "I didn't think you'd want to work with your magic after what happened."

"I know how important it is that I practice," she said shyly. "You've only knocked me over the head with that emphasis."

He grinned and leaned against the rail of the terrace. "Of all the things I've said, I'm glad you've at least walked away with that imprinted on you."

Saoirse returned his grin and strolled towards the terrace stairs. She stepped up to where he was standing, and Emrys became highly aware of how close she was now. He could see just how much of her hair was stuck to her forehead and temple with sweat. Cautiously, he raised his hand and brushed the wet, limp bits of hair out of her face. His hand lingered on her cheek and for a moment, he was tempted to close the space between them. He hungered to taste her lips again. They hadn't kissed since Seraphina's office, and he craved her more and more each day.

"Emrys," she whispered in a husky voice. Her tongue darted out and licked her lips. Her gaze was locked on his, and a slow smile crept across her face. "I'm proud of myself."

He let out an uneven, breathy laugh. "I'm proud of you, too."

Saoirse rose on her toes and claimed his mouth with hers. This kiss was much more passionate than before, and Emrys wasn't going to let her pull away so quickly this time. His arm slid around her waist and pulled her close. Her body melted into his, and she let out a little sigh.

Saoirse's fingers slid into his hair, and her nails scratched along his scalp. Gooseflesh rippled all over his skin, but he didn't have the energy to care. Saoirse tasted too good to stop, even briefly. Her tongue slid over the seam of his lips, and he didn't hesitate to part them. He relished the feel of her tongue exploring his and the little noises she made that went straight to his cock. There was just enough sense in his head to not push any further than kissing her, but the urge to toss it aside and ravish her on the terrace was a mighty temptation.

Saoirse was the first to break their kiss, pulling away and breathing heavily. Her lips were a brighter shade of pink than they were a moment ago, and she had a dazed expression dancing on her face. "I..." She chewed on her swollen bottom lip.

Emrys pressed his forehead against hers. She swallowed audibly and tried again.

"I..." She sighed and brushed a kiss over his lips. It was much sweeter than the last. "I think I feel worthy."

Heat rushed through Emrys's body, and he pulled her into him, holding her. She nuzzled her face against his chest and sighed. Joy flooded him once again, and he sent up a silent prayer of thanks to the gods. Saoirse felt worthy of him for once, and they were nearly back to where they were prior. Just a bit more assurance, and he felt confident in sharing the truth with her. He had to tell her so that Kieran could no longer hang anything over him. He just hoped he didn't lose Saoirse by doing the right thing.

Saoirse stepped through the doorway of the little dress shop in Cogwick. She hadn't gotten to visit the week before, but Andromeda had been gracious enough to bring samples and take her measurements after tea with the duchesses. She invited her to her shop to have a final fitting before the dinner, and Saoirse was downright giddy to visit.

She didn't know exactly what she expected from a dress shop that Andromeda owned and managed, but it surprised her how simple it was when she walked inside. Rolls of jewel-toned fabric were hung on the wall to her left, and glass cases showcasing accessories and jewelry sat to her right. Saoirse stepped closer to the case and admired the items on display. She wondered to herself if Andromeda would loan one to her for the next evening. There was a beautiful teardrop amethyst pendant wreathed in diamonds that would compliment her dress.

Saoirse's gaze roamed to the two mannequins that flanked the glass case. One was dressed in a wedding gown that looked a few decades behind the current fashion, the other clothed in a lilac day dress that looked more in line with the trends. Both looked to be made with a meticulous attention to detail. The seams were sewn in precision-quality straight lines, and the lace and beaded details didn't have a stray thread in sight.

"Saoirse," a sweet voice she recognized said.

Saoirse turned around to see Calliope seated on a round, tufted stool. Her ornately carved cane leaned against the wall behind her. Saoirse smiled at the duchess. "Good afternoon, Calliope."

"Good afternoon." Calliope returned the warm smile. "Are you also here to pick up a gown?"

"A fitting, actually."

"Andromeda really is burning the midnight oil." The duchess giggled. "Tomorrow is the dinner, and she's just finished my dress and still has work to do on yours. That boireann is going to work herself into the grave."

"I do it because it makes my friends happy." Andromeda's voice came from behind Saoirse. "If you were a mere customer, I would tell you you were all out of luck for something last minute." Andromeda squeezed Saoirse in a side embrace. "Let's get you dressed in your gown."

The duchess led her to a small dressing room at the back of the shop where a deep plum-colored gown hung on a hook. Saoirse didn't get much of a look at the dress before Andromeda was unfastening it. She instructed Saoirse to undress down to her corset and petticoats and guided her through the process of dressing into the complicated gown. Saoirse stepped out into the corner of the shop that had a small platform and several mirrors. She hopped up on the dais and took a long look at the dress before Andromeda commanded her to stay still.

The duchess made a few pins and tucks, giving the dress more shape and accentuating Saoirse's figure. Saoirse noticed the dress was looking a bit plain with only some pleating on the skirt done. But just as she thought that, Andromeda began to rummage in a chest and pulled out rolls of lace and beading. She placed them on a small table nearby and picked up several more pins.

"So how are you and Emrys?" she asked as she reached for a roll of lace and unfurled it. "Has he gotten on his knees to show you just how worthy you are?" Andromeda winked at her in the mirror.

"Andromeda!" Calliope scolded before lowering her tone to a whisper. "We're in a public place."

Andromeda looked around and shrugged. "I have no other customers, and my girls have heard me say much worse in the sewing room."

Saoirse giggled but quickly composed herself so as to not get stuck with a pin as Andromeda placed the lace at her neckline. "We've...made progress."

"Oh?" Andromeda asked, clipping the lace.

"I'm learning I really do deserve more than I think I do," Saoirse answered shyly.

"Oh, I see." Andromeda smirked. "Have you passed into worthy of a good fuck territory?"

Saoirse saw Calliope nervously swivel her head to the door and stifled a giggle. "Not quite, but we've gotten much closer. And I mean more than just physically."

"Vasili will be happy to hear that," Calliope remarked.

Andromeda whipped her head towards the duchess. She made a motion with her hands that Saoirse couldn't decipher.

"Laszlo said he and Emrys had a bit of a falling out," Saoirse said. "Emrys didn't tell me what it was about, just that it was political. Did Vasili tell you?"

"No." Calliope sighed. "He said something about Kieran and the army. But I honestly don't follow court politics well, and he had no desire to talk about it at length, so I left it alone. He seemed to be less bothered by it the next day. He even talked about it cheerily. And Emrys had made the effort to come all the way to Donheath to apologize. It's all water under the bridge."

Saoirse gave a small smile. It was the same amount of effort Emrys had put in with her. He cared for her and anticipated many of her needs before she even knew them. "I'm happy they were able to remedy that."

"I am, too." The duchess sighed. "It was a hard night. I hate when he detaches and I can't do anything to help. But he gained some clarity after a good night of sleep and having local discussions. He isn't a pushover, but he isn't a stubborn mule either."

"No, the stubborn mule would be Cyprian." Andromeda chuckled. She lowered to her knees and pinned up the hem of Saoirse's dress.

"Does that make Laszlo the pushover?" Calliope giggled.

Andromeda snorted in amusement. "Hardly. If he were a pushover, I'd own half this territory, and you'd catch me in council meetings more often than tea."

The duchess instructed Saoirse to spin so she could hem another portion of her dress. Saoirse obeyed and turned two more times before Andromeda was finished.

"Alright," the duchess said "Let's get you out of the gown so my girls can finish the alterations. I'll have it ready and sent to you first thing tomorrow morning."

They returned to the dressing room where Andromeda helped her carefully removed the gown without sticking herself or dislodging the pins. When Saoirse was dressed in her day clothes again, she emerged to see Andromeda carrying a blush pink lace dress.

She handed the gown to Calliope who positioned it strategically in her arms. "Are you sure you don't want one of my girls to take it to your carriage?" Andromeda asked.

"I'm leaving now if Andromeda doesn't have anything else she needs from me." Saoirse looked to the duchess who shook her head. "I can help if you'd like me to."

Calliope grabbed her cane and hoisted herself to her feet. "If it won't put you out."

"Not at all." Saoirse smiled at her, and the duchess returned it.

"Alright," she said. "If you could carry my gown out, one of the footmen can get it into the carriage."

Saoirse delicately took the gown from Calliope's arm and bid Andromeda farewell. She followed the duchess outside, Calliope's cane clicking against the sidewalk as they walked the few feet to her carriage. A footman greeted her and opened her door, handing her up into the vehicle. Saoirse transferred the dress to him and watched as he gingerly placed it on the seat across from Calliope.

"I'm looking forward to tomorrow night," Calliope said once the footmen stepped aside. "Dinner is going to be spectacular, and I can't wait to have all you celebrating with us."

"I hope you and Vasili get to enjoy every moment of it." Saoirse smiled.

"We will." Calliope winked at her and punctuated it with a giggle.

Saoirse giggled with her and waved goodbye before heading to her own carriage. The warm feeling in her chest she had whenever she spent time with the duchesses filled her again, and she recognized it was a similar feeling she had when she spent the same kind of quality time with Emrys. She smiled to herself at that realization and felt a giddy shiver run through her as she anticipated tomorrow's dinner party.

When *Saoirse arrived* home, she slipped into the drawing room to pass through to the council room, looking for Emrys. She was cresting on that warm rush of emotions, and she wasn't ready to come down from it. She wanted to spend the rest of the afternoon with Emrys, maybe even spend more than just a few hours of quality time.

Saoirse strolled inside but stopped in her tracks when she heard the creak of one of the chairs. She spun around to find Kieran's oily grin flashing at her.

"Your Highness." Kieran rose and stalked towards her. "It seems like you just can't stay out of my path."

"What are you doing here?" Saoirse asked, taking a small step towards the door.

"I've been summoned," he answered simply. "Believe it or not, I don't come to this house to share a cup of a tea and enjoy a lark."

"Not that you're welcome to do that," she murmured.

Kieran narrowed his eyes at her. "Are you too good to be found enjoying an afternoon with lowly me?" He took another step towards her. "I'll remind you who pled for me to stay. You knew then what you were worth. And you were terrified of finding less." He closed the space between them and reached out, stroking his thumb over her cheek.

Saoirse froze under his touch. She didn't think about batting his hand away until it was no longer touching her. She fumbled through her memories to remember at least something she had practiced with Emrys. When she came up short, she began to angle herself towards the door. "I've come to my senses now." She took a step backwards in the direction of the hall. "I deserve nothing less than what Emrys gives me." She turned and tried to make a break for the door, but she wasn't quick enough.

Kieran grabbed her arm like he had a few nights ago. "You're deluding yourself," he growled.

His grip triggered her mind to recall the technique to pull an unwanted hand like his off her arm. She reached for Kieran's pinky and nearly got her free hand on his. But a quick motion from Kieran had her arm being jerked behind her. He pushed her towards the wall and leaned against her with his weight pressed on her back, pinning her against the wall. She cringed as she felt the faint throb of pain in her shoulder, and she found it hard to breathe with her ribs being crushed against the wall.

"You tried to disarm me?" Kieran hissed in her ear. "I thought you were more polite than that." Saoirse could sense his anger boiling, and she felt the same fear she had when they were romantically involved. While he had never physically threatened her like he was now, she had feared it from the aggressive way he would speak and the damage she had witnessed him inflict on various objects.

"Get off of me, Kieran," she said through gritted teeth. She pushed against him, but she had no leverage against his size.

"I don't think that's very polite either." Kieran's hand skimmed over her hip. "I would have thought Eamon taught you better manners than this." He fisted her skirt, and she felt the hem of it rise up her calf. "You really think you deserve someone like the Crown Prince with such ill manners?"

Saoirse gritted her teeth, refusing to take the bait he was dangling in front of her.

"Besides, I've heard he's been neglecting you." Kieran's hand slid higher up her leg, the thin fabric of her combination standing between her bare skin and the palm of his hand. "Tell me again how you're worthy of his affections? I would think someone who found their wife worthy would see to her needs whenever they arose." He slipped his hand into the slit of her combination and palmed her arse. Saoirse wanted to fight against his grip and his words, but she knew it would only bring on worse treatment. "I warned you it was a matter of time before he learned his mistake. It's only a matter of time before he begs me to take you off his hands."

Kieran's middle finger stroked the length of her quim, and Saoirse tried to resist the urge to panic. She clambered to think of anything that could help her in this position. Her instinct was to scream for Emrys, but Kieran would easily find a way to silence her. Besides, Emrys had just healed from the injury she had given him and—

Saoirse focused on calming her rapid heart rate as Kieran's lips touched her neck. His fingers continued to stroke between her legs, but she disconnected her mind from the touch. She knew she would only have one chance to act on her idea, so she had to think it through carefully.

She wiggled her free arm out from between her body and the wall and reached back for any part of Kieran within grasp. She grabbed what she presumed was his arm and called forth her magic. She knew she shouldn't have let fear stoke her magic, but considering Kieran was her target, she had a feeling Emrys would forgive her for it. Her magic licked under her palms, and unlike when she was practicing with Emrys, she let the fire manifest.

The smell of burning linen hit her nose before the sound of Kieran's cry hit her ears. His grasp slipped on Saoirse, and he stumbled back a step, just far enough for Saoirse to slip away towards the door.

"You bitch!" She heard him yell as she hurried into the hall. She didn't dare turn back to witness what kind of damage she had left. She desperately wanted to put as much distance between her and Kieran as she could.

Her heart pounded in her chest as she reached the bottom of the stairs and grabbed the banister. She haphazardly gathered her skirts in her hand to keep from tripping over her hem and prayed she was sure-footed enough to not tumble on the stairs. When she finally reached the second floor landing, relief washed through her when she saw Emrys emerge from their suite.

Alarm hit Emrys as he took in the look of crisis on Saoirse's face. She threw herself into his arms and breathed heavily as his arms came around her.

"Saoirse, what's wrong?" he asked.

Before she could answer, footsteps pounded up the stairs. Her body went rigid in his arms, and her breathing turned shallow. Kieran came into view on the landing with a wild look in his eyes, and Emrys felt a growl rumble in the back of his throat. Kieran's shirt sleeve was burned near the cuff. and red, seared skin showed through the singed hole.

"Go to our quarters," Emrys murmured to Saoirse.

She nodded and slowly slipped out of his arms. Her footsteps were light and quick down the hall, and Emrys stared Kieran down until he heard the click of the door close behind him.

"Have you learned your lesson about leaving her alone yet?" He nodded towards Kieran's ruined shirt sleeve.

"We were merely having a discussion," Kieran sneered. "Then she decided my arm would look better branded with her magic."

"I highly doubt she did that unprovoked," Emrys spat. "I don't know how many times you need to be told, but leave her alone."

"I'll do what I damn well please." The general tugged at his ragged shirt sleeve and winced as his fingers brushed over his blistering skin.

"You've done nothing but become a problem since she arrived."

"I'm not the one hiding secrets from his wife. I'd keep her on a leash if you wish to keep those secrets private."

Impulses of protection boiled inside Emrys. He was sick of Kieran interfering with him and Saoirse. This damn threat he held over Emrys's head had not only nearly ruined his friendship with Vasili but his relationship with Saoirse as well. Damn it all. He didn't care anymore. He didn't care if Saoirse rejected him for it. Emrys wasn't going to let Kieran control him any longer.

"Leave her alone," Emrys said through gritted teeth. Frost coated his palms, and he wouldn't hesitate to launch it in Kieran's direction if needed.

A slimy grin spread on the general's face. "Make me," he provoked.

Emrys let out a low growl before launching the ice gathered in his palm at Kieran's chest. He reeled back with an "oomph."

"You know the consequences of that," Kieran said breathlessly.

Without thinking, Emrys retorted, "There are no more consequences. I told her. You have nothing to hold over me anymore." He prayed his lie wouldn't come back to bite him. Kieran could still let it slip thinking Saoirse knew. But that was a consequence Emrys would have to consider later. "Now, leave her alone before I escalate this to Cyprian and Alastair."

The general bared his teeth before shoving at Emrys's chest, causing him to stumble back a step. "You don't get to push me around," Kieran growled.

Emrys's anger bubbled up, and he shoved him in return. "You don't get to push me around either."

Kieran grabbed Emrys's waistcoat, but Emrys acted on instinct. He broke the hold the general had on him and let his magic coat his fist before aiming it at Kieran's jaw. The layer of ice protected Emrys's fingers but had left a mark on the side of Kieran's face.

Kieran grabbed at his jaw and swung his other arm towards Emrys, hitting him in the side of his ribs with his magic. As Emrys was doubled over in pain, Kieran grabbed onto the back of his waistcoat and lifted a knee into his stomach. Emrys tried to push the general away, but he was in a position that didn't provide him sufficient leverage. In response to Emrys's attempts to separate himself from Kieran, the general led Emrys in a direction that resulted in his hip being slammed into the wall.

"What in Annwn is going on?" Alastair's voice boomed in the hall.

Emrys finally got the strength to push Kieran off him and forced himself to stand upright. However, his ribs ached in protest. Out of the corner of his eye, he caught sight of the blooming bruise on the side of Kieran's face.

Alastair stared at the two until Emrys finally spoke up. "Nothing to concern yourself with, Father." He rubbed at his sore ribs. "Kieran was just about to leave."

Kieran glared at Emrys, but Emrys stared back, daring the general to contradict him. He might have nearly bested Emrys, but Kieran wasn't likely to stay at the house after being caught brawling in the hallway. Kieran bared his teeth at Emrys before turning towards the stairs without even an acknowledgement to Alastair.

"Emrys, do you want to tell me something?" Alastair asked once Kieran was out of sight.

Emrys met his father's waiting gaze, but he wasn't about to explain at length how Kieran had been blackmailing him and how he had physically just fought for Saoirse's honor. "No," he murmured. "I don't." Alastair continued to stare at him, unconvinced, but Emrys refused to budge. "If you'll excuse me, I need to check on Saoirse."

Before his father could say anything else, Emrys turned and took long strides down the hall towards his quarters. Kieran had done something to Saoirse, and with how shook up she was the last time he had laid a hand on her, Emrys knew he shouldn't delay checking on her any longer.

Saoirse felt numb as she stood in the middle of the sitting room. She gripped the back of the sofa, the feel of the hard corner digging into her palm helping to ground her. Her blood and magic pounded in her veins. Using her fear to feed it resulted in a struggle to keep it reined in.

As she struggled to keep her breathing even, she felt every emotion wash through her, yet she felt completely emotionless at the same time. How did she let this happen again? How could the gods have let this repeat? She was tired of this game they were playing with her life. For every two steps she fought to move forward, something always pulled her three steps backward.

She snapped back to where she was when she heard the knob of the door click open. She whirled and was relieved to find it was Emrys. He shut the door behind him and closed the distance between them.

"Are you alright?" he asked, cradling her face in his hands.

Saoirse took in a shaky breath. "He grabbed me again. I tried to remove his hand from me like you taught me, but he countered it. I had to resort to using my magic to get him off of me." She wanted to vomit at the thought of recounting exactly what Kieran did to her.

"You used your magic?" A corner of Emrys's lips twitched. He looked like he was holding back a thread of excitement that she used her magic successfully.

Saoirse nodded. "It was the only other thing I could remember."

His whisper of a smile faded into concern. "I'm sorry you had to defend yourself at all." He pressed a kiss to her forehead. "But hopefully this taught him not to do it again."

"I hope so, too," Saoirse whispered. She wrapped her hands over his forearms and within moments felt a chill against them. She hadn't realized her magic was still lingering until Emrys responded with his. With a bit of effort, she spooled it back until she could no longer feel it thrumming in her veins.

"Can I do anything for you?" Emrys asked.

"Can you go back in time and keep Kieran from being born?"

He gave a huffed laugh. "I've been trying to do that for decades."

Saoirse gave a genuine smile. Her chest still felt like she was on the verge of drowning, but it felt good to smile. Emrys had a knack for making her smile during moments where she couldn't fathom doing so.

"I think I'll take a bath," she said, dropping her hands and slowing separating herself from him. "Traveling makes my skin feel like it has a layer of grime on it." It wasn't completely false. She did prefer to bathe after traveling, but she wanted to scrub her skin until she could no longer feel Kieran's touch that lingered on her body.

"Alright." Emrys reached for her hand and brought it to his lips for a quick kiss. "I'll see you downstairs for dinner, then?"

"Yes, of course." She nodded.

The rest of Saoirse's evening consisted of her fighting her own thoughts once again. Flashes of the events of earlier intruded in her mind. She wasn't trying to forget about it, but she was trying not to relive it every waking moment. Forgetting was what she had done with Odysseus, and it had ended with effects that still haunted her.

That night, she didn't even pretend like she was sneaking into Emrys's room like she usually did. She joined him like she owned his bed as much as he did. As expected, he didn't put up a fight and welcomed her into his arms.

Saoirse's thoughts didn't completely calm, but they seemed to cease being erratic. She adjusted against Emrys, hoping to leech more of that calm aura from him. Nothing changed, so she continued to writhe until Emrys's hand pressed against her stomach.

"I know you didn't come here for that," he murmured.

Saoirse's cheeks heated. "Sorry," she whispered.

His lips brushed over her shoulder in response. "Is what happened today bothering you?"

She turned in his arms and felt the pinch of tears when she met his emerald gaze. She nodded and bit back her bottom lip, willing her tears not to spill. If she could just hold them back this once...

"How can I help relieve it?" he asked.

Her tears threatened to spill again, but for a whole different reason. She opened her mouth to speak, but her throat felt clogged. Emrys's reaction was completely different from how her brother and Cressida had responded. She received a scolding and lecture, causing her to lash out with her magic and lock herself away until she could block out the memories.

While Emrys didn't know all the details of what happened to her, he showed that he didn't need them to comfort her. His foremost concern was Saoirse's wellbeing. It always had been.

"This might sound silly," she whispered, finding her voice. "But I'd like to feel your weight on top of me."

"Nothing you need is silly." Emrys kissed her cheek and rolled her onto her back. He maneuvered over her and laid his head on her shoulder, his torso splayed over hers at an angle. He didn't put his entire body over hers, but it was enough that Saoirse felt that extra layer of calm she had been looking for.

She stroked the outline his bare shoulder blade and let her fingers mindlessly wander along his ribs. Emrys flinched at her touch.

"Are you alright?" she asked.

He took a long pause before answering. "I got into a bit of a brawl with Kieran."

"What?"

"When I saw his shirt was burned, I knew he had done *something* to you. I couldn't let him get away without defending you. He accused me of pushing him around when I threatened to involve the court, and we got carried away from there."

If he hadn't been applying weight and pressure to her chest, Saoirse would have felt the full force of an ache. "Emrys," she whispered. "You don't ever have to do that for me."

He lifted his head, and that spark zipped through her when their gazes met. "I would go to the ends of the earth and otherworld to defend you. Especially when it involves Kieran." Emrys shifted and brushed a kiss to her lips.

Saoirse's insides felt like they had been melted. Not only had he gone to great lengths to make sure she was cared for, he had defended her against her assailant. It was beyond what she had ever wanted from her family when her last incident occurred.

Maybe she could forget what had happened. She was safe now, and Emrys made her feel protected as well as comforted. The space in her mind would be much better suited to hold more important memories. If she cleared the incident from her mind, she would be able to move onto a happier life.

26

Rory *buttoned the* last of the small bead buttons that lined the back of Saoirse's dinner dress. She stepped aside once the last button was closed, so Saoirse could see how she looked in the mirror. The dark plum dress had a square neckline and a champagne gold sash around the waist. Intricate beading in the same shade of gold covered the bodice, and a plum-colored lace overlaid the sleeves and floor-length skirt of the dress. She was cinched by the dress at her waist and a bustle gave the back of her skirt volume. She couldn't believe this was the same dress she had tried on in Andromeda's dress shop.

Saoirse's hair had been swept up into an intricate knotted bun on the crown of her head with small curled tendrils framing her face and a pale gold comb tucked in her bun. Andromeda had chosen the color palette of the territory's official colors, and Saoirse didn't have a reason to complain.

"You look gorgeous," Rory said quietly to her.

"Thank you." Saoirse smiled before a soft knock made the boireannaich turn and catch Emrys carefully poking his head into the doorway.

"Are you ready to leave?" he asked. "We're running a bit late."

"How late?" Saoirse asked as she slid her gloves on.

"We're just shy of missing the first course of dinner late."

Saoirse looked over her shoulder at the window as if she could guess the time based on the position of the sun. It had dipped low in the sky and dusk wasn't too far off.

"How long will it take to reach Cogwick?" she asked him.

"Just about an hour," he answered, reaching for her hand. "But I foresee myself losing all sense of time staring at you."

Saoirse felt the spark race up her spine as Emrys kissed the back of her gloved hand.

"You look beautiful," he murmured.

"Thank you," she said, smiling at him. She ran her fingers over the black velvet collar of his swallow-tail suit. He paired it with a pale gold waistcoat underneath his jacket along with a crisp white shirt adorned with a plum-colored bow tie that complimented her dress. Saoirse brushed a kiss over his bottom lip, unable to resist how delicious he looked in formalwear. "You look quite handsome yourself."

He chuckled and kissed her in return.

Saoirse thanked Rory for her help before following Emrys out of the room and through the house to the front door. Outside, Emrys helped her into the carriage, and they settled onto the same bench. In the tight space, she felt the warmth of his body next to hers, and she gave in to the urge to mold her body against him.

"Calliope said this is her fifty-fourth wedding anniversary," Saoirse said as her mind pinpointed every place her body touched his. As much as she tried to not think about the incident from the day before, her mind was hyper-vigilant of her surroundings. "And I know she used to be a High Healer, so how did she and Vasili come to be arranged?"

"We had to find a way for Calliope to qualify for an arrangement," Emrys said. "Arrangements and marriage are solely reserved for nobility."

"So what qualified her?"

"Vasili's mother and Seraphina are to thank for that," he answered. "Since Calliope was essentially Seraphina's daughter—"

"Wait," Saoirse interrupted. "Calliope was raised by Seraphina and Ada?"

Emrys nodded. "She and her older sister."

"Why have neither of you mentioned that?" A smile tugged at her lips, and she began to compile a long list of questions for her friend.

"I thought I had." He chuckled. "I told you about the dukes. I assumed I had told you about Calliope."

"Well, you didn't." Saoirse leaned back in her seat. "Alright, then, go on. How did Calliope become arranged?"

"As I was saying," Emrys continued. "Since she was Seraphina's daughter, she became the top referred High Healer for the court and those adjacent to it. Vasili had just come into his dukedom and suffered an injury from a horseback riding incident. It was bad enough that Seraphina had to send Calliope to heal him and his mother became enamored by her."

"And Vasili didn't?" Saoirse felt the tension pinching between her shoulders relax, and the chatter in her mind hushed to a murmur.

"Oh, Vasili was enamored by her." Emrys chuckled. "But he...he doesn't really prescribe to society's normal functions, especially not then. He was never groomed for dukedom. It fell into his lap when his uncle died. He never saw himself marrying until his mother plotted with Seraphina to find a way to arrange him and Calliope."

"So how did Calliope become qualified for an arranged marriage?" Saoirse asked, enthralled by this story. It was better than the stories of how her brothers were arranged. They paled in comparison to the stories of the dukes and duchesses.

"Seraphina was able to craft a title in the Healer Union that would allow her to marry Vasili," he answered. "It's not exactly following the rules, but none of the dukes exactly followed the rules of arrangements to marry their partners."

"And here I thought you were so romantic with your late-night bargaining session." Saoirse giggled.

He smirked in response. "Yes, I will admit I have been outdone by the dukes in that regard. But..." His grin faded as his words trailed off.

She knit her brows in confusion. What made his words trail away? What was he about to say? Before she could open her mouth, Emrys changed the subject.

"Have I told you about their fifteenth anniversary?" he asked.

"No, you haven't, and neither has Calliope." She forced a soft smile even though her earlier questions still tugged at her mind.

Emrys went on to detail how Vasili had gifted Calliope a crystal sculpture of the home Ada and Seraphina had raised Calliope and her sister in for their fifteenth anniversary. Fifteenth anniversaries were crystal anniversaries hence the crystal sculpture. However, the sculpture was placed inappropriately and caught a sofa cushion on fire when the afternoon sun hit the sculpture at just the right angle.

Saoirse mirrored Emrys's smile as her shoulders shook with quiet laughter. With the bits of information she had gleaned about Vasili and Calliope, this story was very fitting for the couple. Saoirse felt the last bit of tension melt from her body, and she let a grin casually pull at her lips as she drank in the sight of Emrys. In the fading light, the gold in his emerald eyes flickered, and the spark jumped in her body again. Damn that spark. She was half-inclined to explore what that spark wanted to be satisfied, but a carriage wasn't the appropriate place to allow that exploration.

Her eyes dropped to his lips, and she nearly let her self-control snap when the carriage jerked to a stop. She blinked several times, trying not to look disappointed as Emrys opened the carriage door and held out his hand for her. When he handed her down from the carriage, Saoirse took in the gray bricked house with a steel blue roof and carefully placed glass windows in front of her. Long vines of flora crept up the sides of the house and the smell of freshly baked bread wafted out one of the open windows.

Emrys offered his arm to her, and Saoirse wrapped her hand around his bicep. She felt transported back to their first dinner where she made note of how firm and muscular it felt under her fingers. It gave her a feeling that she couldn't place. She felt light and warm, as if she had been familiar with Emrys for more than just a few weeks.

The two approached the door, and Saoirse noticed how well-shined the brass door knocker looked and the smooth click it gave as Emrys tapped it on the door. A tall, rail-thin fireann opened the door and greeted them, welcoming them inside. Saoirse stood in the foyer and studied the inside of the home, resisting the urge to turn in a circle to drink in the aesthetic. She had only been to Andromeda's dress shop, but that had a completely different atmosphere to her home.

As they moved through the house, the simple elegance stood out to Saoirse. It reflected her taste in fashion as much as her shop appealed to all classes of nobility. Light, airy color palettes were used in the dining room and sitting room as far as Saoirse could see, and the rooms had an inviting feeling that wasn't too prim and proper to enjoy. Savory scents floated through the air, and her stomach began to petition her to taste what she smelled.

The duchesses and their spouses were lounging in the sitting room, chatting and drinking pre-dinner cocktails. "Saoirse!" Isolde sprang from her seat and made her way across the room to her friend as quickly as her beaded gown would let her. The pale green gown was covered in almost transparent gold beads, and the lacy sleeves sat off her shoulders with ruffled straps that kept her neckline from slipping too far down.

She pulled Saoirse into an embrace, and her sweet scent of apples and jasmine tickled Saoirse's nose. "We were wondering how late the newlyweds would come."

"The rest of you are too punctual," Emrys commented with a cheeky grin. "I blame Cyprian's overly detail-oriented law school education."

"Next time you find yourself needing an attorney to defend you, I'll remember to be a half-hour late," Cyprian said from the sofa Isolde had vacated.

Saoirse caught Andromeda roll her eyes before standing. Her ruffled, navy blue gown swished as she stood at one of the doorways of the sitting room. On the sofa next to her was a large gray dog with a boxy snout and massive paws. It picked up its head before hopping down to the floor. It shook its coat, and Saoirse was stunned at how tall the dog was. It definitely stood tall enough to come to her waist if not perhaps her chest.

"Before we begin a full-out quarrel," Andromeda said. "Let's at least make it to the dining room."

Everyone followed her into the dining room, most still holding half-full glasses of cocktails. The dog tried to follow them, but Laszlo uttered a command in a language Saoirse didn't recognize, and the dog sat down with a whine.

Andromeda showed the guests of honor where she had reserved their seats at the table, and everyone fell into place around them. Saoirse was seated with Emrys on her left and Isolde on her right. Calliope was directly across from her, seated between Vasili and Andromeda.

The first course of the meal was brought out, and everyone began to indulge in the wine and fresh salad full of seasonal vegetables. "Where are our manners?" Emrys said as he swallowed his bite of food and reached for his wine glass. "We were so wrapped up in eating we forgot to toast." He lifted his glass towards Vasili and Calliope, and everyone followed. "To the couple of the hour, may this next year of marriage bless you beyond even what the gods can measure."

Everyone let out a low laugh and toasted to the couple before sipping their wine. The cranberry red liquid warmed Saoirse's body from the inside out, and she welcomed the involuntary relaxation of her muscles.

"So, Calliope, what did Vasili give you for an anniversary present?" Isolde asked. "I believe fifty-four is the glass anniversary."

"I received the most elegant and ornately decorated vanity with a mirror," Calliope answered with a bright smile. Vasili leaned over and kissed her temple.

"Will we be hearing it rattle this evening?" Andromeda asked with a smirk.

Vasili sputtered as he took a sip of wine at the wrong moment.

"I think we rattled it enough earlier today." Calliope giggled while her husband's face was nearing a shade that resembled the wine in his glass. While Calliope seemed accustomed to Andromeda's inappropriate commentary—at least in a private setting—Saoirse suspected Vasili wasn't accustomed to it at all.

"I think you'll hear more than the vanity rattling." Isolde sniggered as Cyprian choked on his bite of food.

"I thought we agreed to never speak about this subject at the dinner table again," he said as he regained his ability to speak.

"Yes, I believe we did," Vasili said quickly. "Andromeda?"

The duchess sighed and nodded. "Shall we discuss the last couple to celebrate fifty-four years of marriage instead?" Andromeda glanced at Isolde, who gave her an unamused look.

The servants came in and exchanged the guests' empty first course plates with the main entrée. It was a rich-looking medallion of beef with a thick, brown sauce and steamed vegetables that added to the savory scents of the meal.

"Andromeda, you know exactly what I was doing on my fifty-fourth wedding anniversary." Isolde shot back as everyone began to cut into their meat. She turned to Saoirse and explained why Andromeda was bringing up her own anniversary. "I was in St. Clewark visiting my parents when a flood hit, and I was trapped for weeks."

"Oh, that's awful," Saoirse said.

"Not as awful as not getting an orgasm on your anniversary," Andromeda murmured, taking a sip of wine. Isolde fired a glare at her but didn't take any more of her bait.

"Other than making sure your wife orgasms on your anniversary," Vasili interrupted, his face reddening as he said the word "orgasm." "What marriage advice do you have for us at this stage, Cyprian?"

The dark-haired fireann chuckled. "Well, it goes without saying to always let her finish first."

Low laughter circulated around the table again. Cyprian looked to his wife, who shot him an unimpressed look. He kissed between her furrowed brows and added, "And there's never a bad time to tell her you love her."

Isolde's expression melted, and she kissed her husband.

"I don't know, Cyprian," Laszlo said. "Telling your wife you love her after you bring home a puppy without telling her beforehand has proved to be an ill time."

"A dog that weighs three stone is hardly a puppy," Andromeda countered. "But it's not just telling your partner you love them. It's showing them, too."

"And what would be showing love look like for you?" Vasili asked with genuine curiosity.

Andromeda smirked. "Well, you all barred talking about sex at the table, so…"

"Would you count being given the puppy as one of those ways?" Calliope asked quickly. "I'll admit a dog sounds better than the things Vasili brings home to me."

"Badger meat is very tender," Vasili argued. "If you let me cook it for you, I think you'd like it."

Calliope flashed him a polite smile and shook her head in response.

"No," Andromeda answered, trying to smother her laugh. "I wouldn't say being given the puppy felt like love, but Laszlo taking care of him and training him does." Her cheeks became tinged with pink as she looked to her husband. "As well as when he takes care of me."

Laszlo grinned at her and kissed her as Cyprian had with Isolde.

As Saoirse watched the conversation volley between the members of the court, a warm hand covered hers. She looked down and saw Emrys's fingers slipping into her palm. He squeezed her hand three times while he engaged with the dukes. A warmth filled her chest that didn't feel anything like her magic. When it didn't ease, she wanted to rub at her chest to disperse it, but she felt that would be futile. It was a persistent feeling that she had only felt inklings of in the past few weeks.

"I think a well-timed kiss does it for me." Emrys's words pulled Saoirse's attention back to the table. He must have been asked about how he shared love. "I could be in the sourest mood, have my livelihood destroyed before my eyes, and a deep, satisfying kiss could solve all my problems."

"I'll remember that the next time you get upset in council," Laszlo said, causing another eruption of laughs.

Saoirse's gaze fell to her intertwined hand, and she found it hard to swallow. He had been sharing love with her for weeks. That was what she felt bubbling in her chest and spreading through her limbs. It was no wonder the sensation was so foreign. Her family had put in a bare minimum effort to raise her. They didn't think she was worthy of it. But Emrys did. He thought she was more than worthy of a loving effort. He believed she *deserved* love.

"I like spending time with you," she murmured so that just Emrys could hear.

"Hmm?" He turned his attention to her, and she felt her pulse kick higher under his gaze.

"I feel loved when you spend time with me," she reiterated. "When I'm not alone."

A slow smile spread across his face. She lifted their threaded hands and brushed her lips over the back of his. His smile grew wider, and he leaned towards her, pressing a kiss to her lips. The spark crackled in her veins as the seconds of their kiss ticked by. She swore it lasted longer the few moments it actually did, but when he pulled back from her, she wanted to grab for him in any way she could—his coat, his shirt, his face—and pull him back into the kiss.

The discussion continued around the table, but Saoirse barely heard any of it. She and Emrys stared at each other for what seemed like hours as the rest of the room faded away. Was this what the duchesses felt with their spouses? Was this what love and freedom actually felt like, tasted like?

He had never offered it to her because he saw her as unworthy of his love. He offered her freedom because he believed she deserved it. And in that freedom, she was able to explore not only the world she had been locked away from, but herself as well. He gave her ample room to find her boundaries and choose what she wanted. He had never pushed himself on her and respected her choices. She had never felt such desire for someone, and it was because he had the decency to treat her with respect.

As if he knew he was in her thoughts, Emrys leaned towards her and whispered in her ear. "I'll sit with you and listen to you for as long as you like, if that's what it takes to make you feel loved." His breath tickled her neck, and goosebumps ran over her skin.

He pulled back without giving her time to respond, offering a knowing smile before he jumped back into the table conversation. It took Saoirse a moment to pull herself together, but she still spent the rest of the evening stealing glances at Emrys, memorizing his profile, how the muscles of his face creased when he laughed, and the way he smirked when he caught her looking at him. Whatever manifested the spark in her body, it was buzzing through her. As much as she enjoyed spending dinner with her friends, Saoirse looked forward to the end of the evening.

After dinner, everyone returned to the sitting room to relax and enjoy after-dinner drinks. Saoirse sat in an armchair adjacent to Emrys, resting her elbow on the arm and propping her chin with her hand. She drifted in and out of the conversation, but her thoughts continued to drift to Emrys more than they usually did. Her gaze bounced around the room but came back to Emrys whenever she heard his voice. He caught her a few times gazing at him, but she didn't care to hide it. He grinned at her before he returned his attention to whoever was holding the conversation.

The night slowly waned, and when Calliope and Vasili chose to retire to their bedroom for the night, everyone else followed suit. Emrys reached for Saoirse's hand as they made their way up the stairs to their guest room, and she reveled in the personal touch of warmth in her hand.

He led her along the upstairs hallway to a door on the right side at the end of the hall. "How do you know this is ours?" Saoirse asked. No one had given them directions, at least she was fairly sure no one had. She hadn't been paying much attention to anyone but Emrys after dinner.

"We've all spent enough time in this house that we've claimed certain rooms," Emrys answered with a cheeky grin. "And I chose this one because it's the furthest from Laszlo and Andromeda's."

Saoirse giggled and followed him inside their quarters for the night. In the dim light of a small lamp on a nightstand, she could barely make out the space, but there was a four-poster bed in the middle, a small dresser to the right, and a standing mirror on the opposite side of the room.

She located her suitcase at the foot of the bed and plopped it on the quilt to open it, digging around for her nightgown. As she reached for the back of her dress, Saoirse remembered Rory had buttoned her into it, and there was no chance she could unbutton it herself. "Emrys," she said. His attention swiveled to her, and she felt the overwhelming tension that had been building between them all night. "Would you help me out of my dress?"

He nodded and stepped towards her as she pivoted around. He thumbed open the buttons one by one. Every so often, his fingers grazed her exposed skin and made her feel like she was being lit on fire with every brush. "Why do you boireannaich have such tiny buttons on your dresses?" he asked with a chuckle.

"My question has always been why they were put behind us while being so small."

She grinned as he opened the last few buttons and slid it off her shoulders, letting it pool on the floor. The heaviness of the dress struck her once it was off, and she felt lighter. Stepping out of the puddle of lace, satin, and beads, she turned and bent for the dress, but Emrys picked it up before she could reach it. He promised to place it on the dresser while she continued to undress.

Saoirse thanked him and pulled the pins out of her hair. It fell over her shoulders, and she brushed it out with her fingers. She stripped down to her chemise and exchanged it for a silk cream-colored nightgown with lace along the neckline and hem. The hem of her nightgown barely reached her mid-thigh, and the neckline left much of her collarbone and upper chest exposed.

She braided her hair as Emrys perched on the bed, removing his shoes and socks to join his jacket and waistcoat. He glanced at her before quickly returning his attention to his shoes, sneaking peeks when he thought she wasn't looking.

"Do I have a tear in my nightgown?" she asked, turning and

giving an exaggerated look over her shoulder.

Emrys's throat bobbed as he swallowed. "No," he answered huskily. "Just that cheeky little starburst birthmark between your shoulder blades."

Saoirse giggled and reached for a satin ribbon in her suitcase, feeling Emrys's eyes follow her movements. Her fingers worked swiftly to braid her strawberry blonde hair and tie the ribbon around the few inches she left as a tail. She stepped between Emrys's legs and lazily plucked the buttons of his shirt open.

"Someone packed with very specific intentions tonight," Emrys said, skimming his hands over the back of her thighs.

She smirked and pressed a long kiss to his lips. "Want to know a secret?" she whispered.

"Always."

"I brought two nightgowns."

"What?" He chuckled.

"I brought this one," she motioned to the nightgown she was wearing, "and one that is much more..."

"Scandalous?"

"Frumpy."

Emrys's shoulders shook with quiet laughter, and he squeezed the back of her thighs. "I like the one you chose to wear."

Saoirse bit back another smile as she pulled the loose tie from his collar and tossed it towards the other discarded clothes piled near his closed suitcase. Emrys's eyes never left hers while she continued to unbutton his shirt. When she untucked the tails from his trousers, she slipped her hands under his suspenders and felt the muscles of his chest. They were smooth and firm under her palms.

He unbuttoned his cuffs with their gazes locked while Saoirse smoothed her hands over the muscles of his chest. He shrugged out of his shirt, and Saoirse smirked as she slipped her hands under the hem of his undershirt and pulled it over his head.

"What?" he asked.

"It's finally your turn to be undressed."

His lips cracked a smile, and he slid his hands up her hips to cup her arse.

"I knew it was just a matter of time."

He kissed her exposed collarbone and his lips burned a path along her decolletage. Saoirse's fingers traced over his muscles, and his eyes followed the path she drew. Saoirse had seen his bare torso before. She had even been held against his bare skin as she slept. But it had never been this intimate. The tension between them was electrifying, and she couldn't deny herself any longer.

Emrys cradled her face with one hand, inviting her to meet his gaze. "Saoirse," he whispered, his lips a breath away from hers. "Is this happening tonight?" That spark bounced erratically through her, urging her to forego all her hesitations and indulge herself.

She nodded and closed the distance between them, her lips meeting his. Her shoulders melted as he stood and pulled her closer. She felt the heat of his body through the thin fabric of her nightgown, and she wished it wasn't standing between them. She wanted to press her breasts against his skin and feel their shared warmth.

At first, her mind was able to keep track of every touch they shared. She was aware of the path Emrys's hands traced on her body, the rhythm his tongue danced against hers, and the press of his hips on hers, indicating just how much his body was anticipating this. But then, the awareness faded, and she found it difficult to register what was happening. She felt movement against her body, but she couldn't place what the source of the touch was.

Her body also felt like it wasn't hers, like it was being controlled by someone else. She was merely a witness to its actions. Her hands moved stiffly over his body, and her kissing turned sloppy. She tried to concentrate, but her thoughts mingled and mashed together, causing her to lose complete focus on where she was.

"Saoirse?" The question sounded distant.

"Hmm," she hummed, but she could hear it came out more like a grunt.

"Saoirse."

Something soft gently stroked her cheek, and she worked to

open her eyes. Her vision was blurry, but she could make out the concern in Emrys's expression. Her senses started to come back to her, and realization hit her too late.

It had happened again. As much as she had pushed yesterday's incident from her thoughts, her mind felt the need to protect her. It disconnected what she was doing from her conscious state.

Tears burned Saoirse's eyes as she tried to blink them away. She had chosen to suppress what happened to her yesterday for a reason. She didn't want her body reacting like this, especially not with Emrys. Her bottom lip trembled, and she knew her resolve was waning rapidly. A hot tear rolled down her cheek, and that was all she needed for the fuse of her emotions to be lit.

Saoirse's face twisted as a choked sob escaped her lips. She covered her face with her hands and tried to step back, but Emrys's arm wrapped around her, bringing her in tightly against his body. Once again, she was hyper-aware of his touch, and two impulses warred within her, one being to untangle herself from him and lock herself in the bathroom to cry and the other being to press herself as closely as she could to him, grounding herself and letting her emotions take over.

The latter won out, and she gripped his sides, burying her face in his warm skin. Her nails dug into the flesh covering his ribs, but he didn't react. Instead, he ran a hand over the back of her hair and pressed his lips to the top of her head. He murmured words to her that she couldn't hear over her sobbing. She only knew he was talking by the way his chest vibrated against her.

"I'm sorry." The words were garbled as she hiccupped for air. "I'm sorry." She continued to repeat the words until they dissolved into more sobbing.

Emrys didn't respond with empty words of comfort. He merely held her tighter. There was still a piece of her that believed he didn't deserve the hardship she brought on him. She cried for that insecure part of her. She also cried for the person she was before meeting him, the one who didn't know love. Finally, she cried for herself who would no longer know what not being violated by another person felt like. She'd always carry that knowledge, no matter how well Emrys treated her or loved her.

Saoirse felt her body slightly sway side to side, and she realized it was Emrys rocking her. She focused her mind on the rhythm and let it ground her and settle her. Her breathing was still heavy, but her tears had slowed to a halt. Her hands loosened their grip on his sides, and she cringed at the effort it took to remove her fingers from his skin, knowing she most likely left behind crescent moon shaped marks on his flesh. She swallowed before lifting her head up.

He cupped her cheek and wiped at the tear stains on her face. Saoirse's lip wobbled again at the gentle touch, but she kept herself from spiraling into another bout of sobs.

"Why don't we go to sleep?" he suggested quietly.

Saoirse nodded and closed her eyes as his lips pressed a kiss to her forehead. She wanted to apologize again, but she knew what his response would be. Instead, she slipped out of his grasp and let him change out of his trousers and into a pair of pyjama pants.

Emrys pulled back the layers of bedding, and she slid under them alongside him. She felt an arm wrap around her waist, and his body molded against hers. That strange calm that accompanied Emrys whenever he was close wrapped around her like a thick blanket. Her thoughts still warred between wanting to run from being hyper-aware of her body and wishing to be held as tightly as Emrys could manage. His lips gently kissed her bare shoulder, and it helped ground her.

"I want you to know I'm not disappointed," he whispered. "I had no expectations for tonight. I'm just as happy laying here with you."

He stroked her arm with his free hand, and Saoirse reached for it, lacing her fingers with his. She brought his hand to her lips and placed a wobbly kiss against the back of it. In return, he squeezed her hand three times and tightened his arm around her waist. She worked to keep her breathing even as she still fought the impulse to push away from him. Her instinct in the past had been to run, but there was never anywhere safe for her to run to. But now, she finally had a safe place, and she didn't need to run to find it.

Emrys woke as the sun peeked into the room the next morning. His hands and arms were still tangled with Saoirse's, and he tried his best not to move. He wanted nothing more than to stroke the soft skin of her arm, but he didn't want to do anything that would cause her to stir or wake. He wanted her to sleep as long as she needed.

He hadn't fallen asleep until he knew she had succumbed to slumber first. Last night, she had fought her tears and emotion for close to an hour before her body was too exhausted to continue. He wasn't sure what had triggered her to disconnect, but his suspicion had his stomach twisting in knots. He wanted more than anything to use the mating bond to take on the pain that caused her to react like she did, but it would have possibly made it worse since he'd have to explain how he could do such a thing.

Instead, he held her as tightly as he could and let her know she wasn't at fault for anything that happened or didn't happen that night. He tried to focus on the silver lining. While his heart broke and he felt helpless last night, he took some comfort in knowing he had built a sufficient amount of trust with her again. If he hadn't, she wouldn't have tried to initiate anything.

Emrys felt her shift in his arms, and he placed a gentle kiss between her shoulder blades. Saoirse's skin was warm and silky, and if he wasn't in Laszlo and Andromeda's home, he would have stayed in bed holding her for the rest of the day. She turned in his arms, and her hazel eyes met his. Even with the touch of swelling under her eyes, she was beautiful, and his heart pounded in his chest.

"Good morning," he whispered, the early morning rasp in his voice making itself present.

"Good morning," she whispered back.

Their hands were still intertwined, and he took the opportunity to place another kiss on hers. He tucked away the desire to take his chance to kiss every inch of her and instead slowly closed the space between them to give her a proper kiss. She ducked her head before he could make contact, and instead of letting his disappointment flood him, he settled for resting his forehead against hers.

"I'm sorry," she said quietly.

"You have nothing to be sorry for," he reminded her.

"I know you were disappointed." She refused to meet his gaze as she spoke.

"I wasn't." He repeated his sentiment from the night before, every word still genuine. "I had no expectations." He pressed his luck and leaned towards her to brush a kiss to her forehead. She allowed it this time, and he let it stoke his confidence. "I was just happy to be so close to you in this nightgown."

A laugh bubbled out of her, and she finally raised her eyes to his. The lilt of her laugh eased the tightness in his chest, and he gave her a soft smile as she studied him. "How do you do that?" she asked. "How do you make me laugh when all I want to do is dive under these covers and pity myself for eternity?"

"Well, the gods knew I'd be a disastrous fae, so they made sure I had a sense of humor."

She let out another silvery laugh and cuddled closer to him, her head resting against his chest. "About last night," she said quietly.

"We don't have to discuss it," he said when she paused. "At least not here. We can wait until we return home."

Saoirse shook her head. "I don't want to lose my confidence."

Emrys didn't argue with her further. Instead, he dropped a kiss to the top of her head and moved the hand that was around her waist to stroke her hair.

"First, I want you to know, none of it was your fault." Her voice was just above a whisper.

He had tried not to blame himself and let his thoughts spiral last night, so it was nice to hear her confirm it. "I assume it's happened before?" he asked.

She nodded. "I first experienced it—fading out—when I tried to be intimate with someone after Odysseus."

Emrys swallowed. Had Kieran triggered this reaction? He had grabbed her without her permission twice now. Was that all it took? Or...did he do something Emrys didn't even want to begin to think about?

He pushed the question from his mind. He feared he would turn murderous otherwise.

"How did you work through it before?" he asked cautiously. "I remember you being very present on our wedding night."

Saoirse buried her face in his chest. "Stop that," she said with a hint of a giggle.

"Stop what?" Emrys couldn't help the tug on the corner of his lips.

"Making me want to laugh when all I want to do is cry."

"I can't do that." He brushed back the strands of hair that had fallen from her braid and into her face.

She sighed against him. "I don't really know how I worked through it before. Sometimes when I work to focus on what I'm doing, I can keep it at bay. Sometimes it just takes me a minute to remember what I'm doing and I don't experience it anymore." She lifted her head, and her cheeks were stained with a touch of pink. "The only time it didn't cross my mind was on our wedding night."

That didn't quite ease the rest of the tightness in Emrys's chest, but it gave him a bit of hope. It helped explain her reaction last night. Her experience with him had been memorable. Literally. And then, when trying to recreate it, her mind slipped back into its old habits. He'd also be frustrated if his body and mind betrayed him.

A cheeky thought pulled at his lips, and he couldn't resist sharing it. "So what you're saying is you're best when I'm worshipping you and your body?" Before she could duck away from him again, Emrys aimed a kiss for her collarbone and pulled her closer to him.

Saoirse's shoulders shook, and she gave a half-hearted shove at his chest. "You're terrible."

Her laughter spilled out of her as he kissed the crook of her neck, his kisses exaggerated and playful. He could listen to her laugh for the rest of eternity. If it was the only sound he'd ever hear again, he'd be a happy fireann.

Emrys pulled back, and Saoirse's laughter died out, leaving a whisper of a smile on her lips. The mating spark sizzled through him at her hazel stare, and he carefully closed the space between them again. He silently prayed she wouldn't duck away again as his lips neared hers. Thankfully, she didn't, and she allowed him to kiss her slowly and softly. A tingling warmth spread through Emrys's body as they shared the tender kiss.

When they pulled apart, her hazel eyes glistened, and he could read the unspoken words in her gaze. He silently repeated them back to her and welcomed her to stay as long as she wanted in his arms. She scooted as close as she could to him and tucked her head under his chin.

It took another hour before they finally pulled themselves out of bed and dressed in comfortable silence. There was a strange ease between them, and Emrys prayed unceasingly to the gods that they wouldn't take any more steps backward.

28

mrys *and Saoirse* returned to Fearynhurst later that day. She was still shaken by the previous night. Fading out and disconnecting from a partner was something she never thought she'd experience again. She hated that it happened with Emrys, and that he had to witness it.

Her mind raced with thoughts but came to a screeching halt when she spotted a tall figure. Kieran glanced at her but quickly ducked into the council room. Saoirse's heart pounded in her chest, and she felt her limbs vibrate with adrenaline. He hadn't said a word to her, but she suddenly felt every word and touch from their last encounter.

She followed Emrys up the stairs into the quarters and disappeared into her room. She unpacked her things and attempted to erase the incident from her mind. Her hands shook as she pulled her belongings from her suitcase and put them away. Taking a deep breath, she thought of the ways she could quiet her mind and gain a break from her incessant thoughts.

Her first instinct was to leave. Being in Cogwick with her friends and Emrys had helped relieve her for a few hours. But what happened last night held her back from following through with it. She thought of anything that could keep her mind occupied until the urge to panic subsided.

A hot pop in her veins brought her to the best idea she could come up with. Saoirse stepped into the sitting room and called for Emrys.

"Yes?" he asked, poking his head out of his bedroom.

"Can you arrange a lesson for my magic?" She tried to keep her voice even as she spoke, but it wobbled a bit.

"I could probably put something together for tomorrow," he said.

"No, I want to do it today." Saoirse rubbed her thumb in the center of her palm, pressing just enough pressure into it to keep her composure.

"Are you sure you'd be up for it?" he asked. He knit his brows in concern, and it made her thoughts shout louder in her mind.

"Yes," she answered, still shaky.

He stepped out of his bedroom and made his way towards her, studying her. Saoirse swallowed, but her throat was too dry. She needed Emrys to agree soon, or she would complete break down.

"Magic isn't a coping skill," Emrys said.

She felt the dam on her emotions crumble. "Emrys, please," she begged. "I don't want to think. I don't want to feel. I just want to exist without my mind making life feel like a prison of my own doing." A familiar pinch stung the back of her eyes, and Saoirse wanted to sink into the floor. Training her magic wasn't going to help anymore. She wanted to escape and be numb.

"Saoirse." Emrys stepped closer, but it was too late.

Saoirse sunk to the floor, her knees thudding onto the hardwood. She squeezed her eyes shut as hot tears rolled down her cheeks once again. She couldn't fool herself any longer. Nothing was going to erase the incident with Kieran. She'd have to live with the burden of it along with every other traumatic incident she experienced in her life.

Emrys felt helpless watching Saoirse dissolve to the floor. He realized how naïve he was to believe her brave face and assume she was anything remotely close to fine. He knew she was hurting, but he didn't think it was enough to result in her crying on the floor.

A whimper escaped Saoirse's lips, and he felt it like a punch to his gut. His guess of what Kieran did to her crept back from earlier. The previous times he had touched her had upset her but never to this level of intensity.

Emrys crouched down next to Saoirse but wasn't sure whether or not to reach for her. He carefully brushed at a wisp of hair at her temple, measuring how much physical contact she was receptive to.

Saoirse took a shaky breath and lifted her head. Tear tracks stained her cheeks, and her bottom lip wobbled as she turned her head in his direction. He wanted to encourage her to talk about what was causing her reaction, but he didn't want to push her either. His heart hurt as he was torn on what to do or say.

"He touched me," Saoirse said before Emrys could decide what to say to her. Her voice barely audible as she spoke. "He put his hand under my skirts, and he...he touched me." Her face twisted, and a sob shook her entire body.

Emrys was immediately hit with a torrent of his own emotions. His initial reaction was to swear and curse and rampage. He had hoped his guess hadn't been correct, but it sickened him that he wasn't surprised.

The other emotions that hit him made his chest feel heavy. His heart ached as he watched her succumb to her barrage of heavy emotions. She had kept her guard and demeanor up, but now it was eroding before his eyes. He wished she had come forward with this sooner. Maybe it wouldn't have been this painful for her to process. But he knew better than to chastise her for that. He could predict her reasoning, and it all pointed back to her bastard brother.

A wail came from Saoirse as she collapsed further and buried her face in her lap. Her shoulders shook violently with the sobs, and Emrys felt even more helpless. He attempted to reach for her again, but she flinched at his touch this time. He tried to swallow the hurt of being rejected on top of watching his wife, his love, his mate, writhe in complete distress. A whisper told him he had failed her. As a mate, he was bound to protect her and keep her from harm at all costs. It was why the protective instinct came with the bond, but he had failed to act on it. Guilt flooded him, but he pushed it aside to focus on finding a way to help soothe her.

Saoirse slowly lifted her head, sobs still wracking her body, and found the strength to steady herself enough to utter words. "How could it have happened again?" Her voice was raspy, and the words were barely discernible. Emrys's heart shattered hearing the pain in her voice. "I thought I had done everything to prevent it from happening again, but I couldn't stop him." Her sobs intensified, and she leaned into Emrys for comfort.

The ache in his chest eased as he wrapped his arms around her and held her tightly. She wanted his touch now, and he was thankful for that small mercy. "It's not your fault," he whispered. "Kieran is a self-centered, arrogant bastard. You did everything you were supposed to. He's responsible for what he did, not you."

She let out another sob and dug her fingers into Emrys's thigh, trying to find relief from the pain she felt. "Why me?" The words were soft at first, but became more distraught as she repeated them. "Why? Why?"

He knew she wasn't looking for an answer but was trying to release the emotions that plagued her. She collapsed onto his lap and sobbed harder. Emrys stroked her back and hastily wiped away the tear that rolled down his own cheek. Watching her wrestle with her emotional pain was the hardest thing he had ever witnessed. He could do nothing for her.

As he pressed the palm of his hand on her back, he felt the pull to use the bond to soothe her. He had forgone it before, not ready to face the consequences, but the consequences be damned now. He could no longer watch her and remain helpless. He willed himself to steady his breathing as he closed his eyes and concentrated on pulling the pain from her.

Echoes of memories, not his own but Saoirse's, slammed into him, and a different kind of helplessness overwhelmed him. The panic and terror he felt was like nothing he had experienced before. He felt the violation of being overpowered, and he, too, wanted to break down in sobs. Feeling objectified to the point of having his body used for someone else was foreign and bitter.

It hit him that Saoirse had not just experienced this once, but twice. Tears of his own hit his cheeks, and he hastily wiped them away. Taking her pain as his own was more overwhelming than he thought it would be, but he knew it was the only way he could help her at the moment.

Saoirse steadied underneath his touch, and he traced circles with his hand between her shoulders again. She slowly lifted her tear-stained face, and her glassy eyes met his.

"What did you do?" she asked, her voice barely above a whisper.

Emrys felt his heart plummet. This was it. He'd have to confess the bond. He braced himself for her reaction. "I took some of your pain," he answered softly, hoping to buy himself time. He scrambled for a reason that didn't force him to confess their bond. Only mates had the ability to take on each other's pain, and he didn't have the option to lie about it.

"How?" she asked.

Emrys took a deep breath and prepared to confess the bond to her. "It..." His thoughts were running at an excessive speed trying to avoid this conversation. Before, he had just stopped talking when he was close to confessing the bond. If he didn't say anything, he couldn't lie. But that wasn't an option in this situation. But maybe he technically still could. Omission might be a loophole he could take advantage of.

"It doesn't take all the pain," he said. "It doesn't erase what caused it in the first place either. But it can take some of the burden off. And now I carry it, too."

Emrys let out a breath of relief and tentatively reached towards Saoirse's face to wipe a track of tears from her cheek. She blinked at him but didn't ask any further questions. Instead, she nodded numbly at him before slowly pulling her gaze away and staring off across the room.

"I saw him today," she whispered. "When we came home, he went to the council room but just seeing him..." She took a deep, shaky breath and closed her eyes. A tear rolled down her cheek, and he carefully wiped it away again. "I've tried for the past two days not to think about what happened. Today, I just wanted to not think about him for a gods damned moment."

"I understand." Her request made sense now. He was still adamant that magic use wasn't a good coping mechanism because it could lead to bottoming out one's magic, a rare but very real consequence. But he at least understood everything that led to this point.

"I'm sorry," she whispered.

Emrys couldn't help the chuckle that bubbled in his chest. "You're the one lying here wrought with emotional pain and you're apologizing to *me*?"

Saoirse gave a weak laugh and rested her head against his shoulder. "You don't deserve to have to concern yourself this."

"And yet I've chosen to take it on as my own."

She was silent for a moment. Emrys could feel her breathing become even, and she relaxed more fully against him.

"I just keep seeing it, feeling him," she croaked. "I can't stop it."

"I know." He felt the same flashes of memories in his mind. The urge to vomit hit him, and he wondered how she went more than a day feeling like this. "I can feel a fraction of it, and it's not anything I would wish on my worst enemies to experience."

She raised her melancholy gaze to his and attempted to smile. He tentatively placed a hand on her cheek and stroked his thumb on her warm skin.

"If you need to talk or cry or scream about it, I'll always be here to listen and hold you." He took a risk and kissed her forehead, letting his lips linger on her. His chest loosened as she rested her head against his touch.

"Why did you pick me?" she whispered after a long silence. He crinkled his brows in confusion. "Why did you choose me for your arrangement? We both had the option to leave at any time, and I've given you several reasons to since you met me. You deserve better than a broken boireann." Her voice began to crack, and he tightened his grip on her shoulders.

"You're not broken," he told her softly. "Nothing has broken you. You haven't let a single thing tear you into unrepairable pieces. You may fall apart, but I've witnessed you put yourself back together and come back with even more strength." He kissed the top of her head as he heard her take a shuddering breath. "That's why I picked you," he whispered.

She lifted her head, her eyes glittering with fresh tears.

He stopped himself before he could say more and confess too much.

I love you, Saoirse. I love every scar, every tear, every hidden imperfection, and I will love them until my final breath.

Saoirse's bottom lip quivered, but she stretched up and placed her lips against his. He had spent decades waiting for her, waiting for the gift the gods had promised him. He couldn't help but think of how they had created her just for him and somehow he had been created just for her. They had both fallen apart numerous times and pieced themselves back together. But now, they were paired to piece *each other* back together when they inevitably fell apart again. Emrys felt his body sigh at the realization, and a glimmer of hope returned as he held Saoirse in his arms.

Her scent of vanilla and sandalwood filled his nose, and the world tilted around him. She didn't deepen their kiss, but the emotion in her touch struck him. This boireann filled every empty space he possessed, and he never wanted to part from her. If he did, he feared that everything he had worked hard for would fall apart for good.

29

I t *was only* two short days until the next council meeting came. Saoirse should have been relieved to be surrounded by her friends, with a multitude of distractions at her fingertips. But the thought of being in the drawing room had her chest constricting. She clung to Emrys that morning, unable to fathom being alone, knowing Kieran was guaranteed to be in the house today.

Calliope was the first of the duchesses to arrive, and Saoirse reluctantly let Emrys proceed to the council room with Vasili. She followed Calliope into the drawing room and tried to keep her face neutral as she took a seat.

"Rory and Ada continue to outdo themselves," Calliope remarked, leaning her cane against the arm of the sofa she sat on.

"Yes, they do." Saoirse tried to flash a warm grin, but she knew it came off more as a grimace. She quickly occupied her nervous hands by pouring tea. To her surprise, she didn't tremble as she handed Calliope the cup.

She did, however, jump in her seat when she heard the door behind her open. When she saw it was Andromeda and Isolde joining them, Saoirse let loose the breath she was unaware she had been holding. Her shoulders finally relaxed, and she close to feeling at complete ease.

She poured two more cups of tea and handed them to the rest of her friends. Without wasting any time, Andromeda launched into her latest anecdote of the week, one she surprisingly hadn't shared at the Lughnasadh dinner.

Saoirse sipped her tea as she listened to the rest of the duchesses comment and jest about Andromeda's dramatic retelling. She nodded along as Calliope and Isolde shared glimpses into their lives when courting their husbands. Saoirse wished she could be more involved in the conversation, but all she could think about was returning to her bed and falling asleep so she didn't have to be plagued by her brutal thoughts.

"Saoirse," Isolde said.

"Hmm?" Saoirse hummed, a bit dazed.

"Are you alright?"

As she nodded, she felt a buzz of anxiety. She had yet to tell her friends what had happened with Odysseus and hadn't wanted to. Tearing open that old wound had not seemed worth it. But now she was actively hurting from a similar incident and only had Emrys to confide in. Tears welled at the back of her eyes, and she tried to blink them away.

"I'm fine," she croaked, her voice betraying her.

"Are you and Emrys alright?" Calliope asked.

"Yes, we're fine." Saoirse nodded, her voice cracking again.

Andromeda eyed her and leaned forward in her seat. "Saoirse, you do know what secondary magic the gods granted me, don't you?" she asked.

"Andromeda, don't," Isolde warned. "If she doesn't want to tell us, we shouldn't push her."

Andromeda ignored her plea and kept her gaze locked on Saoirse. "The gods gave me the gift of Truth Seeker," she told her. "I can see right through anyone lying."

Saoirse took in a deep, shaky breath before slowly letting it out. She looked at the nearly full cup of tea in her lap and felt the first tear slip down her cheek. "Kieran touched me," she answered in a voice so small it was nearly inaudible. "In this room."

"What?" Isolde and Calliope said in unison.

Saoirse looked up to see Andromeda's eyes widen and her

nostrils begin to flare. "He did what?" Her voice was low and lethal and a shiver ran up Saoirse's back.

"He held me against the wall and put his hand under my skirts," she answered. "I gave him a first-degree burn on his arm to get him to let me go."

A flash of something that looked like lightning danced through Andromeda's eyes before she blinked and stood from her seat. She stalked to the door and disappeared into the hall. Saoirse quickly sprang to her feet and followed her. She heard the rustle of Isolde and Calliope standing, but she didn't wait for them to catch up.

"Andromeda," Saoirse said, following the duchess.

Andromeda didn't turn but kept her pace through the hall to the council room. Saoirse tried to stop her several times to no avail. She could only follow her, silently panicking over what she might do.

The duchess reached the council room and flung open the door. Saoirse stopped shy of the doorway and watched as the duchess stormed into the room. The fireannaich inside went quiet as she made a beeline straight to Kieran and raised her hand.

Before Saoirse could blink, Andromeda slapped the general across the face. Gasps and wide eyes followed, but she kept her attention on Kieran. He sat stunned as she leaned into the arm of his chair and bared her teeth at him.

"Don't *ever* touch another boireann like that again," she spat. "If I hear you so much as breathe near a boireann who makes it clear you are unwanted, you will get slapped with more than just the flesh of my hand." She raised the hand that had just connected with his face and sparks flew between her fingers. Without giving Kieran allowance to respond, Andromeda stood and turned, storming out of the room and back to Saoirse and the other duchesses who had caught up with her.

"Andromeda, I—" Saoirse began, but Laszlo cut her off as he tore out of the room and lunged at his wife.

"Andromeda, what was that about?" he asked as he got hold of her arm.

She turned to him and lightning danced in her steel-gray eyes again. "Kieran is a filthy, no good, lousy pig," she snapped as she wrenched her arm away. "He deserves more than just me humiliating him in front of the court."

"You know that was too far," he argued.

"It wasn't far enough." She crossed her arms and gave her husband a cold stare. "He deserves to be emasculated...fully."

"Andromeda," he chided. "You can't barge in and interrupt a meeting. We are facing threats that are beyond our imagination and an outburst like that can cost people their lives."

"He did that himself. If he had kept his hands to himself and respected Saoirse, I wouldn't have felt the need to punish him."

"That's not your place."

"When it comes to my friends, it is!" Her nostrils were flaring, and sparks of lightning were twining around her arms.

"We'll talk about this at home," he said, trying to take her arm again before she shook him off.

"I'm not going anywhere with you if you plan to treat me like a child." She glared at him and challenged him to call her bluff.

"Fine," he said. "Enjoy your night here alone."

He trudged back into the council room without looking back. Saoirse saw Andromeda's icy gaze waver as she stepped up beside her. She wrapped her arms around her friend and was thankful when Andromeda returned the gesture.

"Thank you," Saoirse whispered to her.

"Only the best for my friends." Andromeda squeezed Saoirse's shoulders.

Isolde and Calliope joined in the embrace, and Saoirse had to hold back a new flood of emotions. It was one thing for Emrys to uphold her honor, but it was another for her friends to do it. She wasn't an afterthought or an obligation. She was a priority to these people, something that was becoming less foreign to her.

Saoirse loosened her grip on Andromeda and the duchesses slowly dropped the embrace. "So, I suppose you're staying with us tonight," Saoirse said.

"Yes." Andromeda let out an exhale. "I suppose I am."

Emrys hadn't believed what he had seen. If he could pay all of his inheritance to watch Andromeda slap Kieran again, he would do it without a second thought. Although, he might lose that inheritance with the way Alastair was fuming.

"Are we finished with our bit of dramatics?" he asked sharply as Laszlo sat back in his seat.

"Yes," Laszlo answered, a sober expression on his face. Emrys had rarely seen his friend so serious. "And I apologize on my wife's behalf."

"If council meetings are going to devolve into theatrics on a regular basis, your wives will have their invitation to this house revoked," Alastair threatened.

"Understood." Laszlo and the rest of the dukes nodded.

Alastair turned to Kieran. "That goes for you as well."

"Me?" Kieran asked. He gave an exaggerated wince.

"Yes," Alastair barked. "You represent this court just as much anyone else at this table does. What you do outside of this room has consequences."

"I didn't ask to be slapped, Uncle."

"I didn't ask for your rebuttal." Alastair straightened his jacket and sighed through his nose. "Shall we get back to the business at hand?"

The council meeting moved along stiffly. No one was willing to speak more than what they needed. The threat to Donheath was stagnant, and nothing much had changed in the other sectors the court managed. Alastair finally dismissed the meeting, and the dukes and Kieran were all too eager to vacate the room.

Emrys stood to leave with them, but Alastair halted him.

"Emrys," he said. "What was that earlier scene about?"

Emrys swallowed. His father wasn't entitled to Saoirse's private life, but the way he scolded Kieran softened Emrys's resolve. "It's not my place to say."

"Did it have to do with the brawl I witnessed between you two a few days ago?"

"That wasn't a brawl."

"Oh, my apologies, you two were just roughhousing like children." Sarcasm dripped from Alastair's words.

"We aren't children."

"You two sure could fool me."

"Why don't you ask Kieran what he did?"

"Because I don't trust he'll tell me the truth."

Emrys scoffed. "You've realized now that he has a propensity for lying?"

Alastair didn't answer but gave an unwavering stare.

"It really isn't my place to say." When his father still didn't respond, Emrys asked, "Am I free to leave now?"

Silence continued to stretch between them, and Emrys eventually stood to make his way towards the door.

"Emrys," Alastair finally said when Emrys was nearly through the doorway. His voice had dropped to a solemn tone. "Would you tell Saoirse that if she's willing, I'd like her to explain what happened?" He turned in his seat to face his son. "Since it isn't your place."

Anger flickered in Emrys's gut. Of course Alastair had little concern for his own son. But Emrys's anger warred with feeling appreciative. His father could have easily paid Saoirse the same minimal attention that he paid Emrys, but he didn't. Instead, he treated her like his own. Jealousy flared in him, and Emrys found himself cycling through each emotion again and again as he left the council room and went on the search for his wife.

He peeked into the drawing room only to find it empty, save for a few half-eaten plates of sweets. The rest of the downstairs was quiet, leading him to look upstairs. When he stepped into their quarters, he found Saoirse and Andromeda on the sofa.

"Hello," he said, leaning on the arm of the sofa and greeting Saoirse with a kiss. "Andromeda, I assume you're staying the night?"

"I'm not quite welcome in my own home at the moment, so yes," the duchess answered.

"If it's any consolation—and please don't repeat this to Laszlo—I could watch you slap Kieran until the end of time."

Andromeda let out an amused laugh. "One of us had to do it." She gave him a cheeky grin and shrugged.

"I'll have you know I boxed his face with my ice," Emrys told her, his ego slightly bruised at her comment.

"Ice?" she repeated, her impressed expression exaggerated. "That's cute. Have you struck him with lightning?"

"No," he answered, with a smirk forming on his face. "But I'd very much like to see it."

Andromeda laughed again as Saoirse's hand slipped into Emrys's and squeezed it three times. He wanted to tell her what his father requested, but his anger and jealousy won out for the moment. While he was happy that so many people adored and cared about his wife, he wasn't ready to face the feeling of being picked over by his father once again. It was selfish, but he was allowed to be a bit selfish when it came to Saoirse. At least, that was his justification to himself.

Rory made up Saoirse's room for Andromeda to stay in that night. With Saoirse staying with Emrys most nights, Andromeda would get much better use out of the room. The two boireannaich sat in the sitting room after dinner and ate what was left of the food from tea. They also broke into the liquor Emrys kept on the bar cart until they were both giggling and spilling their hearts to each other. Saoirse had lit the fireplace, and they sat on the floor in front of it as they talked.

"I'm sorry if I created the argument between you and Laszlo," she said, biting into the last blueberry scone.

Andromeda furrowed her brow and shook her head. "You aren't at fault for anything," she assured her. "Laszlo likes to execute revenge with much more subtle means, unlike me. He knows when to stand up for himself and what he thinks is right, but he rarely goes about it like I do. He says I take drastic measures, but when you're a boireann, sometimes you have to take drastic measures to be heard and taken seriously."

Saoirse smiled at her, understanding how the world could be cruel to boireannaich. "I appreciate you standing up for me," she said as she drained her glass of amber liquor. She wasn't sure if she was becoming accustomed to the burn it gave the back of her throat or if she was a little too intoxicated to care.

"I'll always stand up for my friends, no matter what," Andromeda said with a lopsided, tipsy smile. "I spent many years having to stand up for myself. It exhausted me to the point I almost prayed to Morrigan herself to remove me as a burden on the earth. But I found one person willing to stand up for me, and I have never forgotten how much that has meant to me."

"What happened to them?" Saoirse asked.

"I married him," she said in an exaggerated whisper.

Saoirse smiled at her, and her thoughts drifted to Emrys. He was the first person to assure her what happened with Kieran wasn't her fault. He reminded her nothing she had done warranted Kieran's actions, and the fireann was responsible for his own choices. A blaze that had nothing to do with the liquor warming her insides filled her. She had a renewed determination to keep this incident from taking hold of her life. She had worked too hard to build it with Emrys to let it slip away.

She and Andromeda finally decided to go to bed, and Saoirse swayed as she walked to Emrys's bedroom. She found him as she usually did at this hour, half-asleep and half-naked.

When she walked into the room, he gave her a tired smile. "There you are," he said, sitting up.

She stumbled into his arms and giggled as he caught her.

"Did you and Andromeda get into my brandy?" he asked.

Saoirse nodded and buried her face in his neck. She breathed in his scent mix of musk and bergamot, and if she wasn't already drunk, she would have been from his scent alone.

She began to line the column of his throat with kisses and worked her way up his jaw to meet his lips. She gave him a deep kiss and ran her hands over his bare chest. He responded to her kiss, but his hands stayed cemented where they were at her waist. Her hands continued to roam over him until they lowered to the waistband of his pants.

"Saoirse," he said between kisses. "We're not having sex right now."

She pulled back and frowned, her vision of him swaying. "Why not?" she asked.

"Because you are too drunk at the moment," he said as he tightened his grip on her waist so she didn't topple over.

She pushed him towards the bed until he was lying on his back and crawled on top of him, straddling his hips. "But I want to," she slurred.

"No," he said in his gentle but firm tone. "I don't want to have sex with you in this state just like I didn't want to have sex with you when your mind wasn't completely present."

Saoirse frowned, but his reasoning eventually made it through her mind's intoxicated state. She collapsed on top of him and felt his hand stroke along her spine. "You're too good to me," she murmured.

"I'm glad you think so." He chuckled.

She sighed and pushed herself up just far enough to meet his eyes. The gold in them glittered in the dark room, and the spark bounced along Saoirse's spine. "Emrys," she said quietly. "What if it doesn't go away? What if I can't keep myself from fading out?"

"Then we keep working until you can stay present with me," he said simply. His lips gently kissed hers before continuing. "I will wait for you for as long as it takes."

She felt tears sting her eyes, and they dropped onto Emrys's face before she could stop or swipe them away. He reached for her and wiped the subsequent tears with his thumbs before they could fall. "I don't deserve you," she whispered.

He brought her forehead to his lips and gave a long, lingering kiss to her warm skin. "You deserve all the good things, Saoirse. We both do."

When the sun streamed into Emrys's room the next morning, a pounding headache hit Saoirse as soon as she woke and she buried her face in her pillow to block out the light. Unlike wine, hard liquor could easily bring on a brutal bottle ache. It was much stronger than wine, and fae bodies couldn't process it as well or as quickly. Saoirse groaned as she felt Emrys shift and run a gentle hand over her arm.

"Did I forget to tell you less than a glass of liquor is enough to enjoy an evening?" he asked, a playful lilt mixing with the rasp in his voice.

Saoirse groaned again and blindly shoved at him. He chuckled before rising from the bed and shutting the curtains as tightly as he could. She heard his footsteps move out of the room and back in.

"Take this," he told her.

Saoirse lifted her head from her pillow and eyed the open flask in his hand. "Why?" she asked.

"It's a remedy for bottle aches," he explained as he sank to his knees so he was eye-level with her. "Seraphina made it and filled a flask of it for me. You only need to take a healthy swig of it for it to work."

Saoirse carefully reached for the flask and took a tentative whiff. There was a hint of mint among the strong herbal scent, and she had to keep herself from dry heaving. She brought the flask to her lips and tipped back a swig. Her body cringed at the taste as she forced herself to swallow. "Not exactly the flavor I was hoping for this morning," she said.

Her headache still remained, but she handed the flask back to Emrys. He closed it and placed it on the bedside table before reaching for Saoirse and brushing wisps of hair out of her face.

"You two must have had a good time if you're suffering from such a strong bottle ache this morning," he said with a cheeky smirk.

Saoirse nodded and closed her eyes again, her eyelids too heavy to keep open. Her headache was subsiding, and she started to recall the events of the previous night.

Her eyes flew open, and she stared in horror as she remembered what she did after she and Andromeda agreed to go to retire for the night. "Oh, no." She covered her face with her hands, mortified at the memory. "Did I try to have sex with you last night?" She peeked at him through her fingers and saw Emrys try to stifle a chuckle, but his vibrating shoulders gave him away.

"You did," he said with an amused grin. "You were very hard to resist."

She groaned and threw herself face down into her pillow again. If the way he resisted laughing with that grin on his face was any indication, she must not have been as irresistible as he made her out to be.

A faint knock at the sitting room door saved her further embarrassment by taking Emrys's attention. She felt him kiss the side of her head before she heard his footsteps fade towards the sitting room. The door clicked open and Saoirse listened to the distant conversation between Emrys and who she could only assume was Laszlo.

"Good morning, Emrys," the duke said. "I'm here to collect my wife."

"She's just through there." She heard Emrys inform him. The sound of footsteps crossing the room could be heard through the sitting room. "But I must warn you, she and Saoirse got into the brandy last night, so you might want this." There was a short pause before Emrys continued. "She may not be in any mood to argue either."

"I don't plan to argue," Laszlo said plainly.

"Isn't that always the intention and never the outcome?" Emrys said with a chuckle.

Laszlo also chuckled but didn't answer his question. "Thank you, Emrys," he said.

Saoirse heard the door to her bedroom squeak open across their quarters before noticing Emrys had reappeared. He put his finger to his lips and tiptoed towards her. She sat up as Emrys sat next to her on the bed and wrapped her arms around his waist. They stayed quiet, eavesdropping on Laszlo and Andromeda in case they found interference was needed.

The conversation was muffled between the walls, but Saoirse could make out the deep tone of Laszlo's voice and the gravelly one of Andromeda's. From the way her words seemed to come out monotone, she must have woken up with the same headache Saoirse had.

Pieces of the conversation filtered through and Laszlo didn't sound nearly as harsh as he was the day before. Saoirse caught Andromeda's side of the argument. It was the one she had told Saoirse last night, a time when Laszlo had stood up for her.

There was a long moment of silence before the sound of the bed creaking was the only noise to be heard from the other room. Saoirse's face heated as she realized what their conversation had transitioned into. She turned to Emrys, who she watched reach the same realization, and let out a snort of laughter.

"I can see that argument is over," he murmured.

She giggled and quickly slapped her hand over her mouth. Emrys kissed her temple as the creaking next door intensified, making it harder to ignore. Saoirse's face grew hotter as she tried to push the image of Laszlo and Andromeda enjoying themselves on her old bed. If she wasn't already committed to sharing Emrys's bed, this would have tipped her over the edge.

"Would you like to get some breakfast?" Emrys asked quickly.

She looked up at him and saw he was just as visibly uncomfortable as she was. "Yes, yes, I would." She slid her arms from him and swung her legs over the edge of the bed.

She grabbed her silk dressing gown, foregoing proper clothes in favor of getting out of their quarters as quickly as possible. Emrys also pulled on a flannel dressing gown and followed her out of their bedroom. He dared a glance at the other door in the sitting room and swiftly turned his gaze back to the wall in front of him, his face a bright shade of crimson.

"Don't turn around," he instructed in a low voice in her ear. "They didn't close the door."

Saoirse's face went even hotter, and she forced herself to keep her eyes forward as Emrys quietly opened the sitting room door so they could make their escape.

Once downstairs, they made their way to the breakfast room and were greeted with the same dishes they had every morning. Saoirse hadn't realized just how hungry she was until she dug her fork into her food and couldn't stop shoveling it into her mouth.

A chuckle caught Saoirse's attention, and she swallowed the bite she had in her mouth. "What?" she asked.

"Absolutely nothing," Emrys said, his grin giving him away.

"I'm starved," Saoirse said defensively.

"I can imagine." He sipped his morning tea, hiding his amusement.

She watched him as his grin dropped a moment later and he kept his eyes on his plate. "Emrys," she said gently. "Is something wrong?"

He shook his head. "No, nothing wrong." His gaze shifted to her. "My father asked for you to tell him what Kieran did."

Suddenly, Saoirse's appetite disappeared.

"You don't have to," Emrys quickly added. "But he does seem concerned about you."

"What do you think?" she asked.

"About what?"

"About telling Alastair about...my incident."

He sighed. "He could give two straws about me. But you, he wants you to be treated like the future queen you are."

A shiver ran through her. She knew Emrys was first in line for the throne, but it had never felt like a tangible possibility that she would hold the title queen. "Do you think this would affect Kieran?" she asked.

"I don't really know." Emrys shrugged. "He could be punished or my father could completely ignore it."

Saoirse absently reached for her tea and sipped on it, the flavor barely registering on her tongue. Alastair had treated her well ever since she arrived, Emrys hadn't exaggerated that. But could she manage to take priority over the king's golden fireann?

"There you two are," Andromeda's voice broke through her anxious thoughts. She was wearing her clothes from the day before. Like her hair, they were a bit rumpled. "I wanted to thank you before we left."

"You can thank us by shutting the door next time," Emrys said.

"Apologies," Laszlo murmured. "I didn't think that was how that conversation would end."

"Oh, you didn't?" Emrys smirked as he sipped his tea.

"Thank you for letting me stay last night." Andromeda quickly veered the conversation back to her original intention. "I really appreciate the hospitality."

"Any time," Saoirse told her.

After a quick hug, Andromeda and Laszlo made their departure. In the duke and duchess's absence, Saoirse and Emrys sat in a stilted silence. Alastair's request for her kept pulling at her thoughts. Would it even do anything? Did he have the energy to punish Kieran? Surely he would do more than dismiss her like her brother did in this type of situation.

Saoirse sighed aloud. She was thankful for Andromeda and her willingness to stand up for her. But Saoirse couldn't solely cower behind her friends and husband. She had to stand up for herself as well.

"I'll do it," she said quietly.

"Do what?" Emrys asked.

"I'll talk to Alastair about what Kieran did." She swallowed. "He deserves to know what happens in his own house, especially when it involves the court."

Emrys reached for her hand and squeezed it three times. "I support you completely."

A smile tugged at her lips and that familiar and welcome warmth in her chest flooded through her. She squeezed his hand back and punctuated it with a kiss to the back of it. The words that articulated how she felt were caught in the back of her throat, so for now, she settled for showing him as best she could.

The next afternoon, Saoirse paced the length of the sitting room. She had been confident in her decision the day before but was beginning to doubt herself. Her limbs felt like they were vibrating with electricity, and her heart was pounding viciously in her chest. Emrys came into the sitting room to collect her, and she stopped cold.

"Are you still sure?" he asked her.

"I don't know," she whispered as she wrung her hands. "What if he accuses me of lying?" The question haunted her, eating away at the confidence she had put into her decision. It was what her brother did, and while Alastair had treated Saoirse like a beloved daughter, Alastair was closest with Kieran. She couldn't help but wonder if Alastair had already settled on his opinion about whatever transpired between her and Kieran.

Emrys closed the space between them and wrapped his hands over her upper arms, rubbing them soothingly. "I know," he said softly. "But..." He took a deep breath before continuing. "But he did tell me he wanted to hear this from you because he doesn't trust Kieran to tell the truth."

"He did?" she asked, stunned.

"He did." Emrys nodded and gave her shoulders a squeeze.

Saoirse took a deep breath through her nose before nodding. "Alright, I'm ready to see him." Her fingers interlaced with Emrys's as he led her down the hall to Alastair's office. Her heart continued to pound, and she felt nausea roll through her stomach. She focused on breathing through her nose, willing her stomach to settle as they approached the door.

Emrys rapped on the door before opening it. Alastair was seated behind his desk, but quickly got to his feet to greet Saoirse. She looked to Emrys before entering the office, looking for last-minute reassurance. He kissed her gently and let her pull her hand from his. His gaze told her he'd be close by for support if she needed it, and her stomach mellowed.

Alastair closed the door and motioned for her to follow him. Instead of seating himself back behind his desk, he led her to the sitting area on the other side of the office where two armchairs sat in front of a brick fireplace. He gestured towards one of the armchairs, and Saoirse carefully sat in it.

"Well, dear, how are you?" he asked, taking a seat in the other.

"I've been better," she answered hesitantly.

"I can imagine." He gave her a sympathetic smile, and her heart slowed down to a steady pace. "Well, I'll come to why I've asked you here. During the last council meeting, the Duchess of Cogwick brought something to my attention about Kieran. She gave him a few...*choice* words about being inappropriate. I understand it had something to do with you. Would you want to share what happened?"

She stared at him, swallowing, and collected the courage to recount the incident. "I had come home last week and saw someone was in the drawing room. I thought it was Emrys, but found it was Kieran. I tried to leave the room, but..." Saoirse chewed on her bottom lip. Explaining why Kieran would keep her from leaving sounded out of character without the background of what he had been doing the past few weeks.

"I should add Kieran has been harassing me up to this point," she confessed. "We had a previous relationship six months ago, and I believe that's his reason behind his harassment."

"I know," Alastair said.

"Y-you do?"

"I witnessed him try to kiss you in the hall shortly after the wedding. I intervened as best I could."

Saoirse's jaw dropped a bit. She remembered a blast of wind halting Kieran from pushing any farther than his attempted kiss. She didn't think much of it at the time since she had just been happy to have an opening to get away. But looking back, there really was no way to explain its presence naturally. Of course it had to be magic. It hadn't even crossed her mind to connect it with Alastair since Emrys hadn't inherited the same element of magic.

Alastair had protected her. A now familiar warmth flourished in her chest just like when she was with her friends and Emrys. It compelled her to shake her doubts from earlier and trust him enough to continue.

"When I tried to leave the drawing room, Kieran grabbed me and pinned me to the wall. He then put his hand under my skirts and touched me." Her voice lowered to nearly a whisper as she spoke. She wasn't quite at the point where recalling the incident was getting easier. It just flooded her with fear.

"How did you get away from him?" Alastair asked, a genuine look of concern on his face.

"I tried to disarm him, but he countered it, and that's when he pushed me against the wall," she answered. "I eventually had to resort to my magic, and I burned his arm to get him to let me go."

Alastair's features morphed from concern to empathy, as if he was reliving a similar experience she had just described. "I'm so sorry that happened to you," he finally said, a hint of a shake in his voice. "I hope you know none of it was your fault."

Tears welled in Saoirse's eyes, and she forced them back, refusing to let them spill. She had cried enough over the misfortune of her life. She didn't want to do more of it now. Her throat was too thick with emotion to speak as she nodded.

He studied her for a moment before addressing her reaction to his comment. "You've had someone disbelieve you before, haven't you?"

"Yes," she croaked. "I had it happen before, and my brother blamed me for it."

Alastair pulled his handkerchief from his jacket pocket and handed it to her. She dabbed at her eyes as the tears ultimately pushed past her defenses. "I hope you know that wasn't your fault either, and your brother is a fool for telling you otherwise." Saoirse nodded again as more tears rolled down her cheeks. "I've found it's hard for those who haven't experienced something like this to believe victims of it."

"Thank you," she whispered as she blotted her face again. Her breath was shaky, but she held herself together enough to hand the handkerchief back to him.

"You're welcome." He gave her a warm smile. "I appreciate you trusting me enough to share something so difficult. I understand it's not as easy as one may think."

"It's not," Saoirse agreed. "And it's not getting any easier."

"It probably won't for a while." Alastair sighed through his nose. "But I can tell you your father would be proud of who you grew up to be despite your brother's best efforts."

She cracked a small smile. She had forgotten that Alastair mentioned he knew her father. Saoirse desperately wanted to hear stories of him, but this wasn't the time. She would have to ask Alastair later on.

"Thank you," Saoirse said. "For everything. I've felt more at home here than I did in Ireland. Even in spite of what Kieran has done."

"I'm glad to hear that." Alastair stood and extended his hand. "Well, I better not keep you much longer. I'm sure you have much more exhilarating plans than listen to me blather on."

Saoirse accepted his hand and rose out of her seat, following him to the office door. Her heart felt a little lighter after confiding with Alastair. She was a bit conflicted knowing Emrys had a troublesome relationship with him, but both fireannaich had the same intention to protect her as best they could. If anything, it made her feel more comfortable and secure in the house.

Emrys waited patiently outside the door of his father's office. It felt like an hour had passed before he heard the click of the doorknob and immediately perked up when the door opened to reveal his mate. Her eyes were slightly swollen, and her nose had a rosy tint to it, but she didn't look as fearful and anxious as she had been before stepping into the room. Instead, she looked content, as if the weight of the world had been removed from her shoulders.

Saoirse stepped towards him and wrapped her arms around his waist. He planted a kiss in her hair and embraced her.

"Are you alright?" he asked in a low voice.

She nodded as she pressed her cheek to his chest.

"I hate to ask this, but can I have a few words with Emrys in private?" Alastair asked from the doorway of his office.

Saoirse lifted her eyes to Emrys, and he kissed her gently.

"Go see Ada or Seraphina. I'll find you afterward, alright?"

She nodded and slid her arms from him. He missed her warmth immediately as he watched her disappear down the stairs. Once she was gone, Emrys entered his father's office and debated sitting in one of the chairs at his father's desk.

"I was afraid my assumption would be true," his father said, still standing. "There are going to be consequences for Kieran."

"There are?" Emrys asked, his brows raising in surprise.

Alastair nodded, his expression a mix of anger and resentment. "He deserves more than a black eye from you in the hallway and a slap in front of the court." He leveled a gaze with his son. "I'll be removing him as general."

Emrys thought he misheard his father. His eyes widened as he stared in bewilderment at him. "You are?" he asked.

His father nodded again. Determination gleamed in his eyes, and it made a shiver run through Emrys. "Yes, he's gone too far in the last month, and he needs to be held accountable for his monstrous actions. Between the way he's bullied the Duke of Donheath, engaged in brawls in my hallways, and now what he's done to Saoirse..." Alastair sighed. "I've let him get away with too much."

Emrys's jaw hung open. He wanted to be wary of his father's words, but after seeing the look on Saoirse's face when she left this office, he had little room to doubt Alastair. "I support you, Father."

"Thank you," Alastair said. "I'll let you get back to your wife now."

Emrys nodded and made his way to the door.

"Oh, one last thing," his father said, making Emrys stop in his tracks. "Saoirse is quite lucky to have you as her spouse. I think your mother would be proud of you."

A knot formed in Emrys's throat. He attempted an appreciative smile and nodded. His father rarely brought up his mother, but since Emrys had married Saoirse, Alastair had brought her up several times. It pulled at old wounds, ones that Emrys had thought he had closed decades ago. What had he missed by having his mother ripped from him so young? Would he have made different choices in his life?

Emrys pushed those thoughts away as he always did, and when his father turned his attention to his desk, he slipped into the hall and down the stairs.

He found Saoirse in the kitchen enjoying a cup of tea with Ada and Rory. A warm smile tugged at his lips when he saw her lost in conversation with the house manager and housekeeper. The mating spark made itself known as Saoirse met his gaze and smiled back at him.

"Hello," he said, placing a hand on her back and kissing her temple. "Are you still alright?"

She nodded. "I'm actually starting to feel much better than I have in the last few days."

"Good." He stroked his hand along her spine and felt her tiny flinch, as if she had been hit with a surge of electricity. He knew she had felt the mating spark, and he once again debated sharing the truth.

Saoirse was in a better place than when he took advantage of one of the elements of the mating bond to relieve her pain. But what if she was still emotionally fragile and didn't take it well? She had spent the last week reliving the worst moment of her life. Revealing the bond could pile onto that and cause all the work he put in to gain her trust to unravel.

He shook the thoughts and doubts from his mind and spent a few minutes with Ada and Rory alongside Saoirse. He was caught up on the staff gossip, a favorite pastime of Ada's. But when she offered him his own cup of tea, he graciously declined and bid them goodbye to escort Saoirse upstairs.

"What did your father say?" she asked as he closed the sitting room door.

Emrys crossed the room to his bar cart and poured a glass of amber liquor, hesitating to answer her. "Do you want a drink?" he asked. He needed liquor more than tea after the emotional whiplash his father put him through.

"No, thank you," she answered as she leaned against the arm of the sofa. Emrys sipped his drink and avoided meeting her gaze. "Emrys." Her soft voice was too nice to avoid. He looked up, and she asked again. "What did your father want to speak to you about?"

"He told me my mother would be proud of me." Emrys leaned against the back of the sofa and took a sip of his liquor. He relished the burn in his throat as he swallowed it.

"That was nice of him." Saoirse gave a small smile. "Maybe he does give two straws about you."

Emrys huffed a laugh. "I think he only gives two straws about me because I'm married to you."

"Regardless, he notices you, and he's proud of you."

Emrys stared down into his glass, unable to absorb any truth of her observation. "He's going to punish Kieran," he added.

Silence came from Saoirse. He peeked up at Saoirse to see all amusement had been flushed from her face and her skin had gone pale. "Punish him how?" she asked, her voice beginning to waver.

"He's removing him as general." The words didn't seem real as he spoke them out loud.

"What?" Her hand shook as she raised it to brush the tiny

strands of hair at her hairline. "He-He's stripping him of his rank? Because of me?" Saoirse shook her head in disbelief, and Emrys quickly jumped to explain she wasn't at fault.

"He's done more to warrant this than just what he's done to you. He's been a menace in council meetings and has pushed us closer to a war we could have avoided. He has ignored my father's warnings and hid behind his rank to avoid responsibility."

Saoirse's chin wobbled as she fidgeted with her hair and clothes. "But that's now how he'll see it. He's going to assume it's because of me. I burned him for what he did. You boxed him. Andromeda slapped him. And now he's having his rank removed. He's going to think it's because of me!"

"He's not going to—"

"I don't want to be here," she interrupted. "I don't want to be in this house when Alastair strips Kieran of his position. You can tell me I'm not at fault all you want, but that doesn't mean he won't take his revenge out on me...or you."

Emrys hadn't thought about himself as being a target of retaliation. Kieran could easily turn on Emrys rather than Saoirse. She had a handful of people ready to make his life miserable if he touched her again. But if he made Emrys's life miserable? It would be much harder to prove, and Emrys couldn't guarantee his father would step in like he did for Saoirse.

"Emrys." Saoirse's eyes were wide, and he could see how shallow her breathing was.

He scrambled for an idea. Somewhere he could take her to be safe for a few days. His mind landed on the one place Kieran couldn't go looking for them.

"I know somewhere we can go."

She froze at his words, and Emrys waited patiently for her to confirm how much she trusted him. "Where?"

"Go pack a bag." He leveled a stare with her, waiting for her to agree.

"Where are we going? What should I pack? How many days?"

"Pack whatever necessities you need and make sure they'll last a few days."

"Emrys, I trust you, but where would you be taking me?"

I trust you.

He gained the one thing he had been after since he met her. She trusted him, and he could finally breathe easier.

"A cottage," he finally answered. "Seraphina and Ada own it, but since they live here, it's unoccupied. It's near the North Sea, and Kieran doesn't know anything about it."

She nodded in understanding and contemplated his offer for one last moment. He reminded himself she trusted him and she wasn't contemplating if it was safe. She was contemplating if it was indeed right to flee or not.

"Okay," she said softly. "I'll go pack."

Saoirse wasn't sure what she expected the cottage to look like, but what she found was exactly what she would expect Seraphina and Ada to call home. After riding on horseback for two hours, she and Emrys came to a cottage that was a mile from the beach. While the exterior showed some wear and tear due to its proximity to the ocean, it had been built to withstand what was probably centuries of use. The two stories of cream-colored stones were weathered in places, but the terracotta-tiled roof looked nearly untouched. The only other obvious sign of the home's age was the porch creaking under her boots.

As Emrys opened the front door, Saoirse was greeted by the smell of cloves and other spices. The kitchen was the first room to welcome them. The counters were clean, and the space was small with a simple sink, stove, and table. A cozy dining room was to the left, and a sitting room sat on the other side of the kitchen wall. A large brick hearth was built against the wall and, with the chill of the sea air, Saoirse imagined herself curling up on the worn sofa with a cup of tea and enjoying the dancing flames of a fire.

She turned in place where the dining room, kitchen, and sitting room bled into each other and took in the pale blue walls of the interior and the worn, scuffed floors. She could feel the love of Ada and Seraphina's family woven into every inch of the house.

"There's a bedroom this way," Emrys said, pointing to a door at the opposite side of the kitchen and pulling her from her thoughts. "And three bedrooms upstairs. You're welcome to choose whatever room you'd like."

"I'd like the one down here," she answered.

"Very well. The layout of the house is pretty easy to navigate, and I don't think you'll have any difficulty finding what you need."

He closed the front door and placed their luggage into the downstairs bedroom. When he returned to the kitchen, he rummaged in the cabinets for ingredients to make something for dinner. "I'm not sure what I'll find to make dinner," he commented as he sniffed a block of cheese.

"I thought you said Seraphina and Ada haven't lived here in years." Saoirse leaned her elbows on the kitchen table.

"They haven't, but there's usually one of us who has been here in the last week."

"One of us?" Saoirse asked.

"Ada and Seraphina's children," Emrys answered simply. "We all have full access to the cottage and have an unspoken rule to leave some food in the icebox or cupboards for whoever comes next." He looked over his shoulder at Saoirse with a cheeky grin. "Except for me."

"Why are you the exception?" she asked, the corner of her lip tugging upward.

He returned his attention back to the cabinets and pulled a few things out that Saoirse couldn't make out. "Because I'm the baby, of course."

Her lips pulled up into a full grin, and her shoulders shook a bit. As her giggles settled, she looked around the cottage and noticed how quiet and empty it was. "How did you know no one would be here?"

"I didn't." He turned towards her and plopped a loaf of bread, that cheeky smile still on his lips. "I took a gamble."

She huffed a laughed as she shook her head. Emrys found cold cuts of meat and fresh cheese in icebox and added them on the table alongside the bread. He pieced the ingredients together and presented a finished sandwich on a plate to Saoirse. She took a small bite, but her stomach still felt unsettled from earlier.

Her thoughts continued to return to Fearynhurst and every potential reaction Kieran could have. She wanted him to be punished, but she assumed he would get a few responsibilities or privileges revoked, not be stripped of his entire job. With the timing of his latest transgression, there was no doubt he would connect the punishment to her and target her for his revenge.

"Saoirse," Emrys said gently. "You're going to be safe."

"I know," she whispered. "But—"

"No 'but.'" He closed the space between them and cradled her face in his hands. "I will keep you safe as long as you trust me to do so."

"I have no plans to stop trusting you."

"Good." A small grin graced his lips before he pressed a kiss to her forehead.

They continued eating their meager dinner, and Saoirse found herself missing Ada and her staff's indulgent cooking already. Emrys took their empty plates to the sink as Saoirse moved to the sitting room. She shook the anxiety out of her mind long enough to muster a bit of flame to light the hearth. Delicious heat brushed against her, and she smiled to herself.

Saoirse heard the squeal of a kettle in the kitchen and moments later, Emrys appeared with two large ceramic mugs that had lopsided rims. He handed one to her, and she breathed in the comforting scent of Ada's special blend of tea.

"Did one of Ada and Seraphina's children make these mugs?" she asked as she took a sip, feeling warmth inside her as well as outside.

"No, Seraphina did," Emrys answered, fighting a laugh. He took a few steps towards the worn ivory sofa and plopped down comfortably on it. "She took it up long before I was born and I'm sure dropped it not long after. Case in point." He lifted his own misshapen mug.

Saoirse also stifled her laugh, covering her grin with another sip. She joined him on the sofa and stretched her legs out onto his lap. Her fears of Kieran were slowly fading the longer they were in the cottage. They were alone without staff, visitors, or Alastair. The respite was shaping up to feel like a honeymoon.

A new fear struck her, and she hid her shaking hands by sipping her tea. As fulfilling as sharing uninterrupted time with Emrys was, it wouldn't be long before they tried to be intimate. And she would fade out of the moment, interrupting it.

She dropped her gaze to her tea and tried not to let their future disappointment ruin this quiet moment.

"What are you thinking?" Emrys asked.

She glanced up at him, and her cheeks flushed to a rosy shade. "Nothing," she murmured.

"I know it's not nothing. You're thinking so loudly I can't find any peace in this room." His half-smile eased her, and she attempted to return it.

"I'm worried what will happen if we have sex," she answered in a small voice. She didn't mean to say it so bluntly, but she felt compelled to be as forward as possible with the truth.

"You shouldn't," Emrys said.

"What if the same thing that happened at Andromeda's happens here?"

"Then we work through it." He wrapped his hand around her ankle and gave it a squeeze. "We haven't tried since that night, so there's no telling what will happen."

"I'm sorry." Her throat clogged, strangling her words.

"You have nothing to be sorry for."

"But I do. I trapped you in this. I saw a way out of my miserable life and took it. You deserve better."

She braced for his realization and subsequent exit. But it never came. Instead, she felt the warmth of his hand on her calf.

"That's absolutely not true." His tone was gentle, and Saoirse felt the familiar pinch and burn of tears forming behind her eyes.

"It is," she argued, her voice cracking. "You deserve better than the mess I am. You deserve someone who doesn't have the scar of a neglectful family. You deserve better than someone who has nightmares and panics when she sees her former lover. And you deserve someone who doesn't fade away in intimacy. I'm sure you could have found someone that offered much more than I could."

"I am not perfect," he whispered as his hand stroked her leg. "And I definitely don't deserve someone who is perfect."

"But you deserve better than me." Her voice cracked again, but she held back tears.

"Maybe that's true, but I don't want anyone but you." She tried to give him a smile, but it came off as a grimace. "And I want all of you. I want every dark corner and bright spot. I want to love every last part of you."

Saoirse felt her heart drop, and her tears dissolved instantly. Emrys's face remained calm as she stared at him.

"You don't have to feel the same. I don't expect you to. But I love you, Saoirse, and you deserve that."

Love.

He said he loved her. She couldn't think of the last time someone had said those words to her. There may have never been a time she heard those words directed at her. She sat numbly as it sunk in.

As if sensing her overwhelm, Emrys carefully extracted her mug of tea from her hands and moved it to a nearby table. He pulled her into his arms and cradled her in his lap.

He had spoken the words she had come to understand and craved to feel. She had only just learned what those words meant and felt like at Calliope's anniversary dinner. She felt it with the duchesses, Emrys, and earlier that day with Alastair. She had been showered with love since the first arrived at the Fearynhurst estate.

She pulled away far enough to look him in the eyes and felt the words bubble in her chest. However, a thread of fear held them back. She stared at him instead while she tried to even her breathing.

He placed a kiss on her nose and without saying a word, she knew he understood. She wanted to apologize but knew what he would say to it. Her forehead rested against his, and she closed her eyes, enjoying the way their bodies melded and breathed against each other. She heard him whispering, but it wasn't to her or in English. She recognized a few words and realized he was speaking in the Old Language. A smile spread across her face as she translated the few words she could.

To her, it sounded less like a sweeping declaration of love and more like a rambling of his admiration. She caught pieces that echoed the vows they made to each other at their wedding. He promised to show his love in every possible way from holding her when she felt alone to caring for her when she fell ill to listening to whatever ailed her mind. He promised to choose her over and over again, no matter the hardships they faced or the ones that came between them.

Tears pricked the back of her eyes. The whispered thoughts about her worth tried to cling to her mind, but Emrys's words washed them away. He was promising the energy to love her would never run out, no matter her condition. He loved her as she was, scars and all.

Emrys pressed a kiss in her hair when he finished speaking, and the two sat silently tangled in each other on the sofa until the fire turned to smoldering embers, and he carried her to bed.

The cottage was a stark contrast to the estate in Fearynhurst. The obvious difference being it was much smaller and more intimate than the sprawling house. But there were subtle differences that had her falling in love with the cozy beach cottage. It was quiet with just her and Emrys, a different quiet than when they were in Fearynhurst. While their quarters could feel secluded, there was always the fact that someone else was in the home hanging over their heads. There was always the possibility of being interrupted or called on. Here, there were none of those threats or responsibilities.

Every corner of the cottage also revealed how heavily lived-in it was. Books with creased spines and aging glass decorations lined various shelves and flat surfaces. The dining room had mismatched chairs with various levels of distress to them. Nothing in the house seemed new and preserved. Instead, it was comforting and welcoming.

Saoirse thumbed through the books on a shelf in the sitting room and ran her finger over a spine that wasn't quite right. When she pulled it out, it looked like the cover had been torn off and every effort was used to salvage the book. She opened to the first chapter to see bits of writing scrawled in the margins and numerous pages throughout the book were dog-eared.

She tried to decipher the handwriting, but didn't immediately recognize it. As she read through the notes left behind by the book's reader, the chosen words sounded a bit familiar. A smile tugged at her lips as she imagined Emrys reading the book and scribbling his thoughts. Her smile grew wider as she skimmed through the opening chapter of the well-loved book. It was a novel about a love story, one between a garden-loving fae and a guard to a fae prince.

Saoirse took the novel into the kitchen and perched onto one of the stools at the small table as she read.

Emrys emerged from outside in trousers and a dress shirt, the top buttons of his shirt open and his rolled sleeves revealing his forearms. "What have we found?" he asked as he came up to her side. She flashed the well-worn book to him and his laughter filled the room. "Where did you find this?"

"It was just sitting on a shelf in the sitting room." She kissed him in lieu of a greeting.

"You know, this is my favorite book."

"Oh, is it?" she asked with a cheeky giggle. "I couldn't tell by the lack of a cover and all the handwritten notes inside it."

Emrys chuckled and kissed her temple. "You have quite the investigation skills. If you find yourself a widow, you should ask Cyprian for a job."

At the word "widow," Saoirse's face fell. "Please don't joke about that," she whispered.

"I'm sorry." He slid his hand into hers. "I just don't want to share you if I can help it."

She took a shaky breath, trying to calm the urge to protect him at all costs. "I don't ever want to think about you dead."

"I know, and I promise you won't have to."

He leaned down and kissed her gently. The spark danced along her shoulders as she sighed. She threaded her fingers into Emrys's hair and readied herself to fight to stay present. Her bottom slid off the chair, and her heels reunited with the floor.

Emrys pulled her tightly against him as the fog in her mind threatened to roll in. But she concentrated on the feel of his lips against hers, the taste that lingered on his tongue. Her hands slid to the buttons of his shirt and popped the remaining ones open. He shrugged out of his suspenders and let her hands slip under his open shirt.

Warmth seeped into her palms, and she latched onto the sensation to anchor herself in the moment. Her lips traveled along his jaw to his collarbone before pressing a kiss to the middle of his chest. When she lifted her gaze back to him, his eyes had darkened, and she gave him a knowing half-smile.

She felt the beat of his heart under her palm as he smoothed a hand over her hair. "Have I lost you yet?" he asked.

"No." Her smile grew wider just before he captured her lips again. He kissed her deeply, and she fumbled as she reached for the waistband of his trousers. As she unbuttoned the first button, his hand caught hers.

"We shouldn't do this in the kitchen," he breathed.

"Where do you suggest we move to? The sofa?" She giggled and circled the sensitive skin of his lower abdomen. She felt his muscles jump and twitch involuntarily at her touch.

"I was thinking the bedroom would be suitable."

Her smile softened before she bit her bottom lip. Kissing and teasing him in the kitchen was one thing but moving into the bedroom was another. She steeled herself for another fight with her mind as she nodded and let him lead her the few feet to their bedroom.

He positioned her to sink onto the bed, but she shook her head. "You," she whispered, and guided him to sit on the edge of the mattress.

"Saoirse," Emrys said. "You don't have to do this."

"I want to."

She said it with enough firmness that whatever caution he held in his expression vanished. His posture relaxed, and he sank onto the edge of the bed. Saoirse pulled his shirt from his body and was enveloped into a lazy kiss. As he sank back further onto the bed, she followed him down and ran her hands over his bare torso. She traced a single finger over his ribs and counted how many she touched. A giggle escaped her as he shivered when she brushed a sensitive spot on his waist.

Saoirse's thumb traced around his nipple before swiping over it several times until it tightened to a pucker. Emrys sighed against her mouth, and it was all she needed to continue her exploration. Kissing a line from his mouth to his bare stomach, he sank onto her knees. She opened the rest of the buttons of his trousers and clutched the waistband of his trousers and drawers, pausing.

"May I?" she asked breathlessly, meeting his gaze. He rose onto his elbows, and the lust in his gaze sent the spark racing through her entire body.

"Yes," he answered with a nod and a lift of his hips so she could free his erection.

She took her time exploring the length of him, her hand wrapping around him and gauging his reactions to her strokes. His breathing became labored, and the guttural sounds he made spurred her on.

"Saoirse," he said, the words strained. "You have no idea how long I've wanted you to touch me. I've dreamt of you touching my cock."

She grinned at his confession, and something in her motivated an urge to do more. Her tongue flicked over his tip, and he groaned, tossing his head back. She wrapped her lips around him and moved them over his erection in tandem with her hand.

"Brigid's tits." Emrys's voice was hoarse, and his body stiffened underneath her. She removed her mouth from him and stroked him with a fervor she was sure would bring him over the edge. She had never taken so much enjoyment in giving a partner pleasure. It kept her completely focused as she thought of the next action to make Emrys react.

Emrys swore under his breath and moaned at her new pace. His hands fisted the bedding, and Saoirse watched the muscles in his hips and thighs contract and relax.

She got to her feet and leaned over him, kissing him deeply as she continued to stroke him. He sucked in a breath before letting out a grunt.

"Saoirse," he growled as he climaxed, spilling over her hand. She broke the kiss and stroked him until he was drained. His hazy post-coital gaze satisfied her to no end, and she couldn't stop smiling.

"My dreams didn't do that any justice," he told her with a low laugh.

She giggled softly and gave him a long kiss. A hand slid into her hair before it slumped onto the back of her neck. She had sapped every drop of his energy and it endlessly amused her.

When she found the strength to pull herself away, Saoirse rose and washed her hands at the bathroom sink. She plucked a clean cloth from the linen cabinet and ran it under the water. There was only a bit of evidence of his pleasure on his stomach, but she gently wiped it away. He caught her arm as she swiped the cloth over him one last time and pulled her towards him for a kiss. They exchanged smiles that spoke louder than any words could, and Saoirse felt the spark run through her veins again.

Emrys was sitting upright when she returned from tossing the cloth in the sink, his pants and drawers making him modest again. She stood between his spread thighs and rested her forearms on his shoulders, leaning her forehead against his. His hands wrapped around her waist as he stole another kiss from her. Saoirse smiled as a wave of giddiness swelled in her chest.

They sat for a long, silent moment, their foreheads pressed together and their hands mindlessly touching each other's backs. Saoirse traced one of his scars with her finger and lifted her gaze.

"Emrys," she said quietly. He met her eyes, and the spark gave a light zap in her body. "Tell me how you got these."

He stared at her for a few beats before sighing. "I spent my youth ignoring my grief about my circumstances," he began. "I threw myself into whatever Ada and Seraphina put in front of me. It distracted me long enough to push my emotions down to sufficiently ignore it. But that didn't do me any favors as an adult. I don't blame them for how I was raised. They gave me ample opportunities to face my grief and move on from it, but you've learned by now how stubborn I am."

She gave a half-smile. "You? Stubborn?"

He cracked a smile and held her a bit tighter. "I know. It's a shock." His smile faded, and he cleared his throat before continuing. "My adult years were where I suffered the most. I became angry at the gods for the hand they dealt me in life and how they let my questions and requests go unanswered. I picked fights with my father in council meetings and earned lectures about embarrassing the court. They didn't satisfy me enough, so I escalated to stoking the animosity I have with Kieran and making other terrible decisions to try to numb my emotions."

"Like what?" Saoirse asked.

"You don't want to know." Emrys shook his head. "But I'll say that I'm lucky Cyprian is very good at his job—and I still owe him several favors."

She kissed his forehead and felt his fingers drawing anxious circles on her back through her blouse.

"My worst decision was enlisting in the army under Kieran. I don't know when exactly I hit the bottom of my well of despair to do so, but I know at some point I lost any will to live on this earth. I knew if there was anyone who would oblige my death wish with pleasure, it would be him."

A chill ran down Saoirse's spine at those words, and she felt like she was barely breathing as spoke.

"I know you asked earlier not to speak about my demise, but you did ask." He ceased his fidgeting flattened his hand on her back.

Her heart raced, but she nodded. She had asked, and she

genuinely wanted to know.

"I don't remember how long I spent in Kieran's command, but I know I managed to find every punishment he was willing to dole out. Most of them just made me numb, but then he found one that cut deeper than any of them." He met her gaze that was fixed on him and swallowed. "He found whipping gave the effect he wanted on me. Anything else made me disconnect with the world, like you did with intimacy, and endure the pain until it was over."

Saoirse felt a sob clog her throat, but she swallowed it. "You..." She took in a deep breath. "You did it, too?"

Emrys nodded. "One thing I wish we didn't have in common."

She flashed a solemn half-smile. "Fate has a wicked sense of humor pairing us together, I suppose."

He blinked at her before nodding and clearing his throat again. "Once Kieran learned what made me react how he liked, he looked for every reason to do it," Emrys went on. "He and his underlings found any excuse to catch me making a mistake and bring me to be whipped. He would make it a whole production and do it in front of the entire camp. Sometimes I wouldn't be the only one being punished, but most of the time it was only me."

Saoirse pictured him standing in front of a large group, waiting for his imminent pain. She couldn't imagine the anxiety and dread he experienced while he waited for Kieran to punish him.

"He experimented with how many lashes he could give before he did something irreversible. And the more he whipped me, the more endurance I unfortunately built to it. So, he pushed a bit further each time. He kept it right on the cusp of doing enough damage that his favorite play thing was no longer viable. I constantly prayed he would lose himself just a bit more and end everything. My final night with the army was the night he did it."

Saoirse felt her eyes sting. Her lip wobbled, and she quickly sucked it between her teeth. Emrys's hand on her back vibrated, but he sat up strong and tall.

"I was accused of losing a crate of supplies while on shipping duty." His voice had dropped in volume. "Kieran pulled me in front of the entire camp to punish me for it. He completely lost himself in the action, and I did more than just pass out from the amount of blood he spilled from me. Seraphina said I had lost too much, and there was no chance of saving me even if someone had acted immediately."

Saoirse felt like she stopped breathing. Her mind imagined Emrys bloody and despondent surrounded by a group of fireannaich that just witnessed his death. She wanted to fall apart at the thought. How he could sit here and retell this so calmly was beyond her.

"Dying felt different from what I thought it would," Emrys continued. "I felt like I was waking from a haze and was confused as to why I didn't feel any pain in my body. That was until I realized I didn't have a body. Then I found myself in front of the council of gods."

"The gods?" she asked in a hushed tone. It was the only volume she could speak at without invoking a sob.

Emrys nodded.

"All of them?"

"All nine of them," he answered. "They looked me over and took turns sharing their disappointment with me. They lectured me on how I tried to discard my grief and gave up the things I could have achieved."

Saoirse wiped at her face. Her tears were too strong to fight against any longer. "I'm sorry," she whispered.

Emrys reached up and wiped them away for her. "No need to apologize," he said gently. "I've spent a century having to relive and retell this."

Her jaw dropped. "A century?" She could barely recount her story with Odysseus that happened two years ago without tumbling into a panic. Having to repeat it for a century was unfathomable.

Emrys nodded again. "It's gotten easier." He wiped one last tear from her cheek before returning his hand to her waist. "Now, where was I?"

"You were in front of the gods," Saoirse provided.

"Yes. After they shared their disappointment in me, I fell to my knees, or what felt like falling to my knees, and pleaded with them. I pleaded for my life and promised to pursue the things they told me I could achieve for myself and for the kingdom. I pleaded until I no longer had a voice."

"Or what you thought was a voice." Saoirse hoped he would appreciate her attempt at humor.

Emrys huffed a small laugh, and she felt her shoulders relax.

"Now you're understanding." His brief grin slowly faded. "They contemplated their decision in front of me, and I felt like I had been in their presence for hours while they did so. Finally, they granted me a second chance at my life."

Saoirse felt a new wave of emotion hit her. She cupped his cheek and stroked her thumb over his cheekbones as she tried her best to keep her tears back. He reciprocated the gentle touch with more purposeful strokes of his hand on her back.

"Getting a second chance at my life didn't fix everything, though."

She nodded in understanding.

"I still didn't feel whole. My gaping grief I hadn't dealt with in decades continued its attempts to consume me. On several occasions, I found myself trudging through it, working to heal it. Knowing what I was destined to accomplish, and what was promised in return, helped as well. I mentored young fae with their magic, and it helped me mourn the childhood I lost with my parents. I did more in the Northern Fae territories amongst the poor and in need, and it helped me feel less alone in what I lost. I slowly returned to the council meetings regularly and found a voice to speak for those fae I encountered. It's taken decades, and I still feel pangs of grief, but I've come a long way from the person I was that wished to no longer dwell on this earth."

Saoirse took a deep, shaky breath and lifted her head to press a kiss to Emrys's forehead, like he had when she was grieving and stripping herself emotionally bare in front of him. His hands on her waist tightened, and she knew her action did what she intended it to. She slid from his grasp and sat behind him on the bed. His puckered scars laced his back, and she stroked the length of a few of them.

"Did the gods make these permanent?" she asked. She watched the back of his move in a nod.

"No matter how hard Seraphina tried, they wouldn't disappear. I imagine the gods made them permanent as a reminder."

Saoirse began to understand why he didn't hide them. They truly were a reminder of what he lost in his previous life and what he had gained in this one. She kissed the tips of each scar across his back from one shoulder to the other before resting her forehead against his temple.

"I'm glad the gods gave you a second chance," she said quietly.

"I am too," he responded in his softest voice.

She gave a long, gentle kiss to his cheek and felt herself let go of the last fear she still held with him, one she knew couldn't be reversed once it was spoken.

"I love you," she whispered. She felt him still before each muscle under her touch relaxed.

He turned his head to meet her gaze and a gleam of tears outlined the bottom edge of his eyes. "I love you, too," he replied, his voice hoarse.

She closed the thin space between them and kissed him as deeply as she could. She wanted to emphasize her words with actions so that he knew she was being genuine. He responded with his own passionate kiss, and they ended up tangled in each other until neither could remain awake.

Saoirse woke the next morning and found that her first thought wasn't why she was at the cottage. Instead, she had an itch to visit the beach. The salty air had wafted in and out of the cottage for the past two days, and she yearned to experience the beach. The closest she got to being on a beach was taking the ferry here to England. After a pitiful breakfast of eggs and whatever cured meat was in the icebox, she asked Emrys to take her to the shore.

Once they were dressed, he led her along the sandy path to the beach. Looking back towards the cottage, Saoirse felt just how secluded they were. There were no other cottages for miles, and she could barely see the terracotta roof of theirs from the beach. On the shore, there wasn't a soul around.

They both shucked off their shoes and abandoned them near the path back to the cottage. After stripping off her stockings, Saoirse sunk her toes into the sand and grinned at the way it tickled.

She and Emrys fixed their clothes so their hems wouldn't get wet as they neared the water. They held hands as they walked along the shore where the water lapped at the sand, Saoirse squealing whenever the icy water touched her bare feet. She skittered up the shore towards where the water didn't reach, but Emrys pulled her back.

A laugh escaped her as he held her, the water brushing over their ankles. "Emrys, I can't feel my feet," she said through a giggle.

"I think you have a perfectly magical way to fix that," he murmured in her ear.

"You can feel your magic in your feet?" she asked.

"If you try hard enough."

Saoirse couldn't tell if he was being cheeky or not. She tried to call her magic and direct it towards her lower extremities. Emrys's lips brushed the side of her neck, and heat that wasn't her magic ignited in her abdomen. Saoirse reeled her magic back, deciding his comment was more cheeky than serious.

"Has your itch for the beach been sufficiently scratched?" he asked.

"Almost," she answered. The water that lapped at their ankles was slowly progressing up their calves, the icy temperature making Saoirse shiver. "Are you keeping me in this frigid water so I can ask for us to go back?"

"I'm hurt you would accuse me of ulterior motives." Emrys chuckled. He held her tighter against him. "Is it working?"

Saoirse laughed and wiggled in his arms. He lifted her until her feet were no longer submerged and carried her a few feet to dry sand. She turned in his arms and met his emerald gaze. A soft smile graced his lips, and she knew hers mirrored it. Emrys lowered his lips to hers, and she sighed against him.

The crash of the waves and distant calls of sea birds dissolved as he ran his tongue over the seam of her lips, asking for permission to deepen their kiss. She let out a soft moan as he explored her mouth. He tasted like their savory breakfast, and Saoirse had the urge to devour him.

The ambient sounds of the waves and birds filtered into her ears, and she smiled as she kissed him. Emrys pulled back for a moment and searched her face. "What?" he asked tentatively.

"Nothing," she answered with a triumphant grin. "I'm just enjoying this time with you."

He smiled back at her and kissed her deeply again. He rested his forehead against hers as they tried to catch their breath.

"Let's head back to the cottage," he said in a husky voice.

She lifted her gaze up and saw his eyes darken with hunger. There was no hesitation in her answer. They didn't bother putting their shoes and stockings back on as they followed the path back to the cottage. Their shoes were left behind on the deck as they entered the house through the rear door.

Emrys pressed her against the edge of the kitchen counter, and their tongues and lips and hands collided with each other. The spark fluttered through her, and she leaned into its demands. It acted like a magnet, pulling her towards him, and she wondered if he felt it, too. She was stripped down to basic needs when they touched, and the spark was awakened. It always felt like too many clothes were in the way, and she wanted to claw the fabric that stood between them until they were completely bare.

His fingers nimbly unbuttoned her blouse, and his hand slid inside her shirt. Warmth spread over her chest as his palms found Saoirse had foregone her corset, and Emrys groaned. He explored the curves of her breasts, squeezing and pinching, until he finally untucked her blouse from her skirt and stripped it from her torso.

Her thin chemise did nothing to hide the dark circles of her nipples, and Emrys kissed from her collarbone to the swell of her breast. She gasped as his mouth made contact with the sensitive bud of her nipple and licked and nibbled it through the fabric of her chemise.

Saoirse's fingers tore at his suspenders and tore them off his shoulders, giving her the freedom to strip his shirt off. They took turns undressing each other until they were equally unclothed, and Saoirse's heart beat faster at the thought of them both being naked. She shivered thinking about their warm skin pressed together with nothing between them. It was a delicious and tantalizing thought.

Emrys helped her remove her chemise, and then she was bare. Her perked nipples grazed his skin, and the spark in her body turned frenzied. She wanted him. She wanted his touch. She wanted his hands all over her body and his lips following them.

Emrys peered down at her naked form and took a moment to drink in the sight. His chest heaved as he caught his breath, and his eyes darkened. "You're breathtaking," he breathed.

Saoirse felt an intoxicated grin grow on her face as he looked at her from head to toe once more. When he had his fill, he captured her lips again. It was less fevered and hungry, as if he were trying to commit every moment they touched to memory. He gently lifted her off her feet and set her onto the kitchen counter.

She giggled as her bare skin warmed the wood underneath her arse. "What happened to not doing this in the kitchen?" she asked.

"I got impatient." He leaned close to her ear and whispered, "And I'm starving."

Gooseflesh erupted in the wake of his lips grazing her bare skin from her collar to her breast. His tongue lapped over her nipple, and she couldn't help the moan that escaped her lips. Saoirse threaded her fingers in his soft, blonde hair and leaned her head back to rest on the windowpane behind her. He flicked her erect nipple with his tongue and carefully grazed his teeth over it. Her spine arched, begging for more, as Emrys continued his exploration with kisses along her stomach. His lips lowered until he was on his knees, teasing her inner thigh.

"I could spend all day tasting you," he said between kisses on her sensitive skin.

She moaned in response and tightened her grip on his hair. Slick warmth coated her quim as he kissed up to the apex of her thighs. Anticipation thrummed through her as he paused, his lips hovering just over where she wanted his touch. His gaze locked on hers, his warm breath ghosting over the seam of her sex and making her squirm.

"May I?" he asked.

"Yes," she panted, "please."

A slow grin spread on his face before he lowered his lips back between her legs. He kissed her clit running his tongue over her entrance, the touch sending a tingling sensation through her body. Saoirse gasped and mewled as he tested where she needed his touch the most. Her breath hitched when he stroked his tongue along the length of her quim, flicking it over her clit. A jolt of pleasure coursed through her in response. He narrowed his tongue to that small, needy area, and she moaned her approval.

Her mind quieted but didn't fog as her orgasm slowly built. She could feel every touch, every sensation with complete clarity. Emrys pulled his lips from her for a moment but replaced them with a single finger that stroked and circled where his tongue had been previously. She arched her spine again, the change in contact making her plead for more.

His finger moved from her clit to her entrance, and he gradually slid it inside her. Saoirse groaned as he built up a rhythm with his finger. An entirely new pleasure overwhelmed her when he replaced his lips on her clit, and she cried out.

No one had ever touched her with fingers and lips and tongue simultaneously, and her body felt like it was about to rip apart. Her toes curled as she dug her heels into his shoulders and clutched at his hair. His single-minded focus was on her pleasure, and Saoirse felt the edge of it approaching rapidly. Emrys's finger moved faster, along with his lips, intensifying his hold on her.

"Oh, gods," she breathed as the warm wave of pleasure crested through her body. An involuntary gasp slipped from her lips as her orgasm broke over her. She had little time to prepare for it, and her body was immobilized as her climax pulsed through her. The muscles of her body felt like they were tightened for minutes rather than seconds, and she shuddered and mewled as she came down from her orgasm.

Emrys eased her through her climax before pulling away from her. He kissed along the insides of her thighs as she slumped against the kitchen window, trying to catch her breath. She mindlessly combed her fingers through his hair as he rested his head against her thigh and grinned up at her.

"Did you stay with me?" he asked, stroking her other thigh with his thumb. She nodded and smiled back at him. "Good," he whispered. "Because I plan on pleasuring you all afternoon."

She let out a breathy laugh and imagined riding and crashing orgasm after orgasm for the rest of the day. It wasn't the worst way to pass the time.

"No one's ever done that before," she confessed as her breathing evened.

"You're going to stroke my ego with confessions like that." He chuckled low and sultry.

She gave a satiated grin as her fingers slowed their combing in his hair. "I'd like to stroke more than just your ego," she said with a cheeky grin.

His eyes darkened again, and he stood to claim her mouth with his. She reached for the button of his pants, but Emrys wrapped his hand around hers.

"As much as I'm dying to take you fast and dirty right now, we're done with the kitchen," he told her.

The spark raced along Saoirse's spine at his words, and she nodded in agreement. He scooped her off the counter, his hands taking healthy handfuls of her arse, and Saoirse wrapped her legs around his waist. She felt his erection straining against his pants between her legs, and her heart thundered as she realized only a layer of fabric stood between them now.

Emrys gently set her on the bed, and she reached for the waistband of his trousers without a second thought. He didn't stop her this time and even lent a hand in shoving them off his hips and getting them to the floor. Saoirse stared at his erection and noticed how much stiffer he was than the day before.

"May I?" she asked, looking up at him with a sensual grin.

"Yes," Emrys answered, catching his breath. "Please."

Saoirse wrapped her hand around him and gently stroked the length of his erection. Emrys threw his head back as he let out a swear. A grin tugged at her lips, and she moved her hand more deliberately over him. She watched as he groaned and bit his bottom lip. His eyes were glazed over when he lifted his head back up to watch her movements over his cock. Her grin widened until he wrapped a hand around the nape of her neck. He took a fistful of her strawberry blonde hair in his hand and planted a deep kiss to her lips.

"Saoirse," he whispered, his breathing labored. "I won't last much longer if you keep touching me. I want to be inside you."

The spark pinged around the inside of her body in anticipation. Her thighs felt slick again, and she wanted the same as he did. Saoirse slowed the pace of her stroking and slipped her hand off him. Emrys kissed her as she lay back onto the bed. His lips lined a trailed down to her thighs again. He planted himself just above her quim before he worked his way back up to her neck, teasing every inch of her bothered, flushed skin. Kneeling over her on the bed, the tip of his erection hovered so close to her aching entrance.

He longingly kissed her and drew out the moments before they joined. He pulled back from her and studied her face like he had the night before. "Are you still with me?"

"Completely," she said with a nod.

Emrys kissed her again before asking another question. "Are you taking any contraceptive? We can stop if you aren't."

"I'm taking it," she answered with another nod. "I still have a week before I take it again." The contraception she had asked Seraphina for after the wedding lasted four weeks, and she thanked the gods she still had time before needing another.

"Good," he whispered before claiming her mouth again. "Because I plan to come inside you over and over again."

Gooseflesh covered Saoirse's skin, and Emrys stroked the tip of his erection over her clit. She moaned against his mouth and bucked her hips against his. He kissed along her jaw as he continued to move painfully slow against her.

"Are you certain?" he whispered into her ear.

"Yes," Saoirse breathed, her voice a plea. "I need you."

Emrys placed a longing kiss on her neck before whispering in her ear again, "I love you."

"I love you," she echoed, her gaze full of lust as she traced his cheekbones and jaw with her finger.

His lips met hers again as he slowly sheathed himself inside her. She let out a deep moan as he reeled himself back and gently thrust back into her.

Saoirse's unmuted mind allowed her to feel every point of touch and sensation on her skin and in her body. The brush of his skin against hers, the way he filled her in such a satisfying manner, and the crackling warmth of pleasure that spread through her body were overwhelming, but she yearned for more.

"You feel as good as you taste," he said with a growl.

She shivered as gooseflesh erupted over her skin again and small jolts of pleasure rippled through her. Saoirse's hands roamed over Emrys's body as he set a steady rhythm. He swallowed her moans of approval, and their tongues danced in sync with his pace. Her fingers wandered down to his thrusting hips, and she squeezed a handful of his arse. The feeling of the soft flesh in her palms made her understand why Emrys's hands always wandered to her backside whenever given the chance.

"Brigid's tits," he moaned as she squeezed him.

She giggled sensually at his outcry and tucked away his response for the future. In response, Emrys reached between her thighs and began to trace circles over her swollen clit with his thumb. Her breath caught in her throat, and he grinned devilishly at her.

"You're terrible," she said between breathy laughs.

His thrusting quickened as his finger strummed her, and she found her mouth trying to form words; they were strangled by her rising pleasure. "Emrys," she gasped. "Don't stop."

Sweat beaded between Saoirse's breasts and at her hairline as she chased her second orgasm. She was breathless as pleasure tingled through her legs. Every touch between them felt amplified and all-consuming. Emrys's breath also became erratic as he moved against her. The crash of Saoirse's next orgasm hit her hard, and she let out a strangled cry. It was even more intense than the first, and she teetered on the line between pain and pleasure.

She stilled as it coursed through her before her entire body became too sensitive, and she shook from the all the points of Emrys's touch. She felt Emrys thrust into her at a fervent pace until he reached his release. A strangled groan came from him as he thrust deeply, spilling into her. His body collapsed over hers, his cock still sheathed inside Saoirse. He was sticky with sweat, but their mingled breathing as they came down from their euphoria lulled Saoirse into a sense of safety.

Emrys kissed lazily along Saoirse's neck and shoulder as they evened their breathing. Saoirse brushed the hair at his nape, savoring the feelings that coursed through her. "I love you," she whispered in his ear. He lifted his head to meet her eyes, and the spark that usually shot through her seemed to now be a dull buzzing all over her body, as if it had turned her blood into bubbling wine.

"I love you," he repeated back to her. "I love all of you, and I'll never stop loving you."

He pressed a long kiss to her lips and wrapped an arm around her waist. Saoirse leaned into the kiss, savoring the moment. She felt several emotions wash through her as the height of her climax waned. She was able to not only stay present but also enjoy herself the entire time. There was no need to fight her mind to remain in the moment. That had never happened before. Emrys had made it easy to keep from fading.

A desire to cry filled her chest, but it wasn't from sorrow or heartbreak. Saoirse was the happiest and most satisfied she had ever been. Emrys made her feel safe and loved and cared for, things she hadn't realized she was missing in her life. She swallowed the desire and nuzzled her face into the crook of his neck, breathing in his scent. The Fearynhurst estate felt so far away, and if she had her way, she would keep Emrys here and never go back.

Emrys *breathed in* the vanilla scent of Saoirse's skin and sighed. He had been satisfied by lovers before, but Saoirse...she made him never want to leave her side. He had waited half a century to hold her like this and, gods, was it worth every second. His veins hummed as he held her against him, feeling every inch of her bare skin against his. His senses had been more than satisfied with the sex they shared. The taste of her, the feel of her around him, hearing her moan his name, the sight of her luxurious body, and the smell of the bond overwhelmed him and tempted him to stay in bed with her forever. He'd throw away his crown if it meant he could keep Saoirse in his arms for eternity.

Phrases of the Old Language flooded his mind, and he assumed they were the prayer to seal their mating bond to the gods. He had wondered how one got the sealing prayer. Apparently, the gods supplied it subconsciously. He wondered if Saoirse had the same jumbled language running in her mind, but he hesitated to ask.

Sealing the bond would be so easy after having the words whispered in his mind, but he refused until Saoirse knew about the bond in the first place. He had wanted to tell her at many points during their stay, but he never found the perfect moment. He didn't want to overwhelm her with the information after the mess she endured with Kieran and Alastair. There was also the chance that she wouldn't take the truth well. He feared losing her altogether, and losing the love of his life scared him into perpetual hesitation.

Emrys kissed her neck as his hand mindlessly fondled one of her breasts, causing a lilting giggle to escape her lips. He nearly hardened again at the sound. He told himself that if all she wanted to do today was be intimate, he would be more than satisfied with those plans. But the urge to seal the mating bond didn't fade and was becoming unbearable to ignore.

As he sat up, she grabbed his arm. "Where do you think you're going?" she asked alluringly.

"I was going to run a bath," he said, hoping a shred of distance would quiet the desire to seal their bond. He leaned down and kissed her cheek in reassurance.

"I want to join you." She pushed herself upright and met his gaze. "You don't think I'm letting you out of arm's reach, do you?"

Emrys chuckled and kissed Saoirse, unable to disagree with her. She deepened their kiss, and he let loose the moan he couldn't hold back. He couldn't deny her request to join in his bath either. His body ached just thinking of her silhouette wet and dripping with water and soap. The bond be damned. His lust was the one thing more powerful than his will when it came to the bond.

"Stay here," he said as he slid out of her grasp. His blatant arousal was on display as he padded into the bathroom. He ran the water in the tub and set a handful of towels on the ledge of the sink. Once the tub was filled with warm water, he returned to Saoirse and scooped her into his arms. The lilting giggle that escaped her lips hit his ears again, and it took all his self-control not to lay her on the bathroom floor and turn the giggle into a sensual moan.

He stepped into the tub with Saoirse still in his arms and lowered them both into the water. She twisted around and straddled his waist as they settled into the tub. Her body pressed against his, and she wrapped her arms around his neck.

"I love you, Emrys," she said, her forehead resting against his.

He couldn't get enough of those words coming from her lips. The phrase had been held in for so long that he wanted to hear nothing but those words for the rest of his immortal life. He wrapped his hands around her back, holding her against him and never wanting her to move.

"I love you," he repeated back to her. Her lips met his, and he knew there would be very little washing up in the tub.

She rocked her hips over him and paused. "You're erect that quickly?" she asked, holding back an amused grin.

He chuckled and kissed her longingly. "Yes," he answered, his gaze hazy with lust. "That's what happens when I have the most breathtaking wife in the world." He kissed her again, and she smiled against his lips.

Her hips continued to move over him, torturing him with the taste of friction. He lost himself to her, enjoying watching her find what she liked and what made her satisfied. It was what had him fighting his self-control on their wedding night. She wasn't afraid to take what she needed, and it drove him mad with lust.

It made feeling her fade from him when they attempted to be intimate a week ago all the more painful to witness. He still worried she would slip into it again, but the hunger in her eyes and the way she cried out told him she was more than present and enjoying herself with every touch and movement.

Saoirse rose a few inches out of the water and sank back down onto his erection. Her mouth fell open in a breathless gasp, and she slowly rode him, making water slosh up to the edge of the bath.

"That's it," he whispered as he reached for her hips. "Take what you need from me."

He filled his palms with her arse and squeezed her soft flesh. She had found his weakness earlier when she grasped his bottom, and he was curious as to how she would use that knowledge in the future.

She rocked in his lap and grabbed the edges of the tub to support her as she moved. "I love watching you take your pleasure into your own hands," he said.

Emrys leaned towards her bouncing torso and teased her bare breasts with his lips and tongue. As he took her nipple between his teeth, Saoirse gasped. "Brigid's tits," she cried out.

He couldn't help but grin in response. He loved hearing her cry out, especially when she swore. She was such a beautiful little thing that had a dirty mind and mouth.

He thrust his hips with hers, and she cried out again. This time his name came to her lips, and he steadied himself so he didn't climax too early. "I love how my name sounds on your lips." He brought her head down to his and kissed her hungrily. "I almost came just hearing you saying it."

"Oh, gods," she gasped as she continued to ride him.

Her hands gripped the tub until her knuckles turned white. He could feel the pulses of pleasure that signaled she was getting closer to her climax, and he resisted the urge to change his pace to help her reach that satisfaction faster. Instead, he reached between them and circled his thumb against her clit hurriedly. Saoirse nodded and murmured encouragement for him to keep going. It only took her moments before she gasped and arched her spine as her pleasure peaked, her release washing over her.

Emrys felt her spasm around his erection, and he thrust until he found his own climax. He spilled into her as she collapsed into his arms. Their chests rose and fell against each other as her arms wrapped around his neck. He gently stroked along her spine, steadying his breathing and surveying the bit of damage they had done to the bathroom. Water dripped from the edges of the tub, and he assumed the floor around them was soaked. He couldn't help grinning to himself, feeling absolutely no remorse for the mess.

Saoirse's lips pressed against his shoulder, and he sighed contentedly. She kissed from his shoulder to his neck, eventually meeting his lips. Her lips parted, and he welcomed her eagerly. It was short-lived as she broke their kiss to rest her forehead against his. She traced the curve of his collarbone with her finger, and her face looked as contented as his. Emrys's chest flooded with various emotions all over again. Over the last few days, he had gone through a slew of them over her.

He hadn't planned on confessing he loved her, but she was willing to trust him, so he had been willing to take that leap, too.

His love for her hadn't been driven by the mating bond either. He had never cared so deeply or felt so heard and seen by someone he was involved with. Saoirse made him feel safe, as much as he knew he did for her.

"We should probably do what you meant to in here," she said with a cheeky grin.

He kissed her and let loose the chuckle he had been resisting. "I wasn't planning on bathing one bit," he confessed.

"Then why did you try to come in here without me?"

"I don't know what I was thinking." He kissed her again before she slid off his lap.

He kept himself from grabbing for her and keeping her connected to him. Instead, he watched her reach for the soap on the edge of the tub and dip it in the water. She lathered her hands with the unscented soap and covered his chest and shoulders in suds. Her hand gently tugged at his shoulder, encouraging him to turn, and he obliged her. He was all too aware of where her fingers lingered on his body as she moved along his back.

His face heated as he realized how close she was to his scars again. He felt guilty for not telling her the truth until the night before. He hated how hesitant he had been to reveal their history. He had shared it on several occasions to those close to him, but with her, he had lost his nerve until recently. She had bared some of her worst fears and deepest wounds to him, and he hadn't even had the courage to do the same.

His guilt and embarrassment faded as he felt Saoirse rinse the soap from his body and kiss along his shoulders. He could feel her tenderly kissing each scar from one shoulder to the other. Rationally, he realized she wouldn't mock him or be so disgusted with him she would leave, but fear didn't care about rationality. He was relieved when she responded with tender, loving touches and a confession of her own love for him. Whether or not he should have told her earlier, she accepted him and still loved him. That was enough to stifle the guilt he felt.

"What?" she asked.

"Nothing," he breathed as tears blurred his vision. He kissed her deeply, willing the tears to retreat. He took a shaky breath as they broke apart, and he tentatively opened his eyes.

"I love you, Saoirse," he said, his hand instinctively caressing her cheek. His gaze dropped to the soap in her hands, and he reached for it. "Your turn." He forced a grin as the tears melted away instead of spilling.

She handed it over without hesitation, and he lathered his hands with the bar. His hands traced the curves of her body, his palms paying special attention to her breasts and hips. The sight of her skin glistening with soap was more erotic than he thought it would be. He reluctantly rinsed her body and allowed her to turn.

He ran his soapy hands over her shoulders and pressed a kiss to the eight-point star-shaped mark between them. "There's that birthmark I told you about," he murmured. She let out a laugh and splashed water behind her in his direction. He let out a low laugh of his own and continued running his hands over her body. He placed the bar back onto the edge of the tub and rinsed the soap from her skin.

As Emrys washed away the last remnants of soap, he let his hands wander over her body. He reached around Saoirse and slid them from her waist up to her breasts. His palms covered both of them, and he grinned to himself when she responded with a soft mewl. His thumbs swept over her nipples slowly, and he took enjoyment in how tightly they beaded under his touch.

"I could touch and feel these respond so immediately for the rest of eternity." He kissed her shoulder as he gently pinched her nipples, invoking a gasp from her.

Saoirse leaned against his chest, giving him more access to her body, and he stroked one hand down the front of her. He ran his fingers lazily over her quim while she hummed her approval. He unhurriedly kissed along her neck and jaw as he slowly circled his fingers around her clit. Memories of earlier flooded his mind, and he could almost taste her as he teased her.

"I can't get enough of you," he murmured while he kissed her jaw. "I love hearing every noise you make. I especially love hearing you swear."

Saoirse let out a cross between a laugh and a gasp as he moved his fingers faster against her. He continued to kiss along her neck and caress her breast, his fingers fidgeting over her nipple, as he found just the right pace to bring her to her peak. Her breathing became more labored, and her fingers dug into his knees.

"Emrys," she said with uneven breaths. "Don't stop. Please don't—" Her words were cut off as her back arched and her body stilled. A moment later, she sunk back against him, her body shaking in the wake of her climax. Her breathing was labored as she grabbed for Emrys's forearm.

She whimpered, and he slowed to a stop, wrapping his arms around her and dotting her shoulders with kisses. Saoirse slowly came down from the height of her ecstasy and wrapped her own arms on top of his. She leaned her head back against his chest, lazily kissing the area of his neck she could reach. A noise emitted from her that resembled a satisfied purr.

Emrys breathed in the scent of her hair again and sighed contentedly in return. "I've dreamt of this for so long," he murmured against her skin.

"What? Sex in a bathtub?" Saoirse asked.

He couldn't hold back the laugh that rumbled in his chest. "That, too," he said, punctuating his words with a kiss to her jaw. "But no, I've dreamt of this moment, of you, sated and happy in my arms. At times I didn't think it would ever happen."

"Have you never held someone like this?" she asked innocently.

Emrys shook his head in response. "Lovers never stayed long enough," he confessed. "They enjoyed the sex, but they didn't want to stay for the intimacy."

"They were missing out on the best part."

"Indeed they were." Emrys dropped a kiss onto her shoulder and tightened his hold around her waist.

They sat tangled in the tub until it ran cold, and even then it took a moment for them to stir.

"I love you, Emrys," Saoirse said softly.

"I love you, Saoirse." He kissed the tip of her nose.

Saoirse gently stroked his arm as they sat in comfortable silence. The touch was so minimal, so gentle, but it meant so much to Emrys. The casual touches drove him over the edge. He hadn't been lying when he told her physical touching was the way he showed and felt love. To him, it was so intimate without saying a single word.

Saoirse woke beside Emrys the next morning, and the morning chill made her aware that both of them had fallen asleep without a stitch of clothing on. She snuggled deeper under the covers and savored the warmth Emrys's body radiated.

They had spent the better part of the day before exploring each other and learning what brought each other over the edge with the most intensity. Saoirse had never done anything like it before, and while it was blissful, it had also exhausted her. She let her eyes drift close again, but her mind wasn't able to quiet enough to fall back to sleep.

The thoughts she had were odd. They were whispers of phrases in the Old Language, and she couldn't pinpoint where she had heard them or why her mind was stuck on repeating them. She also couldn't translate any of it. A few words stood out to her, but she couldn't string enough of them together to understand what they were supposed to mean.

Saoirse tried to shake the odd thoughts from her mind. Finding it was useless to attempt sleep again, she shifted and brushed her lips over Emrys's collarbone. He didn't stir as she laid her head on his chest and idly traced his muscles with her finger. Her mind kept wandering back to the topic of mates. Nothing could convince her they were real, but she entertained the idea of the gods arranging her fate with Emrys. It was a pleasant daydream. He was everything she needed, everything she had been deprived of for so long.

Emrys stirred, and she was pulled closer into him. His arm held her tightly, and she reciprocated by wrapping her arm around his waist, holding him just as tight.

"Good morning, Princess," he said in that gravelly voice that made the spark in her body jolt.

"Good morning," she purred.

He placed a kiss in her hair, and they lay in tranquil silence for a moment.

It was luxuriously peaceful until a sinking feeling hit Saoirse. "We have to return home soon, don't we?" she asked.

Emrys exhaled and ran his finger along her bare shoulder. "We do," he answered somberly. "I wish we didn't have to. I'd rather stay here with you for eternity." He kissed her forehead and let his lips linger for a moment. "But, unfortunately, this afternoon is the next council meeting. My absence says much more than just being a loving husband."

"I understand," she said, sitting up. Gazing at him from this position made her stomach flutter. He was so relaxed and natural. Nothing was tensing his shoulders or forcing him to wear a mask of nobility. "At least I'll get to see the duchesses."

"Oh, gods," he groaned as he slapped a hand over his face. "They're going to know everything we did, won't they?"

Saoirse giggled and leaned down to share a kiss. "My silence *may* be bought for a price." She gave him a devious grin.

"I don't like that word 'may.'"

She giggled again and tossed a leg over his side so she could straddle him. His hands slid onto her thighs and massaged the muscles there. She ground her hips against him and felt how aroused he was even for the early morning hour. "Are you always like this in the mornings?" she asked.

"Do you want the truth?" Saoirse nodded and waited for his answer. He reached up and threaded his fingers in her hair, bringing her ear down to his lips to whisper, "I never woke up like this until you came into my life."

A shiver ran through her, and she felt her nipples tighten without any prompting. She captured his lips and moved against him until the flickers of pleasure began to hit her.

She reached between her thighs and sank onto his erection. Her mind was fully awake, and it was craving a climax. Their moans mixed together as Emrys's hands slid onto her arse and he thrust up into her. A mangled cry came from her, and she felt the crest of her orgasm climbing. She noticed Emrys lose himself in the chase of release along with her, and his hips moved erratically. The two moved in rhythm together until they crashed into their successive orgasms.

Saoirse rested her forehead against his as they panted and came down from their early morning climaxes. "Alright," she said breathlessly. "I feel ready enough to leave this place now."

Emrys laughed and laced his fingers into her hair, keeping her forehead pressed against his. They grinned with amusement at each other before they willed themselves to get out of bed and prepare to return home.

Emrys strolled into the council room, feeling his confidence higher than it had been in decades. He sat in his usual seat, Vasili and Cyprian already present, and he couldn't hide the grin on his face. He had watched all his friends marry and fall in love with their partners while he patiently waited for his gods-promised mate. Bitterness and jealousy never filled him during that period. He genuinely enjoyed watching his friends find happiness, but it left him hollow as he slowly became the last unmarried fireann in the court.

"What is that smug grin about?" Cyprian asked.

"I would assume by now you'd know exactly what it's about." He smirked as the duke rolled his eyes.

"Did you and Saoirse finally find a private room together?" he asked.

"Better," Emrys said. "We spent the last three days in a cottage near Howgrove Beach."

"Oh, thank the gods," Cyprian groaned. "We've had to watch you pine for your mate for decades."

"Don't forget the moping," Vasili added.

"Yes, and the moping." Cyprian nodded. "I'm glad you finally broke your celibate streak."

"That's probably not the only streak he broke." Vasili snorted and sipped from his whiskey glass.

"So, are you going to divulge any saucy details, or are we going to be left in the dark?" The Duke of Stoneblack smirked, and Emrys rolled his eyes.

"I didn't pry into your sex lives when you were courting your wives, so I expect the same privacy."

"Oh, please," Cyprian scoffed. "You knew almost every detail of our sex lives when we were courting."

"Against my will," Emrys shot back. "I was supposed to be your chaperone while you two courted your wives, and yet neither of you could keep your hands to yourselves."

"Yes, and you did a piss-poor job at it," Cyprian remarked. "All you did was interrupt us at the worst possible times."

"You nearly cost us our relationships," Vasili added.

"I also wish I didn't know as much about you and Calliope as I do," Emrys said, a shiver running through him. He had walked in on Vasili and Calliope discussing oral sex, and it was a memory he wished he could scrub from his mind. "There's a reason I didn't participate in that conversation you wanted to have with us about sex."

"Well, I came just at the right time," Laszlo said, entering the room. He chuckled as own innuendo as he stepped up to the bar cart to fill a glass with amber liquid. "What have I missed?"

"We were just discussing how Emrys was the world's worst chaperone when we were courting," Cyprian answered.

Emrys glared sideways at him, but the other fireann acted casually, as if figurative daggers weren't being shot at him.

"Oh, gods, yes, he was," Laszlo said as he took a sip of his liquor. "We had the most awkward dinners when he was in tow."

"I'm glad you all enjoy talking as if I'm not even present," Emrys grumbled.

"Yes!" Cyprian slapped a hand on the table. "Dinners were the worst."

"You think dinner is bad?" Vasili punctuated his words with a sardonic laugh. "Try having breakfast the morning after you've had sex for the first time."

"Oh, yes, that is worse," Laszlo agreed.

Emrys sat back in his seat and shook his head at the ceiling. His friends, as loving and supportive as they were, were the worst when it came to heckling. This was apparently his reward for finally reaching their same level of happiness.

"Emrys, why didn't you have to endure one of us as your chaperone with Saoirse?" Laszlo asked.

"You'll remember I was engaged in less than twenty-four hours from meeting her and got married a week later," Emrys answered. "Besides, I did have a chaperone. Kieran." He sneered the last word, and the dukes cringed. "In hindsight, I wish I *did* have one of you jossers as a chaperone."

The dukes chuckled, but their merriment was cut short as Alastair entered the room.

"Good afternoon, uaislean," he greeted neutrally. "Kieran will no longer be attending our meetings. For the foreseeable future, our information about the threats to Donheath will be through letter and telegram."

The dukes looked between each other, and Emrys schooled his features. He knew why Kieran wasn't attending the meeting, but if his father wasn't going to share the reason, Emrys would keep it to himself. Not that the dukes couldn't piece it together for themselves. Saoirse had obviously shared what Kieran did with the duchesses, and he had little doubt they wouldn't share it with their spouses. The shock that Kieran finally experienced consequences was what probably flabbergasted them the most.

Weekly business was discussed once the news of Kieran's absence settled. A few hiccups were interrupting the normal flow of the territories. Portions of the successful harvest they had just celebrated were now being diverted to the camps, causing delays for other territories. Manufacturing had also slowed due to the uptick in army recruitment. Eventually, everything would balance out again, but for now, the territories would feel the impacts of the foreboding Fomóire sightings.

As they attempted to shift away from topics discussing the impact of the Fomóire threat, a servant scurried in and delivered a piece of paper with ink stains on it. Everyone sat with bated breath as Alastair read the note.

"It's not good news in Donheath," he said. The dukes and Emrys looked between themselves. Vasili, holding a calm exterior, started to go pale. Alastair continued, "A Fomóire has made contact with a camp on the northern border of the territory. There have been casualties."

"How many?" Vasili asked, the shake in his voice betraying him.

"Thankfully, only a few," Alastair answered solemnly. "Seven injuries and three deaths to our army."

The room was silent as they digested the information. Until now, the threat felt merely looming rather than imminent. Emrys assumed it would be weeks or months before there was any real action.

"What is our next move?" he asked, breaking the tense quiet.

"I'll have to refer to my general for that." Emrys opened his mouth to ask who his general was, but Alastair cut him off. "Well, that settles that matter on the agenda. Vasili, I will be in touch with what our next steps are in Donheath."

Vasili nodded and rose from his seat. The other dukes filed out, leaving Emrys alone with his father.

"Who is your general?" he asked once the door was closed again.

"In a certain capacity...Kieran," Alastair answered.

"What?" Emrys felt his body go numb. His initial thoughts immediately leapt to Saoirse. Would she be relieved or upset? She had been terrified of Kieran retaliating, but if he was still in his position, her fears may be pacified. On the other hand, she deserved better than Kieran barely being punished.

"His powers of decision within the court have been restricted, but he remains an authority in the army. I'm in contact with several officers who are privy to what is discussed in council, but Kieran is still in charge of our military."

Emrys felt like he had been punched in his gut, and the urge to vomit struck him. His father had cowered and essentially slapped Kieran on the wrist. Sure, he couldn't make decisions with the court anymore, but he still held power in the camps. Flashes of the punishments he doled out hit Emrys, and the room spun.

"Emrys," Alastair said. "I'm sorry this is not what you expected, but I can't remove a general wholly when we're teetering on the brink of war. I hope you understand."

"I understand perfectly." The high of confidence he had been riding had now deflated. "You'd rather appease your fears than actually hold him accountable to his actions."

"Emrys, that's not—"

"No, it's exactly that. You know what he's capable of, and still you'd rather bow to him and protect yourself than your own flesh and blood!" Emrys's breathing was labored, and he hadn't initially realized he had risen out of his seat. Anger, pain, embarrassment, and a slew of other emotions cycled through him as he stared at his father.

Alastair's face remained neutral and, to his credit, he hadn't darted his gaze away as Emrys dressed him down. "I do know what he can do," he said solemnly. "I know what he did to you."

"What?" His anguish running ice cold in his veins. His head felt like it was underwater, and his lungs seized. He had been under the impression that his father was completely unaware of what happened to him or what Kieran did in his army.

"Ada told me what happened after Seraphina fled from this house as if her apron were on fire." Emrys continued to stare blankly. "I felt responsible for letting you enlist. We weren't in wartime, but I allowed you to put yourself at risk." Alastair took a deep breath and slowly let it out. "I'm sorry, Emrys. I'm sorry that

I've failed you."

Emrys was at a loss for words as he blinked at his father. Words he wished he would always hear, words he killed himself over, didn't hit as hard as he thought they would. Instead, they felt like a pat on the back. They weren't completely cold and spiteful, but they weren't warm and relationship-mending either. His apology was somewhere in the middle, and it fell completely flat.

Emrys rose from his seat and vacated the room without a single word. His head spun, and he was desperate to find his anchor again. He swept into the drawing room and was surprised to find the duchesses still sitting around drinking tea, their husbands picking at the leftover sweets.

"There's the fireann in question," Andromeda said as Emrys moved beside the armchair Saoirse sat in.

His wife looked up to him and beamed, a rosy glow on her cheeks most likely from the amusing topics of conversation that only walls knew about.

"Good afternoon, ladies," he said, unable to keep his voice casual.

"Emrys." Saoirse's face quickly fell. She shot up from her chair and smoothed her hands over his biceps.

"I'm sorry," he said kissing her awkwardly.

She pulled back and stared at him, aghast. Morrigan strike him. He hated that worried expression on her.

"What's wrong?" Saoirse asked. "Is it Kieran?"

"Yes." Emrys shook his head and sighed. "No. I— "

"Ladies, I think I'm going to cut our afternoon short." Saoirse turned to the duchesses, who were already putting their tea cups away and chastising their husbands to stop stuffing their faces.

They gave quick goodbyes and a few congratulations to Emrys as they made their way out of the drawing room.

"Emrys." Saoirse had turned back to him, her eyes still full of worry. "What happened?"

"Let's go upstairs." He took her hand and led her out of the drawing room. His mind barely registered the short journey to their quarters. His head still felt like it was submerged underwater, and his entire body felt like someone else was commanding it.

"Emrys, please tell me something," Saoirse pleaded when he shut the door behind them. "I've never seen you like this, and it's scaring me."

"Kieran is still general," he finally blurted, the words sounding just as unreal as when he first heard them.

"What?" Saoirse froze.

"He's been stripped of some of his power within the court, with a group of officers fulfilling those duties instead, but he still has authority in the army." Emrys sank into an armchair near the fireplace and buried his face in his hands. He heard Saoirse's quiet footsteps come towards him and felt her place a gentle hand on his shoulder. "That's not all." His voice croaked as he ran the conversation with his father over and over in his mind. "My father told me he knew what Kieran did. He knew he sent me to the council of the gods."

Emrys's eyes pinched with tears, and he hastily wiped at his face. Anger and resentment warred with a new wave of grief. He had spent nearly a century accepting that his father was wholly apathetic to Kieran's actions and that was never going to change. His relationship with his father was stiff and professional, and he had made peace with that. This new revelation had now shattered that peace.

Saoirse's hand moved on his shoulder, and soon she was astride on his lap, embracing him. Emrys slid shaking hands onto her waist as she stroked his hair and let him feel the wave of his various emotions.

"He knew, and he did nothing," he said around the clog in his throat. "He knew he killed me and didn't do anything."

Saoirse didn't say anything, but she continued stroking his hair. The feel of her fingers on his scalp grounded him, dissolving some of the numbness.

Emrys sucked in a shaky breath. "He tried to apologize. He said he felt responsible, but I..."

She pulled back when his words trailed off and wiped at his tears. "You feel it's too late?"

He nodded. "I've spent my entire life wanting to hear him take responsibility, but it felt more painful to hear it now. He had so long to say it. Why did it take him that long?"

"I don't know," Saoirse said quietly, cradling his face in her hands. "I'm sorry, Emrys."

"Would you forgive him?" Emrys asked, but quickly amended his question. "Not my father, but your brother. If he apologized for what he did to you, would you forgive him?"

She sat still for a moment, and he could tell she was taking extra care to think over his question. "No," she finally answered, shaking her head. "I don't think any words could make up for what he put me through."

He nodded, feeling a calm wrap around him. He knew it was the bond. It followed him and Saoirse whenever they were together, and he was never more grateful for it than now. Saoirse pressed a kiss to his forehead and combed her fingers through his hair again.

Emrys was understanding why she felt the most loved when he spent time with her, listening to her. It was comforting and peaceful. Her quiet gentleness soothed the ache in his chest. He felt like he could breathe without feeling the sting of pain in his lungs.

"I told you I'm not perfect," he said, burying his face in the crook of her neck.

Her shoulder shook with a silent laugh, and he swore he could hear her smile as she spoke. "And yet, I still want you." she said in a teasing tone. "All of you."

He chuckled and pulled away to meet her eyes. The spark zipped through him as he connected with her hazel eyes, and he wanted to blurt out the truth of the mating bond to her. He wanted at least a bit of his happiness back. But fear strangled him again, and the best he could do was kiss Saoirse deeply, standing with her in his arms.

She kissed him back and groaned as he pinned her against the nearest wall. However, her hand pressed against his chest, breaking their kiss and studying him for a moment. "Emrys, I don't want to do this if you aren't alright," she said.

"I'm alright when I'm with you."

"Are you sure?" Her eyes were filled with a mix of desire and concern. She wanted this as much as he did, but he was sure she would stop him if she sensed he was trying to stamp out his emotions with sex.

"Let me show you how sure I am." Emrys claimed her mouth again, and she slowly parted her lips. He gently placed her feet on the floor so he could trace her curves with his hands. Saoirse moaned as he squeezed her breasts through her corset.

His hands fumbled as he hastily pulled the tails of her shirtwaist from her skirt and tried to unbutton it. She met his same fervor and plucked open the buttons of his waistcoat. They undressed each other at an astonishing pace, and soon Emrys was picking her up in his arms again.

Saoirse wrapped her legs around him and hooked her ankles together at his back. He felt how wet and needy she already was and groaned into the crook of her neck as he kissed her soft, warm skin. Her hips undulated, blindly attempting to align him to her entrance. He finally obliged her, and she sank onto him until he was buried to the hilt.

"Brigid's tits," he groaned as she clenched around his erection. Her nails dug into the scarred flesh of his back, and he half-hoped she'd break the skin to leave scars he could cherish.

He pressed her against the wall as he thrust into her. Her breathing quickly became ragged between moans of agonizing pleasure. Emrys didn't withhold anything as his pace hit a fever pitch, and Saoirse bobbed with his deep thrusts. A strangled cry came from her before she arched off the wall with a gasp. Emrys felt her pulse around his cock, urging him to meet her with his own release. She whimpered as he continued to thrust until the coil of pleasure snapped and flooded him with ecstasy.

He gave a few slow, deep thrusts, spilling what felt like everything he had into her before his own body shuddered, and he stilled. Saoirse still clung to him and dotted his shoulder with gentle kisses, bringing him back down to earth. Thoughts from earlier bubbled back up in his mind, and he couldn't help the scowl that pinched at his brows.

"Emrys," Saoirse whispered. He dragged his attention back to her. "Are you still with me?" A whisper of a smile graced her face, and he focused on the feeling it gave him all over, letting all other thoughts melt away.

"Always," Emrys answered, gently kissing her lips.

He carried her into his bedroom, and they sat tangled on the bed for a few long moments. He savored her warmth before pulling away from her and retrieving a warm, wet cloth from his bathroom. Saoirse tried to reach for the cloth, but Emrys pulled it back while he shook his head. He wiped away what he had spilled into her and kissed the silky skin of her stomach. She combed his hair with her fingers with a dreamy smile on her face. Gods, he loved the feeling of her fingers in his hair and couldn't get enough of it. He wanted nothing more than to feel that for the rest of his immortal life.

"I love you," she said.

He grinned contentedly at her, never tiring of hearing those words in her voice. "I love you, too," he returned.

He set the cloth aside and sat next to her on the bed, wrapping an arm around her waist. Her warm body was a welcome feeling against his chest. He pressed a kiss to her hair and felt her sigh in satisfaction.

Another kiss was planted to her forehead as he leaned back onto the pillows with her in his arms. She snuggled into his chest and idly stroked his skin with her thumb. A knot formed in his stomach as loud thoughts about Kieran and his father warred in his mind for attention. He closed his eyes and gently ran his hands over Saoirse's curves, letting her presence cast at least a glimmer of peace over him.

Despite exhausting himself, Emrys had a restless night of sleep. His one solace was Saoirse sleeping soundly in his arms. After waking up from yet another short spurt of sleep, he found she had turned over and had her arm wrapped around his waist, holding him tightly. He gently lifted her hand to his lips and brushed a grateful kiss over her knuckles. She could argue how imperfect she was until she was blue in the face, but she was perfect for him. Funny how the gods arranged that.

The sun slowly streamed into the room, and Emrys clung to his last attempt at sleep. Unfortunately, Saoirse stirred just as his body was about to give in. Her arm slid from his waist, and he felt her lips press a kiss to his cheek before she vacated the bed. He internally groaned, knowing any attempt at sleep was now ruined.

His eyes squinted as he sat up and rubbed at the throbbing headache at his temples. He hadn't been that intensely emotional in quite some time, and he forgot how taxing it was on not only his mind but his body as well. Saoirse appeared from the bathroom, and Emrys noted she was still nude. Her body radiated heat as she slid back into bed next to him and wrapped her arms around his neck. He turned his tired eyes towards her and attempted a smile.

"Good morning," she said with a kiss.

"Good morning," he mumbled in response.

"You didn't sleep well, did you?"

He shook his head and closed his eyes. Saoirse kissed his achy temple and rested her head on his shoulder, the two sitting in silence for a long stretch of time. It was as close to peace that Emrys had felt since his father made his confession.

"Should we get breakfast?" Saoirse asked, pulling him out of his early morning savoring.

"I think we'll have to put some clothes on."

She made an annoyed grunting sound and sighed. "Maybe it isn't worth it, then."

He let out a laugh and felt some of the stress holding him hostage ease. "I could always feast on you for breakfast." He rolled over top of her and kissed from her lips to just above her naval. Her skin was so enticingly warm and silky. If he skipped breakfast to spend the morning in bed with her, it wouldn't be the worst idea.

Saoirse giggled and threaded her fingers in his hair. "As good of an idea as that sounds," she said. "I think I need a bit more sustenance than that."

Emrys sighed and rested his head on her stomach. She stroked his hair, and he nearly lost all his thoughts. Gods, he had dreamed of mornings like this, the fitful night of sleep notwithstanding.

"I could ring for someone to bring up food," he said.

"Would that still require clothes?" she asked.

"Only on my behalf." Emrys pressed one last kiss to her skin before peeling himself off of her and sliding out of bed. He grabbed his dressing robe and tied the belt around his waist. When he stepped out into the sitting room, he was greeted with a screaming meow from Owen.

"You can't have any of our breakfast," he told the cat as he reached for the bell pull. It took only a few moments before Rory was knocking at the door. Emrys asked for two trays of breakfast, and she promised to have them up quickly. Once she turned back down the hall, Emrys hurried back to his room.

Saoirse was stretched on her side, the sheets only covering her hips. He inwardly groaned and felt the image he was witnessing go straight to his cock. While he looked forward to spending the morning eating breakfast with his wife, his mate, he anticipated following through with his desire to feast on her afterwards. The rest of his day was going to be brutal, but at least he could pull up this image of her to get him through it.

The day dragged at what felt like half-speed. Minutes seemed to tick by like hours, and Emrys could barely focus on a single task. He attempted to read the latest report from the army camps, but it only caused his thoughts to wander to Kieran. He moved on to writing correspondence, however, his mind could barely string together a coherent sentence.

Emrys finally gave up trying to work when he dozed off and his head slipped from his hand, smacking into his desk. Rubbing the swollen bump on his forehead, he retreated from the council room towards the stairs. But the captain of the guard cut off his path.

"Good evening," Emrys said from behind heavy eyelids. He was so close to his quarters that he prayed the guard had little to inform him of.

"Good evening, Your Highness," the guard said plainly. "I've come to find you and ask you to appear in front of your father."

"What for?" Emrys asked.

"I've only been told it's urgent." The guard remained stock-still, not giving away anything of his quest.

Emrys sighed and followed the guard from the council room to the scarcely used throne room. It sat in the middle of the first floor and was usually locked unless the need for it arose. It was last used when Emrys came of age and was crowned as prince. As Emrys was motioned into the room, a shiver ran down his spine when he spotted Saoirse standing in the middle of the room.

His blood ran cold when he looked further to find his father on the pale gold throne and Kieran flanking him. He stood at Alastair's side with a hand on the fireann's shoulder, his beloved pocket watch dangling from his fingers.

Alastair's face unreadable as Emrys approached him. He stopped next to Saoirse and glanced at her from the corner of his eye.

Her spine was ramrod straight, and her expressionless face made him queasy. She was scared, and he could do nothing but endure whatever this meeting was beside her.

"Emrys," his father said coolly. "Do you know why you have been summoned to me?"

"No, sir." Emrys kept his voice from rising. There was no good reason he would be pulled into the throne room, especially with his wife there as well, but hissing and spitting wouldn't get them out faster.

"You don't?" Alastair asked. He straightened his posture and narrowed his eyes at his son. "Someone must know then."

"I know why." Kieran's chilling voice made Emrys shiver. Kieran stared him down, looking like a wild cat who had caught its prey and was intent on taunting it before putting the poor creature out of its misery. "He's conspired to kill you, Alastair," Kieran said.

"That's a lie." The words escaped Emrys before he could articulate a decent response. "I have never conspired to kill anyone."

"Is that so?" Kieran asked, slipping his hands into his trouser pockets and stepping down from the dais. "May I?" He reached towards Emrys, waiting for his permission. Emrys wanted to say no, but he knew he'd come across as guilty if he refused to be searched.

"Yes," he said plainly.

Kieran gave him a devilish grin as he reached inside Emrys's pocket. He didn't search long before he pulled out a vial of clear liquid. Emrys's heart dropped. That hadn't been in his pocket. His trouser pockets had been empty that morning, and he had been in the council room all day. His mind scrambled for a defense as Kieran returned to the dais. He handed it to Alastair, who read the label. His face drained of all color as he looked up at Emrys, bewildered.

"Emrys," he whispered. "This is poison. It's lethal at just a drop. What were you planning to do with this?"

"Kill you, Father," Kieran said.

Father?

Emrys felt like his sleep-addled mind had interfered with his hearing. Did he insinuate Alastair was more than just an uncle to him? Did he think the way Alastair treated him was how he would treat a son?

"You didn't know?" Kieran asked with another devious smirk. Emrys glanced at his father and saw a flash of shame mix with his expression of shock. "Why, Father, why haven't you informed your dear boy about our brotherhood?"

"I'm sorry, Emrys," Alastair croaked. It sounded just as it had yesterday, pitiful and ashamed.

What was going on? Why did his father display such remorse for what Kieran was saying?

"Well, since *he* hasn't given you this information, I suppose I shall take it upon myself to share it with you." Kieran strutted slowly across the dais, that damn pocket watch between his fiddling fingers. "Our father was not as faithful as you may think he was. He and my mother held a secret affair for decades right under poor old Callum's nose. I think our dear Saoirse knows how secret affairs like that go." Emrys glanced at Saoirse, who kept a straight face, but her gaze shot daggers at the general as he let out a low laugh. "You really thought I'd publicly declare my feelings for someone like you, a young and naïve boireann with wild magic? Even if you are a princess, it would be embarrassing for me."

"That seems quite contrary to what you've been saying about me and Emrys." To her credit, Saoirse's response was controlled, but the loathing in her gaze couldn't be missed.

"I was merely stating facts," Kieran said. "Facts that seemed to have resonated quite deeply."

Saoirse didn't retort again.

"In any case," Kieran went on, "my mother fell pregnant from her affair. She told no one that Alastair was the father for fear of being stripped of her crown and banished from the court. Luckily, I came out looking more like my mother, so they both could keep their secret."

"What happened to Callum?" Emrys asked. His mind and his mouth had become two separate entities. He wanted to shred

Kieran apart for embarrassing his mate, but somehow his mouth voiced questions that were more important.

"He was an unfortunate casualty," Alastair said gravely. "He became suspicious and lost his life because of it." Emrys saw his eyes go glassy as he gave his answer, and he wondered if his father had been forced to kill his brother.

The room began to spin and vomit rose in his throat. He held onto his composure as he asked his next question. "And my mother?" he asked. Alastair opened his mouth to reply, but Kieran answered for him.

"She was jealous," he said. "Your mother hated me and the one who was responsible for my entrance into the world. She wanted to spite my mother, and so she seduced our father to get pregnant with you. Without my legitimacy, you would become the heir. She finally had to go so that the rightful queen could sit on the throne."

"Did you kill her?" Emrys's voice went ice cold, and adrenaline thrummed through him. Thoughts of Saoirse and his father's affair still screamed in his mind, but the thought of Kieran killing his mother had his focus narrowed.

"No," Kieran answered. "I was only fourteen. What demented stick asks a child to kill an adult?" Emrys glared at him as he was being chastised. "But your father made the cowardly choice and put her on a ship to let the gods decide her fate on the stormy seas."

Emrys flicked his gaze to his father, who now had a wholly shameful expression on his face. His stomach dropped. There was something he wasn't saying, something it seemed he *couldn't* say. This scene didn't feel right. Kieran was taking hold of the dialogue and keeping his father from saying what he wanted to.

Their father.

Oh, gods. Kieran was his brother. The fact finally sunk in. It explained why Alastair treated him better than Emrys. But his fondness for Kieran had faded the past few weeks, and he had genuine conversations with Emrys. Ones that talked fondly of his mother and angrily about his appointed general. His apology, as hurtful and heartbreaking as it was, seemed genuine.

The room felt too hot, yet Emrys's skin was covered in goosebumps. "Why are you doing this?" he asked through gritted teeth at his half-brother.

"I'm not doing anything, Brother. I'm only shedding light on your true nature to our innocent father."

"Emrys," his father spoke in a weak voice. "You've never had malicious intent towards anyone. What has caused you to do such a thing?"

Emrys held back his urge to deny it, but what proof did he have that confirmed it wasn't true? He had no idea where the vial came from, and his only alibi was Saoirse, who could easily be accused of conspiring with him. He had easy access to Seraphina and her healer's space. It was easy for someone like Kieran to frame him.

"Yes, he and his little mate are quite deceptive, aren't they?" Kieran said. The words were for Alastair, but he directed them to Saoirse.

Emrys felt his body go numb. The room spun faster, and he felt like he might topple over. Kieran had done it. His worst fear had come true. The last person he wanted to divulge this information to Saoirse had revealed their mating bond. Ada, Cyprian—everyone really—had warned him, but he had been too cowardly to talk to her. He watched Saoirse carefully as she digested the confession. Her expression went stony as Kieran witnessed her reaction.

"Emrys," he chastised. "Did you lie to me? Did you lie to *her*?" A slimy grin tugged at Kieran's lips. "Emrys, I told you not to keep things from someone you hold so precious. I believe this means you two haven't sealed the bond either. I wonder what the gods think of that."

Anger and mortification flushed through Emrys's body as he watched Kieran sever all the trust he had built for the second time with his wife, his love. He stole another glance at Saoirse, who held a glassy expression as she kept her gaze on Kieran.

"What are you going to do about this, Father?" Emrys asked, his heart pounding in his throat. He wanted this over with. He wanted to be alone with Saoirse to explain everything and plead his case as to why he hadn't told her. Visions of her rejecting him outright flashed in his mind, and it took all his strength to keep the sting of tears behind his eyes from coming forth.

"I don't know yet," Alastair answered. "I believe I'll need a few days to think about a suitable punishment. You two will be kept downstairs until I come to a decision."

Kieran's smirk made Emrys's throat go dry. He wasn't thinking of his own punishment, but of what would happen to Saoirse since he had somehow tangled her in this mess. Emrys was about to open his mouth to protest her being punished, but two guards came from behind them and secured iron shackles around their wrists.

The iron shackles felt worse than the iron on the trains. Instead of just the discomfort of suppressing his magic, it felt almost painful. It also amplified the sense of helplessness Emrys felt. He couldn't protect himself or Saoirse, and they were now at the mercy of Kieran and Alastair.

The guards pulled them to a small hidden staircase behind the dais, and Emrys tried to ignore the victorious grin on Kieran's face as they passed him.

The underground of the house was dark and dank. One-half of it was used as servant chambers, a wing that was much more well-maintained than the chamber they were being led into. A small prison sat under the house and, to Emrys's knowledge, hadn't been used during his lifetime.

Until now.

Emrys was herded into a cell, and he immediately slumped against the wall as he heard Saoirse forced into the one next to him. After the guards left, silence fell over the cells and fear grew in Emrys's chest. He knew the repercussions of withholding the truth, and the silence that stretched between them made it all the more painful. He wished she would just get on with her reaction because this...this was much worse than any punishment his father could think of.

The *smell of* mold hit Saoirse's nose as her eyes adjusted to the dim lighting of the dungeons. A steady trickle of water rang through the dark stone chamber, and she nearly slid on the slick stones of the floors as she was shoved into one of the cells. Her iron chains were wrenched from her wrists, leaving her skin red and raw. Her relief was short-lived as an iron cuff and chain were shackled to her ankle, connecting her to a post on the wall. Her cell had a stiff cot against one wall and a brown bucket that she assumed was a toilet. Iron bars trapped her in the small square room and slammed shut with a metallic twang.

She sat on the thin cot and leaned against the gray brick wall. She crossed her arms and told herself she wouldn't cry. But it was the only way she felt she could express all the emotions that she felt swirling in her mind.

Kieran had pulled the rug out from both her and Emrys in a matter of minutes.

Emrys.

Her stomach roiled at the fact he and Kieran were brothers and, subsequently, the relationships she had shared with both of them. Who married the brother of her former lover? She did, apparently. Even if it was unknowingly, it made her feel ill.

Kieran had also revealed another secret, one held by Emrys.

Mate.

The word rang in her head as if trying to claim her attention over all her other thoughts. Kieran had referred to Emrys as her mate. But mates weren't real. They were a lie. Even if Saoirse could entertain the thought of them being real, Emrys had said nothing about them at any point in their courtship, their engagement, or their marriage. If it was true, he had kept it from her yet told others about it. Why? Why didn't he feel the need to share that with her? Why did he feel everyone else was privileged to that information but her?

But mates *weren't real*. They were tools used by abusive bastards like Eamon and Kieran. Maybe he was lying. He had lied about how he felt about her. He had lied about Emrys plotting to kill Alastair. He had lied about his parentage. But Emrys's reaction when the word was uttered made her doubt Kieran was lying in that statement.

"Saoirse."

She heard Emrys's voice from the small window of bars in the wall between their cells after a long, silent moment. She hadn't wanted to speak to him or hear his reasons. But this wasn't going to go away if she ignored it. Somewhere in this mess was the truth, and she needed to find it.

"What makes you think we're mates?" she asked sharply. A short silence followed her question.

"The gods whispered it to me," Emrys answered feebly.

She snorted. It was the same explanation Eamon used on Cressida.

"The gods spoke to him and told him they fated me with him," Cressida would always recount. She would follow it with a swoon, as if it was the height of romance to be told something so outrageous. How did the gods even speak to their creations?

"You know, when the gods resurrect someone, they like to keep account of them and make sure they didn't choose poorly," Emrys said.

"I'm sure they appreciate you lying," Saoirse mumbled. "How do they even 'whisper' to you? Wouldn't that just be a thought?"

"No, it's different," he said. "Even if I explained it, would you believe me?"

She wanted to say no, but she wasn't in the mood to give him the satisfaction of guessing her reaction correctly.

He exhaled heavily and continued. "They promised me a mate when I had proved I had been a worthy investment to them. They watched over me and were pleased with my actions. They saw how it had transformed me and my outlook on my life. They saw how I saved myself and others, and they wanted to reward me. They whispered to me when you entered the world."

"And how did you know it was me?" she asked. "Did they give you my name and all the details of my person?"

"No, I only knew you existed," he answered. "They gave me no details. I had to wait until their hands intervened and put you in my path. Your proposal—or your brother's proposal, I should say—amongst other potential brides stood out to me. I kept count of how long since I heard the whispers, and when I saw your age, I took the chance. I felt the mating spark the moment I saw you. That first spark was everything to me."

Saoirse's hot anger flushed cold. That damned spark. He had felt it, too. It was one strike against her refusal to believe mates were real. She never felt it with Kieran or anyone else she had been involved with, only with Emrys. Whenever he looked at her, whenever they touched, whenever they made love, it was there.

But mates weren't real.

"Why didn't you tell me?" The angry heat in her tone was slowly fading. She fought against entertaining the idea of mates being real. She couldn't let herself wonder about it. Because if they were real, wouldn't the gods have whispered to her, too? Why didn't she get to experience that hope for all those years she lived in misery?

"You told me bluntly you didn't believe they were real," Emrys answered, shaking her from her thoughts. "Besides, I wanted to build your trust first. That felt more important to me."

"But you kept it from me." Both things stung. Her spouse thinking they were mates and him feeling the need to keep it a secret hurt worse than anything Kieran or her brother had ever done to her.

"Would you have agreed to marry me if you knew?" Emrys asked. "If instead of offering you our bargain, I told you we were fated to be together, would you have agreed to marry me?"

"I would have taken my chances in the Matron House," Saoirse answered. "At least there they would be honest with what my relationship was with them."

"I wanted to tell you." His voice dipped into desperation. "There were several times I nearly did."

"And what stopped you?"

A long pause hung between them. "I didn't want to lose you. I was willing to ignore the bond if it meant I kept you."

Saoirse's anger boiled again. "Congratulations, Emrys," she said. "You've made yourself such a martyr that you turned into a complete dog in the manger."

"I'm sorry," he said softly. "I'm so utterly sorry for destroying your trust. I ruined everything."

"Yes, you did," she said, ignoring the pity he was laying on himself. She was too angry to allow it to persuade her into sympathy.

Emrys let out a heavy exhale. "I have nothing to lose at this point," he murmured. "I should also confess that what I did after you told me about Kieran...assaulting you, that was the bond."

Saoirse froze. That was the second blow to her resolve. It was one she couldn't explain away as easily as the spark. Coincidence and pure attraction could have created what she felt was that connection between them. But Emrys soothing her pain in an instant? That had no explanation.

"So you lied about that, too?" she asked, her voice wobbling.

"I didn't lie exactly," he said. "I omitted it like I did with the bond as a whole."

"Omission is the same as lying." Her words cracked, and she felt the familiar pinch behind her eyes.

"I know," he said quietly. "I'm sorry."

Saoirse bit down on her wobbling lip, willing herself to keep her composure. "Mates aren't real," she whispered. She hoped saying it would make it feel true again. But even though Emrys's omission hurt her deeply, she couldn't deny the details he was describing. She couldn't wave them away as accompanying lies either. They described things she experienced that she had never made known to Emrys. If he were lying, he wouldn't be able to guess things with such detail.

A tear escaped and rolled down her cheek. She sniffed and hugged her knees into her chest. Her grip was slipping on her belief, and she felt the little control she had left dwindling. She couldn't even turn to Emrys for comfort because he was the culprit of her spiral.

"For what it's worth, my love is real," Emrys murmured. "I didn't fall in love with you because of the bond. It only led me to you. I fell in love with you regardless of what the bond told me, and I will love you to my last dying breath. Mates or not, accepting the bond or not, nothing will change that."

Saoirse stared at the dark stone ceiling and wiped at her tears. She wanted to be able to say the same, but pain had bruised her heart. Her love was buried under anger and hurt, and there was no telling what it would take to uncover it again. Saoirse had had her heart broken before, but this time it had been shattered, the pieces too sharp and jagged to consider mending back together.

They didn't speak the rest of the night or most of the next morning. Saoirse started to curse Kieran every time she lay on the thin mattress of the cot in the cell or used the wooden bucket she had for a toilet. The food delivered for breakfast was anything but appetizing. Various colors of mashed food and a stale piece of bread were the only substances she was served, and hope for dinner being better waned with each bite.

Occupying her time was another curse to the general. Neither she nor Emrys knew when Alastair would pull them out of their cellar imprisonments to deliver what he saw as suitable punishments. For all they knew, Kieran would prolong Alastair's decision, and he would never come to one, keeping them in the cells to rot. She tried not to think about that fate.

In exchange, she thought about the previous day and all the things Kieran had revealed. She had learned too many things all at once, and they bounced around in her mind, leaving her at sixes and sevens. What she wanted to know most was if Emrys was just as surprised by it as she was or if he had omitted to her those details as well.

"Emrys," she said, trying to keep her voice neutral. She didn't want to tilt at him, nor did she want him to think she had silently forgiven him. She only wanted answers. "I need to know for my own sanity. Did you know about anything else Kieran revealed yesterday? Did you know he was your brother?"

"No," Emrys answered immediately. "I knew nothing about that. It was as new to me as it was you."

"So Kieran didn't convince you to marry me?"

"Not at all," he said. "He tried to make comments about you, but I didn't want to hear anything from him, good or bad. I made the decision on my own."

A month's worth of relief washed over her. She had a strong inkling Kieran had been lying about his involvement with her arrangement. But now that she knew about the bond, she realized it was true for a different reason.

"You mean you made it because of the bond," she corrected bitterly.

"Partly, yes," he answered. "As I said, I wasn't certain you were my mate, but I felt drawn to your proposal. I took a leap of faith, and it paid off."

Saoirse took a deep breath, continuing her resolve to not tilt at him. "Since you didn't know Kieran was your brother, I assume you didn't know about your father's affair."

"I was oblivious to it," Emrys answered. "I was too young for my mother to divulge that to me, and the time I did spend around Kieran's mother, I was unaware of anything between her and my father. By the time I was an adult, she had disappeared and no one explained to me why or how."

Saoirse found that curious, but now wasn't the time to dive into Emrys's past. "And the poison?" she asked.

"My pockets were empty when I walked into the throne room," he said quietly. "Kieran is nothing if not a showman." He gave a dry laugh before clearing his throat awkwardly.

A terrible thought struck Saoirse, and she willed herself not to let her emotions crash over her instantly. "What will happen to you?" she whispered.

"Exactly what you think will happen," he answered woefully. "Kieran has done it once before. This is his attempt to make it permanent."

Saoirse tried to swallow the emotion clogging her throat, but it was no use. Kieran was cruel to strike a blow between her and Emrys and then tear Emrys away from her with no chance of reconciling. She felt betrayed by Emrys's omission, but she would never wish his demise because of it.

"I'm sure this isn't the time," Emrys said. "But sealing the bond would have given us a higher chance at fate deciding in our favor."

"You were right. It isn't the time." A tear spilled onto her lap, frustration and sadness mingling. "I don't even know what sealing the bond is."

"It's a prayer ritual," he provided. "It grants mates a higher chance of surviving the pitfalls of the world. I've had the words echoing in my mind since we—since the cottage."

A third blow to her belief regarding mates. At this point, her resistance was threadbare, and she could only cling to it with desperation. She let out a choked sob and slumped onto her side on her mattress. She attempted to calm herself with deep breaths, but it was no use. Between her betrayal and Emrys's dwindling time left, she was inconsolable, and she remained so until her body was too exhausted to remain conscious.

38

Three days went by before anyone other than the guards watching over them or the servants plagued with the task of delivering meals came down to the cells. Emrys knew Kieran was only drawing this out to torture him and Saoirse. He didn't need Cyprian's knowledge of the law to know his punishment was death. This was Kieran's retaliation to his demotion. Even though he still had authority, he had lost the power he held in the court, power he wouldn't trade for anything.

It made Emrys suspicious that Kieran chose now to reveal what he knew about his—their—father. But his motive wasn't entirely clear. Revealing himself as Alastair's first born did nothing but toss away valuable knowledge he could hold over the king. It was probably why Alastair had favored Kieran for as long as Emrys could remember.

But why reveal it? Emrys was destined for death for what Kieran framed him with. Kieran would automatically take his spot as next in line for the throne. Did he know something worse about their father that kept Alastair from stopping his theatrics? When they had been pulled into the throne room, his father looked like he was being held against his will. At times he even looked like he wanted to say more, to defend himself from the picture Kieran was painting of him, but he couldn't.

The longer Emrys waited, the longer he held out hope that

Ada or Seraphina would come storming down and rescue him and Saoirse. But no one came. There wasn't even a clatter of someone attempting to free them. Kieran had something devious planned, something he couldn't have plotted just in the last week.

Emrys tried miserably to ignore the feeling of his unwashed body and the stale clothes he had worn for almost four straight days. He imagined Saoirse felt the same way. As he had the thought, a whimpering noise came from the cell next to him. He tried to ignore it until he heard the whimper again.

"Saoirse," he said cautiously. "Are you alright?"

"I'll be fine." Her voice sounded pained, and he felt the urge to knock down the stone wall that sat between them with his bare hands. If only the protective instinct of the mating bond came with the strength that would quench it. "It's only cramping from my cycle."

She let out a small groan of pain, and he couldn't sit and do nothing any longer. He stood and pressed himself against the iron bars of his cell. He could feel his magic physically deflating with the amount of iron being pressed to his body.

"Oi!" he called to the guards that stood at the foot of the stairs. "Don't you hear her in pain? Do something for her." The guards turned their attention away, and Emrys felt his anger boil in his veins.

"Emrys, it's fine," Saoirse said weakly. "It'll go away soon."

He sat back on the thin mattress and tried to settle himself. He hated feeling helpless when it came to her, and his helplessness mingled with anger when he remembered why she was in a cell next to him. He rubbed at his face and tugged on his hair, unable to do anything else. His stomach dropped when two guards came to get him and Saoirse moments later. This was it. His destiny was about to be revealed to him in a mere moment.

Their hands were shackled with iron chains once again, their ankle cuffs removed temporarily. They were tugged up the stairs to the throne room again, and the stark contrast of the bright afternoon sun pierced Emrys's vision. He squinted while his eyes adjusted.

He and Saoirse were shoved in front of Kieran and Alastair. Emrys tried to stand tall and seem unfazed, but watching Saoirse's pained and fearful expression nearly destroyed him. He had to plead for her innocence and let her walk away freely. She didn't have a lifelong rivalry with Kieran and didn't deserve to be punished. He was willing to take twice as much punishment if it meant she wasn't harmed.

"I hate the putrid smell of prisoners after lunch," Kieran remarked.

Emrys clenched his jaw to not sneer at him and instead faced his father. "Do you have our punishments?" he asked flatly.

"Yes, Emrys, we have come to a conclusion of how you'll be punished," Alastair answered, his face unreadable once again.

Emrys's heart raced, and he stole a sideways glance at Saoirse. She looked as if she were holding herself together, but he knew there was physical pain from her cycle she was battling on top of whatever emotional pain Kieran was inflicting on her with his presence.

"You will be sent to Donheath to join one of the army camps there."

"What?" Emrys didn't understand. His punishment had been clear since the moment evidence was found on him. He couldn't tell if this was by the fate of the gods or part of a darker plan that Kieran had plotted.

"Your punishment is to be under my command," Kieran answered, a slimy grin on his face. Emrys's stomach became unsettled. "You should thank me, Brother. I begged for your life."

"Why?" He didn't know why he kept asking questions, but he couldn't help pushing for answers. This was a drastic change from a cut and dried policy.

"It would be quite the spectacle for the beloved Prince of the Northern Fae to be executed for a devious crime," Kieran explained. "It would cause unwanted attention to the court, especially from that solicitor duke. So, Father and I came to a compromise. You get to live, but you will live out your days in my command."

Emrys's stomach threatened to purge his slop from breakfast. Kieran would most certainly attempt to kill him in that camp. He hadn't negotiated for Emrys's life. He had made a bid for it.

Emrys watched Saoirse as Alastair's gaze turned to her to deliver her punishment. Conspiracy was a much more fluid crime. It depended on how much the conspirator knew and how involved they were with the larger crime. He couldn't predict Saoirse's punishment, and with how much leeway he had been given with his sentence, he had to try to negotiate her freedom.

"Don't punish her," Emrys said. "She had nothing to do with any of this. She doesn't deserve whatever punishment you have for her."

Kieran chuckled darkly at his plea. "One last attempt at rescuing your mate?" His voice dripped with malice and his grin was devilish. "I applaud your sacrifice, Emrys, but how can we know for sure she wasn't involved? Do you not share everything with her? Well, you share *most* things with her." He continued to smirk as he uttered her punishment on behalf of their father. "You were going to be sent off to the Matron House, but I'm feeling just as heroic as your sweet mate."

He stepped off the dais and closed the gap between him and Saoirse. He curled his fingers under her chin and tilted it so her gaze met his. He stroked his thumb over her bottom lip as he spoke. "You can keep to my bed, and when your beloved mate meets the gods again, you can marry me and keep your future crown as queen."

Her expression went cold, and Emrys was stunned by the steady, icy voice that came from her lips as she answered. "I'd rather be a Matron," she said with a sneer.

"Fine," Kieran said, dropping his hand from her face. "Enjoy being a whore." He slid his gaze over to Emrys. "Maybe I'll bid on her for a night of sweet reunion."

Emrys tried not to show his reaction, but the thought of Kieran touching Saoirse again made his blood boil. Kieran smirked and stepped back onto the dais. The guards roughly grabbed Emrys and Saoirse, leading Saoirse back towards her cell and Emrys towards the hall. It seemed that his punishment would be effective immediately. Emrys's mind swirled with thoughts of his new life in Kieran's army camp and Saoirse being torn away from him to live her worst nightmare.

Suddenly, Kieran's voice filled the throne room again. "Why is there blood on your clothes?" he demanded, stopping both guards in their tracks.

Emrys looked over to see a red stain on the back of Saoirse's skirt. He watched as Saoirse twisted towards his half-brother, her gaze filled with fire.

"I'm on my cycle, you ignorant prick," she spat.

Emrys held back his shock and pride in her answer. She had nothing left to lose, and he could tell that the fire in her spirit was roaring to life. Her magic might have been incapacitated, but he knew her tongue could pierce deeper than her fire could.

Kieran made a disgusted noise. "I'm thankful I wasn't born a boireann."

"Is that what you're thankful for?" she retorted. "I thought you'd be thankful you didn't have such an immature bride who would embarrass you in front of the court. But I've seen now you're capable of doing that all by yourself."

Emrys couldn't hide his smirk. Danu bless her. She was amazing. Alongside watching Andromeda slap him, Emrys could listen to Saoirse belittle Kieran until the end of time.

The guard dragged Saoirse towards the stairs before Kieran could respond. Emrys caught the brief look she shot over her shoulder to him before her attention was forced to the stairs at her feet. It was one that sprang new hope in his chest. It told him that while he had hurt her, she held him with a higher respect than Kieran. It was a low threshold, but Emrys would take whatever she would give him. Maybe it would even lead to a chance of being forgiven.

That was if he lived long enough to earn it.

Saoirse *lay on* her sad excuse for a mattress and stared blankly at the wall in her cell. Her heart was shattered as if it were made of glass. She couldn't let herself think of what Emrys's fate in the army camp would be, but the weight of knowing what happened the last time he was in Kieran's hands sank her further into her thin mattress.

When her cell door opened, she didn't know how much time had passed. It could have been minutes or it could have been hours, but she was too numb to estimate. A pair of guards roughly handled her after unlocking the iron restraint on her ankle, but they didn't chain her arms. They restrained her hands behind her, and she was too dazed to take it as either a small pleasure or an insult that they thought they only needed their strength to hold her back. She complied nonetheless, knowing her alternative was being Kieran's personal sex slave until he wanted to toss her aside for someone else.

The guards pushed her up to the main floor of the house and out through a servants' entrance to a carriage. It was a sleek, dark carriage with few ornaments on it. It had to be a carriage sent by the Matron House. They were known for having very plain accommodations. Saoirse wasn't sure how the finances were handled in the House, but she assumed any surplus in profit was not spent on the boireannaich that served the House.

She barely registered being hoisted inside and the door shutting behind her. The carriage lurched forward, and she finally let tears fall down her cheeks as she accepted her fate.

The sun was dipping below the tips of the forest, and Saoirse learned it was near dusk. Her stomach growled, and she realized they hadn't fed her dinner before leaving.

Bastards.

She hoped the Matron House was more caring than the guards, but her hope was minimal. She would at least be able to bathe and change into clean clothes even if they were Matron robes. A shiver ran down her spine at the thought of donning the navy blue robes and red bonnet. She had rarely seen Matrons in Dublin, but they always looked the same, their heads hung low, their gazes avoiding anyone but the families they were contracted to help.

Saoirse pushed away the thought of having to bed strangers and pray to the gods they bless her with a child for them. She swallowed the panic that began to rise with the realization of bedding unknown fireannaich against her will. Instead, she sent a prayer to the gods that she could find a way to flee the Matron House and end up somewhere safe.

The sun dipped behind the trees, and Saoirse sat in the dark carriage for a bit longer before it stopped abruptly. Lamps illuminated a brick, gothic building covered in vines of ivy, and lights inside were stifled by dark tinted windows. The carriage door was opened, and she was allowed to step out of it of her own will. With nothing around the Matron House except for a dark, foggy forest, the footman must have assumed she wouldn't attempt to bolt the moment she was given a chance. Saoirse walked up to the tall black painted doors and before she could reach for the door knocker, the doors opened. A tall, thin boireann with aging features answered the door and crinkled her nose at the sight of Saoirse's soiled appearance.

"Come," she ordered sharply.

Saoirse followed the boireann into the dark house and barely glimpsed the halls before she was shoved into a washroom. Several pipes hung from the ceiling and snaked down the wall, connecting to knobs that controlled them like a faucet. Several drains sat on the floor, and thin opaque curtains separated the stalls of showers. The boireann disappeared, shutting the door behind her. Saoirse took a deep, shaky breath as her surroundings settled into her. She was truly here.

Silently, she stripped off her clothes before turning one of the knobs of the showers and stepping under the stream of water. Ice cold liquid hit her skin, and she jumped at the shock. Playing with the knobs did no good. Cold was the only temperature she had access to. She gritted her teeth and stepped back into the stream of icy water.

Scrubbing at her body to remove the thin layer of dirt that clung to her skin was nearly impossible without a washcloth or soap. The cold water numbed her skin, and she shivered while her teeth chattered. In the silence of the washroom, she heard the door open again and watched as a short boireann in dark blue robes entered. She set towels on a stool and laid a matching set of navy blue robes next to them.

Saoirse's entire body vibrated from the cold as the boireann dug in a nearby closet. She emerged with a large brush and a bar of soap. The boireann drew back the curtain of the shower and Saoirse tried not to act as embarrassed as she felt. The brush was lathered with soap and scrubbed over Saoirse's body.

The coarse bristles scratched at her skin, and she winced at the rough scrubbing. However, the dirt began to slosh off with the icy water, and Saoirse was thankful to feel clean for once. The boireann gestured with her hands, and it took Saoirse a moment to realize what she was doing.

Mute. The Matron was mute and used her hands to communicate. Saoirse wondered if that was what brought her to the Matron House. She would be a perfect candidate for a career of being bedded against her will, with no voice to complain or cry for help.

The boireann copied her hand movements again, and Saoirse paid closer attention this time. She made circle shapes with her hands and moved them before opening her fingers. Saoirse realized she was signing about her magic. She focused on the sliver of emotion she could still feel and manifested a flame in her palm. The Matron jumped back and held up a hand to stop her from manifesting larger flames.

"Sorry," Saoirse murmured. She drew back her magic, but let it linger in her muscles. The iciness of the shower faded, and the room filled with steam. The Matron had been telling her to use her magic to keep herself warm while she showered. How she knew her magic element was fire Saoirse didn't know, but she was thankful for the advice.

The Matron moved onto washing Saoirse's hair and dragged over a stool to reach her height. She ladened her hand with shampoo and worked it through the Saoirse's strands. The sensation of clean hair was almost worth the embarrassment of having a stranger bathe her. She came to realize how little privacy the Matrons were given. Their bodies were not their own, and anything private was sure to be exposed at some point. It was something Saoirse would have to adjust to sooner rather than later.

The boireann rinsed Saoirse's hair and shut the water off. Saoirse dried off her body with one of the towels while the boireann squeezed the excess water from Saoirse's hair with a second towel. She combed the knots out, and while the tugging and scraping of her hair was painful, Saoirse was thankful it was at least clean. The boireann finished by running her hand over Saoirse's hair and instantly drying it under her touch. Saoirse wasn't sure if the boireann also had high fae fire magic, or whether it was mid fae practical magic, but she was thankful for the small pleasure of being taken care of.

"Thank you," Saoirse said to the Matron as she turned for the door.

The boireann gestured with her hands and nodded with a small grin. She left the bathroom, and Saoirse had nothing left to do but dress into her new uniform. The robes were oversized and shapeless, allowing for the potential growth of an offspring, and completely unflattering. Matrons were to be devoted to their craft of bedding and producing heirs for fae who were unsuccessful at doing it themselves and were to be unattached to partners.

At the thought of a partner, Saoirse's mind drifted to Emrys, and she had to push him away to keep herself from crying. She couldn't think about him right now. It would make her first night in the Matron House that much harder.

She stepped out of the bathroom and found the tall boireann who had greeted her at the entrance of the House was waiting for her. "This way," she said curtly.

Saoirse followed her silent footsteps down the narrow hallway as the dark wood floors beneath their feet creaked. The walls of the hallway were covered with black brocade wallpaper, and the sconces that illuminated the hallway did a minimal job at providing light. The boireann stopped at a door on their left and opened the black-painted door.

Saoirse stepped inside and saw six tall bunk beds lined either side of the room. Each one had a thin mattress—although not as thin and frail as the mattress in her dungeon cell—gray sheets, and a few beds had personal items decorating them. The boireann stalked off down the hall before Saoirse could turn and ask her which bunk was hers. She scanned the room for a bed that looked untouched and found one near the back wall.

"Are you our new girl?" a voice asked as Saoirse approached the unoccupied bed.

She nearly jumped at the sound of another boireann. The Matron had soft features and rich, dark brown hair. She was sitting on the bottom bed of one of the bunks reading a book by the dim candlelight on her nightstand.

"Yes," Saoirse answered. "I'm Saoirse." She offered her best attempt at a smile. In return, the Matron beamed back at her, jumping to her feet.

"I'm so happy I finally get to be the first one to meet a new girl," she said. "I'm Althea."

"It's nice to meet you, Althea," Saoirse said. "Is this bunk available for me to take?" She gestured towards the bunk at the back of the room, and Althea nodded vigorously.

"Oh, yes, that's the last empty one in this room," she answered.

"Great." As Saoirse climbed the wood ladder, it groaned underneath her. She sat on the mattress and relished that it was at least thicker than the cot she had slept on for the last few nights.

Althea stepped next to the bed and kept her gaze on Saoirse. "So, what great misery brought you here?" she asked.

Saoirse's chest tightened. "It's a long story," she said quietly.

"We've got nothing but time here." Althea shrugged.

Saoirse met the boireann's gaze and studied her beautiful features. She wondered how long she had been here. Had she fallen pregnant before? Had clients used her services? Althea looked at her with an expression that longed for friendship and interaction with another being. Saoirse wondered what might keep Althea from making connections with the other boireannaich in the House. But Saoirse also had little choice in friendship, and she, too, was desperate for a connection.

"Well." Saoirse sighed deeply. "I was married."

"You were?" Althea asked, her eyes growing wide. Saoirse nodded. "So you're nobility?"

Saoirse chewed on her bottom lip. "Something like that."

"What happened to your husband?"

"He..." She didn't know how exactly to explain her husband's cousin, turned half-brother, framed him for attempted murder and now had him awaiting his fateful end in an army camp. "He was taken from me."

"Oh." Althea's face fell. "I'm sorry. I shouldn't have pried like that. Of course something happened to him. How else would you be here?"

"It's fine." Tension in Saoirse's shoulders melted. It seemed Althea genuinely wanted another person to talk to. And Saoirse needed to talk. "It's a part of my life. I don't want to keep it in the shadows."

A warm smile graced Althea's face. "You had a husband," she mused. "I could only dream of a husband. But being a Matron, there isn't any room for that."

"If you weren't a Matron, would you pursue finding one?" Saoirse asked.

Althea shrugged. "I wouldn't know. I've always been a Matron."

Saoirse knit her brows. The Matron must have sensed her confusion and curiosity from her silence.

"I was born in the Matron House," she supplied. "My mother was successful with a client who was an earl. But a few weeks later, his wife discovered she was pregnant. He chose that child over me."

Saoirse felt like that cold shower from earlier had sprayed on her again. Althea had known nothing outside the Matron House. She wanted to press her with more questions, but she knew it wasn't an appropriate time to pry.

"I was raised in the House," Althea continued. "Because I was high fae, I was seen as an ideal Matron. I was groomed to be successful, but..." She sighed. "I've yet to fulfill my purpose successfully."

"I'm so sorry," Saoirse whispered.

Althea flashed a sad smile and nodded.

Saoirse's problems with Emrys now seemed small in comparison. She had been spoiled in contrast to Althea. But for someone who was given a terrible hand in life, Althea still seemed welcoming and friendly. Saoirse admired that.

"It's not all bad," Althea said, her cheerfulness slipping a bit. A long beat of silence passed between them before she changed the topic. "If you don't mind my asking, what was your husband like?"

"He..." Saoirse searched for the right words to convey Emrys. Her ruminating anger brought his flaws to mind first. "He was cocky and a bit too cheeky at times. He was a bit selfish and vain, if I'm honest."

Her eyes fell to her left hand and the glittering gem on her wedding ring. The House hadn't confiscated it, and she had never been more grateful for something so small. It was a reminder of his promises—his promises to love her until his dying breath. And that last breath might be coming sooner rather than later. He had been saved from an instant death, but it was only a matter of time before Kieran dealt him his true punishment. She didn't want to remember him for his flaws in that case.

"But he listened well." Her voice cracked. "And he was protective."

She looked over to see Althea hanging on her every word.

"Did you love him?" she asked.

Saoirse wished she could give her answer directly to Emrys. Maybe if she said it out loud, the gods would intervene with him. She would do anything to have the chance to tell Emrys how she felt herself. Even if she wanted to throttle him for being an idiot. At least he was *her* idiot.

"Yes," she answered softly. "I still love him."

Althea gave a genuine smile, and Saoirse returned it until a wave of pain hit Saoirse's abdomen and it wasn't from how much she missed Emrys. She took a deep breath, trying to let it subside, but she doubled over from the intensifying pain instead.

"Are you alright?" Althea asked.

"Yes, I'll be fine," Saoirse gritted out. "I started my cycle this morning and I've had cramping."

"I have something to help that." Althea lunged for her bed and began to rifle through a small wooden box filled with what looked like bags of herbs. She fetched a cup and pulled a tea cozy off a very plain teapot. Placing one of her herb-filled bags in the cup, she poured the hot water over it and handed the teacup to Saoirse.

"The healers also have serviettes to use for your cycle," Althea said. "It's probably best you ask them for some. You can't serve clients while on your cycle, and they keep track of those things."

"Thank you," Saoirse said, sipping her tea. It wasn't instant relief, but she felt the cramping slowly ease. "How do you know pain remedies?"

"I spend most of my days in the garden or with the healers," Althea said. "They've taught me what herbs to use as simple remedies for pain, nausea, and headaches. I keep a small collection of my own, so I don't need to bother them if I have any of those ailments. I would love to be a healer, though. It feels more honorable to help people stay alive than to increase the population."

"Could you ever leave and become a healer?" Saoirse asked.

"No one leaves the Matron House," Althea said, and her voice sounded defeated. "They make it completely unimaginable."

Saoirse's chest tightened to a point where she felt like air was nearly impossible to get into her lungs. Her last shred of hope dissolved like a wafer. She was going to die a Matron and Emrys would die at the hands of his enemy.

Again.

O*ver the next* four days, Althea became Saoirse's closest friend in the Matron House. She showed her the kitchen, the best washrooms, and described how the process of clients worked. Saoirse being in the midst of her cycle kept her from being immediately placed on the list of biddable Matrons, but she only had a day or two left before it would finish and she was eligible. She tried not to think of when that day would come, otherwise her lunch would make a second appearance.

Saoirse also learned Anastasia, the Head Matron and boireann that spoke no more than three words upon Saoirse's arrival, ran a tight ship within the Matron House. Althea explained all the Head Matron's quirks to help Saoirse navigate the Matron House and avoid any missteps. Mealtimes were served on a prompt schedule and dawdling from Matrons wasn't tolerated, Anastasia did bed checks each night at different intervals so no one could predict when she would be checking, and Matrons were barred from certain activities that may hinder their fertility or pregnancy. The knowledge made daytime manageable, but it reminded Saoirse of living in her family's estate, tiptoeing around her brother to not set him off.

Nighttime was a different story. Sleep was hard to find, Saoirse learned, and she wasn't alone as several other Matrons in her room stayed up late or tossed and turned throughout the night.

One Matron woke the entire room with a fit of screaming in the middle of the night on several occasions. Each time, Saoirse heard another Matron soothing her and helping her through her panic from whatever horror haunted her in her sleep. Saoirse wanted to ask Althea what it was about, but none of the other Matrons acknowledged the outbursts the next morning.

Althea helped occupy Saoirse's empty time by showing her the herb garden she attended. Saoirse felt transported back to her youth at her family's estate, watching the gardeners tend to the fruits and vegetables of the season, learning about how they grew, and what purpose they served the earth.

"Althea," she said, watching the Matron tend to a plot of thyme. "Can I ask you something?"

Althea nodded as she dug her hand deep into the earth. Sprouts began to slowly grow and mature, and Saoirse became enthralled with the magic this boireann possessed.

"That one boireann who has been screaming in the middle of the night, has she always done that?" she asked.

"No," Althea answered with sorrow in her voice. "Emmeline is one of the more popular Matrons. She's had four pregnancies since she arrived a few years ago. But that also means she doesn't get the kinder or gentler clients. Matrons end up with the highest bidder, not necessarily the client with the most need. She doesn't talk about it, but everyone else does. Apparently, a client tried to go for a second round, which isn't allowed but hardly enforced. The rumor that went around was that when she struggled against him, his wife thought she was trying to harm him and almost killed her."

Saoirse gasped and Althea nodded, agreeing with her horrified response. "Does that happen often?" Saoirse asked.

"No, but it happens enough that we've been trying to work with Anastasia to protect us better," Althea answered. "Our efforts haven't gone very far. Instead, she's implemented sedation upon the next appointment for anyone who returns from a client with a complaint."

Saoirse's jaw dropped in horror. "Does she sedate Matrons

often?"

Althea shook her head. "She only uses it for Matrons who have a record of misbehaving in the House or with clients. It keeps them from attempting escape during appointments."

"That's awful." Saoirse swallowed, hoping she could keep herself in line to at least avoid being sedated.

"We've managed." Althea shrugged. "We've come up with ways to deter clients from trying anything and avoiding sedation. Having the footman tell clients we're on a strict schedule, even though we technically aren't, or tingeing our robes with juices from fish, all sorts of methods we've found to make clients adhere to their supposed rules."

"Do they not sign contracts?" Saoirse asked.

"No, only we do," Althea answered. "We're kept to a much higher standard than clients are. We aren't to engage in activities that could result in losing a pregnancy, fight against clients no matter what they do to us, or attempt to keep the child, amongst other rules."

Saoirse's heart broke for the boireannaich in the House. They were merely wombs with no recognized personhood. It wasn't right. Clients should be held just as accountable as Matrons.

"Have you experienced that?" she asked. "Since you haven't been able to fall pregnant?"

Althea paused, her gaze averted from Saoirse as she planted more seeds. "No," she finally answered in a small voice. "I haven't had a Matron client in quite some time."

Saoirse knit her brows. If Althea wasn't actively fulfilling Matron duties, why was she still here? Saoirse would have thought someone who wasn't useful to the Matron House's main purpose would be let go in favor of someone who could.

"The gods truly have a sense of humor." Althea's sad, low laugh pulled Saoirse from her thoughts. Althea finally looked up from her gardening work and even with a half-smile, tears glittered in her eyes. "I was groomed to become a Matron to give others an heir as a gift, but I can't even produce one." Her laugh became shaky, and

Saoirse reached out a hand to stroke her shoulder. Althea closed her dirt-covered hand around Saoirse's and gave her a watery smile.

She finished her gardening, and Saoirse followed her inside to deliver the harvested herbs to the healers. When she first stepped foot in the healers' office in the Matron House, Saoirse noticed it was nothing like Seraphina's office at the Fearynhurst Estate. It was a much larger room with several beds set along the walls, each with a curtain available to draw around it for privacy. With the main purpose of the House being to encourage and maintain pregnancy, it was no surprise the healers were given more space to work in the House.

Althea greeted the Head Healer and began to empty her basket of herbs. Saoirse studied the room, and a sudden pang of longing for Seraphina struck her chest. The healer had become a mother to her like she had to Emrys. Saoirse tried to distract herself by imagining Seraphina's response to Alastair's punishments. The boireann would probably rip into the army camp and the Matron House, scooping her pseudo-children up and storming out before anyone could stop her.

Saoirse's gaze scanned over the small cots set up along the wall and the sound of a curtain being pulled caught her attention. Her heart dropped in her chest as golden brown skin and tightly coiled curls came into her view.

"Calliope?"

The boireann whirled, and her eyes grew wide in shock. "Saoirse," she breathed. She quickly crossed the room and engulfed her friend in an embrace.

It took all of Saoirse's strength not to collapse in her arms. She welcomed the familiarity and had to hold back her relieved tears.

"What are you doing here?" Calliope asked.

"It's a long story." Saoirse sighed and felt a shred of joy thread through her. "But I'm so glad to see you."

Calliope released her embrace and glanced at the healers sitting at their desks. She quietly pulled Saoirse out of the office and into the empty hall. "What happened?" she asked once they were far enough away from the healers. "We came to tea, and you weren't there. Vasili told me you and Emrys aren't living at the estate anymore. No one would answer our questions. Seraphina and Ada didn't even know where you went."

Saoirse's chest pinched at the image of her friends looking high and low throughout the estate for her. It proved they truly cared for her and that Kieran had really kept everything tightly sealed if even Ada and Seraphina didn't have answers for the duchesses. "It was Kieran," Saoirse whispered. "I told Alastair what he did to me, and he stripped Kieran of his responsibilities in the court. He did this in retaliation. He framed Emrys for attempted murder of Alastair, and I'm fairly sure Kieran influenced Alastair's decision in his punishment. He sent me here and Emrys to one of the army camps in Donheath."

Calliope stared at her in disbelief. "I need to get you out of here," she said. "I'm going to tell Anastasia you're coming with me."

Saoirse smile gratefully, but then thought better of it. She caught Calliope's arm before she could get too far.

"No," Saoirse said quickly. "If she thinks I'm trying to escape, things could turn bad for me. Anastasia is very finicky and doesn't let anyone leave easily."

If Anastasia thought she was escaping, she could relay it to Alastair, and gods knew what would happen if Kieran got wind of it. She wouldn't put it past him to bid on her and keep her from going with Calliope. Saoirse swallowed the bile that crept up her throat at the thought of being contracted to Kieran.

Calliope paused, and Saoirse could tell she was thinking of how to free Saoirse without raising suspicion. She finally gave a slow nod. "I understand," she whispered. "But I'm going to get you out of here. I have to talk to Vasili, but it shouldn't be an issue."

"What shouldn't be an issue?" Saoirse asked, noting how cryptic Calliope was being.

She ignored her question and squeezed her into another hug, leaning towards her ear. "Stay safe—don't argue if you get a client from Donheath."

Saoirse's heart hammered in her chest. Calliope was carving her a way out. She pulled back the tears that threatened to fall and composed herself. She had to convince the House they only had a short, lively conversation. She could hold on for a few more days. She could hold out for her rescue.

Emrys adjusted better to the army camp than he had expected. His will to live made him want to follow the rules and avoid being punished. The officers, while following Kieran's orders, weren't as bloodthirsty as Kieran was and didn't hold lifelong animosity towards Emrys. He didn't get much news about what was happening in the court, but whispers had suggested that Kieran was now taking on Emrys's responsibilities. He wasn't sure what the story was being spun about his absence, but he hoped it was one he could easily dismantle if he ever got free.

Freedom. It seemed so foreign, yet Emrys craved it. He dreamed of leaving the camp and finding Saoirse to break her free of the Matron House. But nothing he schemed in his daydreams was realistic. They would likely end with his demise at best and Saoirse's alongside his at worst. It was almost more practical to pray for a miracle. Actually, that was all he had been doing since arriving at the camp. He prayed and nearly begged the gods to save him and Saoirse daily.

In the camp, Emrys noticed everyone kept to themselves and their work, especially when Kieran was present. While he had taken Emrys's place in the court, Kieran refused to give up control of his army. Emrys expected nothing less, and given Kieran's paper-thin temper, it was clear Kieran had allowed the power to inflate his ego.

The late summer sun warmed the camp, and Emrys slipped into his tent to put on a dry shirt. He was only given three khaki-colored uniform shirts, and even with the use of his magic to cool himself, he sweated through his shirt by the end of the day. He had gotten to know the boireannaich who laundered and mended the camp's clothes already with how often he needed his uniform shirts cleaned. At some point he wouldn't be able to maintain the daily cycle of dropping off and picking up his clothes, but the hassle was worth the reprieve from discomfort.

Emrys reached for his canteen and gulped the cold water. He had frozen half of it that morning so that it didn't warm while sitting in the sun. With his torso free of his sweat-soaked shirt, he debated pouring the water over himself to feel even more refreshed. A full-fledged bath was out of the question, but he wasn't sure if wasting his water was worth it.

He refused to drink anything but water in the camp. Within the first day, Emrys learned the potion Kieran implemented in the army was in any beverage besides water. It had an unnatural metallic taste to it, and Emrys sensed it upon his first sip of tea. Water was the only beverage that didn't have the tainted flavor, so he chose it over anything else.

Emrys was still wary of the potion's use, and after witnessing the effects of it in the camp, he was convinced it was the worst idea Kieran could implement. While it did boost immunity from head colds and granted more physical strength, it also caused members of the camp to have short fuses, and petty brawls broke out multiple times a day. Aggression was already a guarantee with this many fireannaich crammed in one place. Adding something unnatural like the enhancement potion only amplified it. With how the members of the camp reacted while taking it, Emrys could only imagine the side effects for those who were discharged from the army and were brusquely cut off.

The tent flap flew open, and Emrys's bunkmate, Silas, stormed inside. He kicked the leg of his cot in frustration and let out a swear.

"Something go wrong?" Emrys asked, putting his canteen down.

"How in Cernunnos's Wilderness can ye stand this shithole?" Silas asked, his brogue more pronounced than usual. He was a tall, muscular fae that was less than half Emrys's age. Even with his occasional outbursts, Emrys saw himself in the fireann. Silas was angry at the world for the hand he was dealt and looking for any excuse to heighten that anger and let it fester.

"I've seen much worse, trust me," Emrys answered, trying to defuse him.

One of the officers burst into the tent, fury raging in his eyes, and pointed at Silas. "Laurent," he barked. "You're on guard duty tonight."

"Ach, I'm not doing that," Silas snapped back. "I did guard duty yesterday."

"I wasn't asking if you wanted to do it. I was commanding you." The officer stepped up to him and looked down his nose at him. "You don't want to find out what happens when you question authority."

"Maybe I do," Silas replied, standing up taller in defense. "How do ye plan to teach me to listen?"

"Silas," Emrys warned. "It's not worth it."

Silas slid his stormy blue eyes to him, and Emrys saw a muscle in his jaw feather as the fireann bit back his rage. "Fine," Silas spat. "I'll be there in a moment."

"I volunteer my help as well," Emrys said, pulling on his fresh uniform shirt.

The officer narrowed his gaze at him. "What are your duties for the rest of the day?"

"At any moment, Fomóire could invade this camp. Would you really rather have me on dish cleaning duty?" Emrys argued.

The officer's nostrils flared, but he didn't argue further. "Fine." He turned on his heel and stalked out of the tent.

"Why would ye volunteer yerself?" Silas asked as he grabbed his pack and loaded it for guard duty.

"Because I know why you argued with the officer," Emrys said. "You're not afraid of the punishments."

"I'd rather be beaten than suffer another night guarding this shithole," Silas murmured. "Dagda save me, maybe one day one of those beatings will end it all. Wouldn't that be lovely?"

"And that's exactly why I volunteered." Emrys tied his pack closed and shouldered it.

Silas pulled his pack onto his back, and the two turned out their lamps. They headed out into the thick summer evening air towards the north end of the camp. Emrys wiped at the sweat on his brow with his shirt sleeve. So much for a clean, dry shirt.

"What did ye mean by 'that's why ye volunteered'?" Silas asked as they trekked to the open area on the edge of the camp.

"Because I've thought like you have before," Emrys answered. "And I don't want anyone else to endure what I did. Life is worth living, even in this shithole."

"I know that," Silas grumbled. "Kieran and the rest of them just make life in this gods-forsaken camp miserable enough to find any way out."

"Of course he makes life miserable." The fireannaich set their packs down once they reached the boundary of the camp and settled in for the night. "I don't think I've gotten more than four hours a sleep in a night because of how many hours he's made me work. My body is in agony from the amount of labor. Nothing about this camp is enjoyable. But he only makes our lives miserable because he's too miserable in his own life to experience it alone."

"Then ye see my point." Silas dug around in his pack before pulling out an apple. He turned it over in his hand and then bit into it.

"Sure, but your time here isn't indefinite. There's plenty of life to enjoy outside this camp." Emrys's thoughts wandered to Saoirse, and he swallowed the emotion that crept up with them. She was his joy, and he had destroyed it. He prayed every night before he passed out from exhaustion that she would forgive him and let him prove he was worthy of her again.

Silas snorted. "Ye're real convincing with that sad look on your face."

"I'm in a different situation than you," Emrys said. "When is your contract up?"

The fireann shrugged. "Whenever living on the street sounds better than this."

"You don't have an end date?"

Silas shook his head. "I'm here 'til I'm dead."

He continued to chew, a silence stretching between them. Emrys wanted to fill it with conversation, but the realization they were in fact in the same situation made it difficult. The only difference was Emrys hadn't chosen to be in the army. He had a life, a mate, a home. He had been dragged here to be tormented. Silas had chosen it for—he wasn't quite sure why he had chosen to join the army but being fed and having a place to sleep probably had to do with it.

"Oi, daydreamer." Silas's brogue shook Emrys from his thoughts. "The prince of misery himself is headed our way."

Sure enough, a figure was approaching them. The setting sun kept Emrys from making out any identifiable details, but by the haughty swagger, he knew it was Kieran. Eventually, the general's sharp features came into focus, and Emrys steeled himself.

"Fearynhurst," Kieran barked. "What are you doing out here?"

"I volunteered night watch with Laurent," Emrys answered steadily.

"That's not what was assigned," Kieran sneered.

"Your officer didn't have any qualms about it." Emrys leveled his gaze with Kieran, challenging him to argue with the authorities he had put in command.

"Get back to your assigned duty."

"Will clean dishes really stop the Fomóire? Because last I checked, guard duty had better odds."

Kieran flared his nostrils. "You know the consequences of abandoning your post."

"If ye're hard-pressed to find a clean plate, ye know ye can clean one yerself," Silas said.

Emrys tensed. He knew how far he could push Kieran before it caused harm, but Silas was currently having a hard time finding that line.

"Watch it, Laurent." Kieran turned his attention to the fireann. "I know you questioned your commanding officer earlier. Don't think I'm not aware of what goes on in my camp."

"Aye, but I'm here, am I not?" Silas shrugged, seemingly unfazed by the sharp stare Kieran had on him. "If ye wanted an army that followed orders blindly, ye should have necromanced one."

"That's enough from you." Kieran lunged for Silas, but Emrys scrambled in front of him.

"Kieran, he's doing what you commanded." Emrys held up a hand to halt him. "That doesn't warrant punishment."

"Talking back does." Kieran tried to grab for Silas again, but Emrys shot a chunk of ice at Kieran's hand. He knew he shouldn't have used his magic. The result was immediate consequences, but Emrys would rather endure them than watch Silas attempt to numb himself through Kieran's punishments.

Kieran's dark gaze pierced through Emrys. "You know what the use of magic results in, Fearynhurst."

"Yes," Emrys said flatly. "I do."

"Camp center. Now." Kieran pointed back towards the heart of the camp.

Emrys scrambled for a way to delay his punishment. He was willing to throw himself in front of others to save them, but he still had nightmares about the last time he was in the center of Kieran's army camp. "You want me to abandon guard duty? You'd have these fireannaich lose another capable body?"

Kieran bared his teeth before he took a deep breath and his composure changed. "Fine," he said. "You and Laurent finish guard duty, then at sunrise, you will learn not to use your magic against authority."

With that, Kieran stormed back towards the camp, and Emrys let loose the breath he hadn't realized he had been holding. He moved back to Silas's side and ran a hand over his face. He only made it four days without being punished. And he had done the worst action to receive consequences.

"Ye're high fae?" Silas asked, breaking the quiet between them.

Emrys turned to him and knit his brow. "What?"

"Ye conjured ice," Silas observed. "Only high fae can conjure elements."

"Yes, I'm high fae."

"Ye don't usually see your kind here." Silas shrugged. "Most of us are common or mid fae."

"Which are you?" Emrys asked.

"Neither," Silas answered. "I'm demi-fae. My father was human and my mother was common fae. He lied to my mother, let her believe he was common fae, too. But when he aged at a faster rate than she did, she found out he was human, and he ran off. Not before I was born, though. I ended up bein' the one she took her anger out on."

Emrys studied him for a moment. He really had been dealt a bad hand in life. He had more reason than Emrys ever did to want to end his misery. It still didn't mean he should.

"I'm sorry," Emrys said quietly. "That couldn't have been easy to endure."

Silas shrugged. "Like ye said, I endured it. That's enough, isn't it? I made it here to tell the tale."

"You did." Emrys nodded.

"Well, tonight is gonna be a long night, eh?" Silas took a final bite of his apple before tossing it towards the trees behind them.

"That it is."

Another pause lingered between them. "Aside from keeping my dumb arse from dying, what's keeping ye going?" Silas asked. "What's on the other side of this camp waiting for ye?"

Emrys breathed a laugh. "What else? A boireann."

"Aye, a boireann, eh?" Silas laughed. "It's always a boireann."

"Not just any boireann, though." Emrys smiled to himself at the thought of Saoirse. "My mate."

"Ach, ye have a mate? And ye're here in this shithole?"

Emrys couldn't help but laugh. "Trust me, if I had my way, I wouldn't be here."

"What made ye leave her?"

Emrys was silent for a moment. He hadn't revealed his identity to anyone. It would come with more questions that he wasn't willing to answer.

"Or did *she* leave ye?" Silas amended.

"It's difficult to explain," Emrys finally answered. "But it was my fault, not hers. I broke all her trust. She had every right to be upset."

"And ye left her?" Silas asked, stunned. "Ye didn't fight for her to forgive ye?"

"I didn't have the chance." Emrys sighed. "Besides, she wasn't anywhere near ready to forgive me and, if I'm honest, I don't deserve it."

Silas made a Scottish noise.

"What?" Emrys asked.

"I just don't understand ye. Ye have a boireann, a *mate*, and ye do something foolish and instead of groveling and begging her forgiveness, ye run away to the army."

"I don't remember asking you for your opinion." Emrys tried not to scoff, but Saoirse was a sore subject for him at the moment.

"No, ye didn't," Silas said pointedly. "But I'm going to give it to ye anyway."

Emrys loosened a sigh. As much as it pained him to relive those moments with Saoirse, he hoped it distracted Silas to steer him away from his thoughts of being better off dead. At least for tonight.

"Ye pity yerself too much." Silas jabbed a finger in Emrys's direction. "Ye should have apologized 'til ye couldn't take another breath. Instead ye pitied yerself and gave up."

"And what authority does this advice have?" Emrys asked curiously. Maybe Silas did have a partner back home. That was an angle he could work with to keep the fireann from his careless actions that would lead to his demise.

"I made my living off making boireannaich feel good," Silas said proudly. "I learned all sorts of things about their feelings."

"So what you're saying is I made things worse?"

Silas shrugged. "If I learned anything from my line of work, it was that there's never a wrong time to grovel."

Emrys mulled over his words. He hadn't had any chance to talk about what he did to Saoirse since arriving at the camp. If he was home, he knew his friends would have torn him to shred for what he did. They would have been even more brutal than Silas. It would be a resounding 'I told you so' from each of them. But he didn't have them here to kick him back into line. Thankfully, Silas had nothing to lose by telling him what he had done wrong. Emrys found that invaluable in his current situation.

"Thank ye, by the way," Silas mumbled.

"For what?" Emrys asked. If anyone should be sharing gratitude, it was him, not Silas.

"For keeping me alive," Silas said sheepishly. "At least for tonight."

"No thanks necessary," Emrys said. "But if you'd like to return the favor," he turned to face the fireann, "if Kieran gets beyond fifty lashes on me tomorrow, alert the healers immediately."

Two *more days* passed before Saoirse's cycle ended, and Anastasia informed her she had received a bid. Saoirse schooled her features as the Head Matron explained where she would be going, unintentionally confirming that Calliope's plan had been enacted. Anastasia listed off a series of rules for Matrons, and Saoirse noticed there were very few, if any, for clients, just like Althea had said.

One thing Saoirse worried about was a time limit. Was she expected back at the Matron House after a certain amount of time? Would someone come looking for her? Anastasia only mentioned she was to return in a "reasonable amount of time," which surprised her, considering how strict Anastasia was in the house.

Saoirse showered and was given fresh robes for her appointment. She sat on the edge of Althea's bed as the Matron braided her hair.

"Make sure you meet the wife before being taken to the bedroom," Althea advised. "Keep your eyes on her or the floor in her presence. Wives can be very jealous, even if they're the ones who sought out our services in the first place. Learn her name if you can. Hers is going to be much more important than the client's. If you call out her name when you need help, she's more likely to blame her husband than you."

Saoirse sucked in her bottom lip and nodded. Althea didn't know her connection to the Duke of Donheath or his wife. She wouldn't be providing any services tonight. Instead, she would be escaping the House.

Althea tucked the tail of Saoirse's braid into her hair, creating a neat, plaited crown around her head. Saoirse enveloped her in an embrace, knowing this would possibly be the last time she would see the boireann. She had been in the house less than a week and already found herself attached to Althea. Silently, Saoirse vowed to herself to find a way to give Althea the same freedom she was being given.

The dark carriage that had brought her to the Matron House was sitting outside the entrance awaiting her. She found it curious that there was no person to ensure she didn't try to slip away. But then again, Anastasia didn't hesitate to sedate Matrons if they gave her an inkling of misbehavior. Saoirse climbed into the carriage, thankful she had all her senses still intact.

She took deep breaths as the carriage pulled away. Freedom was within her reach, but she worried about the rest of Calliope's plan. Beyond smuggling Saoirse out of the House, what did the duchess have in store? Surely the Duke and Duchess of Donheath had more power than the Matron House if anyone came looking for her once Anastasia noticed she didn't return.

The carriage bumped along the road for at least an hour until they turned onto a smooth, paved drive. The sand-colored home with a flat roof came into view and Saoirse felt her heart leap in her chest. She was here. She was closer to safety than she had been in over a week. The footman opened the door for her, and Saoirse stepped out onto the pavement.

She tried to keep her pace even as she walked to the front door, but her excitement and relief was propelling her towards the door as fast as she could go. Gently, she rapped on the door and waited in anticipation to be welcomed inside. A small maid answered the door and greeted her with a bow of her head. She motioned for Saoirse to enter and directed her through the house. They reached a small sitting room, and Saoirse almost flung out an arm to grab onto the maid as her legs wanted to give out and drop her to the floor.

Sitting in a velvet navy blue armchair with a large white dog laying at her feet was Calliope, but she wasn't alone. Andromeda and Isolde sat on a matching navy blue loveseat, their expressions a mix of relief and empathy. Saoirse disregarded any of the self-restraint she had left and flung herself at her friends. They stood and enveloped her in a tight embrace. Saoirse let her tears fall as she was surrounded by people she loved. A chorus of gratitude that she was all right and questions of what she was doing as a Matron rang through the room.

Saoirse composed herself and loosened her grip on her friends. She wiped the elated tears from her face as she made her way to one of the empty armchairs and took a deep, steadying breath. The duchesses sat transfixed as she caught them up on the reason she was currently wearing Matron robes.

"That bastard," Isolde sneered. She sat back in her seat, her nostrils flaring, and her arms crossed over her chest. "Andromeda, I wish you truly had struck him with lightning when you slapped him."

"Trust me, I regret it as well." Andromeda frowned. "But we can't do anything about that now. What are we going to do about getting Emrys out of the army camp?"

"To begin with, it was illegal to put him there in the first place," a deep voice from the doorway said.

The boireannaich turned their attention to the tall, wide figure of Cyprian, and Isolde scowled at him.

"I thought you and Vasili were busy discussing the latest harvest contracts," she said.

"We were, but when he told me who his guest was, I had to see for myself." He shrugged and nodded at Saoirse.

"What do you mean Emrys was illegally put in the army camp?" she asked.

"Well, first, Alastair had no right making a judgment on his own about whether Emrys actually had the intention to poison him, especially with Kieran involved." Cyprian strode into the middle of the sitting room. "Second, drafting him into the army camp is not a consequence for such an action. Now, before you sigh in relief, the actual consequence is much more dire." Saoirse frowned at his words but let him continue. "Lastly, Kieran is currently in violation of the rights of the Northern Fae Court by refusing to sign the papers that would release Emrys until a full investigation and court case can be conducted."

"Is Kieran at fault even though the decision came down from Alastair?" Saoirse asked.

"He could be if it's found he tampered with evidence. But if anything, his violation for not releasing Emrys would get him in quite a bit of trouble."

She let out a breath. Even if they were to investigate Emrys, Kieran would be in a much worse position as details were dug up.

Isolde sighed and rested her chin in her palm, her eyes dreamy as she stared at her husband. "I love when he talks about legal proceedings," she mused.

Andromeda rolled her eyes as Cyprian smirked at his wife. "So, what are we going to do about Emrys?" she asked. "Kieran has taken his place back in council meetings and seems to have a strong influence over Alastair. If he refuses to sign those papers, is Emrys trapped there until someone...." she lowered her voice, "takes care of Kieran?"

"Andromeda!" Calliope scolded.

"What?" Andromeda asked defensively. "Don't tell me you don't think that's a viable option."

"Andromeda, I'm not defending you if you commit murder," Cyprian told her.

She rolled her eyes and slumped back into her seat.

"So, what *are* our options?" Saoirse asked.

"Our hands are tied at this point." Cyprian tried to give her his most sympathetic look, but she was reaching her breaking point.

Her entire being roared with anger, and an urge to level the earth until she got Emrys back filled her thoughts. She had denied the belief in mates, but everything she had experienced with Emrys chipped away at her fortitude. The moment she had laid eyes on

Emrys, that spark struck her, something she couldn't ignore. It was only satisfied with Emrys, and, if she was honest with herself, *she* was satisfied with Emrys.

He gave her room to find her freedom and let her experience all the instincts she had been forced to ignore. For the first time, she had control of her own life, and it was because he had given it to her. He was patient and thoughtful and loving.

Love. He had taught her what love was, what it looked like, and how it acted. He had omitted his knowledge of the bond because he would have rather loved her endlessly than tried to introduce something she was averse to.

Saoirse had grappled with that frequently over the past week. She came to understand his reasoning, even if it did cause her pain when he was finally forced to reveal it. He'd have to make it up to her for that. But when all was said and done, she did love him, and she was willing to do anything to have him back and safe in her arms.

"Fuck doing it legally," she said more harshly than she intended. The entire room turned in her direction, and she leaned into the growling rage inside her. "You said it yourself—Kieran isn't playing by the rules, so why should we? Emrys is going to die in that army camp if we wait around for Kieran to do the right thing."

"Saoirse, what are you suggesting?" Vasili asked from the doorway, his voice startling Isolde and Andromeda.

Laszlo appeared with him and made his way to the bar cart, filling a glass tumbler with a knuckle's worth of amber liquor as if the room wasn't filled with tension. "We should go take him out of the camp ourselves," he said plainly.

Cyprian let out a loud, heavy sigh and murmured a prayer to the gods.

"Are you suggesting we wear trousers and pretend we're fireannaich recruits?" Andromeda asked.

Calliope looked to her husband, who shook his head. "Oh, no, don't you look at me," he warned. She pursed her lip ever so slightly and raised her brows to make her eyes look rounder. Vasili swore under his breath. "Fine, I'll go through my wardrobe."

"Wait," Isolde said, stopping him in the doorway. "How do we plan to get into the camp? We can't exactly stroll up in makeshift uniforms and pretend we're members of the army. Doesn't Kieran have guards? Don't you think they're going to want some kind of identification to verify us?"

"My wife is right," Cyprian said. "When I've met with him, the guards took extensive measures to make sure I was who I said I was. They're not just going to let you in because you vaguely look like recruits."

"Then we smuggle them in." Laszlo shrugged as he sipped his drink.

Cyprian let out a groan and wiped a hand down his face.

"How?" Calliope asked.

"You're still a working High Healer, yes?"

"I volunteer for work, but yes, I'm still practicing."

"Then you and Vasili load a covered cart with food for the camp and these three in tow." He gestured to his wife, Isolde, and Saoirse. "No one would question the duke gifting and delivering meat and produce to the camp and the duchess offering to heal more complex injuries as signs of goodwill. Meanwhile, the three madcaps can slip out of the cart and search the camp for Emrys."

He took a swig of his drink as the room stared at him, speechless.

"What if I find Emrys in their healer tent?" Calliope finally asked. "I can't exactly smuggle him out on my own."

"Fine, take one of the other boireannaich with you under the guise of your assistant," he suggested. "The guards will give more leeway for the overseers of the land and overlook you bringing an assistant. It would be against their interest to question you."

"What if we run into Kieran?" Saoirse asked. "If he spots me, it'll completely ruin any chance we have at rescuing Emrys."

"I won't let that happen," Laszlo assured her. "I'll glamour you and Isolde so you won't look recognizable or out of place."

"Glamour?" she asked, her brows furrowing.

"Secondary magic," he answered. "It's the ability to make

things appear as something else."

"Like shifting?"

"Not exactly. The object doesn't take on a new form, it just appears to. When I glamour you, you'll remain yourselves but appear to look like plain fireannaich in the camp." Laszlo moved his hand in front of his face, and his features changed to resemble Emrys's.

Saoirse's eyes went wide. "That's frightening."

"It can be quite erotic, actually," Andromeda commented.

Saoirse turned her horrified gaze to Andromeda, who held her hands up in defense.

"I can promise you he has never glamoured himself to look like anyone in the court before, during, or after sex," she said.

"Oh, thank the gods," Cyprian murmured, his eyes looking up towards the ceiling.

"What if something happens, and the glamour comes off?" Isolde asked. "It only works in close range, doesn't it?"

"That's correct," Laszlo confirmed.

"I'll distract Kieran," Cyprian offered. Everyone whipped their attention to him. "I'll go alone in my personal carriage with the documents he needs to sign. No one will question my actions. They've seen me four times since Emrys has been there."

"What if he dodges you again?" Isolde asked.

"Mo Stoirín," he said as he cradled her face with one of his hands and gave her a soft smile. "I'm a lawyer. I can argue for hours. I would think by now you knew that much about me." A blush crept over her face as she conceded his point. "Besides, if I can get him to agree, this entire ludicrous plan will be off my conscience for being extremely illegal."

"Would we be bringing him back here?" Vasili asked. "I feel like this would be one of the first places Kieran would look, making all our efforts moot."

"We could take him to our territory," Isolde suggested.

"Absolutely not." Cyprian shook his head.

"The cottage," Saoirse said, remembering the one place Kieran wouldn't think to look. "Kieran doesn't know that it even exists.

We'll take Emrys there."

Laszlo raised his brow in a bit of surprise but nodded nonetheless. "So, we agree on the plan, then?" he asked. "Speak your concerns now or forever hold your peace."

"I have one question," Saoirse said, locking her gaze with his. The corner of her lips pulled up into the first genuine smile she felt in a week. "When do we leave?"

Between Andromeda, Isolde, and Calliope, Saoirse was able to change out of her Matron robes and into clothes she was more familiar with. She felt relieved to be in clothing that flattered her figure and wasn't scratchy and billowy. Thoughts of the Matron House still nagged at her, but being surrounded by her friends, she felt safer about potential repercussions.

The four boireannaich gathered in Vasili and Calliope's bedroom, where several pairs of trousers and shirts were laid out for them to pick through as their makeshift army uniforms.

The pair of trousers Isolde picked were too long for her short legs and the hem of them engulfed her feet. "Don't worry," she said. "I can shorten them." Vasili groaned, clearly concerned over losing a pair of trousers. "I can always just take a pair of Cyprian's pants to modify."

"I think I like that idea more than you mutilating my trousers," he said.

Isolde shrugged and returned the borrowed trousers. Saoirse chose her outfit as a knot of anxiety grew in her stomach. Their plan was risky, but with Emrys's life at stake, she'd take the risk over worrying about his life while Kieran kept the law tangled up.

Her thoughts continued to drift to the mating bond and a question that had nagged at her since she arrived at Calliope's. Saoirse held her tongue, however, keeping her focus on the task at hand. She would find her moment to voice her question eventually.

After their wardrobe was picked, everyone settled into the dining room for dinner. It wasn't as lively a conversation as it was at Calliope's anniversary, but it was still better than the meals in the

Matron House. It wasn't solemn and morbid in Calliope's dining room, but rather it was comfortable and familiar.

Saoirse and the duchesses enjoyed glasses of wine in the sitting room after dinner. She stared down at her glass, her questions sitting on the tip of her tongue. Her friends chatted casually around her as her anxiety built. Did they know about her bond? Could they help her understand it? Could they answer if it would save Emrys?

A lull in the conversation fell over them, and Saoirse took her chance. "There's something I didn't mention before." The duchesses gave her their full attention. "Emrys confessed to me that we have a mating bond. Well, actually, Kieran did, but Emrys didn't deny it. In fact, he tried to prove it was true."

A few brows rose, but their reactions were nothing near what Saoirse would expect if they didn't know anything about her and Emrys's bond. "I'm assuming by the lack of shock on your faces you all knew."

"We did," Andromeda answered carefully. "He told all of us he was being paired with a mate. When Laszlo and I were courting, he learned you finally existed in the world."

"You all knew when you first met me?" Saoirse asked.

"We had been waiting for you as long as Emrys had," Calliope said. "We just prayed you would be a fit for us as well as him."

Saoirse huffed a disbelieving laugh. "The dukes as well?"

"Yes," Isolde answered. "We were actually quite peeved they met you before we did."

"I truly was the last know," Saoirse murmured. She set her glass on the nearest side table and stood, pacing the room toward the fireplace.

Hurt hit her all over again. It didn't sting nearly as much as it did with Emrys. It was his truth to tell, but everyone had spent the last month hiding his secret.

"We wanted desperately to tell you," Andromeda said, stepping up next to her and placing a tentative hand on her shoulder. When Saoirse didn't shake it off, Andromeda came closer to her. "But it wasn't our place to tell you. At least, most of us felt that way." The duchess shifted her gaze back towards the boireannaich sitting on the sofa.

"In my defense, I thought she knew," Calliope said. "I assumed once they were married, he would tell her."

Their words barely penetrated through Saoirse's mind. She had an inkling her friends knew, but it was one thing to suspect it and another to find it true. Saoirse stared into the fire, watching the flames dance and lick at the logs. It made her think of her magic and the hours Emrys spent with her, helping her learn how to master it. She still was nowhere near expert with it, but she had control over it now.

Saoirse had wondered if the attention he gave her was because he felt compelled by the idea of the bond or if he did it out of kindness. Surely his initial motives were driven by it, but anything beyond their marriage arrangement had to be genuine, didn't it?

"Did you all accept me because you were told I was Emrys's mate?" Saoirse asked.

"Not at all." Isolde shook her head. "We didn't have any stake in you, so if we didn't like you, we wouldn't have come around unless it were necessary. We weren't afraid to tell Emrys that either."

"But luckily we adore you," Andromeda whispered to Saoirse with a grin.

Her friends' omissions didn't sting quite as much as Emrys's, but there was still a bite to their collective lie. If they could omit that to her, what was stopping them from lying further to her? She panicked for a moment as her mind correlated her friends with how Kieran had fooled her. But something whispered to her the two weren't equal.

Andromeda risked her whole reputation in the court to defend Saoirse. Calliope and Vasili chanced repercussions with the Matron House by sneaking Saoirse out of it. All of them were willing to infiltrate an army camp to reunite her with her husband. If their love and friendship wasn't genuine, Saoirse wouldn't be here in the sitting room with them.

A genuine smile tugged at her lips as she turned to face

Andromeda. "I still don't know if I believe the bond is real," Saoirse confessed.

"You seemed fairly adamant it wasn't real before," Calliope offered. "What changed?"

Saoirse opened her mouth to answer, but she came up short of an answer. "I don't know," she finally said. "When it was revealed, I felt betrayed by Emrys. He knew this and chose not to tell me? Why couldn't he be honest with it?"

"We're just as guilty as he is." Andromeda stroked her hand over Saoirse's shoulder. "And while we can't speak for him, he was probably scared."

"I second that," Calliope said. "I've seen him with boireannaich before, and he's never gone to such lengths for them as he has for you. I'm sure the thought of losing you for any reason had him scared out of his wits."

"What if that was just him believing the bond?" Saoirse asked. "If he thought I was a 'gift' from the gods, wouldn't he do anything to keep from losing me, including lying?"

"Didn't he offer you a life away from him when you were married?" Isolde asked.

Saoirse's eyes widened. "How do you know that?"

The duchess chewed on her bottom lip. "Cyprian," she answered shyly.

Saoirse sighed. When she looked around the room, it was obvious that only Isolde had made herself privy to that information. "It's true," Saoirse said. "He offered me complete freedom if I chose to marry him. Living on my own was a decent compromise between living under my brother's scrutiny and marrying into a family that included Kieran."

She thought back to those first few days. Emrys had been genuine in his offer, and she had been the one to expand the bargain to convince her to stay. She had asked for that and got exactly—if not more—than what she requested. But that still didn't prove the bond was real.

Saoirse looked between the duchesses, her thoughts bouncing

between belief and disbelief. When her eyes fell on Isolde, she remembered something the duchess had divulged to her.

"Isolde," Saoirse said, her voice small. "I asked you before, and you said you didn't know what color tie mates have. Was that true?"

"No," Isolde said apologetically. "I do know mates and their tie shade."

Saoirse tried not to let her heart sink at finding another lie from her friends. "Do Emrys and I have a tie that's the shade mates have?"

"You do," Isolde answered with a nod. "I saw it at the wedding. I had seen the color before, but never connected it to a mating bond. And whenever I saw the two of you together, it never waned or thickened. That isn't typical of threads. Neither is being unable to tamper with it. Some ties I'm able to strum to spark something between two people, but this tie wouldn't even let me touch it."

Saoirse's heart thundered in her chest. It was yet another piece of evidence she had a hard time denying. But what if Isolde was lying again? She didn't know how to trust them now, and she hated that.

"Andromeda," Saoirse said weakly. "I hate asking you this, but—"

"Yes," Andromeda said. "She's telling the truth." She held out her hand in front of Saoirse. "If you want to see for yourself, touch my hand. Truth seeking triggers primary magic. If Isolde was lying, you'd feel a shock of my magic."

Saoirse tentatively lifted her hand and placed it in Andromeda's. Nothing close to a shock touched her. All she could feel was the warmth of Andromeda's palm.

Saoirse's resilience had finally been shattered. She couldn't ignore it any longer. There was too much for her to deny. She sank into the closest chair, Andromeda's arm still around her.

The bond was real, and her mate was in trouble.

"It is real," she whispered. "Everything I thought of mates truly was false. They're real, and..." she swallowed. "I could have helped save Emrys." She looked at her friends, who had worry painting their features. "What else can you all tell me about mates?"

"Isolde probably knows the most," Calliope offered.

Saoirse dragged her gaze to Isolde. She had confessed her parents were mates, and that lie still stung. "Why didn't you just tell me you knew a pair of mates before?"

"I'm sorry," Isolde said. "I knew if I told you about my parents, you'd ask about them, and I was sure if I started talking about their bond I would let something slip on accident."

"Would you like to make it up to me?" Saoirse asked. Isolde nodded emphatically. "Then tell me all you know about mates."

"I don't know all the intricacies of their bond," she said. "But I can tell you what I've witnessed between them."

"Have either of them ever...harmed the other?" Saoirse asked. It was the question that haunted her the most. Her brother had convinced his wife they were mates, but Saoirse only ever saw him treat her cruelly. Even though Emrys had never shown her the same behavior, she still worried it was inevitable.

"Never." Isolde shook her head. "My father has never raised a hand or his voice to my mother. They may argue and have spats, but they always find a way to come together afterwards. Their relationship is the healthiest I've ever witnessed, and I thank the gods every day I have a husband who treats me like my father treats my mother, even without a bond."

"And sealing the bond?" Saoirse asked, the other burning question that ate away at her. "What's involved in it?"

"I'm not sure," Isolde answered with a slight shrug. "My parents never discussed it with me."

"I've heard it's a ritual," Andromeda interjected.

"A ritual of what?" Saoirse asked. "Emrys told me a prayer was involved, but he didn't say much else."

"I've heard it involves fucking," Andromeda said mildly. "And something with blood."

Saoirse shivered at the image that the description gave her. Sex with Emrys had been some of the best intimacy she had shared with anyone, but the thought of mixing other elements had her wary.

"And if we don't seal the bond?"

"I'm not sure what happens," Isolde said softly. "I don't think it's necessarily anything devastating, but I don't think it brings the best outcomes either."

Saoirse's stomach roiled at the thought of what condition she might find Emrys in tomorrow. Now she wished Emrys would have told her sooner. Would she have accepted at first? Certainly not, but she would have had better circumstances to come to terms with it. She closed her eyes and prayed the gods would show mercy. They only needed to protect Emrys for one more day.

The next morning, Saoirse dressed into her disguise. For a fleeting moment, she had a twinge of sympathy for fireannaich as she twisted awkwardly to button her suspenders. If it wasn't for the half-dozen layers boireannaich had to wear to be acceptably dressed in society, her sympathy may have extended further.

After pinning her hair and stuffing it under a military cap Vasili had obtained, she met the rest of the court in the sitting room. Isolde and Laszlo were dressed in makeshift military uniforms as well, except Isolde's bust was very evident under her khaki shirt. Hopefully, Laszlo's glamour could disguise it.

"The cart is packed," Vasili announced, entering the sitting room. "I positioned the crates so that we can hide you three without any suspicion if they decide to check the cargo. Cyprian, is your carriage prepared?"

"Yes, I'll leave a half-hour after the rest of you," he answered.

"Why?" Isolde knitted her brows, confused.

"I told Emrys the next time he needed legal counsel, I'd be a half-hour later."

Isolde rolled her eyes and reached for his ear, pulling him towards the exit of the room. Cyprian protested and pried her fingers away from him. He huffed as he tried to defend himself and followed her out of the sitting room, rubbing at his ear. The rest of the group followed out to where Vasili's cart was. As Calliope and

Andromeda were climbing into the front of the cart, Cyprian came over to help Isolde into the cart.

"Isolde," he said as she disappeared inside the cart. Her head poked back out as the mention of her name. "Please do not do anything that will draw attention to you."

"Why are you directing that at me alone?" she asked.

"Because I know you," he replied. "If you three find Emrys, you need to get him out of the camp with as little commotion as possible. We're already treading on dangerous ground sneaking into the camp and taking him without express permission. If any of us get caught, we will all be facing worse than being sent to the Matron House or army camp."

A shiver ran down Saoirse's spine. The three promised Cyprian to stay as inconspicuous as possible, and the duke sighed. Saoirse couldn't tell if it was out of regret or relief.

As she watched Isolde disappear back into the cart, the distinct sound of carriage wheels on cobblestones were heard in the distance. She assumed it was Cyprian's carriage pulling around but quickly realized his carriage was sitting in front of the cart and unmoving.

"We have to go," Vasili said, hurrying towards the cart. He hoisted the boireannaich into the front of the cart and hurried back to the back. "Get her in the cart." Vasili motioned for Laszlo to help Saoirse into the cart. "The Matron House carriage is here, and we can't let them see Saoirse."

Saoirse's heart plummeted. She was finding out exactly what happened when a Matron stayed too long with a client.

Both Laszlo and Cyprian grasped her waist and hoisted her up into the cart. Saoirse grabbed onto the first thing she could reach and clambered inside. She scurried in the dim lighting towards who she assumed was Isolde and flung herself into a sitting position. Isolde wrapped an arm around her shoulder and squeezed her upper arm.

Outside, a pounding sound and shouts could be heard. Saoirse gulped at the air, never thinking she would be so thankful to be in the back of a cart with crates of vegetables and meat. She couldn't imagine what the repercussions would be for her if they had caught her. She was sure being sedated would be the least of her worries.

Laszlo threw himself into the cart and hollered, "We're in! Let's go!"

The cart lurched, and Saoirse had to brace herself against a nearby crate to keep from toppling over. Outside, she couldn't tell how many vehicles were moving, but she continued to hear shouting over the pounding of hooves. She was half-tempted to peek out the canvas flaps, but she refused to risk being seen. Eventually, the shouting became more distant, and the cart slowed to a steady beat.

Saoirse let out a slow breath as she alternated between holding herself against the motion of the cart until her muscles ached and letting the cart toss her from side to side. Her body crashed into the crates that sat around her, and she kept telling herself it was better than whatever fate she just escaped. Besides, she would soon be reunited with Emrys. Anything outside of those facts she shoved aside and put up a mental wall to keep them from tainting her hope.

"Laszlo," she said, hoping to distract herself. "When will you place the glamour on us?"

"As soon as we get inside the camp," he answered. "My range is good for about fifteen feet. Anything beyond that will cause it to slip. So I'll need you and Isolde to stay fairly close to me."

Saoirse nodded before she realized she was blocked from his view by crates and darkness. "Understood," she said.

"Isolde?"

"Yes, understood," the duchess replied.

They were jostled around for several more minutes before they came to a halt and heard voices that didn't belong to anyone in the front seat of the wagon. Saoirse couldn't make out any of their words, but the conversation at least didn't sound hostile. The cart pulled forward again, but at a much slower pace than before.

She didn't see him enact his power, but a fuzzy veil of magic fell in front of her vision. Looking down, her hands were no longer slim and petite. Instead, her fingers were stubbier and a few faint scars littered the backs of them. This was what being glamoured felt like. She didn't know what she expected, but it was much less invasive than she imagined.

The wagon crawled to a stop and Vasili opened the canvas flaps, allowing bright sunlight to stream in. He whisper-shouted at them to move quickly as soldiers were on their way to help unpack the cart.

Saoirse squinted and scrambled over the crates. Vasili helped her down from the back of the cart, and her feet landed with a thud. She felt the impact sting in her ankles but ignored it. Isolde and Laszlo followed, the three quickly making themselves look useful by taking the crates Vasili handed them.

Saoirse looked next to her at Isolde to see what her glamoured appearance looked like, and it was eerie. The duchess's small, soft features were now sharp and angular. Her nose was wider and her lips thinner. Her blonde hair was now dark and cropped short on her neck. Even her bust had been glamoured to look completely flat. If Saoirse came upon her without knowing Isolde was glamoured, she wouldn't have recognized her.

The three of them created a conveyor line, with Saoirse taking the crate from Vasili and handing it off to Isolde, who passed it to Laszlo. Camp soldiers met them and took the crates Laszlo had piled up, and they quickly emptied the cart.

As the camp soldiers took inventory of the cargo, the trio slipped away to search the rest of the camp before the soldiers could look too carefully at them. They passed Andromeda and Calliope, who were being escorted to the healer tent. Andromeda shared a quick glance and a slight nod before turning her attention back to Calliope and their escort.

The camp was a maze of tents and small fire pits. Each tent looked the same—dirty pale canvas erected into structures that could fit two, maybe three bodies inside. The smell that lingered through the camp wasn't pleasant either. Saoirse tried not to breathe in the overwhelming scent of unwashed bodies and burnt food in order to not to gag.

The three wound through the camp, keeping an eye out for

Kieran in case Cyprian hadn't cornered him in his tent to distract him yet. Isolde, the least subtle of the three, swung her head from side to side, looking for the familiar hair or face of Emrys.

"Isolde, stop scanning the camp as if you have an assassin on your tail," Laszlo murmured.

"I'm looking for anyone who might look like they know where Emrys is," she hissed in reply.

"And how would they look like they know Emrys?" he asked.

"I don't know." She shrugged. "They would just...stand out. Like him." She pointed to a tall fireann with long, dirty blonde hair making his way between two tents and grinned. Her pace picked up despite Laszlo's efforts to stop her.

Saoirse watched as the duchess interacted with the stranger, her heart pounding with anxiety. If they were caught by anyone, regardless of their rank in the army, they would surely be turned into Kieran.

"Hello," Isolde said to the fireann, trying to deepen her voice. The glamour only extended to their appearance, not their voices.

"Hello," he said, running his gaze over her curiously. "Are ye lost, lad?"

"Yes," she said quickly. "I just arrived with the latest batch of troops."

"Aye, welcome," he said flatly. "Can I help ye find where ye're going?"

"I was looking for a member of this camp," she answered. "We were in the army decades ago and I heard he had enlisted again. I was hoping we'd be in the same camp for a second time. Fate is funny like that." She forced a chuckle, but it came off like a cough.

The fireann eyed Isolde, unsure of how to perceive her. Saoirse held her breath, praying he wasn't a troop that was wrapped around Kieran's finger. "I can't guarantee I'll know him," the fireann finally said.

"It's worth a guess, right?" Isolde asked, playfully elbowing him.

The fireann leaned closer to her and examined her face. Saoirse's heart was about to beat out of her chest as she watched. If someone looked closely enough, could they notice the layer of glamour?

"Are ye wearing rouge?" he asked in a hushed voice.

Saoirse snapped her head towards Laszlo. "Does your glamour not cover rouge?" she whispered with a hiss.

Laszlo shrugged. "I don't glamour boireannaich that often."

She slapped a hand to her forehead as she watched Isolde flounder.

"I-I can't—" Isolde stammered.

A grin spread on the fireann's face. "Ye're not supposed to be here, are ye?" he whispered.

"Of course I'm supposed to be here," she said, her voice quivering between her normal pitch and the lower one she had adopted. "I told you—"

"It's alright." He smirked. "I don't care. Ye could wreck every tent in this camp, and I wouldn't blink an eye. Tell me who ye're looking for."

Isolde stared at him blankly for a moment before shaking her head. She opened her mouth to ask her questions when another member of the army came upon them.

"What are you two doing standing around?" he asked. His lapel was decorated, and his clothes looked much more pristine than the other members Saoirse had seen milling about the camp.

"Icarus," Laszlo intervened, gripping Isolde's upper arm. "Very sorry, officer. I've been training new recruits, and this one seems to have slipped away. You know how they are."

The officer looked at him curiously. "And who are you?"

"Sergeant Laurence Ozias," Laszlo said without missing a beat. "I transferred over from one of the camps on the eastern border. I've been assigned to train some of the new recruits."

The officer still looked weary of Laszlo and his cover. His face finally relaxed and morphed into recognition. Thinking he recognized Laszlo, Saoirse acted before the officer could speak. She summoned her magic and tossed a small flame towards the ground, lighting the grass on fire.

"Did you do your training at—"

"Oh, my," Saoirse interrupted, deepening her own voice. "We better find someone to extinguish that before it gets too big."

Saoirse watched the officer attempt to stomp on the fire as she grabbed Laszlo. She pulled him away towards the center of the camp.

"'Oh, my?'" Laszlo asked. "You realize we're in an army camp not afternoon tea, don't you?"

"What was I supposed to say? Cailleach's quim?"

"It would be much more believable if you swear." Laszlo turned to his other side and stopped cold. "Where is Isolde?"

Saoirse looked around him and also realized they were short a person. She turned in a circle, looking around the camp, but she wasn't anywhere to be found. "Morrigan strike us," she grumbled.

"We have to find her. She's definitely outside the range of my glamour." Laszlo pulled Saoirse in yet another direction in the camp.

Now, on top of finding Emrys, they had to track down Isolde before someone else found her. Saoirse looked between the tents, but only saw grubby army camp members. She sighed in frustration. None of them looked like her husband either.

"Cogwick."

Saoirse's skin crawled at that voice. It was one she hadn't heard in over a week, and she had thanked the gods for that small reprieve.

She and Laszlo slowly turned to face Kieran. Saoirse swallowed as she noticed his scowl. Where was Cyprian, and why wasn't he keeping Kieran distracted? Saoirse quickly scanned the camp and saw Cyprian approaching. She let out a small breath in relief. Hopefully, he could steer Kieran away from them so they could keep looking for Isolde and Emrys.

"What are you doing here?" Kieran asked.

Saoirse prayed her glamour remained intact as he came closer. His focus was on Laszlo, and she assumed if her glamour had worn off, Kieran would have reacted immediately. As a precaution, she kept her mouth tightly shut.

"I was told my nephew had enlisted," Laszlo said. "I hadn't seen him in quite some time, so I thought I would visit."

Kieran's brows furrowed. "I didn't know you had a nephew."

"I do," Laszlo said, his voice growing louder. Saoirse wondered if he was lying and if his volume was a tell. "He's going to be an upstanding recruit." Laszlo clapped his hand on Saoirse's shoulder, and she nearly buckled under it.

"This is your nephew?" Kieran asked.

Saoirse froze as Kieran scrutinized her. She felt sweat prickle on her brow as he looked her up and down.

"Kieran," Cyprian's voice broke Kieran's focus, and he turned away from Saoirse.

"It's Your Highness," Kieran corrected him coolly.

Saoirse could sense the restraint Cyprian enacted as he stared down at the general. She was sure if he wasn't here on alleged business he would roll his eyes.

"Your Highness," Cyprian said tightly. "Shall we step inside and continue our discussion from the other day?" He gestured to the large tent a few feet behind Kieran.

"I don't believe we have anything new to discuss," Kieran said plainly.

Cyprian opened his mouth to retort, but something behind Saoirse and Laszlo caught his gaze. Saoirse dared a look over her shoulder and saw Isolde with the fireann she talked to earlier. Water manifested from her fingers as she and the fireann evaded other members of the army. Mud splashed as they chased the two, and Saoirse inwardly groaned. Apparently, Isolde had not heeded her husband's words as well as she should have.

Without thinking, Saoirse broke away and ran after Isolde. She heard her name called but kept running to her friend. Her magic crackled in her veins, and she conjured a blast of fire to the grass in front of the fireannaich chasing Isolde. The flames were short, but they quickly spread. The fireannaich stopped abruptly, and Saoirse headed straight for her friend and her new companion.

"Isolde," Saoirse called as she caught up with her.

"Saoirse!" Isolde's eyes were wide. "Your glamour is gone. What were you thinking?"

"What were *you* thinking?" Saoirse asked back. "You lost your glamour long before I did."

"Silas knows where Emrys is," Isolde said.

"Who is Silas?"

"Aye, that would be me," the fireann said. "Emrys is my bunkmate."

Before relief could settle in her, a shout caused her blood to run cold.

"You little bitch!"

She whirled to see Kieran storming towards them. Quickly, she conjured enough of her magic to lob a grapefruit-sized ball of fire towards him. Kieran moved his hand, his element of wind batting away at her fire. But instead of extinguishing it, her fire fed off of it and landed on one of the camp tents. The flames ate away at the canvas, leaving the charred structure and burning belongings behind.

"How did you escape?" Kieran demanded, seemingly unaware of the destruction he just caused.

Saoirse started moving backwards, Isolde and Silas stepping back with her.

"If you've come here to save your little mate, it's too late." A wolfish grin graced Kieran's face.

A protective urge roared inside Saoirse. She didn't want to hear anything else he had to say. She lobbed another ball of fire in his direction, but just as before, he diverted it, causing more tents and grass to flare up. Her strategy was quickly becoming futile. Her only option left was to run.

She grabbed Isolde and pulled her behind another large tent. If they could run along the edges of the camp, they had a chance of making it back to Vasili's cart. As they came around the other side of the large tent, a hard blast of air hit Saoirse in the side of the head. She stumbled to a stop, her ear ringing. When she turned in the direction of the air that hit her, she found Kieran reeling back his hand to blast more of his magic.

She could feel the blood and magic pumping in her veins as she thought of Kieran's last words to her.

"It's too late."

No, it couldn't be. He had lied time and again about Emrys to manipulate her, to get his way. But not this time. Saoirse would end his games, once and for all.

She mentally named every emotion coursing through her—anger, love, fear, relief—and let it feed her magic until she felt it thrumming throughout her entire body. Saoirse felt her magic cracking beyond what it normally did. It almost felt like it was trying to break free of her physical body.

Saoirse focused on manifesting her magic, and she mustered the largest mass of fire she ever had, its size growing larger than a ripe pumpkin. Her only thoughts were of stopping Kieran and finding Emrys. Emrys, who without a second thought took the time to teach her and help nurture her magic. Emrys, the one person who had an endless abundance of patience. Emrys, her mate.

With a grunt, Saoirse put every effort into launching the flaming sphere straight towards the general. For a moment, she stood in awe and pride of her accomplishment. She wanted to double over to catch her breath and let her heart rest for a moment.

But those thoughts were short-lived as Kieran met her flames with his magic and tossed it towards the tent she and the rest of the group had filled with crates of food earlier. It instantly caught fire like the other tents had. Saoirse let out a swear as she watched the inferno ravage the tent and its contents. She glanced at Kieran and a spike of panic struck her. His attention was fixed on the mess tent, a furious scowl on his face. He barked orders at the army members around him, and Saoirse saw the opportunity to slip away.

She pulled Isolde, and the two ran the length of the tent, the fire on their heels. Silas trailed behind, and if he didn't know Emrys personally, Saoirse would have barked at him to flee in the opposite direction. His height and build was too conspicuous. It was almost like he was a flag for the army to follow.

But just as Saoirse was about to lose her patience with Silas, the cart that had brought them to the camp came into sight. Saoirse saw Laszlo and Andromeda helping Calliope hoist a body into the back of the cart, and her heart leapt. The mating spark burst inside Saoirse, and she knew it was Emrys they were loading into the cart. A sob rose up in her throat. They had done it. They had rescued him.

Saoirse watched as Laszlo and Andromeda climbed into the back of the cart, but before she and Isolde could reach them, it pulled away.

"Wait!" Saoirse called out. "Stop! Wait for us!"

The cart didn't halt. Instead, it made its way as quickly as it could out of the camp. Saoirse swore and took heavy breaths. She looked around the camp before looking to Isolde. They were stranded. Their only option out of the camp was now gone.

"What do we now?" Saoirse asked frantically. "How do we get out of this camp?"

Isolde's mouth hung open, speechless. Saoirse's heart sank, and tears pinched her eyes. Emrys had escaped, but she was now left to face Kieran. She wanted to crumple to the ground and sob. She had gotten so close to reuniting with Emrys, but now, she was stranded in a burning camp with Kieran hunting her down.

Her thoughts spiraled as the sound of roaring fire filled her ears. Her mind immediately jumped to the worst conclusions about why they had were stranded. What if they pulled away with Emrys and without them because he—no, Saoirse couldn't finish that thought. Kieran had been lying about it being too late. It couldn't be too late. They had found him. The gods couldn't forsake them like this.

"Mo Stoirín," Cyprian called.

Saoirse had never been so happy to hear the duke's voice. She and Isolde turned to see him motioning for them to come towards him. Saoirse sprinted in his direction. Once past the short side of the burning mess tent, she caught movement in the corner of her eye and saw Kieran racing towards her. She blindly shot more of her magic in his direction without caring for how much more of the camp she burned down.

She heard a fireann cry out, and she dared to look who she had hit. Kieran was desperately patting at flames that were quickly licking over his waistcoat and shirt. She must have gotten a lucky shot and hit him between his responding blocks.

She and Isolde finally reached Cyprian, with Silas tailing close behind them. A darkness suddenly enveloped them that made the late morning seem like early evening. It brought Saoirse to a halt, and she stood in awe as she watched more shadows manifest from Cyprian's palms.

"Alright," he said, turning his attention to them. "Stay close and follow me."

Saoirse nodded and kept her gaze on the back of Cyprian's light blue waistcoat as they moved through the shadows. Shouts of the camp behind them could still be heard, but they didn't sound like they were getting closer.

Saoirse didn't know how long they hustled through the camp, but they eventually made it to a carriage. The shadows subsided as Cyprian opened the carriage door, handing the boireannaich up inside. Saoirse collapsed onto the bench with Isolde and Silas across from her. Cyprian lumbered inside and shut the door before tapping on the ceiling.

Saoirse watched the camp burn brighter as the carriage lurched forward. Flames licked the sky as the fire grew bigger. As the camp was about to vanish from sight, she saw something bolt up from the blaze and soar into the sky. Smoke trailed behind it as it moved westward, and Saoirse squinted to try to make out its shape. It looked almost bird-like, and she wondered if someone had shifted and escaped. Surely it wasn't Kieran. Was it?

The camp vanished behind the trees, the only evidence of it being the billowing smoke pluming up from the forest. Saoirse leaned back in her seat and felt her body crash. She held back tears, but apparently did a poor job of it as Isolde reached over and squeezed her knee.

"It's alright," she said softly. "He's alright."

"But—" Saoirse throat tightened. She couldn't muster up the courage to say it aloud.

"He's not," Isolde assured her, as if reading her thoughts. "I saw ties between you two. I can't see them if one is—isn't alive."

Saoirse nodded, hoping Isolde was right.

"Isolde," Cyprian said as they turned onto the road. "Who is this?"

Isolde glanced at the fireann next to her before returning her gaze to her husband. "Silas," she answered.

"Why is he in our carriage?" A muscle tensed in his jaw as he tried to say the words calmly.

"He is—was—Emrys's bunk mate. He was helping us find him."

"So you decided to kidnap him?"

"If we left him, he might not have survived."

"Which I appreciate, hen."

A blush stained Isolde's cheeks at the pet name. Saoirse stole a glance at Cyprian, who looked like he was one step away from lunging at and throttling Silas. Isolde had been adamant she and Cyprian weren't mates, but the duke could have fooled Saoirse with how easily he became jealous.

"I also appreciate ye burning that shithole to the ground." Silas said to Saoirse.

She tried to muster a grin, but it came off as a grimace. Nothing could ease the pain in her chest, not until she could confirm for herself that Emrys was alive.

Time passed slowly as the carriage was near silent except for the squeak of the carriage wheels and the beats of the horses' hooves. Cyprian kept a glowering stare on Silas while Isolde gave him a challenging one. Meanwhile, Silas sat stiffly, looking very uncomfortable. Saoirse didn't blame him. Cyprian was an intimidating fireann to those who were unaware of the rest of his personality, and she would be nervous too if she were on the receiving end of his glare.

The scent of saltwater eventually drifted into the stuffy carriage, and Saoirse sagged ever so slightly in relief. Their original plan had gone completely off the rails, but they were finally at their ultimate destination. She was that much closer to reuniting with Emrys and finding for herself if he was still breathing and still maintained his spirit. Until the carriage stopped outside the cottage, Saoirse prayed unceasingly that her mate was still alive.

The rescue team from the carriage clambered through the door of the cottage. Andromeda immediately flung herself into Laszlo's arms, and the two embraced tightly in their reunion.

"Who is this?" she asked as her eyes fell on the fireann they had picked up.

"He's Isolde's kidnapping victim," Cyprian answered flatly.

"We didn't kidnap him. He willingly came with us," she argued. "Besides, everyone says *you* kidnapped me when we first met, and that's an exaggeration."

"That was different," he grumbled.

Cyprian went on to argue the difference between the way he so-called kidnapped Isolde and the way she kidnapped Silas. However, Saoirse was too distracted to pay attention to any of it. She instead turned to Vasili.

"Where is he?" she asked, more concerned about finding Emrys than asking why Vasili left them behind.

"He's in that bedroom." He gestured to the downstairs bedroom. She moved towards the door, but Vasili cut in front of her. "Saoirse, he's been badly injured, and he's been in and out of consciousness since Calliope found him. She's working on healing him, and I think you should let her work without distraction."

"Vasili," Saoirse said, her voice lethally calm. "Unless you want your wife to work on you next, you'll move out of my way and let me see my husband."

He visibly swallowed before slowly stepping aside. Saoirse took a deep breath as she gently turned the knob of the door and peeked inside the room. Emrys was half-dressed on the side of the bed. He lay face down with his back exposed to Calliope, who was seated at his bedside.

The duchess didn't acknowledge Saoirse as she continued to clean and dress his wounds. Saoirse's heart twisted as she got closer. She stepped around to confirm what she had feared. New slashes crisscrossed his back, mingling with his scars. They looked fairly fresh, and Saoirse swallowed the bile that crept up her throat. They slowly bled as Calliope tried to dress them. The sleeves of her dress were soaked with blood as she worked, and several red-stained cloths sat in her lap.

Saoirse took her time moving to the empty side of the bed and held her breath as she watched for any sign of consciousness in Emrys's face. His face was smushed into the mattress but she could see his eyelids were heavy, but his breathing was luckily steady. She sat carefully on the bed and threaded her fingers through his. His skin was still warm, and the tightness in her chest began to ease. She exhaled the breath she had been holding as she found more and more signs of him surviving this. Kieran wouldn't win again.

She leaned over and carefully brought the back of his hand to her lips. Tears stung just below the surface, but she fought them back. The gods had answered her prayers. Emrys had made it out of the army camp alive.

"Saoirse." His voice was rough, but his emerald eyes flittered open. The gold flickered around the edges of his eyes, and she gave him a watery smile as her tears infiltrated her resolve not to shed any. Her hand squeezed his hand three times, and he gave her a weak smile.

"I'm here," she whispered, combing the wildness of his hair with her fingers. It was oily and caked with dirt, confirming how unsanitary everyone was in that camp.

"Are you wearing trousers?" he asked, the corner of his mouth twitching upwards.

"Yes," she said with a small, shaky laugh.

"I don't want you to ever wear anything but trousers from now on," he said, the twitch turning into a full smirk. "Your arse is too well hidden under all those petticoats."

Saoirse let out the relieved laugh that bubbled in her chest and pressed her forehead against his. "I'll try to work them into my wardrobe." She giggled as her tear fell onto his cheek, and she quickly wiped it away.

His amusement slowly faded back to unconsciousness, and she tried not to let her heart sink. This was only temporary. He would be back to himself soon. She pressed a long kiss to his forehead before turning her attention to Calliope.

"I've gotten the bleeding to stop. I just need help to dress the wound." The duchess rose to her feet slowly. She winced and braced her hand on the bed.

"Are you alright?" Saoirse asked softly.

Calliope nodded. "I expended what little energy I began the day with getting him into the wagon. I'm going to be needing more than just my cane for the next week."

Saoirse's memories returned to the sight of the wagon riding off without her and Isolde, and she couldn't help the question that came to her. "Why did you four leave without me and Isolde?" she asked.

"That was Vasili," Calliope said as measured and cut the lengths of cloth. "He thought you two were with us. By the time I was able to tell him you weren't and get him to stop, Andromeda and Laszlo couldn't find you two, and the camp was nearly incinerated."

"He's lucky Cyprian found us," Saoirse murmured.

"Yes, he is," the duchess agreed. "When Laszlo told him you started the fire, he quickly learned not to cross you again."

Saoirse gave a half-smile. "I don't mean to intimidate your husband."

Calliope waved her hand. "He might mean well, but he needs to learn his lesson every once in a while. Unrelated, if you ever want a well-bred horse or the pick of the next harvest, he won't hesitate to oblige."

Saoirse let out a huff of a laugh before turning her attention to Emrys. She watched as Calliope soaked the strips of cloth in saltwater and laid them over the open wounds. Emrys's hand and face twitched, but he didn't stir otherwise.

"He's alright," Calliope assured her. "His body is just reacting to the sting from the salt. It's not pleasant, but it eventually passes."

Saoirse nodded and smoothed her thumb over Emrys's brow as if it would soothe his pain. A memory surfaced at the thought of relieving his distress. Emrys said he had used the bond to take on some of her pain after what happened with Kieran. She wondered if that would work now. But she had no idea where to begin to use that ability. Did she simply will it while touching him? That seemed to be how he had done it.

As Calliope finished up dressing Emrys's wounds, Saoirse noticed he was still twitching, and his face had contorted even further. She couldn't watch him writhe like this. She had to try to use the bond. With her hand still clasped in Emrys's, Saoirse shut her eyes and tried to will the bond to siphon his pain to her. For a few minutes, nothing happened. As she was about to give up, she took deep steadying breaths and visualized the pain transferring from his body to hers.

Slowly, a prickling pain scratched at her back as she felt the fear flood her mind. She gritted her teeth, but refused to let go. The pain intensified, and Saoirse began to feel dizzy.

"Saoirse." Calliope's voice broke through to her, and Saoirse gasped as she opened her eyes.

She looked at Emrys, whose face was now relaxed. His hand was limp in hers, and if she didn't witness his chest rising and falling with breath, she would have panicked that she had just sucked the life out of him.

Saoirse reluctantly turned her attention to Calliope, who had moved around the bed and was staring at her bewildered. "I'm alright," Saoirse whispered weakly. "I was just using the bond."

Calliope nodded and patted her on the shoulder. Saoirse hissed in pain. While she determined it was necessary, she vowed to never use the bond for this purpose lightly.

After a moment, Calliope made a gentler yet more effective argument for Emrys's rest than Vasili had and escorted Saoirse reluctantly out of the room. The pair joined everyone in the sitting room, where Cyprian paced in front of the fireplace. Isolde looked tense and nervous as her eyes followed her husband's back-and-forth movement.

"What's going on?" Saoirse asked.

Cyprian paused to acknowledge her with a tight stare before he returned to pacing.

"He's contemplating if burning down the army camp elicits Emrys's discharge or if he still needs to petition for it," Vasili informed her quietly.

"If it does, Silas is also clear and we all walk away with fewer court cases," Cyprian said.

"And if it doesn't?" Saoirse asked.

Cyprian stopped his pacing. "Then we choose which to petition for...and which to hand over for corporal punishment."

"There's also the matter of me escaping the Matron House," Saoirse said.

The duke ran a hand down his face. "Yes, but that's a bit easier. You were there against your will, which is against the code of the House. It's an easy argument to clear any charges."

"But what about Emrys?" Isolde asked. "He was in the camp illegally. That should be an easy argument too. If the camp burning down doesn't assure his release, Kieran could sign the papers you need in order to release Emrys, and then we can petition for Silas."

"Yes, that would still be a valid option if we hadn't taken him from the camp without permission." He gave her a sarcastic smile, and Isolde scowled once again.

"But Kieran is dead," Saoirse said.

Everyone's attention turned to her in shock.

"At least, I think he is." She remembered the shape she saw fly from the camp. She couldn't be sure it was Kieran, but she couldn't sure it wasn't him either.

"How?" Andromeda asked. She sat perched on the arm of the chair Laszlo sat in.

"I—" Saoirse swallowed. Saying the words out loud were harder than thinking them. "I hit him with my magic and, the last I saw him, he was unsuccessfully trying to extinguish it."

The room fell completely silent.

"That doesn't guarantee he's dead," Calliope said quietly.

"It doesn't guarantee he's alive either," Saoirse argued. "We won't know until the dust settles about the camp."

"There's still the legal matter of—"

"Cyprian, why don't we worry about this until Emrys is fully conscious," Saoirse suggested, struggling to handle more than one crisis regarding her husband.

He grunted as he sunk into an armchair and rubbed his hands down his face in frustration.

"How is he?" Laszlo asked. His hand traced idle circles on Andromeda's back.

"He's stable," Calliope answered. "He's no longer bleeding, and I dressed his wounds. He was whipped as punishment and was bleeding too much to care for it on his own."

"He was whipped because of me," Silas offered tentatively.

Saoirse's attention shifted to him, and she tried to keep her protective instinct restrained. "Why?"

"We were on night watch, and Kieran came up, finding trouble where it wasn't, like he always did. I mouthed off a bit, and Emrys kept him from grabbing me. Unfortunately, he used his magic, and the consequences for that was the whip."

Saoirse took several deep breaths. She reminded herself that Emrys was alive, and that was all that mattered. She leaned against the wall for support. Between the excitement of the day and using the bond, her body felt like it had been run over by a train.

"What do we do about Silas?" Andromeda asked.

Cyprian opened his mouth to answer, but Saoirse beat him to

the next legal discussion he was about to launch into.

"We keep him here," she said plainly. "Until we can find out what the damage to the army camp means, we keep him with us. We certainly can't drop him back at the camp in the shape it's in. Nor can we hand him over to a different camp. It's best we keep him somewhere that won't draw attention."

"Thank you," Silas said in a quiet voice. His clear blue eyes met hers, and some of her anger melted as she witnessed the fear and gratitude in his gaze. She had seen that look before, and it had been from the fíreann recovering in the bedroom behind her.

Her curiosity tugged at her, wondering what led Silas to the camp. Was it the same reason as Emrys the first time? Or was he devoted to the territories? His casual brogue told her he wasn't from England. How *did* he end up in the hands of the army?

"You're welcome," she said, pulling herself from her thoughts. There would be time to find answers to her questions later. For now, Emrys was at the top of her priorities.

"So, for now, we just wait for Emrys to wake up?" Isolde asked.

Saoirse nodded and quickly wiped at the rapid-pooling tears at the corner of her eyes. They kept coming no matter how hard she tried to rein them in, and soon she couldn't keep fighting them anymore. Calliope took her in her arms while Saoirse succumbed to her emotions. The pain Saoirse took on from Emrys had become numb as every other emotion flooded her.

Soon she felt two more pairs of arms wrap around her and shield her in a warm cocoon of their bodies. Her sobs came harder as she realized she had more than just Emrys to lean on. In just a matter of months, she had a family of people who were ready and able to support her, and it meant more to her than words could describe.

That evening, Saoirse stretched herself along Emrys's side and listened to the even rise and fall of his breathing. The skin of her back pinched in pain as she lay down. Calliope had helped her investigate the pain earlier and found there were thin marks criss-crossing Saoirse's back in a similar pattern to Emrys's. There was no blood, but the skin was very tender.

Saoirse mindlessly ran her finger over Emrys's arm while her erratic thoughts about the day quieted to a murmur. She was realizing now it was probably the bond that did that—calm her when she was in vicinity of Emrys. The arm she was casually stroking stretched towards her, and she quietly gasped.

She lifted her gaze and saw Emrys's eyelids barely open. "Hello," she said softly. "Are you fully awake, or are you still drifting?"

"I think I'm fully awake," he said with a groan. His attempt to push himself upright caused him to draw in a sharp breath. Saoirse eased him down and shifted so her head was laying in his line of vision. He lifted a hand and stroked his thumb over her cheek. "You're here."

Saoirse chuckled softly. "Do you know where 'here' is?"

Emrys scanned the room before nodding. "Yes," he answered with a weak smile. It slowly faded, and his gaze fixed on Saoirse. "I'm sorry," he said, his voice growing stronger. "I should have told you about the bond. You deserved to know, whether or not you accepted it was true, and I should have accepted however you reacted. But I was selfish, and I will never know the pain I caused you. All I wanted was you, no matter the cost. Now, I'm paying that cost."

"Is it worth it?" she asked.

He shook his head. "No, I nearly ended back where I began. Thinking back, having you be upset with me seems like a much more sufferable consequence."

Saoirse combed her fingers through his filthy and smoothed his brow. "I don't know how I would have reacted," she said. "But you're right. It probably wouldn't have ended with you being whipped again."

"Saoirse," he said softly. "I appreciate you rescuing me."

"I'm sure you would have done the same for me," she replied. "Even if you were upset with me."

"I'm so sorry. I want to prove I won't do it again. I'll spill every secret I have if I have to. Even ones that belong to the dukes."

Saoirse's lips twitched into a grin. "I have no doubt you'll prove your promise." She wove her fingers with his and kissed the back of his hand. "You've proved your promises before."

"Will you forgive me if I do?" he whispered.

"I forgive you now."

"What?" Emrys jerked upward, but his injury caused him to wince and collapse back to the bed. "You forgive me?"

Saoirse nodded as she grinned wider. She shifted closer to him and brushed her lips over his. The smell of his unwashed body triggered a repulsed reaction, but she stifled it. He was alive, and that was all that mattered to her.

"I used the bond," she whispered.

Emrys raised his brows.

"When Calliope was treating you, you were twitching and writhing in pain," she recounted. "I had no other way to soothe you, so I used the bond."

"You believe it?" he asked.

"There was too much about it that I couldn't ignore." Saoirse fidgeted with a loose thread on the blanket she was lying on. "I might not have responded well initially, but I accept it now."

Emrys wove his fingers into her hair and pulled in for another kiss. The mating spark buzzed inside Saoirse, even as she realized how chapped his lips were and the unwashed smell on his body grew worse. When she pulled away, she felt complete peace for the first time in days. Neither she nor Emrys was perfect, but they chose each other during every moment of every day. It was more than Saoirse could say about any other relationship she had, even with her family.

She gazed at Emrys's dreamy expression and tilted her head in curiosity. "What?" she asked.

"I was just thinking of the last time I woke here in this condition," he answered. "And I thank the gods I'm a better fireann now than I was then. That version of myself couldn't even imagine having a wife, let alone one that is as phenomenal as you. But he deserved you even less than I do."

A soft blush stained Saoirse's cheeks, and she settled close to him. She rested her head on his shoulder and wove her fingers with his. They lay in silence for several long beats, the sound of their tandem breathing the only sound to be heard. That was until a steady creaking above them filled the room.

"Who else is here?" Emrys asked.

"Everyone," Saoirse answered with a giggle. "The dukes and the duchesses, as well as your bunk mate that Isolde picked up from the camp."

"Silas?" Emrys asked.

She nodded. "He agreed to help us find you, but I sort of burned down the camp, and Isolde didn't feel right leaving him behind."

"You did what?" he asked, surprised.

"Kieran caught us in the camp, and I was willing to do anything to save you. I struck most of the camp and even successfully hit Kieran with my magic."

Emrys stared at her, stunned. "I think I'm indebted to you for a lifetime."

A giggle slipped from Saoirse. "I look forward to all the ways you plan to thank me."

He craned towards her and pressed a kiss to her forehead. "Whatever you want, it's yours."

They lay for a few moments in silence. The creaking above them had silenced and a calm quiet stretched between them.

"Are you alright?" Emrys asked.

Saoirse knit her brows in confusion.

"You mentioned you used the bond," he clarified. "I know what it does to the one who uses it. You used it to relieve my pain, which means you experienced it instead."

"I have a few cuts on my back," she said with a nod. "They didn't bleed, but Calliope says they'll heal easily and without a trace that they were ever there."

Her thoughts drifted back to the array of emotions she felt while Calliope cared for his wounds. She had been relieved that he was alive, but her heart ached watching him helplessly. Saoirse's bottom lip wobbled, and her eyes stung as she lived those moments again. She sniffed, hoping it would resolve it, but a tear dripped down the side of her nose.

"Oh, no, no, no, don't cry," Emrys said, clumsily reaching for her face. "I'm not in any position to comfort you the way I want." He attempted to wipe at her tears but nearly poked her eye instead.

Saoirse couldn't help but giggle. They both were a disastrous, uncoordinated mess. Saoirse tried to bury her face and calm her giggles in Emrys's bicep, but she reeled instantly from his smell.

"Gods, you smell absolutely terrible," she said.

Emrys's shoulders vibrated. "I'll save you from knowing just how long I haven't bathed."

"We've only been away from a proper bath for a little over a week," Saoirse said, pulling away from him until her urge to gag settled. "Surely, you couldn't have become this foul in that time."

"You would be surprised, Princess."

Saoirse's heart did a little leap hearing the honorific. She never thought hearing it would have such an impact on her. It healed a little something inside her.

"We'll find some way to remedy that," she said.

"No, I think I'll keep the smell." He gave her what looked like a cheeky grin. At least that's what Saoirse assumed he was aiming for. Having half his face smushed into the bed granted her only so much of his expressions.

"You're awful," she giggled.

"I would think you would be well aware of that by now."

Saoirse's giggles had subsided, but she couldn't wipe the grin off her face. It was the first time she felt alright in days. And bantering with Emrys gave her hope that he would be alright, too. They both would be alright.

The *dukes and* duchesses stayed in the cottage for a few days before returning to their territories was necessary. Calliope stayed behind to care for Silas, who was experiencing withdrawal symptoms from the enhancement potion Kieran was giving to the entire army. He had chills and fevers on top of nausea and fatigue. The duchess experimented with herbs Seraphina kept in the cottage, searching for a remedy. Some worked better than others, but mostly the fireann spent his days in a miserable state in one of the upstairs bedrooms.

Calliope worked tirelessly on Emrys's wounds, making sure they were healing properly and stayed clear of infection. Saoirse assisted her as she attended to the impromptu patients until Silas was stable enough to care for himself. Between Calliope's work and Saoirse's use of the bond, Emrys began to heal within two weeks. His wounds had closed into bright red, angry scars that stood out amongst his thicker, fully healed ones.

After assessing everyone's progress, Calliope made the decision to return home to Donheath. Just before she left, she gave instructions to everyone about how to take care of themselves. She made a stock of Silas's remedy to keep his symptoms at bay and a balm for Emrys's wounds. Saoirse diligently applied it to Emrys's back three times a day. She tried to determine if his wounds were becoming lighter in color as the days went by, but his healing progress had slowed tremendously.

Emrys sat at the table in the kitchen with his back exposed to Saoirse as she applied the dollop of balm to his skin. She methodically massaged it into his skin from his shoulders down to his waist. He didn't flinch as she administered it, and Saoirse noted that as progress. His skin was still tender, and he occasionally winced as he moved about the cottage, but he was much stronger than he had been when they first brought him to the cottage.

Saoirse replaced the lid on the balm and kissed Emrys's cheek, resting her chin on his shoulder. Her anxiety continued to calm as she witnessed him grow stronger, but she couldn't help thinking about the repercussions waiting for them. She trusted Cyprian's expertise, but it didn't mean the process wasn't going to test her fortitude.

"I can hear you thinking," Emrys said.

She huffed a laugh and wrapped her arms around his neck. "Are you able to read my mind now?"

"No," he said, clasping his hand over her arm and giving her a gentle squeeze. "I just know when you're quiet, that's when your thoughts are the loudest."

"I've had a lot to think about, your health being one of them." As important as clearing her and Emrys of any wrongdoings was, having him back and whole took priority for her.

"I've told you I'll be alright." Emrys stroked his thumb over her arm in a soothing rhythm.

"And I've told you that won't stop me from worrying." Saoirse punctuated her sentence with another kiss to his cheek.

"Now you're starting to sound like Ada," he chuckled. "I think I strained that boireann's every last nerve."

Saoirse giggled and nuzzled her face into the crook of his neck.

"What other thoughts have been plaguing you?" he asked.

She let out a sigh. It was no use keeping it to herself. "The bond," she answered quietly.

That made Emrys straighten a bit. She lifted her head, and he shifted to face her more, his arms coming around her waist.

"What about the bond?" he asked.

Saoirse could tell he was holding back more questions. While she had accepted the bond was real, he still tiptoed around the topic as if he was afraid to spook her.

"I've been wondering what sealing it would entail," she confessed. "I keep thinking where we would be if we had done earlier and—"

Emrys shook his head and cupped her cheek. "Don't go down that road," he said gently. "None of this was your fault. It's mine."

"I know." Saoirse's gaze dropped to his collarbone. "But I'd like to prevent it in the future."

"Well," Emrys said, tucking a loose strand of her hair behind her ear. "I've told you already that sealing the bond includes the prayer we both hear in our minds."

She chewed on her bottom lip. "During sex?"

He paused before nodding. "Yes, during sex."

"And is there blood involved?" she asked.

A snort escaped from him. "Who told you there was blood involved?"

"Andromeda," Saoirse answered.

Emrys chuckled again. "She was grossly mistaken. There is no blood, fae or otherwise, involved in sealing a mating bond."

She attempted a smile, but her thoughts about sealing the bond were too heavy. She had really only come to accept the bond two weeks ago. Shouldn't she allow herself more time to adjust to it? However, that thought was always accompanied with fear that keeping their bond unsealed put them at risk of experiencing something like this again.

"Emrys." Her voice was just above a whisper. "I want to seal the bond."

His expression turned blank, and his hands went completely still "You do?" he asked. She nodded, and he continued to stare at her. "Are you sure?"

"I think so," she answered, feeling guilty for not being completely confident in her answer. She closed her eyes and sighed in frustration. Why was she still so hesitant? Nothing physically would change. It was just a string of words to promise the gods they would stay bonded to each other as long as they drew breath. It wasn't an intimidating promise or anything.

"We don't have to," he said softly, his thumb brushing her cheek. "We can stay just as we are. It neither damns us nor rewards us. We just...exist."

Slowly, she opened her eyes to meet his. The mating spark sizzled through her as she took in a deep breath. "I'm not scared of the bond," she said, reassuring herself more than anything. "I *want* to seal it with you. I want the peace of mind that you have an extra inch of protection."

He smiled and gently pulled her closer to press a kiss to her forehead. "I want that protection for you, too." He kissed her nose. "I want to know you have the gods protecting you when I can't." He brushed a kiss over her lips. "Everything I've had to watch you suffer with reminds me how cowardly I was not to tell you about it."

"It could have helped you, too," Saoirse added.

Emrys shook his head. "I'd endure as many rounds of lashes it would take to ensure you were safe."

"Emrys." A quivering plea seeped into her voice. "Please don't talk like that."

"You have to know I'm not afraid of dying," he said. "The otherworld doesn't scare me. What does scare me is losing you."

She swallowed the emotion that clogged her throat in response to that admission. "Can we seal the bond today?"

His smile grew wider as he nodded. He kissed her again, deeper and more purposeful. It sent the spark in her body bouncing down her spine until it settled in her lower abdomen. It was as if the spark knew what their decision was and was eager to fulfill its purpose.

Emrys broke their kiss and stood, wrapping his arms under her bottom. He only winced slightly at the movement, and Saoirse almost demanded he put her down. But it was too late as he carried her towards their bedroom. She saw the hunger in his eyes and knew nothing was going to keep him from pleasuring her the way he wanted to. He set her feet on the ground and shut the bedroom door before they started their languid exploration of each other.

His fingers expertly opened the buttons of her blouse one by one at an agonizing but erotic pace. He ducked his head towards her collar and covered her skin in kisses as he slid her blouse off her shoulders. Saoirse lost herself to lust and greedily explored his bare skin, eliciting a sigh from him against her skin. She moved to the drawstring of his pyjamas and teased the skin above the waistband.

Emrys groaned and dug his fingers into the layers of her skirts before proceeding with unbuttoning them. He continued to undress her, and Saoirse gave him relief from her teasing by untying his pyjama pants and letting them crumple to the floor, leaving nothing but the mating spark between them. It pulsed in her veins as she guided him towards the bed, first sitting, then laying back onto the mattress. He kissed from her sternum to the base of her throat and along her collarbone.

His fingers slid between her thighs and gently caressed her. Saoirse bit her bottom lip as warm pleasure grew in her belly and spread towards her limbs. He alternated between long strokes over the length of her quim and tracing circles around her clit.

"How long have you been thinking of this?" he asked.

"Since I decided to trust you again." Her voice was breathy as her focus remained on the shapes his fingers traced over her.

He groaned as he easily slid a single finger inside her. "Your body is so eager." He nipped at her breast and pulsed his finger in and out of her. "There wasn't a night that went by in that camp that I didn't dream of you naked."

Heat flushed her face and neck at his confession. Knowing he thought of her in this state, it made the spark seem tame compared to what her body did in response.

He kissed his way up to her lips and captured her mouth for a long moment. "Saoirse," he breathed. "Are you sure you want to continue?"

"Yes." She nodded. "Yes, I want to do this."

A hungry grin graced his lips as he added a second finger inside her. She moaned against his mouth as he kept a slow pace with his fingers. He lowered his lips to the side of her face and whispered in her ear.

"The prayer has been invading my thoughts ever since we first made love," he said.

Gooseflesh covered her exposed flesh at his rasping voice in her ear. "It's been in my mind, too," she whispered back.

"Good." He continued to kiss her neck and move his fingers inside her.

She mewled at the pleasure he gave her with just his lips and fingers. When he pulled his fingers free, she missed the fullness they gave her. That longing intensified as he met her gaze and wrapped his lips around his glistening fingers, taking a long taste. The mating spark jolted, and she wanted nothing more than to be connected with him. She wanted Emrys and only Emrys.

"Once I'm inside you," he said, the husk in his voice making her ache for him deepen. "We can start the prayer."

She nodded and subtly parted her thighs wider. He pressed more kisses along her neck and shoulders and trailed them down her bare body to just above where she ached for his touch, his lips, his tongue. But that wasn't what they were building up to. Saoirse reached for his hips and filled her palm with his arse. He gave a cross between a groan and a chuckle as he grinned knowingly at her. His erection teased her entrance, and her body felt like it would combust from anticipation.

He hovered over her but paused to gaze deeply at her face. A different kind of warmth washed through Saoirse, and her anxiousness to physically connect with him came to a simmer. She gently traced the muscles of his neck and shoulder with the pad of her pointer finger. His body shivered in response, and she gave him a luscious grin.

"I love you," she said.

He pressed a kiss to her lips and sighed contentedly. "I love you, mo chroi."

My heart.

Saoirse pulled him close and claimed his mouth. The rest of the room melted around her. The only thing she could recognize was Emrys and the heat between them. As they kissed, he slowly slid himself inside her. She mewled as he set a steady pace that stoked the fire of pleasure in her core.

"Whenever you're ready," he whispered to her.

Timidly, Saoirse mumbled the words that had been echoing in her mind. Emrys began to recite them with her, his strong voice giving her more confidence. She tried to be mindful of their volume, but as they continued, his pace became more vigorous, spurring her to speak more fervently.

She wrapped her arms around his shoulders, feeling the wave of her pleasure building in her body. Saoirse desperately held onto it until the prayer was finished. She and Emrys continued to recite the words, but their words were broken into segments between gasps and whimpers of pleasure.

His speech became more disjointed and hurried as his thrusts matched his hastiness. Saoirse echoed the words between her pants as her body inched towards the edge of her climax. The last phrase of the prayer fell from Emrys's lips and Saoirse mirrored them, one at a time, as her climax crested and crashed over her.

Her body felt suspended in the release, the spark shattering and invading every crevice of her body before she came back to earth and shook under Emrys. He met her in ecstasy shortly after and buried himself deep inside her as he spilled his release.

They both went limp, their breath mingling as they panted. Emrys lazily kissed her throat as she gulped down air, a thin layer of sweat covering her body. When he pulled back to meet her gaze, she gave him a satisfied smile told him all he needed to know, and he mirrored it with his own. He claimed her mouth once more, and Saoirse parted her lips to deepen their kiss.

Their post-coital kissing was unhurried as they both came down from the high of their climaxes. Saoirse relished the feeling of her limbs tangled with his and the glow she felt after sex. Emrys broke their kiss and pressed his forehead to hers.

Other than a faint buzz under her skin, Saoirse didn't notice any difference. "I don't feel any different," she told him.

"Me neither," he replied as he dropped a kiss to her shoulder. "But the gods are much more subtle than we give them credit for."

Saoirse let out a soft laugh and cradled his cheek in her hand, tracing his cheekbone with her thumb. "I love you, Emrys, my mate," she whispered with a grin.

"I love you, Saoirse, *my* mate," he echoed.

Emrys *felt a* euphoria that was unlike any other. He lay with Saoirse resting her head on his chest and the mating spark a quiet buzz throughout his body. He felt several emotions at once and didn't know if he should cry or laugh or coax forth another round of sex with Saoirse. She nuzzled her nose into his chest, and he chuckled at how such a simple gesture made him feel like the world was bursting with fireworks around him.

He truly and honestly would have been content to just have Saoirse in his life and never seal the bond. The gods may have gifted her to him, but he fell in love with her regardless of the mating bond. He loved every piece of her and, if given the chance, he would live through all the hurt and pain he endured again if it led to this level of contentment.

His mind replayed the last few minutes, and he knew it would be easy to get himself ready to go another round. He had held himself back as he said the pieces of the prayer to her, especially as she'd melded the words with her gasps and moans. Being away from her made her touch and noises that much more impactful on his body, and he'd had to keep himself in check in order to finish the prayer and seal the bond.

"Emrys," Saoirse murmured, pulling him out of his lustful thoughts.

"Yes?" He stroked her hair and kissed the crown of her head.

"Can I ask you something?"

"Always."

"Am I allowed to make laws? Or at least have a say in them?"

"I don't see why not," he answered. "What kind of law did you want to propose?" His curiosity piqued at the idea of Saoirse getting more involved in the court. She had made it clear it wasn't where she wanted to be on council meeting days, so he was ready to fully support any interest she showed.

"I want to propose abolishing the Matrons," she answered.

"Are you asking this to avoid their repercussions?" he asked, trying to keep his tone playful. Saoirse had informed him of the Matron House footmen who came to remove her from Vasili's estate and how Cyprian had yet another case to resolve.

"No," she said, shaking her head. "It's more for everyone else in the House. None of them deserve to be put through what the House does to them."

The playfulness evaporated from Emrys. "That's quite a feat," he gently warned her. "It would take a load of effort from more than just our court. I would never deter you from getting involved in politics, but that's something we may never see in our lifetime."

Saoirse dropped her gaze to the bedspread covering them. "I want to at least make changes," she amended. "I want to protect those boireannaich. Some of them have experienced..." Her words trailed off, and Emrys reached for her hand, tracing circles on the back of it with his thumb.

He knew what the Matrons were for and how easily their jobs could be abused. He was beyond thankful for fate intervening and conspiring to have Calliope help rescue Saoirse from the House. He didn't want to even entertain the thought of the nightmare it would have been if she had to fulfill her duties of the House.

"Can I also have one request?" She lifted her gaze back to his, and the warmth and longing glittering in the gold of her hazel eyes made his body feel weak. He would give her anything she wanted if he could guarantee that he could fulfill her whims.

"You can have as many requests as you like," he told her.

She loosened a breath, and her fingers trembled slightly. "There's a Matron I want to free," she said.

Emrys felt a little stunned at her words. Saoirse being freed was one thing. She shouldn't have been there in the first place, and Cyprian had a strong legal argument to clear her. But besides smuggling her out as Calliope did, Emrys didn't know how Matrons could *be* discharged from their Matron duties. Could they even be discharged? He would have to add those questions to Cyprian's growing caseload.

Emrys opened his mouth to reply when a distant knock on the front door caught his attention. His heart pounded in his chest as he ran through several possible people who could be outside the cottage. Andromeda had promised to quietly share the information of their whereabouts with Seraphina and Ada. In case they needed to reach Emrys before he was safe to return to Fearynhurst, he wanted to make sure they knew where to find him. Neither of his adoptive mothers would risk coming to the cottage unless there was an emergency.

The other possibility was guards or army officers coming to retrieve him from his hiding place and thrust him in front of the army authorities to face punishment. He attempted to swallow, but his throat felt tight.

"Emrys," Saoirse whispered.

He ignored her inquiry and silently stood from the bed to grab a pair of trousers. As he made his way towards the front door, he carefully peeked through and caught sight of a short boireann with dark hair.

He breathed a sigh of relief as he opened the door and greeted Ada. "Mamanna," he said, his heart still pounding against his ribcage. "What are you doing here? Is everything alright?" She shook her head, and he noticed the distress in her expression. "What's wrong?"

"Your father," she breathed.

His father? Was he sick? Did Kieran harm him? Was he in legal trouble for what he did to him and Saoirse?

"What about my father?" he asked quietly.
"He's dead."

ACKNOWLEDGEMENTS

When I was 12 years old, I wanted to be an author. Little did I know just how much went into becoming one. I started Wicked Heir as a NaNoWriMo project in 2020. My first draft is far from what I've now released to the world, but I couldn't be prouder of it.

But I didn't do it alone. I want to first thank my editor, Bryn Schut, for taking me on as a client and accepting my behemoth of a project. Thank you for assuring me I did in fact not write a pile of garbage and seeing the story I wanted to tell even when I hadn't quite gotten there yet.

Next, I want to thank the person who has watched my book evolve and grow since day one. Lauren, thank you for encouraging me to keep going and cheering me on when I decided to self-publish Wicked Heir. You've loved my characters—some more than others—since you first met them on the page, listened to me lament about plot holes, and let me ramble about story ideas for hours. I wouldn't be here without your support and input.

To my parents, thank you for all your love and support. When I announced I wanted to publish a romance book, you didn't question it or deter me. Instead, you've supported me and celebrated with me. You both have always supported my wildest dreams, letting me follow whatever my heart felt led to. Words can't describe how grateful I am for that.

To all my friends who are my biggest cheerleaders, I know you might not understand all the intricacies of writing and publishing, but you've fully supported me every step of the way. I love all of you and don't know where I would be without you always cheering me on.

And finally, to you, the reader, thank you for spending your time with my characters and all their misadventures. I hope you've fallen in love with them as much as I have and look forward to reading more of their shenanigans.

ABOUT THE AUTHOR

Gwen Alyson has been writing romance stories since she got her first crush on a boy in middle school. She works as a marketing analyst by day and writes fantasy stories about love and adventure by night. She lives in Southern California with her six cats and enjoys their company while she consumes her favorite romances. When she isn't working, writing, or reading, Gwen enjoys time with friends and planning her next Caribbean cruise vacation.

For updates on Gwen's books, sign up for her newsletter at gwenalyson.com.

9 7 9 8 9 8 8 0 0 2 7 1 0